"Release me," Heather said, finding her voice through her fear. **"Send me home to England."**

Heather stared into his cold blue eyes. Never before had she been so close, so alone, or so vulnerable to a man.

"The pampered life of a noblewoman is behind you," Khalid said, his eyes warning her to remain silent or suffer some unnamed but hideous punishment.

Heather's eyes narrowed, her anger rising like a sudden gust of wind, all sign of her previous fear gone.

Surprised by the defiance in her gaze, Khalid cocked a dark brow at her. "Your eyes scream rebellion," he said. "Nevertheless, you are mine and will serve my every whim and need. Do you understand your position?"

"Beast." The word slipped out before she could swallow it.

Khalid leaned closer and said in a harsh voice, "Yes, I am known throughout the Empire as the Sultan's Beast and feared for it. Grown men quake at the mention of me and mothers discipline their children by invoking my name."

"You mean, as in 'the Sultan's Beast will get you'?" In spite of herself, Heather smiled, thoroughly beguiling her captor.

Khalid gave himself a mental shake. His intrepid captive was entirely too beautiful. If he wasn't careful . . .

Desert Eden

Patricia H. Grasso

A Dell Book

Published by
Dell Publishing
a division of
Bantam Doubleday Dell Publishing Group, Inc.
666 Fifth Avenue
New York, New York 10103

The trademark Dell® is registered in the U.S. Patent and Trademark Office.

ISBN: 0-440-21304-5

Printed in the United States of America

Published simultaneously in Canada

April 1993

10 9 8 7 6 5 4 3 2 1

OPM

*Dedicated with love to Constantino and Helen Grasso,
the best parents in the world*

*And, to Sharon "Shasha" Winn, who peeled me off the
ceiling when my writer's insecurity had me crawling up
the walls*

Chapter 1

Sparkling sunbeams danced across the gentle swell of the waves as they rolled almost leisurely toward shore.

With her arms resting on the starboard railing of the French ship *La Belle Beaulieu,* seventeen-year-old Heather Elizabeth Devereux looked toward the distant figures on the beach. Guarded by the Devereux men-at-arms, the dowager countess stood with the kindly Sir Henry Bagenal, Queen Elizabeth's emissary to the Devereux family since the late earl's death seven years before. Sir Henry was a second father to Heather, and she would miss him almost as much as her mother.

Heather knew her mother would watch until the ship disappeared over the horizon. After all, Heather had stood by her mother's side and waved good-bye to her sisters when the queen sent them into marriage outside England. And now Heather, the youngest, would be the last.

Though reluctant to leave England and all she held dear, Heather knew her duty and pasted a cheerful smile on her face for the sake of her mother who'd had no choice in the matter. Her sisters, Kathryn and Brigette, hadn't wanted to leave England either but had found happiness with their foreign husbands.

Heather doubted she would be so fortunate. The comte's miniature proved he wasn't half the man her handsome brothers-in-law were. Bad luck being a ward of the crown, to be sure.

"It's not too late."

"For what?"

"Too late to change your mind about exiling yourself with me," Heather said, turning to April, her cousin and tiring woman.

"Marrying a French nobleman is hardly exile," the other girl replied. "Besides, I've always shared your adventures."

"Why, Cousin," Heather said with an impish grin, "I thought you hated adventures."

"Living in France is the sort of adventure I will enjoy," April replied. "A safe one."

"We've a long journey ahead of us," Heather teased her. "Something more dangerous could be awaiting us."

"Like what?"

"Maybe pirates?"

"Heaven help us," April said, making a quick sign of the cross for protection. "Though, I'm certain you'd relish a confrontation with pirates."

Heather and April lapsed into thoughtful silence. Though England was still in the distance, both felt lonely for home. Lady and tiring woman made a fetching picture as they stood at the railing and caught their last sight of England.

Petite and curvaceously slim, Heather possessed an uncommon, startling beauty of which she was unaware. Enormous emerald green eyes shone from her delicately shaped oval face. Her complexion was ivory silk and her small, upturned nose sported her only imperfection, a sprinkling of fine freckles. Her crowning glory was the luxuriant mane of copper hair.

Brown-haired and blue-eyed, April was of average height, several inches taller than her cousin. Her simple prettiness pleased the eye rather than startled. And much to Heather's consternation, no freckles marred the bridge of April's nose. She was the image of her mother, the late earl's second cousin.

"Mademoiselle," Captain Armande called as he advanced on them. The two girls turned and watched him approach. The Frenchman was short and stout with greasy-looking black hair and mustache. A toad of a man, Heather decided.

"I will escort you to your cabin now," Captain Armande announced. "Please to follow me."

"No, thank you," Heather said, refusing. "We want to catch a last glimpse of England."

"But we are pulling up anchor to leave," he argued.

"Then pull it up," she said. "We are staying here until our home vanishes from sight."

Clearly irritated, Captain Armande turned on his heel and walked away, muttering under his breath about the English lack of manners. The Comte de Beaulieu, hard man that he was, would soon discipline this petite brat and cure her of her rudeness. At least, the captain hoped so.

The girls turned back to the shore and gazed at the retreating figures on the beach. Heather sighed. Apparently, her mother was not going to wait for the ship to vanish over the horizon.

"Do you think we'll fall off?" Heather asked. Teasing her cousin always lifted her spirits.

April was puzzled. "Fall overboard?"

"No, off."

"Off what?"

"Off the edge of the world," Heather replied, wearing a solemn expression. "Do you swim?"

"No, do you?"

Heather shook her head, saying, "I guess that means we can't abandon ship before it goes over the edge."

April paled and her voice rose in alarm. "Then, you think there's a chance—?"

Heather burst out laughing, a sweet melodious sound that drew the attention of the French sailors. "Don't be foolish, April. The world is round, not flat. Besides, my mother came from France."

"The countess crossed the Channel, but we're sailing all the way around into that sea."

"The Mediterranean," Heather supplied. "Trust me, Cousin. There's no edge to fall off."

"How do you know?" April asked, relieved but unconvinced.

"Richard's tutor explained the matter to us in one of his lessons," Heather told her.

April relaxed, then asked, "But, how does *he* know?"

Before Heather could answer, Captain Armande stood beside them again. "Mademoiselle, I insist you go to your cabin now. Your presence on deck distracts my men from their work."

"My dear Captain Armande," Heather said, feigning haughtiness. "I am Lady Heather, not mademoiselle. Furthermore, my servant and I will go below when I am ready, not before. Am I not the future Comtesse de Beaulieu? Are you not merely an employee of my betrothed, the Comte de Beaulieu? You will refrain from giving me, your future mistress, orders."

Suppressing the urge to slap her, Captain Armande scowled darkly and walked away without another word. Heather winked at April, who swallowed a horrified giggle.

"Forgive me for referring to you as my servant," Heather apologized. "Lord, but I detest these French. Except my mother, of course."

"You never met anyone French until you boarded this vessel," April reminded her.

Heather grinned. "True, but it was an instant dislike."

"You should be polite to your betrothed's people. After all, they'll soon be your own," April said. "Besides, the queen has done well by you. She could have sent you to a wild land like she did to your sisters."

Heather thought of her sisters, Kathryn in Ireland and Brigette in Scotland. She shrugged, saying, "My sisters have had something that civilized France cannot offer."

"Such as?" April asked.

"Adventure."

April rolled her eyes.

"Who is better suited to adventure than I?" Heather asked. "You know I took weaponry lessons with my brother and am more than capable of defending myself. But, do I get the chance to face a challenge? No! The queen sends me to staid old France where my only purpose will be to breed an heir for the ugly Comte de Beaulieu."

"Well, I am thankful to be going to a civilized country," April insisted. "And the Comte de Beaulieu is a fine-looking man. Let's see his miniature. Do you have it with you?"

Reaching beneath her dark woolen traveling cloak, Heather pulled the miniature out of her skirt pocket. Lady and tiring woman bent their heads together to study the painted image of the French nobleman's face.

Thirty-year-old Savon Fougere, the Comte de Beaulieu, stared at them from the miniature. His reddish-brown hair matched the mustache that grew beneath his long, pointed nose. His face was thin and his eyes were dark, almost black. The comte's expression was that of a man with a pike stuck up his ass.

"The comte is a handsome man," April said, masking her distaste for his appearance. "I'm certain the artist's brush has done him an injustice. 'Tis impossible for paintbrush and canvas to capture the nature of a man.''

"Fougere resembles a weasel," Heather said baldly. "And I cannot like those cold, serpent's eyes of his. He looks like a man without tender emotion."

"Don't mistakenly judge the man's character by his looks," April advised.

"If he's not to my liking, I'll do what Brigette did—run away."

"Lady Heather," Captain Armande called, bearing down on them. "As captain of this vessel, I say it is time for you to go below." Never in his wildest dreams had he thought to play nursemaid to a couple of English maidens. And who would ever imagine they could irritate him so?

Heather looked toward the shoreline. It wasn't there. England had vanished from sight. Heather felt a moment's panic, then shrugged her shoulders, saying, "Very well."

As the two girls turned to follow the captain, April touched her cousin's arm. "Do you think we'll ever see England again?" she whispered, a hopeful tone in her voice.

Heather cast her cousin a sidelong glance and her lips twitched with merriment. "If I am dissatisfied with the comte, I'm certain we will," she replied, then sighed with exaggeration. "I fear 'twill be a long walk back to England."

Captain Armande opened the door and ushered them into their quarters. "This will be your home for the next two weeks," he said.

Their cabin was slightly larger than a horse's stall and dreary, one tiny porthole being its only source of sunlight. A decrepit cot hugged the wall beneath the porthole, and opposite the cot stood a rickety table with no accompanying chairs. The chests containing their belongings had been neatly stacked on one side of the room. At a right angle to the cot was a large piece of canvas slung by cords from supports at each end.

"What's this?" Heather asked, leaping onto it in the most unladylike fashion. Amazingly, it swung back and forth.

Captain Armande's expression softened and his lips twitched into what might be taken as a smile. "It's called a hammock," he said. "Your woman can sleep on it."

"I'll sleep on the hammock," Heather said, noting her cousin's horrified expression. "It looks more comfortable than that sad-looking cot."

"During the voyage, you and your woman are permitted on deck to take the air between two and four each afternoon," Captain Armande informed them. "The men's quarters are below deck, strictly off limits to you. And your meals will be served to you here. Any questions?"

"Where will we eat?" Heather asked, her eyes green slits of displeasure as she stared hard at the Frenchman. "There are no chairs."

"The table can be pulled across to the cot." Hoping to quell the rebellious streak he recognized in the young Englishwoman, Captain Armande pasted on his sternest expression. "Any infraction of these rules will be considered mutiny."

"Are we the comte's guests or his prisoners?" Heather challenged.

"Lady Heather, these rules ensure your safety," the captain said, then turned to leave.

"Captain Armande?" Heather's voice stopped him. When he turned back, she smiled as winsomely as she could. "Beaulieu is located on the Mediterranean and enjoys fair weather all year, but beyond that, I know nothing of my new home. Can you tell me something more?''

''I am needed on deck and haven't the time,'' he said, then opened the door to leave.

''Why did the comte not travel to England himself to fetch his bride?''

Captain Armande turned around. ''The comte does not explain himself to me. Besides, a powerful man like the comte has many enemies who would assassinate him if he left Beaulieu and traveled by sea.''

''Fougere is a coward?'' Heather blurted out.

April gasped. Captain Armande left without saying another word and slammed the door on his way out.

''How do you dare to voice such a vile thought?'' April cried.

Heather glanced at her cousin's shocked expression and smiled. ''If it looks like a weasel and acts like a weasel, then it *is* a weasel.''

Favorable winds sent *La Belle Beaulieu* flying down the Strait of Dover and the English Channel into the open Atlantic. In spite of the forbidding overcast into which the ship had sailed, Heather leaped off her hammock when she heard the bells announcing the time.

''Two o'clock,'' Heather said, already feeling her confinement. ''Let's go.''

''Above deck?'' April asked, staring out the porthole. ''The sky looks threatening.''

''A little water never hurt anyone,'' Heather replied, throwing her cloak over her shoulders. ''Are you coming or not?''

Duty demanded April accompany Heather. Reluctantly, she grabbed her cloak and followed her cousin.

''Return to your quarters,'' Captain Armande shouted as soon as they appeared on deck.

Heather whirled around to confront the toad. "You said we are permitted to take the air between the hours of two and four."

"The weather is too inclement," the captain snapped as the clouds yawned and rain pelted them.

"Bloody bugger," Heather swore and raced after her cousin for the protection of their cabin.

The next day dawned blindingly sunny. No inclement weather would mar their outing that day.

At precisely two o'clock, Heather and April arrived on deck. Instead of basking in the glory of the sun's warming rays, Heather advanced like a soldier on the unfortunate French captain.

"Washing with sea water is disgusting and intolerable," she reproached him. "My servant and I require better accommodations."

Captain Armande ignored her complaint and walked away.

Fair weather also favored their third day at sea. This time Heather complained, "Eating my meals off a rickety table while I sit on the edge of an uncomfortable cot is stealing my appetite away."

Again, Captain Armande ignored her.

Two days later, *La Belle Beaulieu* passed through the Strait of Gibraltar and burst into the Mediterranean Sea, then changed its course and sailed north by northeast toward the southern coast of France. A warm breeze, gentle as a lover's caress, delighted Heather and April. The sun heated their faces, and its rays danced across the top of the water, changing the sea's color from dark blue to green.

"Perhaps, his disposition is sunny," April said as the two girls studied the comte's miniature.

"Is this the face of a good-natured man?" Heather

countered, cocking a perfectly shaped copper brow at her cousin. "If God, in His mercy, is going to intervene, He'd better hurry."

"You haven't even met the comte," April said. "Give him a chance."

Heather moaned as if in pain.

"What's wrong?" April asked.

"Marrying the comte means I'll be required to sleep beside him each night and submit to his desires. The thought is too revolting for words. Oh, why couldn't the queen have ordered me to marry someone handsome?"

"I'd forgotten about *that*," April said.

Heather grinned unexpectedly, her smile as bright as the sun over the Mediterranean. "Before we reach Beaulieu, I must think of something that will make me decidedly unappealing to the comte. I hope my freckles make him ill."

April stared at her cousin's exquisitely lovely face. Freckles or not, Heather was a beauty. There was no chance the comte would be repulsed. Unless . . . "Perhaps, the Lord will intervene," April said. "The comte might prefer men to the company of women."

"What?" Heather couldn't credit that.

"Some men do," April insisted. "I overheard several of your brother's men-at-arms say so."

Heather burst out laughing.

But, she wasn't laughing the next day after passing a restless night on the hammock. Even the sun couldn't lighten her mood.

"Sleeping on an infernal contraption that swings back and forth with my every movement is unendurable," Heather regaled the Frenchman.

Captain Armande ignored her.

Precisely at two o'clock the following day, Heather and April went above deck. "Enough is enough" etched

itself across Heather's face as she scanned the deck for
the captain. Enduring another day of such unsuitable
conditions was out of the question. Perhaps, tears would
soften the captain's attitude.

With her cousin in tow, Heather looked everywhere,
but the captain was nowhere to be found. Stopping one
of the sailors, Heather asked in French, "Please, where
is Captain Armande?"

The sailor smiled and shrugged. When asked, several
of the other sailors gave her the same reply.

At four o'clock when they started to go below, April
spied the captain but said nothing. Apparently, Captain
Armande had tired of listening to her cousin and decided
to avoid her.

Heather felt like a mistreated prisoner, and her
thoughts of her betrothed were neither kind nor loving.
When she finally met him, Savon Fougere was going to
get a rather large, nasty piece of her mind.

Late one morning on the eighth day of their journey,
Heather decided she'd had enough of close confinement.
Was she not the future Comtesse de Beaulieu? She could
go anywhere at any time she liked.

Heather rose from the hammock where she'd sat and
brooded since breakfast. With determination stamped
across her face, she marched purposefully toward the
door.

"Where are you going?" April asked, looking up
from her needlework.

"Above deck."

"You cannot. It's not afternoon."

Heather glanced back at her cousin and arched a perfectly shaped copper brow at her. "Oh, no? Watch me."
With that, she reached for the door latch.

"Ohhh!"

Something rammed the side of the ship so fiercely,

the force of it sent Heather reeling across the cabin toward the cot. With a cry, she landed on top of her cousin.

Heather covered April's mouth with her hand to stifle her scream, ordering, "Listen."

The sounds of alarm drifted down from above deck. Men's shouts and the ringing of clashing swords reached their ears.

"W-What is it?" April asked.

"Our adventure."

"W-What d-do you m-mean?" April stuttered with fear.

"From the sound of it, we're being attacked," Heather answered. "Though I'm certain there's nothing to worry about."

"Attacked?"

"Shhh!"

Heather pressed a finger across her lips in a gesture for silence, then leaped off the cot and raced for her chest in the corner of the cabin. Kneeling in front of it, she opened the lid and reached inside. After fumbling about for several minutes, Heather pulled out a jewel-hilted dagger, a gift from her brother, then stood and hurried toward the door. If only her mother hadn't forbidden her to take her sword along!

"Where are you going?" April demanded.

"Above deck to see what's happening."

"Don't leave me here," April whined.

"Come along, but stay behind me," Heather said. "And whatever happens, don't grab my arm. Understand?"

April nodded.

Heather opened the door a crack and peered outside. No one was about. Hugging the wall, they proceeded slowly down the passageway toward the stairs. Above deck, a man shrieked in agony, and then all went silent.

April whimpered.

"Shhh!" With Heather in the lead, they climbed the stairs and stepped on deck, then gasped in unison.

A giant of a man, standing well over six feet, blocked their way. Easily the meanest-looking man they'd ever seen, the pirate was bare chested and wore baggy black pants tucked into black leather boots. His dark hair hung long on his neck and he sported a well-manicured beard. In his enormous hand he held a sword that curved, the likes of which Heather had never seen.

"Keep your distance," Heather warned, waving her ridiculously small dagger at him. "If you value your life, don't come any closer."

The giant smiled and held up his empty hand in a submissive gesture, then turned, calling over his shoulder, *"Kapudan!"*

Heather spared a quick glance around her. Dead or dying, French sailors littered the deck. Captain Armande, guarded by two fierce-looking pirates, stood a little distance away and watched his cargo being transferred to the other ship.

Heather looked back at the giant just as he was about to take advantage of her inattention. She growled as menacingly as she could and pointed the dagger at his throat.

"Kapudan!" the giant shouted. This time he wasn't smiling.

Chuckling at the incredible sight of a tiny woman holding at bay his second-in-command, the young pirate leader strode toward them. In his mid-twenties, the pirate captain was tall, broad shouldered and narrow waisted. His clean-shaven face was well tanned from exposure to all kinds of weather.

"What have we here?" the captain said in French, his black eyes gleaming with the unexpected amusement.

"None of your business," Heather snapped in French.

"You are French?" he asked.

"No."

"Then, what?"

"What I am is none of your concern," Heather replied.

Caught by her tempestuous beauty, the captain could only smile at her audacity. The woman's fiery hair matched her flaring temper and fearless spirit. She would make an interesting and spicy addition to his harem.

"I am Malik ed-din, known to my enemies as the Shark's Spawn," the captain introduced himself. "I am the grandson of the renowned Khair ed-din, also called Barbarossa."

"Baba who?" Heather asked, unimpressed.

The captain and his giant exchanged amused glances.

"And you are?" Malik prodded.

Heather drew herself up to her full height, five feet and two inches, and answered in English, "I am Heather Elizabeth Devereux, cousin to Elizabeth Tudor, Queen of England."

"You are a rare and exquisite flower ready to be plucked," Malik remarked in English, surprising her. He held out his hand, saying, "Come. I will escort you to my ship."

"An English rose has thorns that prick," Heather said, waving the dagger at him. "Keep your distance."

"Don't anger the man," April whispered behind her cousin's back. "Turks are notoriously dangerous."

"Who is that hiding behind you?" Malik asked.

"My cousin April."

"How do you do, my lord," April offered, peeking around her cousin. "A pleasure to make your acquaintance."

"The man is not making a social visit," Heather said to her cousin.

Two ripe beauties to add to his collection, Malik

thought and mentally rubbed his hands together. He took a step closer.

"Stop," Heather shouted, pointing the dagger at him. "I still hold this and am unafraid to use—"

In a sudden flash of movement, Malik kicked the dagger out of her hand and sent it sliding across the deck. "The blade is gone, my beauty," he said, stepping closer. "What will you do now?"

"This vessel belongs to my betrothed," Heather announced. "The Comte de Beaulieu's retribution for this will be severe."

Malik's smile vanished. Now Heather smiled, pleased with the result of her desperate threat.

"Rashid," the captain said and nodded at the giant. His second-in-command pulled April from behind Heather and held her in his grip of steel.

Malik walked leisurely around his beautiful, bad-tempered captive and looked her up and down, making Heather feel like a horse he was considering purchasing. A rare beauty, he decided, but her betrothed's identity changed the situation completely. Malik could not keep her when he knew another who would want her more. Ah, well, the cousin was a pretty little bird who would console him in his loss.

"You are truly the weasel's betrothed?" Malik asked, hoping he'd heard wrong.

"The Comte de Beaulieu is no weasel," Heather insisted, indignant.

"Apparently, you haven't met the man," Malik returned, then announced in a loud voice, "Heather Elizabeth Devereux, I claim you in the name of Khalid Beg, imperial Ottoman prince."

"People do not own other people," Heather said.

"Of course they do," Malik corrected her. "Masters own their slaves, do they not?"

Heather lifted her upturned nose in the air. "We do not keep slaves in England," she informed him. "Our servants are free men and women."

"You are not in England anymore, little girl," Malik said, cocking a dark brow at her. Without waiting for her to reply, he called to his watching men, "Keep off-loading that cargo." Turning back to Heather, he ordered, "You will come with me now."

"No."

"The fate of these barbarians is no pretty sight for the eyes of a delicate lady," Malik said, preferring reason to brute force where women were concerned. "I will take you and your cousin to my ship where you will be safe."

"No," Heather refused, unaware of what was to happen.

"You would bear witness to the justice of the imperial navy?" Malik asked.

"You mean, imperial pirates."

Malik shrugged. The English beauty would go along quietly once the first infidel went down. He turned and nodded at his men guarding the French captain.

One of them stepped back a few paces while the other lifted his scimitar in the air. In one swift motion, Captain Armande lost his head.

Heather stared in a horrified daze at the severed head. Glazed with shock, her emerald eyes lost their sparkle.

"Papa . . . " she mumbled, then fainted. Expecting such a reaction, Malik broke her fall and lowered her to the deck.

Without warning, April kneed the giant's groin and escaped his hold when he doubled over in surprised pain. She ran to her unconscious cousin.

Spitting mad, April turned on the pirate captain. "Look what you've done. Her nightmares will keep me awake for a month."

Malik glanced at his man and snapped, "Quit grinning, Rashid. I'll carry the lady and you take this little bird."

Malik lifted Heather into his arms, slung her over his shoulder, and started down the gangway. Without a word, Rashid grabbed April and tossed her ungently over his shoulder, then followed his captain.

When she opened her eyes, Heather saw April staring down at her. The worry shadowing her cousin's expression became cautious relief.

"How do you feel?" April asked.

"Better than Captain Armande, I'm sure."

April smiled, her relief complete. If her cousin could make morbid jokes, she must be feeling better.

Without moving, Heather scanned her surroundings. The cabin glowed softly with lamplight and the filtered sun from two portholes. More spacious than their cramped quarters on the comte's ship, the cabin was large enough for a *real* bed as well as a sturdy-looking table, complete with two chairs. Colorful pillows were scattered on the floor on one side of the room. Beyond that, Heather could see no more.

"Let me sit up," Heather said. She looked around the cabin, then remarked, "Being the Turk's prisoner appears more luxurious than being Fougere's guest."

April pointed to the chests that sat in one corner of the cabin. "They've even brought us our belongings."

"Don't be a blockhead," Heather said wryly. "Our possessions are pirate booty. The greedy buggers wouldn't leave anything behind."

Suddenly, the door swung open. Malik paused, filling the portal, and then sauntered in.

"I see you have recovered," he said in French, more comfortable with that language than English.

"The comte's ship and crew?" Heather asked.

"Violence upsets you," Malik replied, "and I never make the same mistake twice. Let us speak of more pleasant things, my beauty."

"I am not yours. As I said before—"

"And as *I* said before," he interrupted, "you are mine by right of conquest."

"My betrothed will pay a generous ransom for my safe return," Heather said.

"There will be no ransom," Malik replied.

"But—"

"Whatever price you put on yourself would fall far short of your true worth."

"Listen to me," Heather began, glaring at him.

"Silence," Malik shouted. The delicate English flower was exquisite but infuriating. If Khalid didn't kill her first, this one could be capable of piercing the shield that guarded his friend's heart.

"My cabin is yours," Malik told them. "Make yourselves comfortable. Remember, escape is impossible. There is no place to go. Naturally, guards will be posted outside the door."

"There's no need for that," Heather said, her voice oozing with sweetness. "We wouldn't dream of making your misbegotten, contemptible life more difficult."

Malik smiled with patience, thinking the English beauty played a child's game of taunting. She was trapped and knew it. What else could she do but try to wound him with her tongue?

"Do English ladies play chess?" he asked. "We could enjoy a game this evening."

"I'd as lief play chess with a snake," she said, irritated by his indifference to her insults.

"I can see that Khalid must school you on proper manners," Malik said, heading for the door.

"What's a Khalid?" Heather asked.

Malik paused, his expression becoming grim. In an ominous voice, he told them, "Khalid is the Sword of Allah." The door clicked shut behind him.

"Oh, my Lord," April moaned. "What in God's name is the sword of Allah?"

"Never mind about that," Heather said, sounding more confident than she actually felt. "We must plan our escape."

"Plan our escape?" April cried. "We're in the middle of the *damned* sea! There's nowhere to go!"

"Vulgarity is unbecoming of you," Heather chided. "Besides, a tiring woman does not yell at her lady."

"She does when the lady endangers her life."

Never had Heather seen her sweet-tempered cousin so angry. It was definitely a nice change.

"This is all your fault," April accused her.

"My fault?"

"Well, you're the one who wished for an adventure."

"Calm down," Heather said. "When we get to wherever he's taking us, we'll escape. Trust me to get you home."

"Home?" April echoed. "To England?"

"Yes, I've decided I won't marry that weasel."

"But, the queen—"

"We'll worry about the queen later," Heather said. "You don't drink a skin of wine in a single gulp, do you? No, you swallow it one sip at a time."

"Escaping a ship full of Turks is impossible," April said, sitting beside her cousin on the bed. "How can you be so relaxed about this?"

"I'm relieved I don't have to bed the weasel," Heather answered.

"There are worse things in life than marrying an ugly man," April remarked.

Heather glanced sidelong at her. "So, you finally agree the comte is a weasel?"

"Bedding the weasel is preferable to slaving for a heathen Turk," April said. "We'll never see England again."

Heather stood up and crossed the cabin to her sea chest. Dropping to her knees, she rummaged around inside and pulled another dagger out, then returned to the bed and hid it beneath the pillow.

"We'll ambush the next Turk who walks through that door," Heather said, sitting down. "All we have to do is wait."

Heather lay back on the bed. Relief and uncertainty warred inside her. Eventually, Heather found release from the conflicting emotions in sleep, but fear kept her cousin awake.

April walked to one of the portholes. She stood there a long time and watched the sun's rays play on top of the waves. Everything beyond the ship was water. Even if Heather managed to capture one of the Turks, escape was impossible. There was nowhere to go.

"Papa," Heather mumbled in her sleep.

April whirled around and stared at her.

"Papa," Heather moaned again, curled herself into a ball and wept.

Racing across the cabin, April nudged and then shook her cousin, ordering, "Wake up. It's only a dream."

Heather opened her eyes and focused on her cousin, then sat up. "Papa's dead because of me," she whispered in a voice that ached with loss.

"That's not true," April said, the pain in her cousin's voice tugging at her heart.

"I keep thinking, if only I had—"

"What's done is past," April interrupted. "Fix your thoughts on getting us away from these heathens."

Heather nodded. Hadn't she reviewed over and over

the horrifying events of that fateful day? In a thousand nightmares and daydreams the bloody scene of her father's murder played again. She'd even taken weaponry lessons with her brother, but her skill with daggers and swords had come too late to save her father.

"Someone's coming," April whispered, hearing the sound of boots outside.

Heather grabbed the dagger from beneath the pillow, dashed across the cabin, and pressed her back to the wall. The door swung open. A man carrying a tray of food entered and walked toward April. Reaching the center of the cabin, the pirate stopped short when he felt the sharp point of a dagger pressed to his back.

"Gently hand my cousin the tray," Heather ordered in French, hoping he understood. "Then turn around and take us to your captain."

"No need for that," a voice filled with laughter sounded behind her. "I am here, at your service."

Heather froze. It was then she felt the tip of a dagger pressed to *her* back.

"Drop your weapon," Heather said, "or I will kill your man."

The captain chuckled. "I have many men aboard my ship. Losing one will be no problem."

"For God's sake, don't anger the Turk," April pleaded. "He'll kill us."

"Turn around slowly and hand me your dagger," the captain ordered.

Heather did as she was told. Smiling, the captain and his giant stood there.

The captain said something in Turkish. The man set the tray on the table and hurried out. The giant headed for the sea chests and scattered their belongings on the floor in his search for weapons. Satisfied there were none, the big man left.

"*Bon appétit,*" the captain said with a broad grin and backed out of the cabin, being sure to lock the door on his way out.

"Bloody bugger," Heather shouted, hurling a goblet at the door.

"What will we do now?" April whined.

"A minor setback," Heather said, sitting down on the edge of the bed. "We'll use plan B."

"Which is?"

"I don't know," Heather said with a shrug. "I'll think of something."

Enjoying fair winds, the ship *Saddam* sailed east and passed through the Dardanelles to the Sea of Marmara where the captain's villa was located near Gallipoli. Heather and April remained imprisoned in the cabin, their only visitors being Malik and his second-in-command, Rashid. The demeaning task of serving the ladies their meals and seeing to their few needs went to Rashid. His very size, not to mention the scimitar at his side, encouraged their cooperation.

"Look," Heather called from where she stood at the porthole.

April put her needlework down, crossed the cabin and peered outside. "Land."

In the distance, rolling green hills rose gently beyond the bleached white sands of a beach. Amazingly, what looked like soldiers' tents dotted those verdant knolls, and an enormous villa loomed behind the tents.

"Where are we?" April asked.

"I have no idea." Intending to find out, Heather crossed the cabin and tried to open the door. It was locked. "I'm certain we'll find out soon enough," she said, then sat on the bed.

"Perhaps we're better off not knowing," April said, returning to her needlework at the table.

The dinner hour came and went with no sight of Rashid with their food. The sounds of the pirates off-loading their booty drifted down to Heather and April. By early afternoon, they were beside themselves with worry. Startled by the sudden sound of the door being unlocked, Heather and April tensed and looked nervously at each other.

Malik, carrying a tray in his hands, walked in and smiled at them. His appearance at that time of day made them instantly suspicious.

"Are you trying to starve us?" Heather asked.

"Certainly not," Malik said, then gestured to the tray that held two crystal goblets. One contained a pink liquid, but the other was almost colorless. "I've brought you refreshment. It's a drink called sherbet and made with fruit juice. The pink is flavored with rose petals and the other is made from a lemon."

Malik handed the rose petal sherbet to April and the lemon sherbet to Heather. "Drink up," he urged. "You will eat when we arrive at my home."

"This is bitter," Heather remarked, but took another sip. Lord, she was hungry.

"Mine isn't," April said.

"Have you never eaten lemons?" Malik asked, looking out the porthole. "Their taste is tart."

Heather set the empty goblet on the table and crossed the cabin to stand beside him. "What will happen to us now?" she asked.

"The villa is mine," Malik told her. "The tents are Khalid's. At times, he insists upon living in the manner of his ancestors."

"Then wouldn't a *cave* be more appropriate?"

Malik looked down at her and said, "Khalid is a man the likes of which you have never met."

"What has this Khalid to do with April and me?"

Heather asked, then yawned loudly and stretched, feeling relaxed.

"He has nothing to do with April," he answered, noting her movement, "and everything to do with you."

Gazing up at him through strangely blurred vision, Heather could not have cared less. A wonderful feeling of lethargic well-being made her indifferent. "How so?" she asked, crossing the cabin to sit down on the bed.

"I am gifting Khalid with you," Malik said matter-of-factly. "April will remain with me."

"Oh." Too drowsy to care, Heather flopped back on the bed.

"You cannot separate us," April cried. "How will we—?" She broke off. "Heather, he means to separate us."

When Heather only shrugged, April realized something was terribly wrong. She raced to the bed and nudged, then shook, her cousin. "Didn't you hear him?" April shouted. "He's going to separate us."

"Calm down," Heather said, patting her shoulder. "I'm not deaf, you know."

"What have you done?" April demanded, turning on the pirate.

"Pull in your talons, little bird," Malik said with a smile. "I have merely given your mistress something to ease her transition."

"See," Heather mumbled, then closed her eyes in sleep.

April rounded on the pirate and opened her mouth to speak.

"Be silent," Malik ordered, cutting off whatever she would have said. "I show your mistress a kindness by letting her sleep throughout what is to come. Be thankful for small mercies." With that, he left the cabin and locked the door behind him.

Chapter 2

The last ray of sun dropped below the western horizon, leaving the early evening sky awash with shades of dusky lavender. The Sword of Allah, anticipating the arrival of his guest, stepped from his palatial tent and stole a moment of solitude to enjoy the muted beauty of twilight.

Khalid Beg, imperial Ottoman prince, appeared every inch the well-honed soldier that he was. Standing two inches over six feet, Khalid was broad shouldered and narrow waisted. His hair, a thick mane of ebony, hung low on his neck; and disconcerting sky-blue eyes, his great-grandmother's legacy to him, glittered from his clean-shaven and well-tanned face. Marring his near perfectly chiseled features, an angular scar slashed across the length of his right cheek from his temple to his sensuously formed lips and gave him a frightening, dangerous aura.

Always alert to the unexpected, Khalid felt encumbered when he wore the robes favored by the Ottomans. His brocaded, flowing robes remained in his home near Istanbul where he felt at ease with his surroundings. On this particular night, Khalid dressed like a magnificent corsair. He wore baggy white trousers tucked into soft kidskin boots and a white cotton shirt with sleeves that gathered at his wrists. Sheathed at his side was a jewel-hilted dagger.

"Merhaba!" called a familiar voice. "Hello!"

Khalid turned to see Malik and his man Rashid approaching. The two longtime friends greeted each other with affection and went inside the tent. Rashid and several of the prince's men followed but remained in the tent's antechamber. Walking into his private quarters, Khalid gestured Malik to sit down on the pillows set beside the small table.

One of the prince's men entered with their supper of mutton grilled on a spit, accompanied by saffroned rice with sweet green and red peppers. There were pickled cucumbers, stuffed grape leaves, peaches, and figs. After placing a decanter of rosewater on the table, the servant bowed his way out.

Malik cast his friend a mischievous smile and pulled a decanter of wine from beneath his shirt. He filled his crystal goblet and then held it up in a silent offering.

Khalid shook his head. "The Koran strictly forbids the consumption of alcohol."

"You sound like a holy man," Malik said. "Besides, Sultan Selim has a taste for the fermented juice of the grape and, I hear, is considering an invasion of Cyprus because of their legendary wines."

"Do not repeat this," Khalid said, "but I have moments when I wonder if my uncle is the true issue of my illustrious grandfather."

Malik chuckled. "Murad is no better."

"My cousin is as obsessed with women and gold as his father is with wine," Khalid conceded.

"You would have made a good sultan," Malik said.

"Voicing that thought is treason," Khalid warned, glancing sidelong at his friend. "Besides, I descend through the female line and am faithful to the sultan in all things, no matter his flaws."

"I cast no aspersions on your fidelity," Malik said.

"However, you do possess many of your grandfather's virtues."

"Unlike my grandfather, women hold no sway in my heart," Khalid replied. "Devious creatures by nature, the weaker sex needs a firm, guiding hand lest they become uncontrollable."

"Even Khurrem and Mihrimah?"

"Especially my late grandmother and mother," Khalid said. "Uncle Mustafa could have become a great sultan but, as you know, fell prey to my grandmother's machinations. And, Mihrimah is no better than her mother."

"The fig falls beneath the tree," Malik replied.

Khalid nodded in agreement, then changed the subject. "Tell me of your travels while I was in Istanbul."

"We caught one of Fougere's ships," Malik dropped casually.

Khalid's expression darkened at the mention of that name, and unconsciously, his thumb stroked the scar on his face. "I will eventually cut out the weasel's heart for what he did to my sister and brother."

"Not to mention your face," Malik added.

"My face is of no import."

"We seized very valuable cargo."

Khalid arched a brow at his friend. "Such as?"

Malik grinned. "You will see for yourself after we've eaten. I have selected a special gift for you."

"The only gift I desire is the weasel's head," Khalid told him. "Or his balls."

"You will desire this gift when you see it," Malik said. "Trust me."

Their conversation turned to other matters concerning the empire. When they finished eating, two men entered. One cleared the dishes, and the other offered them bowls of warm, scented water to wash their hands and soft linen cloths to dry them. Then, the two friends rose from the table to stretch their legs.

"Tell my man that it is time," Malik ordered one of the servants.

Rashid returned a few minutes later and strode into the tent's inner chamber, pausing to hold the flap aside so his master's men could enter. Four of them carried a rolled up carpet slung across their shoulders. Behind them came six of the prince's most trusted warriors.

"A carpet?" Khalid asked.

"The gift is inside." Malik nodded at his men. Ever so gently, they lowered the carpet to the floor. Two began to unroll it until the edge of the unraveled carpet touched the prince's booted feet.

Khalid stared in surprise at what the carpet contained, the most exquisite piece of womanhood that he had ever seen. Clad in a transparent silken chemise and asleep, Heather appeared like the mythical goddess of love that he'd read about while studying at the prince's school in Topkapi Palace. The tantalizing curves of her flawless body begged to be explored. Having never seen a red-haired woman, Khalid stared at her crown of copper hair that rivaled the natural glory of a fiery sunset.

Enchanted by the beauty sprawled at his feet, Khalid knelt beside her and reached for the soft silkiness of her cheek. Though his touch was light, Heather's eyelids fluttered and opened to reveal disarming emerald eyes.

Heather stared in a daze at him.

Khalid smiled at her clouded expression.

When her vision cleared, Heather found herself staring at a dark-haired, blue-eyed stranger. An ugly scar marred what would have been an incredibly handsome face. In the next instant, she focused on Malik, standing behind him, and then realized she was almost naked. Faster than the blink of an eye, Heather snatched the dagger at Khalid's side and pressed its sharp point against his throat, surprising him and everyone else.

"Get up," she ordered in French.

Angry surprise registered on the prince's face. With his hands held open, Khalid stood up slowly. He did not actually fear her, but thought her badly shaking hand might slip and inadvertently do him injury.

Heather ignored the cramps in her trembling legs as she rose unsteadily, dizzy from the sleeping draft she'd been given. In her right hand, the dagger pointed ready to pierce him. With her left hand, she tried vainly to shield herself from his gaze.

Khalid and Heather stared into each other's eyes. He seemed bemused; she trembled with fright.

It was then Heather felt the cold caress of steel pressed against her back and froze. Without moving a muscle, she looked first to the left and then the right. Six men, with their daggers poised to skewer, surrounded her. That unspeakably horrific memory arose in her mind's eye and blurred her vision. "Don't!" she cried, and fainted. The dagger fell harmlessly to the carpet.

Khalid caught Heather before she fell and carried her to his couch, then drew the coverlet up and sat on the edge. Over his shoulder, he ordered the others to leave. Only Malik remained behind.

"She's as wild as an untamed mare," Khalid said in a voice filled with wonder.

"And as cantankerous as a camel," Malik added.

"What is she?"

"English."

"Indeed, this is a rare gift," Khalid said, "but I have no need for a clinging woman to slow me down."

"I would hardly call her behavior clinging," Malik remarked. "Besides, this woman is special."

"You took her off Fougere's ship?"

Before Malik could answer, Heather regained consciousness. Her startling green eyes opened and stared up at her captor.

"How do you feel?" Khalid asked in French, his voice stern.

Careful to keep the tops of her breasts covered, Heather sat up and asked, "Who are you? Why do you need an army to subdue one small woman?"

"I see that you do feel better." Khalid reached out to brush his fingertips against the silkiness of her flushed cheek, murmuring, "Soft . . . lovely."

Heather slapped his hand away.

Khalid scowled.

"My betrothed will pay—" Heather began.

"You have no betrothed," Khalid interrupted her. "You are my property and will forget your past life."

"I belong to myself," Heather cried, unable to believe what she was hearing. Her anger overruled her fear, and she added, "The Comte de Beaulieu will cut you up into a thousand tiny pieces."

Her words drew an instant reaction from him, but not the one she'd hoped for. His expression darkened ominously and the scar on his right cheek whitened in a sure sign of fury.

That forbidding transformation drew an instant reaction from her. Realizing she'd gone too far, Heather paled and trembled uncontrollably. Oh, Lord! Would she never learn to keep her mouth shut?

"The Comte de Beaulieu?" Khalid asked, looking at his friend.

Malik nodded. "I snatched Fougere's intended wife."

Khalid stared at Heather as if she'd suddenly grown another head. Finally, the corners of his lips twitched and turned up in a mockery of a smile.

"Release me," Heather said, finding her voice

through her fear. "Send me home to England. I have done nothing—"

Khalid leaned close, and nose to nose with her, growled, "Silence."

Heather shut her mouth.

Khalid turned to Malik. "Leave us now."

"Stay," Heather cried, her panic rising.

"Leave us."

"Stay!"

Like a baited bear, Malik snapped his head from one to the other. Then he smiled. The imperial Ottoman prince had met his match in the English queen's cousin.

Khalid reached out and covered Heather's mouth and nose with his hand.

Heather couldn't breathe. She went wild, fighting for freedom. Finally, she understood his point, and her struggles ceased.

Satisfied, Khalid removed his hand and said to Malik, "Please, leave us."

"Khalid—" Malik began.

"Destroying this remarkable gift is not my intention," Khalid cut off his protest. "She is more valuable alive than dead. Now, leave me to enjoy this exquisite gift from the sea."

The operative word was *enjoy*. Malik opened his mouth to protest, but then shut it. After all, he intended to "enjoy" the pretty little cousin that very night. This woman's safety was his concern no longer. Malik nodded and left.

Khalid stared into enormous green eyes that shone with apprehension. Her uncommon beauty attracted him. Though she was truly magnificent, Khalid knew she had to be as evil as her betrothed. Evil or no, he would use her. It was fitting after what Fougere had done to his sister.

Heather stared into his cold blue eyes. Never before had she been so close, so alone, or so vulnerable with a man. Recognizing the unmasked hatred mirrored in his expression, she trembled with fright.

Khalid noted her trepidation. Though he had little reason to like women and the Koran permitted corporal punishment, Khalid had never struck one. In his personal philosophy, hurting weaker, helpless creatures was unmanly and dishonorable. However, he felt no aversion to frightening them when the need arose. Real strength of character lay in training a slave without using physical force, especially when that slave was a woman as spirited as this one.

"The pampered life of a noblewoman is behind you," Khalid said, his eyes warning her to remain silent or suffer some unnamed but hideous punishment.

Heather's eyes narrowed, her anger rising like a sudden gust of wind, all sign of her previous fear gone.

Surprised by the defiance in her gaze, Khalid cocked a dark brow at her. "Your eyes scream rebellion," he said.

Heather's mouth dropped open. "How can you know my thoughts?"

"Silence," Khalid growled. "You are mine and will serve my every whim and need. Do you understand your position?"

Heather refused to meet his gaze. She remained silent and fixed her eyes on the wall of the tent behind him.

"Look at me when I speak to you," Khalid ordered, grasping her chin in his hands and forcing her to meet his gaze. Green eyes and blue eyes clashed in a fierce battle of wills.

Looking at him disturbed Heather. She dropped her gaze and said, "I understand your words."

"Your continued good health depends upon perfect obedience," Khalid told her.

Heather's head snapped up. "Are you going to murder me?" she asked. "Or worse?"

"Lesson one: A slave never questions her master," Khalid informed her. "Understand?"

"Perfectly." Heather's expression told him that she understood but did not accept.

"You're not as unintelligent as you appear," he baited her, then added when she opened her mouth to reply, "Lesson two: A slave speaks only when spoken to. Understand?"

No one had ever taken that tone with her before. Heather had trouble finding her words.

"Well?"

"I understand."

Khalid patted her hands. "This pleases me."

Heather promptly wiped his touch off on the coverlet, a gesture not lost on him. If she'd been a man, Khalid would have applauded her courage and then killed her, but he was a warrior. His experience did not extend to willful women, reluctant as he was to using physical force against a weaker creature.

"My name is Prince Khalid which means the Sword of Allah," he told her, his expression stern. "But you will call me lord or master."

Heather said nothing, but rebellion shone from her eyes.

"What are you called?" Khalid asked.

"Heather Elizabeth Devereux."

"Such a big name for so small a woman. What does it mean?"

"Heather? Why, heather is a wildflower."

"Appropriate," Khalid remarked. "And the other part?"

"Devereux is my family name, and Elizabeth is in honor of my cousin, the queen of England," Heather told him, hoping that invoking the queen's name would win her an immediate release.

Khalid seemed unimpressed. "But, you are commonly known as Heather, the wildflower?"

"Yes."

"I will change it."

"Change what?"

"Your name," Khalid said. "That word *heather* feels uncomfortable on my tongue. Besides, your new life requires a new name."

"I like my name," Heather said. "I can't answer to any other."

Khalid shrugged. "You are probably too slow in the mind to remember a new name anyway."

"Slow in the—"

"Silence."

"I want to go home," Heather said, ignoring his command.

"Your home is with me," Khalid said. "Forget Fougere."

Heather snapped her eyes shut and wished, I want this adventure to end. He was still there when she opened her eyes again. "I want to go home to England," she told him in a forlorn voice. "I have caused you no injury."

Khalid stared at her, his expression softening for the briefest moment. "Your father would seek vengeance on me," he said, steeling himself against her. "I have too many enemies as it is."

"My father is dead," Heather said in a choked voice.

"Then I need have no fear on that account." Khalid correctly calculated that his callousness would anger her.

"Beast." The word slipped out before she could swallow it.

Khalid leaned close and said in a harsh voice, "Yes, Wildflower. I am known throughout the empire as the

Sultan's Beast and feared. Grown men quake at the mention of me, and mothers discipline their children by invoking my name.''

"You mean, as in 'the Sultan's Beast will get you'?'' In spite of herself, Heather smiled, thoroughly beguiling her captor.

Khalid gave himself a mental shake. His intrepid captive was entirely too beautiful. If he wasn't careful . . . The little barbarian was Fougere's intended. She would pay for the weasel's crimes against his family.

"I wish to inspect my gift,'' Khalid said brusquely, rising from the edge of the couch.

Heather shrank back. "You what?''

"Get up and let me see you.''

Heather shook her head and pulled the coverlet up to her chin.

"I said, get up.''

Again, Heather shook her head. Her knuckles whitened from clenching the coverlet so tightly.

Khalid reached out to pull the coverlet back, and a tug of war ensued. Within mere seconds, he whipped it out of her hands.

Heather leaped off the couch. Sprinting past him, she raced around the table, and cursing in Turkish, Khalid gave chase.

Spying his scimitar propped against the side of the tent, Heather lunged for it. In one swift motion, she grabbed it and whirled around to confront him.

"Be careful, slave, or you will cut yourself,'' Khalid warned, then baited her, "Consider yourself lucky to be my concubine instead of the weasel's wife.''

His words hit their mark.

"Concubine?'' Brandishing the heavy scimitar high above her head, Heather flew at him in a rage and swung with all her strength.

Khalid sidestepped to safety. The weight of the weapon toppled Heather forward, headfirst, and the scimitar dropped from her grasp. Khalid caught her before she landed on it. He shoved her down on the carpet and fell on top of her. His body covered hers completely.

"I can ravish you here where we lie," Khalid said, nose to nose with her. "Or, you can stand for my inspection."

Shaking in fear, Heather nodded quickly. She'd never been this close to any man and would have agreed to almost anything to get him off her.

Khalid stood. Reaching down, he grabbed her wrist and yanked her ungently to her feet.

Villain, Heather thought, rubbing her wrist.

"Stand still or I will call my guards to hold you," Khalid said.

Beneath his gaze, Heather suffered the worst humiliation of her seventeen years. She felt like the concubine that he said she was. Shame forced her to fix her gaze on the carpet.

Deliberately, Khalid circled her and perused her body as if consigning it to memory. What he saw inflamed his senses. Heather's angel face topped the body of a goddess. Her luxuriant mane of copper hair cascaded below her waist like a fiery veil, and the swell of her breasts played a teasing game of peekaboo with his mesmerized gaze.

"Petite but not too small," Khalid murmured, circling her without touching. "Nicely rounded buttocks . . . inviting hips created to entice a man and bear his young."

Heather folded her arms across her chest, protecting herself from his gaze. Her face flamed with embarrassment.

"A virgin?" Khalid asked, touching her burning cheek with the palm of his hand.

Though seemingly impossible, Heather's complexion reddened even more. "Yes," she whispered, mortified by his asking.

"Speak with honesty to me," Khalid warned. "There are ways to learn the truth of the matter." His piercing, blue-eyed gaze seemed to see to the very depth of her soul.

Heather stared at him blankly. She had no idea what he was suggesting.

Khalid read the innocence in her expression. Satisfied, he ordered, "Drop your arms. I wish to see your breasts."

Shocked, Heather could only stare at him.

"My guards are outside," Khalid reminded her. "Shall I call them?"

Heather dropped her arms.

Staring at her, Khalid warred against his raging desire but lost the battle for control. He reached out and cupped one soft mound through the silken fabric.

Heather instinctively slapped his hand away.

"Lesson three: Slaves do not strike their masters," Khalid said.

"People do not own other people," Heather cried.

"Who told you that lie? I will cut his tongue out." Again, Khalid reached for her breast.

"No!" Heather slapped his offending hand.

Her insolence broke his control. Grabbing her, Khalid yanked her off her feet and pressed her against the masculine hardness of his body. His mouth swooped down and captured hers in a brutal, punishing kiss.

The feel of him pressing against her stomach made her nearly insane with fear. Heather went wild, kicking and clawing for freedom.

Khalid released her abruptly and sent her crashing to the carpet. Never had he forced himself on a woman, and though provoked, he wasn't about to start now.

Long, silent moments passed as Khalid and Heather stared at each other. Fear and revulsion leaped at him from her emerald gaze.

Khalid looked her up and down, from the top of her head to the tips of her toes. When he leveled his gaze on hers once more, contempt had etched itself across his features. She was the weasel's betrothed, not a gift from Allah.

"I'd sooner mate with a leper," Khalid said, then brushed past her to leave. He paused before disappearing outside and said, "You need harbor no fear for your dubious virtue. Go to sleep."

Stunned, Heather stared after him. Immediate escape was necessary; he could change his mind and ravish her. She refused to be any man's concubine, much less his slave. She'd rather be dead.

"Damn," Heather swore softly. How could she escape with no clothes? Though she wasn't above stealing his, Heather realized she would be unable to locate April in the night. Her shoulders slumped at the thought of waiting until morning. She yanked the coverlet off the bed and wrapped it around herself.

Tension and fear had dried her mouth, giving her an almost unendurable thirst. Looking around, she spied a half-filled bottle on the table.

Heather raised it to her lips and gulped a healthy swig. *Wine!* The one drink in the world she detested! Pinching her nostrils together, Heather took a sip. She grimaced at the taste but swallowed it. At least, her mouth felt better.

Heather convinced herself that she was relatively safe for this one night. If the monster's intent was murder or rape, he would have done so already. Uncertain of what she should do, Heather sat down on the bed. Tears welled up in her eyes and streamed down her cheeks. Oh, why had she ever wished for adventure? She was powerless to end it when she wanted.

When Khalid stormed out of his tent, he stopped to speak with his second-in-command, Abdul. "Set guards around the tent," he ordered. "No one goes in or out."

The older man nodded and grinned knowingly. "I will lay down my life to keep the little barbarian safe until you prepare yourself for the next battle. Beating her might help."

Khalid failed to see the humor in his man's words. He leveled a scathing look on Abdul and walked away.

The rhythmic sound of crashing waves and the purifying, salty smell of the sea drew Khalid. He walked to the beach and looked up. Accompanied by hundreds of glittering stars, a tangerine moon rode high in the velvet indigo sky. A peacefulness that eluded Khalid pervaded the night.

Alone with his thoughts, Khalid wondered how best to handle his incorrigible captive without hurting her. His fearsome reputation encouraged others to do his bidding, but this slip of a girl was ignorant of his past, that he'd ordered the slaughter of hundreds of innocents.

Am I back to that again? Khalid asked himself. Will I never enjoy peace of mind?

Always second behind his older brother, Khalid had been too eager for his mother's dubious praise. A fledgling commander in his grandfather's service, he'd ordered his warriors to destroy those defiant villages that refused to submit to the will of Allah. Grant them no mercy, he'd ordered his warriors.

How Khalid regretted those words, his lack of understanding of what those orders meant! The gruesome slaughter of those women and children had earned him the name "Sultan's Beast." Gazing upon the carnage, he'd vowed never to raise his hand in anger to a woman or child.

That vow hadn't been necessary. The legend of the Sultan's Beast grew and spread throughout the empire until few dared to gaze upon his face for fear of incurring his wrath.

The approbation he'd seen in his mother's eyes hadn't been worth the lives of those innocents, and it hadn't lasted either. She blamed him for the death of his brother at the Comte de Beaulieu's hands. She taunted him about the disfiguring scar he'd taken when his brother died.

Khalid gave himself a mental shake and turned his thoughts to the problem at hand. How was he to train such an ignorant captive? She didn't even know to drop her gaze in the presence of men. Why, she'd boldly stared him straight in the eye as if she were his equal.

Beautiful and brave, Heather intrigued him. She was unlike any woman he'd ever met. No man had ever had the courage to argue with him, much less threaten him with his own dagger and scimitar. Though she feared his strength and power, his wildflower gazed upon his disfigured face without revulsion, a thing his own mother was unable to do.

His wildflower? What in Allah's name was he thinking? The Englishwoman was the weasel's betrothed, and he must never forget that. Attempting to force her out of his mind, Khalid began reciting verses from the Koran.

It didn't help.

Two hours later, Khalid returned to his camp. He dismissed the guards surrounding his tent, then arched a questioning brow at his second-in-command.

"No trouble," Abdul reported gravely, then ruined it by adding, "She's saving her strength for the next battle. Take my advice and beat her into submission."

Without a word, Khalid went inside. The light from

the candle on the table bathed the inner chamber with an eerie glow. Curled on her side, his captive was asleep on his bed.

Lesson four, Khalid thought, mocking himself: A slave sleeps on the floor, not in her master's bed. He would school her in that in the morning.

Turning away, Khalid snuffed out the candle. He sat on the edge of the table and removed his boots, then stood up and pulled his shirt over his head. Khalid reached for the top of his pants, but a sound from the bed drew his attention.

"No, Papa, no," Heather moaned, caught in a nightmare. Then she began to weep softly in her sleep.

Khalid lay down beside her and gathered her into his arms. "Rest easy," he whispered, stroking her shoulder and arm. His presence and touch quieted her, but he didn't let go.

The Ottoman prince and his English slave have one thing in common, he thought wryly. Demons stalk their thoughts.

Without thinking, Khalid planted a kiss on the top of Heather's head. He tightened his protective embrace, then closed his eyes and slept.

Chapter 3

Heather awakened disoriented, but as she focused on her surroundings, the humiliating memory of the previous evening came rushing back to her. The sounds of morning drifted in from outside as the prince's men prepared themselves for a new day. Heather sent up a quick prayer of thanks that she was alone. But, where was the beast?

This seemed the perfect opportunity to escape. She had to get out of the camp and rescue April. Was her cousin still on board the ship? Or had the pirate carried her off? Never mind, Heather decided, she would search the ship first. But how? One step at a time, she told herself.

Heather rose from the couch. She knew she needed food and clothing.

The sight of her captor's breakfast on the table made her stomach growl. There were flaky rolls, jam, honey, sheep's cheese, and black olives.

Grabbing a roll, Heather broke it into two pieces. She smeared jam onto one half and gobbled it down, then dipped the other piece in the honey and devoured that too. Ignoring the olives, Heather took a hunk of the cheese and another roll to eat while she searched for something to wear.

Suddenly, voices sounded in the tent's outer chamber. Heather leaped onto the couch and pretended to sleep.

Peeping from beneath half-closed lids, Heather saw two servants walk into the tent's private chamber. Without sparing a glance in her direction, they cleared the table and left.

Heather waited several minutes before rising. Then she heard it—*his* voice raised in anger at someone outside the tent.

Mustering her courage, Heather decided to get up and search for clothing. Again, she heard footsteps in the outer chamber and snapped her eyes shut. Opening her eyelids a crack, Heather saw her captor advancing on her. Though her heart pounded frantically, she forced herself to shallow breathing in simulated sleep.

Khalid stood beside the couch and stared at his startlingly beautiful captive. She appeared undisturbed by his men. Though he knew he would be victorious in the end, Khalid actually looked forward to her awakening so their battle could begin again. Turning away, he walked back outside.

Heather opened her eyes. What should she do? Escape was now or never.

Leaping off the bed, Heather dropped the coverlet and raced for the discarded clothing that her captor had worn the previous night. She pulled the white cotton shirt over her head. Its bottom edge fell to her knees like a short nightshift.

Next, Heather stepped into his pants and yanked them up, then tucked the shirt inside. She let go, and the pants dropped to her ankles. With a silent curse upon her lips, Heather pulled them up again and grabbed a nearby cord of leather. After tying it tightly around her waist, she rolled each pant leg up. *Success!*

Heather considered taking his boots but guessed that their flopping on her much smaller feet would slow her down. Better to go barefoot than be caught, she decided.

Heather hurried to the rear of the tent and dropped to her knees. Leaning her head against the side of the tent, she listened to silence and prayed that no one stood outside. She lifted the bottom edge a crack and saw no boots, then crawled on her stomach into the world outside her captor's tent.

Ahead of her stood Malik's villa, and behind was the center of Khalid's camp. The beach and the ship lay beyond the camp. Intending to skirt the perimeter of the camp and head for the beach, Heather scurried noiselessly from the back of one tent to another until she was well away.

Meanwhile, Khalid stood outside his tent and watched Malik approach. He smiled and raised his hand in a greeting.

"I could hear your roars from my terrace," Malik said, then glanced at the tent. "How is she?"

"Alive, well, and sleeping," Khalid answered. "I was reprimanding two of my imbecile servants who entered my tent without permission."

Malik grinned. "Wore her out?"

Khalid shrugged.

"I am keeping the cousin."

"What cousin?" Khalid asked.

"Your captive's cousin accompanied her," Malik explained. "I claim her for my own."

"Do what you will."

Malik gestured to the tent. "What will you do with her?"

"Make her my slave."

"And Fougere?"

"We will send him a message by way of the Dey of Algiers and the Duc de Sassari," Khalid said. "When he hears what I have planned for her, Fougere will leave his hiding place to regain his betrothed and revenge himself on me. It is a matter of pride."

"Weasels have no pride," Malik replied.

"Fougere will come," Khalid predicted. "And we will be ready."

Both Abdul and Rashid descended on them at that moment. Khalid's man had a plate of rolls for Heather's breakfast, and Malik's second-in-command carried Heather's chest from the ship.

"I thought your slave would need her belongings," Malik said.

Khalid nodded. "If I kept her undressed, she would certainly become a distraction to the many men who parade in and out of my tent." He took the plate of rolls from his man, ordering, "Abdul, carry the chest."

Inside his private chamber, Khalid stopped short and looked around in disbelief. The tent was empty.

"Where is she?" Malik asked.

"Gone."

"Without clothing?"

"It appears she wore mine," Khalid said. He had to admit the woman had pluck. "Allah be praised, I took my dagger out of harm's way this morning, and the scimitar is too heavy for her."

"The scimitar?" Malik echoed.

"Last night she tried to split me in half."

Malik chuckled.

"I advised you to beat her," Abdul said, shaking his head in disapproval. "Should I sound the alarm?"

"No, she cannot have gone far," Khalid replied.

"I will help," Malik offered. "But where should we search?"

"Abdul, take Rashid with you to the villa. She may have gone there to search for her cousin, but if you find her, do not harm her." Khalid turned to Malik, saying, "We will search the beach, in the event she thinks to swim to freedom."

On the grassy knoll overlooking the deserted beach, Heather lay flat on her stomach and surveyed the scene in front of her. Several unattended dinghies had been pulled up on the sand, and the ship stood at anchor in the bay.

Heather wondered how many men were on board. Though it appeared deserted, she was certain the captain had left guards. Heather decided to make a run for one of the dinghies and row out to the ship. She was only sorry she had been unable to steal a knife.

The image of the prince formed in her mind. What was he doing at that moment? When he discovered her missing, what would he do? And, more importantly, what would he do to her if he caught her?

One, two, three, Heather counted, but fear of the water kept her rooted to the spot. She'd never learned to swim. How could she climb into that boat and row out to the ship?

Calm down, Heather told herself. There was nothing to fear but drowning in the sea. Then Heather thought of April. What torment was her cousin suffering at the hands of that pirate? April could be injured or worse. That thought spurred her into action.

Heather leaped to her feet and raced down the slope to the beach. After dragging the dinghy into the water, she climbed into it and set the oars in place, then began rowing to the ship.

"There!" shouted a masculine voice.

Heather looked toward the shore, and her heart sank to her stomach. Khalid and Malik were running down the slope to the beach. After stopping to pull his boots off, Khalid dove into the surf and began swimming toward the dinghy.

Bad luck that the beast could swim, Heather thought

and rowed faster. Unfortunately, he swam faster than she rowed.

As Khalid reached the dinghy and started to hoist himself inside, Heather lifted one of the oars high in the air to hit him. With lightning quick reflexes, Khalid grabbed the oar and pulled it and Heather out of the dinghy.

"Help!" Heather screamed, and sank.

Khalid dove under the water and yanked her up by her hair. He turned her around in his arms and swam back to shore, then dragged her to safety on the sand.

Heather coughed and choked, then lost the swallowed seawater and her pilfered breakfast. Finally, she looked up the long length of her captor and said, "I thought you were drowning me."

"I saved your worthless life," Khalid said in a purposefully menacing voice.

Tears welled up in Heather's eyes. "My life wasn't worthless until I met you."

"That is debatable," Khalid said. "Your punishment for this will be severe."

Heather shrank back. "Will you murder me?"

"Probably worse." Khalid stared at her for a long moment. "However, I never succumb to rash action. I think first, which you apparently never do."

"I'm responsible for my cousin," Heather tried to explain. "I need to see her."

Khalid cocked a dark brow at her. "Lesson five: A slave makes no demands upon her master."

"That is lesson four, not five," Heather said without thinking. "When I have trouble with numbers, I use my fingers. It's perfectly acceptable."

Khalid's lips quirked as he fought a smile. "Lesson four is A slave sleeps on the floor, not her master's bed."

Heather looked at him blankly.

"You escaped before I could school you in that," Khalid said.

Heather glanced at Malik who was grinning at them, obviously enjoying their verbal sparring. "April is well?" she asked, then looked toward the ship.

Malik's gaze followed hers. "April is settling into her new home and adjusting to her new life better than you. I am keeping her."

Heather couldn't believe what she was hearing.

"Enough talk," Khalid said, then reached down and lifted her into his arms. He turned her around and tossed her, headfirst, over his shoulder.

Heather struggled. With the flat of his hand, Khalid whacked her upturned derriere. That seemed to solve his problem.

With his captive slung ignominiously over his shoulder, Khalid sauntered into his camp, and all the men milling about laughed. Khalid leveled a commanding look at the watching warriors, and all but Abdul dispersed.

"Beating her would work," Abdul muttered.

Heather cried out in protest at the man's words. Khalid whacked her backside again, then set her down on her feet. He gestured to Abdul who dumped a bucket of cold water on her.

"*Oh!*" Heather shrieked.

Abdul poured another bucket of water over her head.

"*Oww!*" she squealed.

"You were covered with sand," Khalid said. "I do not want my new carpet ruined."

At a gesture from the prince, Abdul reached for another bucket.

"Wait," Heather cried. "I am sandless."

"Speckles of sand still cover your nose," Khalid said.

"They're freckles," she insisted.

Khalid grasped her chin in his hand and drew her close. He rubbed the bridge of her nose with his fingertips. "Correct. Go inside and await your punishment."

Temporarily surrendering to his will, Heather obeyed his command. The prince refused to grant her wish to see her cousin, and she was powerless to force the issue.

Khalid watched her disappear inside his tent. Would she ever bend to his rules? He refused to beat her into submission; he carried enough guilt around with him. So, what in Allah's name was he going to do with her?

"Bring her to the villa this afternoon," Malik invited. "She can bathe in luxury and visit her cousin."

"My slave does not deserve the privilege of visiting her cousin," Khalid replied.

Malik smiled. "But the cousin does."

"I refuse to reward her bad behavior," Khalid said. "When I leave here, they may bid each other farewell."

Malik nodded.

"One more thing," Khalid added. "I require the services of a fast-working goldsmith."

"Whatever you wish," Malik said, then left.

Khalid steeled himself for the oncoming confrontation with his recalcitrant slave and went inside his tent. The hint of a smile touched his lips when he looked at her. Through the wet cotton shirt she wore, he could see every tantalizing curve she possessed.

"Where did you think you were going?" he asked.

Heather sighed. "Home."

"Your home is with me."

"My home is in England."

"You thought to get to England in that—?"

"I would have followed the coastline."

"You have the intelligence of an oyster," Khalid said, pointing a finger at her. "Unspeakable dangers lurk outside my protection."

Who is protecting me from you? she wondered, but said, "Don't prisoners always attempt escape?"

"You are no prisoner."

That confused Heather. "I'm not?"

"No, you are my slave."

Before Heather could react to that, Abdul walked in and handed Khalid a towel. "Do you want me to hold her down while you chop her fingers off?" the man asked.

"Chop my fingers?" Heather cried.

"The punishment for thievery is the loss of a few fingers," Khalid informed her. "You stole my clothing."

"I *borrowed* your pants and shirt," Heather lied. "I did intend to return them."

"You borrowed but forgot to ask my permission?"

Heather nodded quickly.

"You see, Abdul," Khalid said. "She stole nothing, merely borrowed. Leave us now."

"I still think you should beat her," Abdul said as he left.

"Dry your hair," Khalid ordered, throwing the towel in her face. "You have had an exhausting morning and need rest. Will you eat first?"

"I've already eaten," Heather said in a small voice.

Khalid stared at her blankly.

"There was food on the table," she explained.

"You *borrowed* my breakfast?"

"Yes."

"Your belongings are in the chest over there," Khalid said, tapping the tip of her upturned nose. "Get out of that wet shirt and go to bed."

"Not until you leave."

Khalid raised his eyebrows at her demand and silently refused to leave.

"At least, turn around," Heather said. Then, "Please."

"How can I refuse when you beg so prettily?" Khalid turned his back on her.

In a flash of movement, Heather whipped the shirt and the chemise over her head. She dashed to the couch and yanked the coverlet up.

Khalid turned around and cast her an inscrutable look, then sauntered across the tent to her sea chest, warning, "Entertain no thoughts of escape. You will not catch my guards unaware twice." He opened the chest and dug past her gowns, then pulled out a nearly transparent silk and lace chemise.

Khalid considered the flimsy garment, then walked over to her and ordered, "Hold your arms up."

"Why?"

"Do it."

When she obeyed, Khalid slipped the garment over her head. Heather watched with enormous green eyes as he pulled the coverlet back, smoothed her chemise into place, and gently pressed her back on the couch.

Without disgust or hate in his expression, Khalid stared down at her. Desire lurked in his eyes, but inexperience blinded Heather to it.

"I take no pleasure in punishing you," Khalid told her. "You will never see your cousin again." With that, the prince left the tent.

Shocked, Heather sat up and stared at the doorway. The longer she sat there, the more furious she grew.

Suddenly, Heather leaped off the bed and dashed across the tent but stopped short at the doorway. Common sense prevented her from fleeing outside.

"Get back here, Your Highness," Heather shouted for

attention. "I must speak to you about seeing my cousin."

No one answered her summons.

"Can you hear me, Your Majesty?" she yelled. "I demand an audience."

Again, no answer.

How dare he ignore her! She was the daughter of a belted earl. Why, she was the queen of England's fifth cousin!

"You heathen son of a bitch!" Heather bellowed in English, a language the prince was unable to speak.

For one brief moment, Heather considered yelling "fire," but then thought better of it. Instead, she walked back to the bed and sat down.

Her throat hurt. Tears of angry frustration welled up in her eyes and spilled down her cheeks.

Feeling abused, Heather lay down and cried herself to sleep.

"Wake up," Khalid said for the third time, standing beside the couch. When Heather ignored him, he reached out and shook her, then yanked the coverlet back.

"Sweet Jesu," Heather grumbled, pushing several wisps of copper out of her eyes.

"You cannot sleep the day away," Khalid said. "The sun is high. It is time for you to bathe and eat. Afterward, you will feel ready to face your new life."

Heather glanced at the wooden tub that had been set up while she slept. Steam rose from the water. "I don't want a bath," she said.

"You smell like low tide."

"You smell no better."

"Do not lie," Khalid said, grasping her upper arm. He forced her out of the bed and over to the tub.

"Bathing is impossible without a tiring woman," Heather argued, stifling a yawn.

"What is that?"

"A lady's maid."

"Slaves do not keep their own servants," Khalid informed her.

"How difficult life must be for a slave," Heather said. "But, since I am not—"

"Judging from your behavior, you are no lady," Khalid added, interrupting her.

That woke Heather up. "I refuse to listen to your insults another moment." She turned her back on him in a gesture of dismissal.

With an angry growl, Khalid whirled her around. Heather stared unwaveringly into his piercing blue eyes.

"The beast's snarl does not frighten you?" he asked.

"Sometimes," she answered honestly.

"You will bathe," Khalid said, fingering the top of her chemise, "or I will bathe you."

"I do want a bath," Heather admitted. "I appreciate your kindness, but I need my privacy."

"I am never kind," Khalid said. "I grant you this one favor. When I return, you will be in the tub. Understand?"

Heather nodded.

Khalid added, "And, you will remove the chemise before getting into the tub."

Again, Heather nodded. She would have agreed to almost anything to get rid of him.

"Well?" he asked.

"Well, what?"

"What do you say for this favor?"

"Thank you."

Khalid cast her an admonishing look.

"Thank you, my lord Khalid." Heather nearly choked

on the words. Her mutinous expression told him what she really thought.

"You are welcome, slave," Khalid said, then left. Outside, he called for his second-in-command and ordered, "Send a message to Mihrimah."

"Your mother?" Abdul asked, surprised.

"Tell her to purchase a French- and English-speaking eunuch at the slave market," Khalid instructed. "I want him at my home by the time we arrive there."

"A eunuch?" Abdul echoed, bewildered.

Khalid glanced at his tent, saying, "She needs someone to care for her."

"A slave with a slave to serve her?" Abdul was shocked. "Have you lost your mind? Perhaps you have forgotten what the weasel did to Birtryce?"

With two hands, Khalid grabbed Abdul and lifted him into the air by his collar. "You presume too much on our long-standing friendship," he warned, anger whitening the scar slashed across his cheek.

"Your pardon, my lord," Abdul apologized. "I will send the messenger at once."

Khalid released his man and touched his shoulder. "I have forgotten nothing, Abdul, and will never rest until my sister's and brother's deaths are avenged."

Abdul nodded and left.

When Khalid returned to his tent, Heather sank lower in the tub, but he did not spare her a glance. Instead, Khalid inspected the contents of her sea chest.

Khalid pulled a skirt and blouse out of her chest, then turned to her, saying, "When you finish, wear these. Later, more suitable clothing will be provided."

"Nothing is wrong with the clothing I own," Heather said. "As you can see, they were made from the finest fabrics."

"You own nothing," Khalid told her. "Everything that was yours is mine." He held the skirt up to shake out the wrinkles, but something fell out of its pocket. When he picked the small object up and looked at it, the scar on his face whitened in a sure sign of growing fury. Staring at him from the painted miniature was his enemy, Savon Fougere.

Khalid stared hard at the miniature in his hand and then at Heather. Her uncommon beauty and refreshing spirit had almost enticed him into forgetting that the weasel was her betrothed. *Almost.*

The terrible expression on her captor's face frightened Heather, and she cowered in the tub. Still, she was unable to look away. At that moment, Khalid's expression was that of a vicious beast.

Holding her gaze captive, Khalid crumpled the miniature in his bare hand. He threw it down and crushed it into the carpet with the heel of his boot. Without a word, Khalid stalked out of his tent.

Heather decided it was the right time to end her bath. She climbed out of the tub, then quickly toweled herself dry and donned her chemise, skirt, and blouse.

Heather retrieved the ruined miniature from the carpet and examined it. Having his face crushed improved the weasel's appearance, she thought. But, what should she do with the miniature? Her position was precarious, and she didn't need the sight of the weasel angering her captor.

Then, Heather saw it—the perfect hiding place. Her emerald eyes sparkled with merriment. Marching across the tent, Heather deposited Savon Fougere in the chamber pot.

With no way to occupy herself, Heather sat on the edge of the couch to wait and ponder her situation. Why did the Turk hate Fougere? What had her betrothed done that was so horrible? Khalid's image rose in her mind's eye. The prince was an unusually attractive but dangerous man. In the future, she needed to be wary.

After what seemed like hours, four servants under Abdul's supervision removed the wooden tub. Abdul cast her a contemptuous look and followed them out.

Alone with her thoughts, Heather fumed. How dare that man look at her in such a despicable manner! Who did he think he was?

A servant, carrying a tray of food, walked into the tent and stared at her. Behind the man stood Abdul, his expression grimly contemptuous.

"You will eat," Abdul ordered, then turned to the servant. "Set the tray down."

"Your attitude insults me," Heather said, advancing on them. "Take the food away. I will not eat."

"Put the tray on the table," Abdul told the servant, ignoring her order.

As the man moved to set the tray down, Heather whacked it out of his hands. The tray and its contents landed on the carpet.

Abdul leveled a deadly look on her, then gestured the servant out and followed him.

Instantly sorry, Heather had cause to doubt her own sanity.

Khalid appeared within seconds. "Clean this mess," he snapped.

"It was an accident," Heather lied.

"Do not strain my patience," Khalid warned. "Ending your misbegotten life appeals to me at this moment."

Kneeling, Heather picked the food off the carpet and placed it on the tray. There were flaky pastries, pickled cucumbers, a roasted pigeon, and grapes.

"Set the tray on the table," Khalid ordered. Then, "Eat."

"What?"

"Is your hearing impaired?"

"I refuse to eat dirty food."

"Wasting Allah's bounty is intolerable," Khalid said, drawing and pointing his dagger at her. "You threw the food on the carpet and will eat every bite."

Wearing a sullen expression, Heather grabbed the roasted pigeon and took a bite. "Are you happy now?"

"You have the manners of a swine," Khalid said. "Do not talk while you eat. In fact, do not speak to me at all."

Heather suffered the powerful urge to toss the pigeon at him.

"Do not even consider it," he warned.

"I have no utensil to use," Heather said.

"Only a fool gives a madwoman a knife." Using his dagger, Khalid carved the pigeon into small, edible pieces for her.

"What's that?" Heather asked, pointing to one of the dishes.

"Pickled cucumber."

She pointed at the pastry. "And this?"

"Baklava. It is filled with nuts."

Heather bit into the baklava, then chewed slowly and swallowed. She took another bite.

"Delicious," she announced.

"I am so relieved that you like it," Khalid said dryly.

Beneath Khalid's supervision and ready dagger, Heather ate everything on the tray. At his master's bellow, the hapless servant whom Heather had harassed brought a bowl of warmed water and left it on the table in front of her.

"Finish," Khalid ordered.

Though full to bursting, Heather decided to refrain from arguing this one time. After all, the beast still held his dagger on her. She lifted the bowl to her lips to drink.

"*No!*"

Startled, Heather looked up.

"Use this water to wash your hands, my little barbarian."

Heather blushed, the humiliation of being thought ignorant too much to endure.

"If you ever throw another tantrum as you did earlier," Khalid warned, "I will beat you beyond recognition. Do you understand?"

Heather nodded.

"You will speak when spoken to, slave," Khalid ordered.

"I understand," she mumbled.

"What?"

Irritated by his overbearing manner, Heather made an exaggerated show of kneeling in front of him. She bowed her head until it touched the tip of his boots, and in a voice oozing with sarcasm, said, "I hear and obey, my high and mighty lord. As always, your wish is my command."

Khalid patted her head condescendingly. "Much better, slave. You are learning. This pleases me." Then he stood and left the tent.

Heather stared at his retreating back and wished she had the courage to throw something at him. Instead, she raced to the back of the chamber and dropped to her knees, then lifted the tent's bottom edge and peeked outside. *Boots!* What looked like hundreds of boots.

With a curse on her lips, Heather stood and marched across the tent to sit on the couch. Apparently, the insufferable lout had learned his lesson and ordered every available man to surround his tent lest she escape.

The thought of the prince's entire army set to guard one tiny woman made Heather smile. She flopped back on the couch and waited for whatever would happen next.

Chapter 4

The heavenly aroma of food drifted across the tent and made Heather's nose twitch. Rousing herself, Heather opened her eyes. Unaware she'd awakened, her captor sat on the pillows beside his table and ate supper.

Heather yawned and stretched. Her stomach growled loudly, protesting the many hours since lunch.

Khalid's gaze locked on hers in an intimate stare. Heather looked away in sudden shyness. Knowing he'd watched her sleeping made her feel vulnerable.

Suppressing that uncomfortable feeling, Heather rose from the couch and walked across the tent to the table. She was hungry. Their fighting could wait until after she'd eaten. Heather started to sit down opposite him, but his voice stopped her.

"Remain where you are," Khalid said.

"Why?"

His piercing, blue-eyed gaze fixed on hers. "You will stand because I order it."

Heather refrained from sitting. Ignoring her, Khalid continued eating.

Two could play his game of aloofness, Heather decided. Ignoring him in return, she stared at the food on the table.

That was a strategic blunder. There were sizzling chunks of mutton grilled on a spit, artichokes in vinegar, saffroned rice with sweet peppers, flatbread, grapes, peaches, and figs.

The sight and smell of her captor's dinner made Heather's stomach growl again. Khalid stopped chewing and cocked a dark brow at her.

"I'm hungry," Heather said, plopping herself down on the pillow opposite him. She masked her embarrassment with a puckish grin.

"Your pleasure must await mine." Khalid stared at her for a long moment. What kind of people raised her to be so disobedient? he wondered. Did she think to rule him with a smile? If so, she was mistaken. Did she even understand what being his slave meant? Apparently not. She would begin her training in the morning.

The plate nearest Heather was filled with figs. Casually, she tried to pilfer one, but he slapped her hand lightly.

"Men do not eat with women," Khalid informed her, "and slaves do not sit at the table with their masters."

"Men and women do not share their meals?" Heather asked, surprised.

Khalid nodded.

"How barbaric."

"It is the refined custom of a civilized country," Khalid said. "You are the barbarian, not I."

Refusing to argue lest she lose her supper, Heather remained silent. There would be time enough—after she'd eaten—to set the infidel straight.

Satisfied with her seeming submission, Khalid resumed his meal. The angry rumble of Heather's stomach broke the silence.

Khalid lifted the tiny bell on the table and rang for his man. Almost instantly, the hapless servant whom Heather had earlier harassed brought a bowl of warmed water and a towel. While Khalid washed his hands, the servant removed his empty plate. A moment later he returned for the water and towel.

"You bring slave's food," Khalid said in halting English to his servant who stared at him blankly.

"You speak English?" Heather asked, surprised.

"I learned many things at Topkapi's prince's school," Khalid replied, switching back to French. He looked at his servant and repeated his order in Turkish. The man nodded and left.

"Why do you speak French so well?" Khalid asked her. "You are English."

"My mother is French." Heather stared in anticipation at the mutton and rice. Her mouth watered. Deciding she could not wait for a plate, Heather reached for a chunk of mutton, but Khalid tapped the back of her hand.

"I have not given you permission to eat," he said.

"May I?" she asked.

Before Khalid could reply, his servant returned and set a bowl on the table in front of Heather. She stared in dismay at its contents. Accompanied by a contemptibly small piece of flatbread, the bowl contained what looked like steaming mush.

"What new torture is this?" Heather asked, her gaze rising to meet her captor's.

"Your supper," Khalid said. "It is called couscous and made from—"

"It appears someone took sick." Heather pushed the bowl away and pointed to the mutton and rice, saying, "I need that."

"You think to eat the same fare as your master?" Khalid countered, feigning appalled surprise. He pushed the plates of mutton and rice toward her.

Heather picked up a chunk of the mutton and was about to pop it into her mouth when his voice stopped her.

"You give no thanks for this favor?" Khalid asked.

"You are the very soul of kindness, my lord Khalid," Heather said, irritated by his overbearing manner but too hungry to argue.

"I like the sound of my name on your tongue," Khalid said, then stood and started to leave.

"Where are you going?" Heather called over her shoulder.

Khalid paused at the tent flap and in a long-suffering voice said, "I told you before, a slave never questions her master."

"Must I eat alone?" The question slipped from her lips, surprising her. What in God's name was she thinking? This dangerous man held her captive, yet for some unknown reason, Heather didn't want him to leave.

Khalid was surprised and pleased. "You desire my company?"

Heather blushed. "I am unused to dining alone."

Khalid sauntered back to the table and sat down again. His beautiful captive was beginning to feel her isolation, and that was the first step in training her to do his bidding.

Heather ate slowly and savored each bite. Without thinking, she licked the mutton grease from each fingertip.

The blatant sensuality of her gesture was not lost on Khalid. He felt his manhood tingle and stretch as if awakening from a long slumber. To relieve his mind and other vital parts, Khalid baited her, "I still believe you possess the manners of a swine."

Heather frowned at him.

Khalid pulled her plate away, saying, "You appear more amenable when hungry."

"I'm sorry," Heather apologized, dragging the plate back.

"Tell me about yourself, slave."

"What is it you want to know?" Heather popped a chunk of mutton into her mouth, then licked her finger-tips with great deliberation.

Khalid struggled against his arousal. "Tell me about your life before we met."

"You mean, before your friend abducted me," she corrected.

Khalid shrugged. "Whatever."

"My father was the Earl of Basildon," Heather told him. "He passed away several years ago. My sisters, my brother, and I became wards of his cousin, Queen Elizabeth. My sister Kathryn is the oldest and lives with her husband in Ireland. Next comes Brigette who wed a Scottish earl. My brother Richard, now the Earl of Basildon, is the youngest."

"And your mother?"

"Lives at Basildon Castle, my home."

"Your home is with me," Khalid corrected her.

Heather frowned at his words.

"Do you love the Comte de Beaulieu?" Khalid asked, unable to bite back the question.

"That weasel?" Heather spoke without thinking.

Khalid threw back his head and shouted with laughter.

Blushing, Heather tried to amend herself, "I mean—"

"I know what you mean," Khalid said. "Your sentiments match mine."

"Loving a man is unnecessary," Heather repeated her mother's words. "A woman need only bear her husband's heirs and manage the efficient running of his household."

Khalid nodded. "Our countries share that custom."

"Tell me about your country," Heather said.

Before Khalid could reply, Abdul entered, saying,

"Lord Malik sent this to you." He set a tray on the table between them and then left.

The tray held small pastries, the likes of which Heather had never seen. Each was rounded, firm, and topped with a walnut.

"May I?" Heather asked, reaching for one.

Khalid nodded. "Your manners are improving."

Heather took a bite of the pastry. A smile of pure pleasure appeared on her face and enchanted the man sitting across the table from her. A delightful mixture of chopped almonds, pistachio nuts, and coconut filled the sweet pastry.

"Delicious." Heather took a second bite. "What is it?"

"Young girl's breasts."

Heather choked on the pastry.

Khalid smiled at her.

"What is it really?" Heather asked, returning his smile. The prince was a handsome man when he smiled. Too bad he didn't smile more often.

"It is called 'young girl's breasts' because of—"

"Stop," Heather cried, laughing.

"Slaves do not order their masters," Khalid said, wagging a finger at her. "You are incorrigible."

"I apologize," Heather said, then ruined it by giggling.

Interrupting them, Khalid's servant walked in and placed a bowl of warmed water in front of Heather. Beside that, he set a small plate of green sprigs.

As Heather washed her hands, Khalid picked one of the sprigs up and chewed on it, saying, "The mint will freshen your breath."

Heather lifted a sprig of mint to her mouth and tasted it tentatively, then chewed on it. "How did you get that scar?" she asked. "In battle?"

Her casually asked question ruined the easiness of their supper. Khalid's expression changed dramatically, and the scar of which she'd spoken whitened in a sure sign of anger.

The Sultan's Beast had returned.

Khalid stared at her coldly. Startled by his sudden transformation from pleasant host to threatening beast, Heather was unable to look away.

"Your weasel gifted me with this," Khalid said in an awful voice, stroking his scarred cheek with his thumb.

"My God," Heather gasped.

"The goldsmith has arrived," Abdul informed his master, walking into the tent's inner chamber.

Without another word to her, Khalid stood and went outside.

Watching him, Heather wondered when and why her captor and her betrothed had met on the field of battle. The French and the Ottomans were allies of sorts and had been united in their hatred of the Spanish for a long time.

Within minutes, Khalid returned but paused inside the doorway. He gazed at his captive and for the briefest moment wished that she weren't his enemy's betrothed. Steeling himself against her, Khalid stared forward.

Heather felt his presence but refused to look at him. His scowl was too frightening. If she remained quiet and still, his anger would dissolve and he would leave her alone.

Khalid read the wariness in her expression and knew that he must outwit her lest she be injured fighting him.

"Look at me," Khalid said.

Heather turned her head and saw his black kidskin boots planted on the carpet beside her. Her gaze traveled slowly up the long length of him, rested for a moment on the gleaming object he held in his left hand, and continued on. Finally, her emerald eyes fixed on his chiseled features.

"Stand up," Khalid said, offering her his right hand. "I have a gift for you."

"A gift?" Heather gave him a surprised smile, then placed her hand in his and stood.

"See." He held up a delicately woven bracelet of gold for her inspection.

Heather offered him her left hand. Khalid fastened the bracelet around her wrist. He produced a tiny key that was attached to a chain necklace and locked the bracelet on her wrist. Finally, Khalid placed the chain around his neck.

Confused, Heather watched him.

From the waistband of his pants, Khalid pulled a long rope chain of gold. It looked suspiciously like the sort of leash that a dog would wear.

"What are you doing?" Heather cried, shrinking back.

"Ensuring myself an undisturbed sleep," Khalid replied, attaching the leash to her bracelet.

"No!" Heather kicked his shin and dashed to the back of the tent.

Vowing to squeeze the life's breath from her beautiful body, Khalid gave chase and cornered her there. He grabbed her and yanked her against the hardened length of his muscular body.

"Now, Wildflower—oooop!"

Heather kneed his groin and flew past him as he swore and doubled over in pain. She stopped short at the doorway and looked back. Khalid, with murderous intent gleaming from his eyes, was advancing on her.

"I'm not trying to escape," Heather insisted as tears began streaming down her cheeks. "I can't bear being tied." She picked up a pillow and threw it at him, but he deflected it with his arm and closed in on her.

Sobbing, Heather grabbed another pillow. With a beastly growl, Khalid threw her down on the carpet and fell on top of her.

Heather shrieked like a madwoman and tried to claw his face. Khalid easily captured her hands and yanked her arms over her head, effectively pinning her beneath him.

In a desperate effort to get him off, Heather thrashed and bucked like a maddened creature. Knowing he had her, Khalid waited for her to tire as he knew she must. Her struggles lessened and then ceased.

"Please, release me," Heather wailed. "I can't bear it."

Khalid lifted his weight off her and got to his feet. He stood there and watched her weeping.

Something is terribly wrong here, Khalid decided. People do not react so strongly without good reason.

"It is time to sleep," Khalid said, reaching for the leash.

"I am no animal to be chained," Heather sobbed. "Take it off."

"So you can escape in the night? I think not. Come."

"No."

"*Inchallah*," Khalid muttered. "It will be as Allah wills." He pulled the leash and dragged his struggling captive toward his couch.

"Stop," Heather cried. "I will not be chained to the bed and ravished."

Ignoring her, Khalid managed to get her across the tent and fastened the leash to his couch. With his hands on his hips, Khalid turned to her and said, "I leave you untouched. Go to sleep."

"Here?"

"A slave's proper place is on the floor beside her master's bed."

Khalid sat on the edge of the couch. He considered ordering her to remove his boots but decided against it. Heather had borne as much as she could for one day, and Khalid knew she was very close to breaking.

Khalid yanked his own boots off, then pulled his shirt over his head and tossed that aside. In the glow from the candle, the golden chain with its precious key gleamed against his magnificent chest. Both the key and his naked chest taunted Heather.

Khalid stood up and reached for the top of his pants. Heather rolled over and snapped her eyes shut.

"Accustom yourself to my nakedness, slave." Khalid lay down on his couch and rolled onto his side to look at his captive's back. "On the morrow, you will begin to serve me."

"I'd sooner serve Satan," Heather mumbled under her breath.

"You will serve me in the morning," Khalid said. "Or I will beat you."

Beat me if you wish, Heather thought, but my thinking will remain unchanged. Revenge will be mine. At first opportunity, I'll slit your throat from ear to ear or plunge the sharpest dagger into your heartless infidel's chest.

Lying there on the carpet, Heather concentrated on the myriad forms her revenge could take. She vowed to escape, but before she left, she would skewer the infidel with his own dagger.

And that was the problem. The disturbing image of Khalid, bloodied and lifeless by her hand, tormented Heather until a troubled sleep finally claimed her.

Unfortunately for Khalid, Allah refused to grant him a peaceful sleep that night.

"No, Papa . . . Khalid." Heather moaned in the midst of a nightmare. *"The blood!"* Heather's piercing shriek rent the stillness of the night.

Khalid bolted up in the bed and stared down at his captive. Curled into a ball on the carpet, Heather wept in her sleep.

Khalid reached down and unlocked the leash, then stood and gently lifted her onto the couch. He lay down beside her and gathered her into his arms.

"It is only a dream," Khalid whispered, stroking her back.

Clinging to him, Heather awakened. The horror of her nightmare glazed her eyes.

"Of what do you dream" he asked.

Heather focused on the man who held her so protectively. "You may chain my body," she said, "but my thoughts belong to me."

"When they disturb my sleep, your thoughts become my problem."

"Ten thousand pardons, master, but I cannot recall what I dreamed."

Khalid's lips twitched at her lie. "You called for me and your father."

At the mention of her father, Heather paled and trembled in her captor's embrace.

"I see that you do remember," Khalid said softly, his arms tightening around her.

Heather tried to pull away. Refusing to let her go, Khalid pressed her against the comforting solidness of his chest.

"I will protect you in the night," he said. "Rest easy."

"You are naked."

"But you are clothed." Determined, Khalid would not budge. He stroked the column of her back.

"Stop touching me," Heather said, lying stiffly in his arms.

Khalid planted a kiss on her forehead. "Close your eyes and relax, Wildflower."

Uncomfortable with the provoking feel and arousing scent of him, Heather remained unyieldingly stiff.

"Relax or I will do my worst," Khalid said.

Heather snapped her eyes shut. Gradually, she relaxed in his embrace, and when her breathing evened, he knew she slept.

What demons stalk her dreams? Khalid wondered. If he ever wanted another peaceful night, he had to know, but his captive wasn't talking. How could he learn what he needed?

Then it came to him. Khalid knew exactly where he could learn his captive's secrets. *The cousin.*

Chapter 5

"What troubles her?"

"I don't understand."

"About what does she dream?" Khalid asked, advancing on the nervous young woman. Frustration hardened his voice.

Terrified by his imposing figure and angry countenance, April paled and stepped back a pace. This is the beast who holds Heather captive, she thought. How had her cousin survived these past two days? April knew that she would have died of fright.

Khalid towered menacingly over her. The whitened knuckles of his tightly clenched fists at his sides matched the facial scar that had whitened with frustrated anger.

"Tell me," Khalid growled.

Frightened, April swayed on her feet.

"You have frightened her," Malik said as she fainted to escape the ogre threatening her.

Malik caught April before she hit the floor and carried her across the chamber. Gently, he placed her down upon the enormous pillows, then looked at his friend.

"Causing her harm was unintentional," Khalid said.

"Please, bring me a goblet of rosewater," Malik said, then sat down beside April and stared at her. Concern etched itself across his features. Would Khalid never learn to take a gentler approach? At times, kindness worked better than fear and threats.

"She bears no resemblance to her cousin," Khalid remarked, handing the goblet of water to his friend.

When April's eyes fluttered open, Malik smiled reassuringly and helped her sit up. "Drink this," he said.

April sipped the water. "Thank you, my lord," she said. "I feel better now." She flicked a nervous glance at her cousin's captor.

Khalid knelt beside her and forced a smile onto his face, saying, "I apologize for frightening you."

"Tell the prince what he wants," Malik ordered, though not unkindly.

"I know nothing," April lied. "How can I possibly know what she dreams? Why doesn't he ask her?"

"She refuses to share her thoughts with me," Khalid admitted.

"Then leave her alone," April snapped, recovering her courage because Malik held her hand. "What she dreams is no business of yours."

"Her nightmares disturb my sleep," Khalid explained, deciding the cousin did possess a smidgen of his captive's spirit. "Knowing their cause will enable me to help her find peace in the night."

"If you want to give her peace, send her home," April said.

"That is a thing I cannot do."

"Cannot or will not?" April asked.

"She calls for her dead father," Khalid said, ignoring her question. "What do you know about him? Why does her father haunt her dreams?"

Though worried by what he'd revealed, April forced her expression to remain impassive. She stared at him blankly and shrugged.

"Share your knowledge with the prince, my little bird," Malik ordered.

"But I know nothing," April insisted, feigning innocence.

"Lovely liar," Malik said. Gently but firmly, he grasped her chin in the palm of his hand and waited until her gaze met his. "On board Fougere's ship, you said your cousin's nightmares would keep you awake for a month."

"I appreciate your loyalty," Khalid said, "but there are ways to force the truth from you."

"When she becomes disturbed, Heather dreams about her father," April told him. "But, I was only a child when it happened.

"When what happened?" Khalid asked.

"Heather was with her father when he died," April said. "Beyond that, I know nothing except—"

"Except what?" Malik prodded.

"We were playmates," April went on. "I remember, Heather wasn't herself for a long time. She screamed for two days and had to be restrained on the bed lest she hurt herself."

Khalid closed his eyes against the remorse he felt. "I can't bear to be tied," she'd sobbed, but he hadn't listened. What kind of monsters were these English to tie a distraught child to a bed instead of holding her close and offering comfort?

"How did her father die?" Khalid asked.

"I don't know the details," April replied. "I was so young. No one answered my questions."

Malik offered April the goblet of water so she could drink, then set it aside. Reaching out, he stroked her pale cheek with the palm of his hand.

"Your cousin is troubled," Malik said. "The prince seeks only to help her find peace and to enjoy an undis-

turbed sleep. I will escort you to his tent. Your cousin
will confide the details to you, and you will share that
information with the prince.''

April nodded. Why did the damn prince care that
Heather suffered nightmares?

"Let us go now," Khalid said.

Malik smiled. "I understand your impatience, my
friend, but the sun is barely risen. Come and break your
fast with me while my little bird refreshes herself.''

Khalid nodded.

Malik turned to April, saying, "I will send someone
to assist you. Be ready in one hour.''

Two hours later, the Sword of Allah and the Shark's
Spawn marched into camp. Between them walked April,
dressed in a black *yashmak*. Worn over her lightweight
caftan, the flowing outer garment covered her from head
to feet. Even her face was heavily veiled so that none
could gaze upon Malik's property.

As they walked through the camp, April flicked a
nervous glance at the prince's watching warriors. Those
hardened soldiers appeared as frightening as their for-
midable leader. Knowing they were unable to actually
see her beneath the shapeless black robe and veil gave
April courage.

"We will await you here," Khalid said, drawing the
outer tent flap back. "Be sure to speak French. You will
find her inside."

"You hope," Malik said as April disappeared into the
tent.

"She will be there." Khalid paused for a moment and
then started into the tent's antechamber.

"Where are you going?" Malik asked.

"To listen to their conversation," Khalid replied.
"Your little bird's loyalties still lie with her cousin."

Malik nodded. Together, they went inside.

April, impressed by what greeted her eyes, paused just inside the palatial inner chamber. Surrounded by enormous pillows, an intricately carved and painted table stood a few feet away, and a luxurious carpet covered the floor.

Her gaze drifted to the prince's couch where her cousin slept. Removing her slippers lest she damage the carpet, April padded across the chamber to the bed.

"Heather," she whispered, nudging her cousin.

Startling emerald eyes fluttered open. Heather focused on the black-veiled apparition hovering over her.

"*No!*" Heather backed away from the threatening vision.

"*Oh!*" April leaped back a pace, startled by her cousin's cry.

"Who are you?" Heather asked in a tremulous voice.

"You fool," April said, whipping the veil off her face.

"April," Heather cried and pulled her down onto the couch. The cousins clung to each other in relief.

"Are you all right?" Heather asked.

"I feel like a walking piece of black gauze," April complained. "You nearly frightened me to death. Are you well?"

Heather nodded. "Why are you dressed like that?"

"It's the custom here for women to be covered completely when they walk about," April explained.

"What strange beliefs they have. I'm sorry I ever wished for an adventure."

"You cannot possibly be sorrier than I am," April countered ruefully.

"Your visit surprises me," Heather told her. "Yesterday, the beast refused to let me see you again because I attempted to escape and rescue you. And now—"

"You did?" April interrupted.

Heather nodded. ''I thought you were aboard the barbarian's ship and nearly drowned trying to get to you. Or rather, *he* nearly drowned me.''

''But, how did you escape his camp? Those men outside . . .'' April shuddered at the thought of the prince's fierce-looking warriors.

'' 'Twas exceedingly easy,'' Heather said. ''These Turks are notoriously simple, you know.''

''The prince doesn't seem simple to me,'' April replied.

''Appearances can be deceptive,'' Heather said, then reached for the golden chain attached to the bed. ''Look, he chains me like a dog.''

''The prince is concerned for your welfare,'' April said, hoping to calm her cousin by changing the subject.

''Worried about me?'' That surprised Heather. ''I cannot credit that.''

''The prince says you cry out in your sleep,'' April said, glancing sidelong at her cousin.

''I did dream of Papa last night,'' Heather admitted, then lapsed into silence.

Feeling like a traitor, April waged an inner battle with herself. Talking about the nightmare could very well help Heather gain peace, but giving the prince that information could cause even more damage if he chose to use it to torment her cousin.

''Sharing your troubles would lighten the load,'' April said.

''I suppose so.'' Heather sighed, and her gaze clouded as if she were transported back in time. ''It is always *that day,* my tenth birthday. Papa gifted me with the dappled gray gelding, and without a thought for safety, I flew without escort outside the walls of Basildon. Naturally, Papa rode after me. But, those men—those outlaws in the clearing . . . Papa shouted at me to ride for help, but—but I froze with fear. *The blood* . . . " Hot tears suddenly streamed down her pale cheeks, and her hands shook.

Watching, April felt sorry she'd asked.

"Bloody and dying, one of the men fell at my feet," Heather continued. "If only I'd grabbed the man's dagger, if only I'd been obedient, if only I hadn't led my father to his death . . . "

"It wasn't your fault," April said soothingly, putting her arm around her cousin's shoulder.

"But, if I hadn't ridden unescorted outside Basildon—"

"The Devereux lands are well guarded," April argued. "You could not have known."

"I should have picked the dagger up and slashed that evil one to pieces. I should have—"

"Stop!" Unable to bear her cousin's tormented anguish, April changed the subject abruptly, asking, "Does the prince keep a harem?"

Heather wiped her eyes with the back of her hand and focused on her cousin's face. "A what?"

"A harem."

"I don't know. What is that?"

"A harem is where a man's women live," April told her.

"What women?"

"It is the custom of this country for a man to live with more than one woman." Imparting her vast knowledge made April feel superior.

That shocked Heather.

"A man may keep four wives and countless concubines."

"Oh, we must leave this heathen land," Heather said. "And the sooner, the better."

"And go where?" April countered. "No man will marry us now."

"Why not?"

"Do you actually believe the Comte de Beaulieu would take you to wife after living with the prince?"

"That weasel?" Heather said. "It's his fault that we're here."

"What do you mean?" April asked.

"The prince holds us for revenge against Fougere."

"What did the comte do?"

"I don't know all," Heather told her, "but that scar the prince wears was a gift from Beaulieu."

April glanced sidelong at her cousin, then remarked, "In spite of it, the prince is a handsome man."

"I suppose, in a mean sort of way," Heather said.

"How did it feel?" April whispered.

"How did what feel?"

"You know."

"If I knew," Heather asked, "would I be asking?"

"I mean, when you shared his bed."

Though shocked, Heather shrugged. If Malik had bedded April, why hadn't the prince tried to bed her? The pirate must have been kind to her cousin, or she wouldn't be able to speak calmly about it. Why hadn't the prince been kind to her?

"How did *you* feel?" Heather asked.

"I was frightened," April admitted, "but my lord was very gentle. Why, he was as breathtaking and romantic as those knights in the stories your sister loved to read."

Heather arched a brow at her cousin. "Brigette was always a peagoose."

"Anyway, by the time *it* happened," April went on, "I was shivering with heat."

"People shiver from the cold," Heather scoffed. "Not the heat."

"*I* shivered from the heat," April insisted. "And the blood—did you bleed a lot?"

"Enough," Heather hedged.

"I like the kissing part, though," April said. "Don't you?"

The image of Khalid arose in Heather's mind. Again, she felt his hardened warrior's body pressing her against him, smelled his clean, arousing masculine scent . . .

"I see that you do," April said with a chuckle.

"Enough of this." Heather masked her embarrassment with irritation. "We must use this time to make our plans. When Malik's household sleeps tonight, you slip away and come for me."

"I couldn't," April refused.

"But you must," Heather insisted. "I cannot come for you. The beast chains me to his bed and—"

Unexpectedly, the tent flap opened to reveal Khalid and Malik. Amusement gleamed from Malik's dark eyes, but the prince was not so inclined.

"You will never escape me," Khalid said in a harsh voice, advancing on them. "Only the truly *simple* can be fooled twice."

"How dare you listen to my private thoughts," Heather screamed, leaping off the couch.

"No," April cried.

Heather advanced defiantly on her captor. She met him halfway across the tent and looked up at his angry expression, hissing in English, "You spying son of a swine."

Without waiting for a reply, Heather rounded on her cousin. "And *you*," she accused her, switching back to French. "You betrayed your own cousin."

"No, no, no," April sobbed. "I—I—I had no idea they were listening. T-t-truly . . ." She dissolved into weeping.

"April knew nothing," Malik insisted, crossing the tent to comfort his little bird.

"Slaves have no privacy," Khalid said, standing close behind his captive. "And what one slave thinks of another is of no importance."

Heather reacted instantly. Whirling around, Heather kicked his shin with her bare foot. Surprised for only a brief moment, he reached out to grab his rebellious slave.

"No," April cried, drawing his attention, giving her cousin time to escape.

Breaking free of Malik's embrace, April hurled herself at the prince and managed to land a few well-placed kicks. Unfortunately, she was also barefoot and the damage to him was minor.

Malik caught her in a moment. He grabbed her upper arms and restrained her.

"I am not *simple* enough to let you escape the same way twice," Khalid baited, his attention on Heather who'd run to the back of the tent. "Though cunning at times, your meager feminine intelligence is no match for mine. And your value, even as a healthy slave, is less than nothing."

His insults hit their mark.

"You bloody bugger," Heather shouted in English. In a dangerously high rage, she escaped his reach and flew past him.

As the other three watched in amazement, Heather vented her full fury upon the prince's tent. She tore the bedding from the couch and then pushed that onto its side. Next, she headed for the table and kicked it over, spilling her breakfast onto the carpet.

Calmly and coolly, Khalid watched his beautiful, high-strung captive turn his living quarters into a shambles. When she reached for his scimitar, Khalid started forward slowly and deliberately. "Enough is enough" etched itself across his chiseled features.

Heather flung the heavy scimitar down and raced for the tent flap. When she would have flown into the outside world, an immovable object blocked her way. Abdul, intent on discovering what the commotion was about, walked into the tent's inner chamber. Heather slammed full force into the warrior's unyielding body and toppled backward onto the carpeted floor.

Malik, April, and Abdul stared in shock at her. Khalid remained expressionless. Never in his life had he met a woman like this.

Kneeling beside her, Khalid verified that Heather was uninjured. Then he yanked her roughly to her feet and held her prisoner in his embrace.

Heather struggled in his arms, but it was no use. His superior strength prevailed.

"I have the information I need," Khalid said, looking at their stunned audience. "You may go."

Abdul bowed his way out. Malik took April's arm and turned to leave, but his friend's voice stopped him.

"Please, return this evening for supper," Khalid invited him, then gestured to April. "Your little bird has the manner of a hawk and should be punished for daring to attack my person."

"Perhaps there is a family resemblance after all," Malik said, hiding a smile. "I can assure you, my little bird will be tutored on proper behavior and this will never happen again. Until this evening, then." With that, Malik drew April outside.

Khalid looked at Heather, ordering, "Clean this mess that you have created."

"No." That word fell between them like an axe.

"Start with the bed so I can sit and watch you work," Khalid said, deliberately ignoring her refusal.

"No." Heather stuck her chin out, and her expression

became mulish. The gauntlet had been thrown, and she refused to let him ignore the challenge.

Khalid towered menacingly over her and considered threatening her with the leash. Knowing her terror, he was unable to make himself say the words. "Obey me, or I will strip you naked and kiss each delectable part of you. My face will nuzzle the valley between your exquisite breasts, and I will suckle their rose-tipped peaks." Then he quoted April, "I will make you shiver with heat."

"I'll clean the mess," Heather cried, hot with shame.

Khalid stared arrogantly at her.

Heather refused to budge.

Khalid reached out and cupped one of her soft mounds. And that got an instant reaction from her.

Heather dashed across the chamber and tried to pull the couch upright. Again and again, she tugged at it but managed only to work up a fine sheen of sweat. Still, Heather struggled on.

Khalid folded his arms across his chest and watched. A smile flirted with the corners of his lips.

"Help me," Heather called over her shoulder.

"You actually expect the master to perform the slave's duties?"

Heather rounded on him. With her hands on her hips, she asked, "Didn't you say that you wanted to sit on this bed and watch me slave for you?"

Khalid was at her side in an instant. He lifted the couch easily and set it in its place, then turned to her and mocked, "You are not as strong or fierce as you believe, Wildflower."

Heather glared at him and then at the couch. Why, she had half a mind to—

"Do not even consider it," Khalid said, reading her expression.

"Consider what?" Heather asked, feigning innocence.

"If you kick the couch over again," he warned, "I will not set it in place."

"Then you will be forced to sleep on the floor."

"Beside you."

That did it. Without another word, Heather picked the coverlet up and spread it across the couch, then fluffed the pillows into place.

"You have potential, slave," Khalid said, sitting down on the couch. He lifted one of his legs toward her and said, "My feet are hot. Remove this boot."

Heather opened her mouth to refuse.

"Remove my boot," Khalid repeated. "And do not speak, or I will throw you down on the carpet and kiss you into silence."

Swallowing her angry retort, Heather bent over and tried to pull the boot off his foot. Like its stubborn owner, the boot refused to budge. Furious, Heather tugged with all her might. The boot came off, but she landed on her rump between her captor's legs.

Khalid lifted his other leg toward her. Heather yanked the boot off.

"Fetch the jar over there," he ordered.

Heather glared mutinously at him. Filled with unmasked hatred, her emerald eyes glittered like exquisite jewels.

"Repeating myself irritates me."

With a silent curse upon her lips, Heather stood up and went for the jar. In a moment, she returned and held it out to him.

"Sit down," Khalid ordered. Then, "Open it."

Heather did as she was told. The jar contained a pale yellow lotion.

"Dip your hand in the jar," Khalid instructed. "Warm the aloe lotion in your hands."

"Now what?" Heather asked, puzzled.

Khalid lifted one bare foot. "Massage it."

"Massage what?" Heather exclaimed, unable to believe what she was hearing.

"Is your hearing impaired?"

"No."

"Then massage my foot."

"No."

"Would you prefer this *simple* Turk strip you naked and massage *your* body with the lotion?"

Heather grabbed his offered foot. She smeared the lotion all over it and rubbed it into his skin, then thumbed the bottom of his foot in a soothing motion.

"You definitely have potential." Khalid lifted his other foot, then baited her, "Be grateful for your position. The life of a prince is much more difficult than that of a slave."

Heather grabbed his foot and started working the lotion into it. Her emerald eyes were green slits of displeasure, but she said nothing.

"Tonight, after I've bathed, you will massage my back," Khalid said. "Do not bother to protest. I know you are anxious to massage my back, but you must understand that a prince is a busy man. I do not have the time to spare at the moment."

Heather's face mottled with rage.

"Finish your chores," Khalid ordered sternly. He pulled his boots on.

Heather remained where she was.

"I said, finish cleaning this mess." Khalid stood up. With mutiny in her eyes, Heather stared at him.

"*Op beni,*" Khalid whispered huskily, leaning down so his lips hovered over hers. "*Op beni* means 'kiss me.'"

Eluding his lips, Heather leaped to her feet and ran to

set the table in its place. On her hands and knees, she began to clean her breakfast from the carpet.

"Abdul!" Khalid shouted.

Obviously listening in the antechamber, Abdul materialized in an instant.

"Guard her," Khalid ordered. "When she's finished cleaning, set up the tub for her bath. Let no man gaze upon her face."

Heather stopped working and glared at him.

"Do not worry," Khalid said to her before disappearing outside. "I will have more chores for you later."

Heather and Abdul glared at each other. Finally, the warrior gestured her back to work.

Heather stared at him and shook her head. Abdul growled menacingly and took a step toward her. Heather resumed her task.

Chapter 6

Khalid returned at midday and surveyed his tent with satisfaction. The chamber was spotless and orderly. His temperamental captive had done her job well.

Curled on her side like an adorable kitten, Heather was asleep on his couch. Apparently, the unaccustomed toiling had tired her.

Khalid studied his sleeping beauty. Petite and curvaceously slender, Heather possessed the body of a temptress designed to entice him. Her shining copper hair cascaded past her angel's face to her lust-provoking hips. Behind closed lids, her eyes were exquisite emerald jewels.

Emeralds represent constancy, Khalid recalled. When this beauty surrendered her heart, she would love completely and forever.

Serene or hissing, Heather inflamed his senses. Khalid never felt more alive than when he was near her. Amazing, how love dropped suddenly into a man's life and filled an empty heart.

What in Allah's name was he thinking? Khalid forced himself to shrug off his tender thoughts. His captive was not meant for him, but to be used for revenge and then discarded.

Regret for what might have been tugged at his heart. If Heather had been anyone else, Khalid would have held her close for all eternity. Strange, he hadn't realized his heart was barren until she dropped into his life. Still, she was Fougere's intended and the only chink in the weasel's armor. If she knew what he planned for her, she would assuredly take her own life.

Khalid steeled himself against his regret. The blood of his sister and brother cried out for vengeance.

Khalid nudged her. "Awaken, slave."

Heather rolled over, turning her back on him, and pulled the coverlet over her head.

Khalid reached out and yanked the coverlet off, ordering loudly, "Awaken."

Heather bolted up on the couch. Her emerald eyes cleared, focused on him, and filled with obvious loathing.

"Slaves do not sleep when they please," Khalid told her, his heart aching at the hatred in her expression. "A slave must always be at the beck and call of her master."

Heather leaped off the couch. "Beck and call?"

Khalid scowled, and his blue-eyed gaze narrowed on her. There was no mistaking his irritation.

"Ten thousand pardons, my lord and master," Heather ground out. "You see before you a docile slave."

Khalid nodded. "You are forgiven."

Turning his back on the angry glint in her eyes, Khalid walked over to her sea chest and rummaged through her belongings. Finally, he pulled out a forest-green gown and returned to drop it down on the couch.

"Toiling has soiled your clothing," Khalid said. "Change your gown."

"What does it matter if I am filthy or clean? More chores will soil me again," Heather replied. "Another gown will be ruined, and the comte will be most unhappy when he learns he must purchase a new wardrobe for me.''

Khalid cocked a dark brow at her. "You will never see the comte again and need not fear his displeasure. Remember, a slave never questions her master's judgment.''

Khalid and Heather stared at each other in silence.

"Well?'' Heather arched a perfectly shaped copper brow at him.

"Well what?'' Khalid knew what she wanted but feigned ignorance.

"Will you leave me alone to change?''

"I told you before, slaves enjoy no privacy.''

Arguing with the beast was useless. Heather turned her back on him and unfastened her skirt, letting it fall where she stood. She pulled her blouse over her head and threw that down too.

Khalid admired the silken column of her back, visible beneath her chemise. His gaze drifted down to her well-turned legs. Even her feet were delicately shaped.

Heather reached for the fresh gown thrown across the couch. Khalid smiled appreciatively at the softly rounded curve of her buttocks.

Desire rode him hard. She was unlike any woman he had ever encountered. Khalid could scarcely control the urge to take her and make her his own.

Dressed, Heather turned around to face him and became mesmerized by his piercing blue eyes. Lust lurked there. And something more, something she failed to recognize. Inexperience blinded her to his budding love.

Khalid lifted his hand as if to caress the softness of her cheek, a gesture that confused and frightened Heather. Khalid realized if he touched her, if he loved her even once, he would never let her go. Khalid dropped his hand abruptly and turned away.

"Abdul," he shouted, and when his man entered several moments later, ordered, "Escort my slave outside. She will cook my dinner."

"I don't know how," Heather told him.

"You will learn." Khalid turned to Abdul and added, "No one may help her."

"I cannot learn if the cook doesn't show me how," she argued.

"You will figure it out," Khalid said. "Even a simple Turk like myself is capable of cooking a meal."

Dismissing her, Khalid turned to Abdul and ordered, "And no man may look upon her face."

"You will be sorry," Heather called over her shoulder as she followed Abdul outside.

A short time later, Khalid sat comfortably on the pillows beside his table and waited for dinner. Smudged and damp from her exertions at the campfire, Heather returned with a tray in her hands. Abdul followed behind.

Heather set the tray on the table in front of Khalid whose eyes narrowed at the disgusting sight. Before him were charred mutton chunks on a spit, watery rice, and artichokes drowned in vinegar.

Unaware of how miserably she'd done, Heather watched with anxious eyes. She always took pride in her accomplishments and genuinely hoped the beast liked her first attempt at cooking.

Suppressing his revulsion, Khalid convinced himself that appearances meant nothing. Food that looked horrible could actually taste delicious. Edible, at least. He forced himself to take a bite of mutton. Though blackened to a crisp on the outside, the mutton was practically raw.

Khalid chewed and swallowed the piece of mutton in

his mouth, then pushed the plate away. "This sheep is still breathing."

Insulted, Heather said nothing, but her lips pursed in anger.

"Undercooked," Khalid said, tasting the rice. "A man could break a tooth on this."

Heather remained silent, but her anger simmered beneath her unhappy expression.

Khalid stared at the artichokes. How could she possibly ruin an artichoke? he reasoned, realizing her pride was hurt.

Against his better judgment, Khalid bit into an artichoke. His eyes flew open wide in surprise at the overwhelming sourness of the vinegar. He threw the artichoke down and spit out what he had in his mouth. Choking, Khalid grabbed his goblet of rosewater and drank, but suppressed the urge to wipe the inside of his mouth with a cloth.

"Are you trying to poison me?" he asked.

"Certainly not, though the idea has merit," Heather said, her simmering anger becoming boiling rage. "I told you I was unschooled in cooking, but would you believe—?"

"For once you have spoken truthfully," Khalid interrupted. "Though I commend your honesty, I deplore your lack of culinary talent."

"Why, you—"

"Perhaps, your talents lie elsewhere." Khalid glanced at the bed, adding, "Shall we find out?"

Heather snapped her mouth shut.

"I thought not. In the future, preparing my meals will not be required, but you will serve them." He looked at Abdul and asked, "What are the men eating?"

"Couscous and flatbread."

"That sounds good to me." Khalid stood and started to leave.

"Use this time for your personal needs," Khalid ordered, watching her face redden with surprised embarrassment. "Naturally, you will serve my guest and me at the table tonight."

"N-n-naturally," Heather sputtered.

Khalid followed his man outside.

Heedless of the fact that a slave's proper place was the floor, Heather flopped down on the bed. Oh, how she hated him! If she'd been smart, she would have poisoned the beast. On the other hand, death by poisoning was too easy. Something more painful and bloody was more to her liking.

Liar, Heather called herself. In spite of her hatred, she knew she could never hurt him; for a reason that eluded her, she never felt more alive than when he was in her presence. Khalid hadn't murdered or raped her, hadn't even struck her. Though a warrior to be admired and feared, could the fierce Sword of Allah be hiding a gentle heart . . . ?

Flickering candlelight bathed the opulence of the prince's quarters in a soft glow that did not quite reach the farthest corners of the tent. Khalid and Malik sat at the table and waited for supper to be served. A crystal goblet of rosewater sat on the table in front of the prince while his friend preferred to sip the wine he'd brought from his villa.

"How fares your little hawk?" Khalid asked in Turkish.

Malik smiled. "Well, but duly chastised. Did you send the message to—?"

Both men turned when the tent flap opened. Abdul walked in, rolled his eyes heavenward, and held the flap aside for the slave carrying the prince's supper.

Heather appeared like an avenging apparition. Wearing a *yashmak* borrowed from Malik's harem, she was covered in black from head to toe. Only her eyes were visible.

Heather crossed the chamber slowly, placed the heavy tray on the table, and began to set their plates in front of them. The main dish was rabbit kebab marinated in olive oil, chopped tarragon, and parsley. Saffroned rice, pickled cucumbers, stuffed peppers, and lightly vinegared artichokes completed the meal.

"I'm suffocating," Heather complained in French as she refilled their water glasses. "Shrouding a body is customarily done after death, not before."

"Did you say something?" Khalid asked his friend.

"No," Malik answered, unable to suppress a smile. The fireworks display that he'd been anticipating all day was about to begin. Watching the prince and his captive was highly entertaining.

"I must be mistaken," Khalid said. "My slave's impeccable manners would never allow her to speak unless spoken to. She also knows that after serving, a well-mannered slave fades into a darkened corner to await her master's call."

Heather cursed inwardly and retired to a corner of the tent. There she seethed in silence. Certain the beast was unable to see her in the shadowed corner of the chamber, Heather unfastened the gauzy black veil and let it flutter to the carpet, then stepped on it for good measure. She absolutely refused to put the damned thing on again. Almighty God! She was an Englishwoman, not a Turkish concubine.

"Delicious," Malik said in Turkish, tasting the rabbit. "Did she cook—?"

"Certainly not," Khalid snorted, flicking a glance toward the corner where Heather stood. Switching to

French, he added, " 'Inedible' best describes my slave's cooking. Why, at the noon meal, she nearly poisoned me."

"By accident or design?" Malik asked, sipping his wine.

Khalid shrugged and said in a disgusted voice, "The artichokes were sour. The rice was brittle. And the sheep, poor creature, was still breathing."

Malik burst out laughing and choked on his wine. Khalid reached out and slapped his friend's back. In the process, wine sloshed onto the table.

Khalid looked at Heather and snapped his fingers for service. She ignored him.

"We need your assistance, slave," Khalid said. "You must learn to give your master's pleasure your undivided attention."

Grumbling under her breath, Heather advanced like a warrior on the table. Khalid noted the battle etched across her perfect features. The evening was becoming more interesting with each passing moment.

"A proper slave never drops her veil," Khalid told her.

"I will never be a proper slave," Heather grumbled.

"Clean this wine and pour more for my guest," Khalid ordered.

Heather knelt beside the table and began wiping the wine up.

"Revenge on the weasel would have been complete if she had married him," Khalid said, making his friend laugh. "Fougere would have met me in open battle to get away from her."

Pouring the wine, Heather wore a grim expression. Before supper was finished, she vowed, revenge would be hers.

"Speaking of Fougere," Malik said, switching to

Turkish so that Heather could not understand, "what is the plan for drawing him out? I was always fond of your sister and want to be included."

"My man carries a message west," Khalid replied, also in Turkish. "The Comte de Beaulieu's betrothed, a prisoner of the Sword of Allah, will be sold at a private auction in Istanbul. The comte, of course, is invited to participate."

That surprised Malik. He knew his friend was attracted to the woman. "The weasel is a coward and will not show," he said.

"Fougere will come to Istanbul," Khalid said, disagreeing.

"What about your slave?" Malik asked.

Khalid stared at Heather who, unaware of what they were saying, glared back at him. The tender expression on Khalid's face proclaimed his budding love for her, but he shook off the twinge of regret he felt.

"What about her?" Khalid said. "She is of no importance beyond enticing the weasel out of his hole and will be sold to the highest bidder."

Malik cast his friend a sidelong glance and said slyly, "If your mind is set, why not sell her to me?"

For a brief moment, fury etched across the prince's chiseled features. Finally, Khalid shrugged indifferently, and the two old friends bantered like a couple of adolescent boys.

"You are incapable of controlling two wild Englishwomen," Khalid said, switching to French for Heather's benefit.

Malik hooted at his friend's insult. "And you are?" he countered, also in French.

Khalid nodded. "Of course."

Heather bestowed a scathing look on them and headed for the tent flap where Abdul stood beckoning her. He handed her the tray with their dessert, two goblets of lemon sherbet.

"You are having trouble with one," Malik said. "Let a master advise you."

Khalid made a show of glancing around the tent. "I see no master of women here," he said. "If I call for a mirror, then I—"

Plop! Plop! The lemon sherbet hitting the table interrupted the prince's bragging.

"Dessert is served," Heather announced. "Will there be anything else, my lords?"

Startled, Khalid and Malik stared at the mass of sherbet on the table and then at her. When the sherbet dripped off the table onto their laps, both men leaped to their feet.

"It was an accident," Heather cried, realizing the enormity of what she'd done.

"See what I mean, my friend?" Malik said, then burst out laughing.

"Train a slave the same as a favored pet," Khalid said, flicking the sherbet from his fingertips onto Heather's face. "If she messes where she should not—"

"A message from Mihrimah," Abdul interrupted, entering at that moment. He handed the prince the missive.

Khalid read his mother's message. Like a gathering of storm clouds, his expression changed into a forbidding scowl. The Sultan's Beast had returned.

"I am needed in Istanbul at once," Khalid said in Turkish to Malik. "Someone tried to assassinate my cousin Murad. The fiend failed but escaped."

"Why would someone try to take the life of the sultan's heir?" Malik asked, shocked. "What madness!"

Khalid shrugged. "I will soon discover the answer to that."

"The *Saddam* will get you to Istanbul faster than a

horse,'' Malik said. ''My crew will be ready for an early morning departure.''

''I will tell the men that we break camp in the morning,'' Abdul said, then left.

''What about her?'' Malik asked.

''My slave accompanies me,'' Khalid replied, then switched to French, adding, ''Send your soiled pants back to my camp. She will not eat again until our clothing is cleaned.''

Malik nodded and left.

Khalid looked at Heather. Lemon sherbet dotted her face—the tip of her nose, her lips, and chin. He picked a towel up and tossed it to her.

''My day is coming,'' Heather muttered.

''Yes, lady,'' Khalid said in an ominous voice. ''It will be here sooner than you think.'' With that, he stalked out of the tent.

Heather could only wonder at his words.

Chapter 7

Peacefulness pervaded the early morning air at the beach. The rising sun streaked the eastern horizon a brilliant orange-red. At anchor in the bay, the *Saddam* lolled on the gentle waves, and overhead, a silent sea gull glided across the sky like a passing fair-weather cloud.

A single longboat had been pulled up on the white sand. Beside it, Rashid and a handful of Malik's sailors talked together in hushed tones. Khalid and Malik stood off to one side and spoke privately.

"You will come to Istanbul for the sale?" Khalid asked, handing his friend the pants his captive had cleaned.

Malik nodded. "Send word if you need me sooner."

"My lord," Abdul interrupted them. "The men are packed and ready,

"Fine. I will see you at home in a few days," Khalid said to his man. "If I need you in Istanbul, I will send word by way of Mihrimah's pigeons."

Abdul nodded and bowed. He turned on his heels and headed back to where the prince's men waited.

"Do you have any idea who would want Murad dead?" Malik asked.

Khalid shrugged, saying, "None to which I would give voice."

Several yards down the beach, Heather and April were

saying their own farewells. Both were covered in black from head to toe.

Heather hugged her cousin and whispered, "I will return and rescue you."

"Do not strain the prince's patience," April cautioned. "Besides, he is definitely more appealing than the weasel."

"Oh, you admit that Fougere resembles a weasel?" Heather asked.

April smiled sheepishly and shrugged. "If we return to England, the queen will only send you away to marry someone else," she said. "Probably, a man even more odious than the weasel."

"Don't worry about that." Heather sounded confident. "I have a plan."

"What is it?"

"I am finished with men," Heather announced. "I intend to join a French convent and devote my life to God."

"*You* in a convent?" April burst out laughing.

"What's so funny about that?" Heather asked.

"Let's not argue," April said, sobering. "It could be a long time before we see each other again."

Heather nodded. "I will miss you."

"Lord Malik has a house in Istanbul and has promised to take me there to visit you," April told her.

"What about his other women?"

"Do you think they'd like to visit you too?" April asked, misunderstanding.

"I doubt it," Heather replied, stifling a giggle. She lowered her voice to a mere whisper and added, "Send word when you arrive and we will escape together."

Unexpectedly, a masculine hand grabbed Heather's shoulder and whirled her around none too gently. Khalid and Malik stood there.

"You will never escape me," Khalid growled.

Heather opened her mouth to reply.

"Defy me in public, and I will be forced to give you a public punishment," Khalid warned in a deadly tone of voice.

Heather closed her mouth and turned to April. She threw herself into her cousin's arms and cried, "Why do I always lose the ones I love?"

"It's not forever." April soothed her, patting her cousin's back. "We will visit each other."

Finally, Khalid drew Heather away and escorted her to the longboat. He lifted her over the side and then climbed in. Rashid and the other sailors pushed the longboat into the surf and jumped in, then took up their places at the oars and began to row.

Looking toward the beach, Heather raised her arm in a farewell gesture to April.

"Saying good-bye to a loved one is always difficult," Khalid said, close to her ear.

Heather said nothing, She cast him a sidelong glance and wondered at the regret in his voice.

As they reached the *Saddam,* Heather looked up at the ship. The longboat swayed one way on the swells while the ship's masts swayed in the opposite direction.

Dizziness assailed Heather, and she grabbed her captor's arm. Khalid looked down at her anxious expression and knew she would be incapable of climbing to the deck.

Much to the amusement of the watching sailors, Khalid lifted her over his shoulder and started up. Heather put up no fight. Reaching the deck, Khalid set her on her feet but refused to let her go.

"Are you ill?" Khalid asked, concerned by her paleness.

"No." Heather shook her head and looked toward the beach. Her cousin had vanished.

"Afraid?"

Heather looked at him. "I—I've never been alone and so very far from home," she admitted.

"There is nothing to fear," Khalid said. "You travel in my company."

"Thank you," Heather said with an impish grin. "That makes me feel ever so much better."

Khalid's lips twitched as if he had the urge to smile but refused to surrender to that feeling. His statement was ridiculous; after all, he was the villain who held her captive.

"I'm hungry," Heather said. "Please, show me to my cabin. I'd like to start cleaning your pants so I won't miss lunch as well as breakfast."

The captain's cabin was as Heather remembered. Spacious, the chamber contained a real bed as well as a table with two chairs. An intricately designed carpet covered the floor, and enormous pillows were strewn about. Two portholes allowed filtered sunlight inside.

"Make yourself comfortable," Khalid said. Without another word, he left and locked the door behind him.

Heather crossed the cabin and stared out one of the portholes at the deserted beach. When would she see April?

Perhaps, her cousin was correct. The prince *was* more attractive than the weasel, and Queen Elizabeth just might betroth her to a more odious man. If she was tied to one end of his infernal leash, the prince had unwittingly hooked himself to the other.

What in God's name was she thinking? She would never submit to the infidel.

Heather yanked the black veil off her face. Next, she

stepped out of the *yashmak* and stomped on it for good measure. Heather plopped down on the bed and began cleaning Khalid's pants while she pondered the bleakness of her future.

Carrying a tray, Khalid returned to the cabin in late afternoon. He unlocked the door and stepped inside. His captive was looking out the porthole. Was she planning her next escape?

"Your pants are clean," Heather said, turning to face him.

"Come and eat," Khalid said, setting the tray of food on the table.

"I'm not hungry."

"If there is no food, you complain that I starve you," Khalid said. "If I bring you a tray, you refuse to eat. There will be no food until I finish my business in Istanbul and reach my home."

"I'll eat."

"I know you do not enjoy eating alone," Khalid said, sitting in the other chair.

Heather looked up from her meal. "When will I be released?" she asked.

"How long are you planning to live?" he countered, wearing that infuriating smile.

"So, you intend to make me your slave?"

"I intend nothing. I have done it."

"I refuse to be part of your harem," Heather announced.

"I do not keep a harem," Khalid said.

"Why not?" Heather asked. Her cousin had told her that men in this land keep many women.

"At the moment, I harbor no love for any particular woman," he told her.

"Surely, the unfortunate woman who bore you holds a place in your heart," Heather said.

Without another word, Khalid stood to leave but paused at the door, saying, "Lady, I have no heart." The door clicked shut behind him.

Apparently, the prince was a motherless beast, Heather decided.

Khalid stood on deck until Istanbul came over the horizon. The sight of the Golden Horn and his uncle's palace never failed to stir him. He shrugged off his thoughts of his beautiful but outspoken captive and concentrated on who would want his cousin dead. Was the failed assassination an isolated act by an unknown fanatic? Or was the assassination attempt the product of a conspiracy? Murad was depending on him to discover the truth.

Who awaited him at Topkapi Palace? Murad, yes. His life and the empire's future tranquility were at stake. Nur-U-Banu? It was her only son's life that was endangered. Sultan Selim? Perhaps, if he hadn't had a previous appointment with wine. Mihrimah? Need he ask himself that? Khalid was certain to find his mother wherever plots were hatched and power struggles fought.

When Khalid returned to the cabin, he heard his captive's moans. She was caught in the midst of that nightmare.

"Wake up," Khalid said, gathering her into his arms.

Heather opened her eyes and focused on him. Glistening sweat beaded her forehead and upper lip. Without forethought, Heather rested her head against the comforting solidity of his chest and clung to him for protection.

In spite of all that has passed between us, she trusts me to protect her, Khalid thought. Guilt for what he had planned coiled around his heart.

"While I am gone, Rashid will stand guard outside the door," Khalid said, stroking her back in a soothing motion. He released her and retrieved the golden leash.

"Do not chain me," Heather cried. "The door is locked, and there is no place to go. Besides, I cannot swim."

Khalid sat on the edge of the bed and tilted her chin up so he could gaze into her disarming green eyes. "You are small enough to squeeze through that porthole and might drown yourself to get away from me. Too many young women lie beneath these waters. I refuse to let you join them in their watery grave."

Heather lifted her upturned nose into the air. "You are not that important."

"Am I not?"

"Do your worst," Heather said, closing her eyes. Trembling and pale, she offered him her wrist.

Like a lamb to the slaughter, Khalid thought as he stared at her stricken expression. His gaze dropped to her badly shaking hand. With a muttered oath, Khalid tossed the leash onto the floor and yanked Heather into his arms.

Her startling green eyes flew open, but Heather had no chance to struggle.

Khalid captured her lips in a passionate, demanding kiss that stole her breath away and made her senses reel. His insistent lips parted hers, and his tongue ravished the sweetness of her mouth, sending ripples of desire dancing down her spine.

Heather, her body on fire with her first kiss, moaned throatily. Unaware of what she was doing, Heather entwined her arms around his neck and returned his kiss in kind.

Khalid broke the kiss and stared with satisfaction at her dazed expression. "Promise me you will do yourself no harm," he whispered huskily, urgently.

"I swear," Heather said, closing her eyes for another kiss.

Khalid smiled softly and pressed his palm against her burning cheek. With that, he turned on his heels and left the cabin.

Shaken, Heather sat down on the bed and touched her lips with her fingertips. *Her first real kiss.* She closed her eyes, sighed dreamily, and tried to recapture the feeling.

In the next instant, Heather burned with shame. Oh, Lord! The villain had kissed her, and she'd enjoyed it, had even moaned and wanted more. Did he affect every woman that way? Or only her? How could she ever face him again?

Twilight's last slash of lavender slid beneath the western sky as Khalid left the ship. He climbed into the longboat and looked over his shoulder at a sight that never failed to inspire him. The domes and minarets of Istanbul, city of intrigue and mystery, rose across the bay behind him. Khalid would not be going into the city proper. Instead, the longboat carried him to his uncle's palace.

Topkapi perched on a promontory overlooking the Golden Horn, Bosporus, and the Sea of Marmara. The name itself meant cannon-gate in Turkish, and located on each side of the palace complex was an enormous cannon. The structure's location and fortification made it virtually impregnable.

Khalid looked toward Topkapi in the distance. Through the fading light, he could distinguish the square towers of the sultan's baths and the octagonal towers of the harem.

The harem, Khalid thought with contempt. How he hated his visits to the harem! Devious and ruthless creatures, the ladies of the harem were like beautiful but poisonous snakes slithering with relentless ambition around their master. Their infighting for the sultan's favor was horrendous and, at times, fatal.

Khalid passed through the harem's carved double doors inlaid with mother-of-pearl. The *agha kislar* escorted him through the winding corridors to his aunt's salon and left him there. Waiting inside the opulent chamber were Nur-U-Banu, the sultan's *bas kadin,* Murad, the sultan's heir, and Mihrimah, Khalid's mother and the sultan's sister.

"So, you have finally decided to help us in our hour of need," Mihrimah said in Turkish, greeting her only living son.

"Khalid," Murad said, his relief evident in his voice.

"Welcome, nephew," Nur-U-Banu added, her eyes alight with true affection.

As many times as Khalid had visited his cousin, the opulence of his aunt's salon never failed to capture his eye. Lavishly tiled and luxuriously carpeted, the chamber featured an enormous bronze brazier, opaque colored glazes upon the walls, and Ottoman mullioned windows that looked out upon a private garden. As mother of the sultan's heir, Nur-U-Banu was most definitely favored.

"I thank you for your welcome, Aunt," Khalid said to his uncle's lovely *bas kadin.* Turning to Murad, he gave his cousin the kiss of peace. Finally, Khalid gave his mother his attention, asking, "Where is Tynna?"

"Your sister is home where she should be at her age," Mihrimah answered. "Do you want her involved in a discussion of murder?"

"No." Khalid looked at his aunt. "And Uncle Selim?"

"Visiting Lyndar," Nur-U-Banu answered, her contempt obvious. "She recently whelped a club-footed runt and named him Karim in honor of your late brother."

"Tell Khalid about the assassination attempt at the bazaar," Mihrimah ordered her nephew.

Khalid turned to his cousin, asking, "Who would want you dead?"

Murad shrugged. "Karim?"

"Infants are incapable of plotting assassinations," Khalid said.

"But his mother could," Nur-U-Banu spoke up. "And Lyndar would dare anything to gain power for her son."

"What do you think, Mother?" Khalid asked.

"Lyndar is too unintelligent for such maneuverings," Mihrimah remarked, then added, "Your scar is not apparent from this angle. Too bad, you could have been a handsome man, and your brother lies in an early grave."

Khalid paled, his lips and disfiguring scar whitening with anger. How could he have forgotten his mother's disdain for him? Her words wounded him as no scimitar could.

"Khalid is the same man he always was," Murad said quietly, appalled that a mother would insult her only living son in such a manner. "Karim died bravely, through no fault of Khalid's."

"My face is of no import," Khalid said to his mother. "No woman could be involved in such a plot. Women wound only with their sharp tongues."

"By law, imperfect sons cannot become sultan," Mihrimah said, ignoring his jibe. "What could she gain?"

"Special boots would hide the child's imperfection from the empire," Nur-U-Banu speculated. "His limp could be explained as a sore ankle."

Murad smiled with love at his mother. "You grasp at camel hairs out of fear for my safety."

"What do you think?" Khalid asked his cousin.

"I have faith in your ability to discover the truth and punish the guilty," Murad replied without hesitation.

The four of them fell silent when a servant entered with refreshments. The girl placed a tray of flaky crescent pastries, sugared almonds, and cups of Turkish coffee on the table, then retreated.

"Malik did not accompany you?" Mihrimah asked.

"He will soon be arriving in Istanbul," Khalid said. "Have you done what I asked?"

"The eunuch awaits you at your home," Mihrimah answered. "Why did you need one who speaks French and English?"

"To care for my English captive," Khalid said, matter-of-factly.

"Your captive?" the other three echoed simultaneously.

"Allah has provided an unexpected chance for revenge against Fougere," Khalid told them.

"You failed to kill him before," Mihrimah said. "What makes you think you are capable of the task now?"

"I hold the irresistible bait that will surely entice him out of his hole," Khalid answered. "Malik captured the weasel's betrothed, a wild heathen of a woman, and gifted me with her. Word has been sent to Fougere that he may purchase her at a private auction next month."

"What does she look like?" Murad asked, always receptive to new bedsport. If she was pretty, he would buy her himself.

"The little barbarian possesses a tongue to rival the sharpness of my mother's," Khalid replied, familiar with the extent of his cousin's lust. "Her hair is the nauseating color of a withered orange, and her eyes are the green of a bitter, unripened apple. Most distracting of all, her face is disfigured by brown spots dotting her nose. So revolting is she to gaze upon, I cannot bear to eat in her presence. A fitting mate for a weasel, though."

"That beautiful, huh?" Murad wasn't fooled for a minute. But, why would his cousin discourage him from purchasing the woman? Did Khalid want her for himself?

"I will come to this auction," Murad said, watching his cousin's reaction. "Unless you want to keep her for yourself?"

"Never," Khalid answered, too quickly.

The others in the salon looked curiously at him. His quick denial of intention announced his interest in the woman. Though they believed he would marry eventually, Khalid had never before shown an interest in anything but war and fighting. Since being scarred, he avoided women and almost never shared his thoughts.

"My slave is unfit for civilized society," Khalid added. "Thus far, the little heathen threatened me with dagger and scimitar, dumped my dinner onto my lap, and swilled down her own food with the manners of a swine. I must waste the next couple of weeks schooling her in proper behavior. In good conscience, I cannot sell such a wild creature to anyone. I keep her leashed lest the empire be toppled during one of her rages."

"Leashed?" Murad burst out laughing.

"Does she bite?" Nur-U-Banu teased.

Mihrimah stared in surprise at the animation in her son's expression and voice. "Why not lock her up and throw away the key?"

"She suffers from horrible nightmares," Khalid answered without thinking. "When she cries out in the night, I soothe her back to sleep."

The three in the salon stared at him in shock. Seeing their expressions, Khalid realized he'd revealed too much and flushed with embarrassment.

"I will definitely attend this auction," Murad announced. "I would view this woman who has captured Khalid's eye."

Masking his embarrassment with irritation, Khalid cast them a quelling look and stood to leave. "I am going home to ponder the assassination attempt. In the meantime, Murad must remain inside Topkapi."

Night had fallen by the time Khalid left the palace and climbed into the longboat. Overhead, a full moon surrounded by thousands of twinkling stars hung in the sky, but Khalid did not notice them. He was too busy thinking of his beautiful captive.

Was it true? Khalid wondered. Did he want to keep his captive with him? In the name of Allah, the witch was Fougere's intended and would murder him in his sleep at the first opportunity. Perhaps, the weasel had meant for her to be caught, and this whole situation was a bizarre trap. No, that was ridiculous. No man would chance losing such a magnificent woman.

Khalid knew he desired his captive. That much was true. But a virgin would bring a high price at auction. Khalid had no intention of bedding her.

His mother's cruel tongue and his own sexual frustration conspired against him and turned his mood foul. Khalid tried to concentrate on the attempted assassination, but each time he did, a green-eyed witch paraded provocatively across his mind's eye. His desire for his captive paralyzed his powers of concentration, and that infuriated him. If Murad was murdered, the fault belonged to Heather.

Entering the captain's cabin, Khalid marched across the chamber, sat on the edge of the bed, and reached for his sleeping captive. "Leave me alone," he growled in Turkish, giving her a rough shake.

Half asleep, Heather opened her eyes and smiled. She

reached up and touched his scarred cheek, murmuring in French, "Are we home?"

Khalid drew back as if scorched by fire. "Your home is in England."

Fully awake, Heather sat up and stared at him. "You agree with me now?"

Without answering, Khalid stood and crossed the cabin to the porthole. For a long time, he gazed at the starlit night and tried to calm his rioting emotions. His mother's contempt always sent him into a rage. The woman in his bed had no part in it.

"Well?" Heather asked.

"Go to sleep," Khalid said quietly.

"You shake me awake and then order me to sleep?" Heather asked. "What insanity is this?"

With his back turned to her, Khalid smiled. She was correct; he *was* insane. Gazing upon the perfection of her face had caused his madness. If the fabled Helen of Troy had launched a thousand ships, his wildflower could launch ten times that.

His wildflower? What in Allah's name was he thinking?

Khalid walked back to the bed and sat down, then reached out to touch his captive's cheek. "I have endured a disturbing interview with my relatives, but it is no fault of yours," he told her. "Forgive me."

Forgive him? His apology shocked Heather speechless for a moment. The beast was actually treating her like a real person instead of a slave.

"Relatives can be unpleasant, even bothersome at times," Heather said. "I understand."

That understatement made Khalid smile. "My mother was born unpleasant," he said dryly.

"You have a mother?" Heather blurted out.

Khalid cocked a dark brow at her. "Of course. Did you think I crawled from beneath a rock?"

Heather shook her head.

"What did you think?" he asked.

"I never pictured villains as having mothers," she answered, then smiled.

"What amuses you?"

"I cannot imagine you answering to a mother . . . or getting spanked," Heather answered, then dissolved into giggles.

"I can assure you, the fierce Sword of Allah is no stranger to parental discipline." Khalid's expression clouded when he added, "Even now, my mother's tongue wounds more deeply than a scimitar."

At that moment, the prince appeared like a hurt little boy, and Heather's heart went out to him. "Her tongue is sharper than mine?" she asked.

"Much." Khalid opened his arms, saying, "It is late. I will soothe you to sleep."

"Are you planning to kiss me again?" Heather asked. "No."

Heather didn't know if that relieved or disappointed her. She snuggled into his embrace and rested her head against his chest. Khalid soothed her to sleep by rubbing her back, then pressed her onto the pillow and planted a kiss on her forehead.

It seemed she had only slept a moment when Heather felt herself nudged awake for the second time. In answer to the gentle nudge, Heather rolled over and pulled the coverlet over her head.

"Awaken, my sweet wildflower," Khalid coaxed.

"Go away," his sweet wildflower grumbled.

"We are home." Khalid yanked the coverlet off.

Disgruntled, Heather sat up and brushed the fiery wisps of hair out of her eyes. "My home is in England."

"Your home is with me," Khalid said. "Stand, and I will help you put on the *yashmak*."

Too tired to argue, Heather stood still while he folded her into the black cloak and headdress. "I'm hungry," she said.

"You are always hungry," he replied, pulling the veil over her face.

Khalid escorted her on deck and carried her down the rope ladder to the longboat. When they reached the shore, he jumped out and lifted her onto the sand.

"My home awaits you, maiden," Khalid said, gesturing toward the top of the cliff.

Heather looked up. Even in the night, the beast's stronghold appeared as if it could withstand a thousand-year siege. How could she ever escape this fortress?

"You expect me to climb the side of that rock?" Heather asked, incredulous.

"There is a path for the less adventurous."

"*Hos geldiniz*—welcome!" a high-pitched voice greeted them.

Heather dragged her gaze away from the castle's battlements. On the sand in front of them knelt a small, rather rotund man. His forehead was pressed to the tip of the prince's boots.

"Stand," Khalid bade him in Turkish.

The short, portly man got to his feet and smiled, eager to please. His hair and eyes were black, his skin swarthy. "I am Omar and wish only to serve you."

"This is Heather, the wildflower," Khalid said in French. "You serve me by serving her."

Omar nodded and turned to Heather, saying, "Please, come with me."

Heather clung to Khalid, a gesture that surprised him. How could he bear to lose the only woman who'd gazed upon his disfigurement without revulsion in her eyes? How could he sell a woman who, apparently, trusted him to keep her safe? That disturbing thought filled him with remorse.

Khalid put his arm around her shoulder and guided her up the path to the castle. Omar followed behind.

"Omar is here to serve you," Khalid explained as they walked. "He will not harm you."

"I am his mistress?" Heather asked.

"You have only to ask, and he will do your bidding," Khalid said.

Once inside the castle, Omar allowed Heather only the briefest glimpse of the torch-lit hall. He whisked her up the stairs to the chamber he had prepared for her.

Heather pulled the *yashmak* off, yawned loudly, and sat on the edge of the bed. Then she looked around. Her chamber was large and decorated with thick carpets on the floor. A warm, cheery fire crackled in the hearth.

Keeping up a steady stream of chatter, Omar rummaged through the sea chests that two servants had carried in. Finally, he pulled out a silken nightshift, the one she was to have worn on her wedding night.

"You are the most fortunate of women to have captured the prince's eye," Omar said in French, advancing on her.

"He captured me," Heather corrected him.

"No matter," Omar replied with an expansive wave of his hand. "You will please the prince and bear his sons. Our fortunes will be made."

"You are insane."

Omar chuckled, unperturbed, and reached to help her disrobe. Heather slapped his hand away.

"Undressing you is my job," Omar told her.

"You will not touch me."

"You need have no fear," the eunuch explained. "I am incapable of performing like a man. Disabled, in a manner of speaking."

Ignorant of his meaning, Heather stared at him blankly, then said, "I prefer to undress myself. Please, leave."

"As you wish." Omar sniffed, his feelings hurt. He left the chamber but waited just outside the door.

Fully clothed, Heather lay back on the bed. No man, disabled or not, was going to touch her. She stared at the hypnotic flames in the hearth, and after a while, slept.

For one hour, Omar waited patiently in the corridor. Finally, he opened the door a crack, peered inside, and smiled. His charge was asleep on the bed.

Noiselessly, Omar entered and closed the door, then hurried over to the bed. He stared at his new mistress's captivating face and mentally clapped his hands together with joy. This sleeping beauty would make him rich beyond avarice.

Omar began undressing Heather until she lay naked to his critical gaze. Spying the golden bracelet, Omar assumed the prince was already devoted to her. He marveled at her angel's face and temptress's body, but the unsightly triangle of copper curls at the juncture of her thighs had to go.

Omar sent up a silent prayer of thanks for delivering this beauty into the prince's hands and, of course, his own. Allah had gifted him with a Christian angel to serve, and he could almost hear the tinkling of gold coins as they dropped into—

The door opened unexpectedly, and Khalid walked in. He'd gone to his own chamber to sleep alone but changed his mind. His chamber had seemed lonely without his copper-haired captive. He'd grown accustomed to sleeping beside her and would continue that practice until she was gone. Besides, if he wasn't there, *she* would miss him.

Khalid stood beside Omar for a moment, and the two

men silently admired the beauty sprawled on the bed in front of them.

"That will be all for tonight," Khalid said in Turkish, dismissing the eunuch. He pulled his shirt over his head and dropped it on the carpet.

"That will be . . . ?" That the prince intended to pass the night with his captive surprised Omar. "She is unbathed," he protested. "She has been neither denuded of hair nor perfumed. This is not the custom. Bedding a woman is not done this way."

"You dare question me?" Khalid reached for the little man.

"However, this is not Topkapi," Omar amended, stepping out of harm's way. "If this is the way you choose, then this is how it will be done." With that, Omar hurried out. Angering the prince was a very unhealthy thing to do.

Khalid gently turned Heather so her head rested upon a pillow, then ṣat on the edge of the bed and removed his boots. He stood to take his pants off, but changed his mind as his gaze drifted over her nakedness. If no clothing separated their bodies, he would be hard pressed to control himself.

Leaving his lower regions covered, Khalid lay down on the bed and pulled Heather into his arms. In her sleep, she snuggled against him.

Like a lamb bedding down with a lion, Khalid thought.

In the morning, Omar would begin schooling Heather in the manners of a proper Ottoman lady. And may Allah have mercy on the little man.

Chapter 8

Heather yawned and stretched, then opened her eyes. She scanned the unfamiliar chamber and remembered where she was, in her captor's stronghold.

The bed's disarray and the masculine clothing in a heap on the floor announced the fact that the beast had slept beside her. Now, however, she was alone. *And naked.* Who—Khalid or Omar—had undressed her the previous night?

Heather donned her discarded caftan. She crossed the chamber to the window, drew the covering aside, and peered outside.

The lightness of the eastern horizon proclaimed the morning's early hour. The bay was empty, the *Saddam* having already begun its return trip home.

Heather's gaze drifted to the beach. Barefoot and naked to the waist, Khalid was working around a dinghy; apparently, the beast had been fishing.

Beside Khalid sat a dog—at least, Heather thought it was a dog—the likes of which she'd never seen. Tall and muscularly slender like its master, the tawny and white beast appeared bred for hunting.

Heather watched Khalid give the dog an affectionate hug and pat. How could a black-hearted villain show a fondness for anything beyond himself? Could there be more to her captor than she had thought? Though he

denied its existence, did his fierce exterior hide a
heart?

Heather studied his broad, muscular shoulders and
back that tapered into a narrow waist. Khalid appeared
like a perfect specimen of manhood as his sinuous muscles flexed with his exertions and then relaxed.

As though feeling her scrutinizing gaze upon him,
Khalid turned toward the castle and looked up. Heather
reacted instinctively and ducked. Shame at being caught
admiring his magnificent physique washed over her,
though she knew he couldn't possibly have seen her.

The door swung open suddenly, admitting Omar. He
carried a tray that contained small triangular-shaped pies,
peaches, and tea.

"I see that you have awakened," Omar said, setting
her breakfast on the table. "Come and eat. Later, you
will bathe."

"I was watching the sun rise," Heather said, sitting
at the table. She reached for a pastry and took a bite.
"Delicious. What is it?"

"Cheese-filled *boregs,*" Omar answered, crossing the
chamber to the window. Nonchalantly, he glanced outside and saw Khalid on the beach below, then smiled to
himself. Apparently, his beautiful little heathen was
more interested in the prince than she cared to admit.

While the eunuch's attention lay elsewhere, Heather
lifted the paring knife from the tray and hid it in the
pocket of her caftan. Pleased with herself, she reached
for the tea and sipped the brew.

"The master adores you," Omar gushed, turning toward her. "Our fortunes are made."

Heather choked on the tea and spit it out.

Omar rushed to her side and slapped her back. "The
prince is correct," he said. "Your English manners are
unsuitable for Istanbul."

"I will be returning to England soon," Heather said, rounding on him.

Ignoring her words, Omar threw the *yashmak* over her shoulders and covered her head with a veil. "It is time to bathe," he said, leading her out of the chamber.

Heather went along without argument. She planned to escape and needed to know the layout of the castle.

"Stinking Christians who did not bathe—no offense to you—built this castle in olden times," Omar told her as they walked down the winding torch-lit maze of corridors. "The prince ordered a bathing addition built when he came here to live."

Omar led Heather past a guard into the baths. It was like entering a new, exotic world. The air was humid from the heated water in the large pool at one end of the enormous chamber. The walls and floor were tiled, and white marble benches were arranged here and there.

Omar whipped the cloak and veil off Heather as two scantily clad slave girls hurried over to help her disrobe. Heather slapped their hands away, and they shrank back.

"I will take care of my mistress," Omar told them in Turkish, then reached for her.

Heather slapped his hand away and pulled the knife from her pocket. "Touch me and die," she warned.

Omar stepped back a pace and said something in Turkish. One of the girls ran to the door and spoke to the guard.

Khalid, still disturbingly naked to the waist, marched into the baths several moments later and surveyed the scene. With her back pressed against the wall, Heather held the eunuch at bay with a fruit knife.

"Allah grant me patience," Khalid muttered in Turkish, advancing on them. To Omar, he said, "Where did she get the knife?"

"I—I—I d-did not know your b-beloved was untrustworthy," Omar sputtered, fearing the prince's wrath.

"She is not my beloved," Khalid snapped. He held his hand out to Heather and said in French, "Give me the knife."

"Where would you like it?" she asked, waving the ridiculously small blade at him.

"I have no wish to hurt you."

"But, *I* have a wish to hurt *you*."

"There is no place to run," Khalid told her. "Accept defeat gracefully."

"I won't have them pawing me," Heather said.

So that was the problem. His Christian captive was uncomfortable with her own nudity, as were all European barbarians.

"I commend your modesty," Khalid said, "but these women are servants who see without really seeing. Besides, your naked perfection is nothing to cause you shame. I know this is true because I have seen it."

"Don't say such a thing," Heather cried, her face coloring a vibrant scarlet.

Khalid sighed in frustration. "Will you allow Omar alone to help you bathe?"

"Let him bathe you."

"I will bathe later." Khalid said something in Turkish to the two bathing attendants and gestured them out, then turned back to his defiant captive.

Khalid and Heather stared at each other in silence for a long time. Their eyes clashed in a fierce battle of wills until she became mesmerized by his intense blue-eyed gaze.

Reaching out, Khalid lifted the paring knife from her hand. He unfastened her caftan and let it drop to the floor, then studied the proud beauty, naked to his smoldering gaze. Desire quickened his pulse and parched his mouth.

Watching them, Omar recognized the irresistible siren's call in Heather's expression and the answering need in the prince's intense gaze. These strong-willed lovers would mate fiercely and produce a dozen fine sons. Allah be praised, his fortune was made.

One of the women returned with a goblet of rose-petal sherbet. She handed it to Omar, who gave it to Khalid.

"Drink this. It will soothe your nerves," Khalid said hoarsely. "Then Omar will bathe you."

Heather drank the sherbet and watched the prince retreat. She handed the empty goblet to Omar. He gave it to the woman and ushered her out.

Omar led a distracted Heather to the washing tub. He lathered her whole body and rinsed, then washed her glorious mane of copper. Relaxed to the point of lethargy, Heather let him apply the almond paste that removed body hair. When he'd rinsed that off with warm water, Omar stepped back to inspect and admire his charge. "Your Venus mound has a deep cleft, the mark of great passion."

After Heather had soaked in the heated pool, Omar toweled her dry and combed her hair until it crackled and sparkled like fire. He led her to a marble bench, covered it with a towel, and ordered her to lie on her stomach.

With skillful hands, Omar began massaging her shoulders, back, and buttocks. The drug-laced sherbet and the eunuch's talented fingers produced in her a wonderfully languorous feeling that prevented her protest.

"The prince adores you," Omar said as he kneaded the flesh of her alluringly rounded buttocks.

"I would hardly call his behavior loving," Heather replied, paralyzed beneath his touch.

"Last night he could not bear to be parted from you," he told her, "but insisted on sleeping beside you."

"The prince doesn't want to lose his slave."

"Slaves are easily purchased," Omar disagreed. "Besides, you must trust my judgment in matters concerning the prince's heart. I am your ally."

"The prince has no heart," Heather said. Then, "Tell me about him."

"Prince Khalid is known as the Sultan's Beast," Omar began. "Though feared and respected throughout the empire, he is disdained by his mother, but I do not know why. Mihrimah, his mother, is the daughter of Suleiman the Lawgiver and his beloved Khurrem, both deceased. Sultan Selim is the prince's uncle; and Murad, the sultan's heir, is his cousin. The prince has one younger sister, but an older sister and brother are dead . . . Roll onto your back."

Lethargic with pleasure, Heather was unable to rouse herself enough to obey.

"Omar said, roll onto your back," another voice spoke.

Surprised, Omar looked up from his task and found Khalid standing beside them. Apparently, the prince was unable to stay away from his beautiful slave.

Heather rolled her over slowly, murmuring, "Khalid."

The provocative sight of her naked perfection and the whispered sound of his name upon her lips conspired against him. His manhood stirred, and he struggled in vain against his rising desire.

"She drank the sherbet?" Khalid asked in Turkish, his voice husky.

Omar nodded.

"Ensuring your safety, they added a mild relaxant to it," Khalid told him.

Khalid traced a finger down the silkiness of Heather's cheek. He turned to the eunuch, ordering, "Leave us."

"But, I have not finished," Omar protested.

"I will finish for you."

"The master massaging his slave?" Omar countered, disapproving.

Khalid scowled and cocked a dark brow at him. Why did these two slaves think they could argue with him?

"As you wish," Omar said, and turned to leave. Khalid never saw the broad, satisfied grin that split the little man's face.

After warming the lotion in his hands, Khalid began massaging her smooth shoulders, but her ripe breasts called to him and beckoned his touch. His hands dropped to her silken mounds and kneaded them with seductive strokes.

Heather sucked in her breath at the amazing sensation of a thousand airy butterfly wings fluttering though her belly, little knowing what she felt was desire. Overwhelmed by his nearness and touch, Heather could not protest; instead, she surrendered to the incredible feelings he was creating. Heather yearned to feel his sensuous lips pressed to hers.

"Kiss me," she breathed.

The invitation was irresistible.

Khalid bent his head, and his mouth captured hers in a devouring kiss. His tongue slipped past her lips, tasting and exploring the sweetness within.

Heather caught fire and squirmed with scorching desire as a throbbing heat ignited between her thighs. Khalid slashed a finger across the jewel of her womanhood, wet and swollen beneath his touch.

Desperate with need, Heather moaned throatily. Spurred on by her sweet surrender, Khalid tormented each of her dusky nipples with his tongue and teeth while his masterful finger continued its gentle assault.

Heather felt her tension build to unendurable heights

and thought she would die. With a cry of surprise, she exploded and then floated back to earth slowly as if riding a billowy cloud. Sated from the unexpected release, she closed her eyes.

Khalid smiled with true affection and planted a chaste kiss on her lips. He wrapped her in the *yashmak* and carried her back to her chamber.

When she awakened later, Heather thought of the prince's intimate touch. Hot embarrassment flushed her face. She hadn't known *that* was what men did to women, had never really thought about it. How could she have surrendered so completely to his touch? Was she a wanton? And, more importantly, how would she face him again without dying of shame?

Heather gave herself a mental shake. She refused to think about facing him now; she would deal with that when it happened. With any luck, she'd be gone before then.

Heather dressed in the fresh caftan that had been laid out for her and headed to the window. The sun rode high in the sky, and the beach was deserted except for a couple of dinghies pulled up on the sand.

Where is Khalid? she wondered. And what is he doing at the moment?

Heather whirled around at the sound of the door opening. It was only Omar, carrying a tray of food.

"The hour has arrived to begin learning the proper deportment of an Ottoman lady," Omar said, setting the tray down. "Table manners will be first."

"I'm no Ottoman."

"But, you are a lady."

"Delicacy is unnecessary for women who do not eat with men," Heather returned.

"Nonsense," Omar said. "As the mother of Prince Khalid's sons, you will certainly be invited to Topkapi."

"I have no plans to become anyone's mother," Heather told him. "What is Topkapi?"

"The sultan's palace," Omar replied. "Come along and sit at the table with me."

Heather stood in indecision for a moment but relented when her stomach growled, her hunger calling out to the food. She sat on a pillow and looked the fare over. "Now what?" she asked.

"Eat," Omar said, plunking his bulky body down on a pillow. "I will correct your deplorable English manners as you eat."

"Correct my *what*?"

Omar pointed at the tray, ordering, "Eat."

Heather swallowed her anger and smiled sweetly at him. This insulting servant was in dire need of a lesson, and she knew exactly how to vex him.

Heather picked several olives up, popped them into her mouth, and chewed. Finished, she turned her head and spit the pits onto the floor between them.

"No!" Omar cried. "Eat one olive at a time. Remove the pit from your mouth daintily and place it on the side of the plate."

Heather nodded her understanding and reached for a handful of roasted almonds, pistachios, peanuts, and hazelnuts. She stuffed her mouth so full that her cheeks puffed out.

"Do not put too much food in your mouth," Omar instructed. "Tiny bites are ladylike."

"What?" Heather opened her mouth and displayed the chewed-up nuts.

Omar grimaced. "Do not speak with food in your mouth."

Heather nodded. She finished chewing and swallowed, then reached for her goblet of rosewater. That went down in one long gulp.

"No guzzling," the eunuch chided. "Take one dainty sip at a time."

"What's that?" Heather asked, pointing to a plate.

"Fried whitebait."

Heather popped a piece of fish into her mouth. Pretending she didn't like it, Heather spit the chewed herring onto her plate. "See," she said. "I used the plate instead of the floor."

"Enough work on table manners for today," Omar said, feeling nauseated. "Our language lesson comes next." He held one index finger up and said, "*Bir.*"

Heather looked at him blankly.

"*Bir* means one," Omar explained. "Repeat, if you please."

"But, I do not please."

"Then repeat, if you do not please," the eunuch snapped, irritated.

"*Bir.*"

"Excellent pronunciation," Omar praised her. She appeared to be a quick learner. Holding up a finger for each new number, he counted to five. "*Bir, iki, uc, dort, bes.* Repeat, please."

Heather pasted an innocent expression onto her face and recited, "Beer, icky, yucky, dirty, bitchy."

"No! *Bir, iki, uc, dort, bes.*"

"Beer, icky, yucky, dirty, bitchy."

Omar held both hands up and counted to ten with his fingers. "*Bir, iki, uc, dort, bes, alti, yedi, sekiz, dokuz, on.*"

Heather smiled sweetly and repeated, "Beer, icky, yucky, dirty, bitchy—on!"

Frustrated, Omar sent up a silent prayer for patience. "Never mind the numbers," he said, then held his arm up and pointed to it. "*Kol.*"

"Cool."

"*Kol.*"

"Cool."

Omar pointed to his eye and said, "*Guz.*"

"Gauze," Heather chirped.

"*Guz.*"

"Gauze."

Omar stuck his tongue out and pointed to it, then said, "*Dil.*"

"Deal," Heather said, enjoying herself.

"No, *dil.*" Omar's voice rose in direct proportion with his frustration.

"That's what I said, deal."

Omar felt like screaming.

Heather could feel her laughter bubbling up.

Omar took a deep, calming breath. He pointed to his nose, saying, "*Burun.*"

"*Burun,*" Heather repeated, and stuck her finger up her nose.

"No!" Omar shrieked, slapping her hand. "Ladies do not pick their nose."

A knock on the door saved Omar from further torment. A servant entered at his call and handed him a message, then left.

As Omar read the note, an expression of sublime joy appeared on his face. He looked up and grinned at Heather.

"Good news, I presume?" she asked.

"The best," Omar said. "The prince invites you to sup with him in his chamber."

Heather never wanted to see the prince again, never mind break bread with him. "Tell the prince I decline his invitation," she said.

"Declining the prince's invitation is forbidden."

"So, the prince summons me to supper?"

"Call it what you like," Omar said with a shrug.

"You will sup with the prince, and if lucky, get with his child."

"I am not *getting* with anyone's child," Heather insisted, appalled. "I am escaping."

"In that case, you had better learn our language," Omar snapped. "Asking directions to England may be necessary."

Heather grinned. "I hadn't thought of that." She leaned over and planted a kiss on the eunuch's cheek, startling him.

"*Bir, iki, uc, dort, bes,*" Heather counted, holding her fingers up.

"Excellent!" Omar exclaimed. "Now, eat an olive like an Ottoman lady."

Heather picked an olive up and placed in her mouth. Finished, she daintily removed the pit and set it on the side of her plate.

"With my help, you will become the perfect Ottoman lady," Omar bragged.

"The better to escape, my good fellow," Heather replied.

Omar smiled and nodded. Let her think what she would. Outwitting Khalid was beyond her capability, and the enamored prince would never willingly let her go.

Omar spent hours and hours dressing and grooming his charge. Finally, when the designated hour arrived, he led her through the maze of corridors to the prince's chamber.

Dressed completely in white, Heather felt like an infidel's bride in an outfit that revealed more than it covered. She wore sheer silk harem pants that gathered at her ankles and sported golden embroidery at the waistband and sides. Her matching, long-sleeved tunic fastened in the front with golden toggles. She wore white satin slippers upon her feet, and a sheer white veil covered her flaming tresses and flushed face. Kohl, outlining her eyes, added a hint of mystery to her innocence. For modesty's sake, the eunuch had thrown a *yashmak* over her shoulders.

Omar knocked on the door and entered at the prince's call. Heather, embarrassed by her behavior at the baths, kept her gaze glued to the floor. Omar dropped to his knees, pulling his charge with him, and pressed his forehead to the carpeted floor.

Slurp! Heather felt something wet against her face. She looked up in surprise at the dog she had seen on the beach that morning.

Slurp! The dog licked her again.

"Sit, Argus," Khalid ordered. Then, "Rise, my slaves."

Omar got to his feet slowly and helped Heather up. Without a word, the eunuch whipped the *yashmak* and veil off her and then disappeared. Heather refused to look at her captor as he crossed the chamber to stand in front of her.

Khalid tilted her chin up and gazed deeply into her disarming green eyes. "I had forgotten how sensitive virgins could be," he said.

"And I suppose you enjoy the vast experience of ruining hundreds of innocents," Heather said, unaccountably jealous.

"Thousands, at least."

Slurp! Before Heather could reply, the dog licked her hand. She looked down at the beast's beast.

Tawny and white, the dog had a long, narrow head that tapered toward the nose. Tall and slender, it sported long, silky ears and a smooth, shiny coat. The beast's eyes, large and dark with a dignified, gentle expression, were most arresting.

"This friendly fellow is Argus," Khalid said.

Heather reached out tentatively and patted the dog's head; Argus reciprocated by licking her fingers. "I've never seen his breed before," she said.

"Argus is a saluki, used for hunting," Khalid told her. "He loves people, especially ladies."

Khalid drew her across the chamber to sit on the enormous pillows beside the table. Argus insinuated himself between them.

Heather glanced around the prince's chamber. Spacious but spartanly furnished, the room contained a bed, a table, and a bronze brazier for heat. It was a warrior's chamber.

"Are you hungry?" Khalid asked, drawing back her attention.

"Yes."

"That was an unnecessary question," he said. "You are always hungry, no offense intended."

Heather looked over the offering on the table in front of her. There were fried sardines, green pepper pickles, yogurt and cucumber salad, saffroned rice, and a minced lamb dish.

"You said that men did not eat with women, nor masters with their slaves," Heather said, tasting a fried sardine. "Why have I been summoned to sup with you?"

"Between an invitation and a summons lies a world of difference," Khalid replied, filling her plate with minced lamb and rice. "Tonight, you are my guest."

"And if I choose to leave?" Heather asked, digging into the lamb.

"Let us be at peace, my reluctant guest."

"There can be no peace between enemies."

"You were not my enemy at the baths this morning," Khalid reminded her.

Heather blushed furiously and changed the subject. "This meat loaf is delicious."

"Yes, lady's thigh is a favorite of mine."

Heather smiled and reached for her goblet of rosewater.

"The molded lamb is round, soft, and smooth like a lady's thigh."

The prince, though disconcerting, was trying hard to be pleasant. Uncomfortable with his disturbing nearness, Heather gave the dog her attention. She offered him a piece of meat and then patted his head.

"Argus is a strange name," she commented.

"Argus is Greek."

"I thought you were a Turk."

"Ulysses, a mighty Greek warrior, returned home from the Trojan War after twenty years and was greeted by his faithful dog, Argus," Khalid told her. "Recognizing his master, Argus wagged his tail with happiness, dropped his ears, and died."

"How sad."

"The story is meant to demonstrate the dog's faithfulness to man, not create a sad mood," Khalid said. "Would you prefer sherbet to rosewater?"

"No, thank you," Heather refused. "I have no wish to be drugged."

Khalid's lips quirked. "And what have you learned from Omar this day?"

Heather stuck her tongue out at him. *"Dil."*

Khalid smiled, amazing his captive with his uncharacteristic good humor. He wasn't behaving at all like the monster she knew he could be. What game was he playing with her?

They lapsed into silence when two servants entered. One man cleared their empty plates and the remnants of their supper while the other served them dessert of Turkish coffee and pastry.

"May I?" Heather asked, reaching for a pastry.

Khalid nodded. "Your manners have improved, slave."

"Slave?" Heather arched a perfect copper brow at him. "I thought I was your guest."

"I stand corrected."

Heather bit into the pastry. It was deep fried with a cream-filled depression in the center. "Mmmm ... delicious."

"So, you like the lady's navel fritters?"

Heather grinned at him.

"The center indentation resembles a lady's navel," Khalid explained. "Now, tell me more about your family and yourself."

Heather stared in silence at him for a long moment. Why did he want to know about her? What trickery was this?

"I lived in the county of Essex all my life," Heather began. "Basildon Castle has been the Devereux home since my great-grandfather came from Wales with the Tudor King Henry VII. As a reward for his loyalty and service to the king, my great-grandfather received in marriage the headstrong heiress of the old lord, namely my great-grandmother."

"Then, you resemble your great-grandmother," Khalid teased.

The jibe was lost on Heather. "No, I inherited my mother's red hair and green eyes," she said.

"And freckles?"

"No freckles."

"You should feel no guilt about your father's death," Khalid said, trying to sound casual.

"My father's death is none of your concern," Heather told him.

"Everything about you is my concern."

"Stop prying."

"Did you love Fougere?" The question came out of nowhere, startling both of them.

"Madly," Heather snapped. Just who did this beast think he was, the Grand Turk?

Khalid cocked a dark brow at her and then changed the subject, asking, "What is this England like?"

"The Garden of Eden."

"Spoken like a loyal Englishwoman." Khalid stood and held out his hand to her. "Come, Eve," he said. "I will show you *my* Garden of Eden."

Heather hesitated a brief moment. Their eyes locked on each other, and without thinking, she placed her hand in his. Khalid led her outside through the arched double doors into a garden.

Created for romance, a full moon hung overhead, and thousands of brilliant stars glittered like diamonds in the perfect setting of a black velvet sky. The fragrances of myriad flowers mingled like lovers and pervaded the night air like an invisible cloud of perfume.

"How beautiful," Heather sighed.

"You appreciate my handiwork?" Khalid asked.

"You have conjured the moon and the stars for my pleasure?"

Khalid shook his head. "No, gardening is one of my hobbies. I enjoy the solitude."

Heather was incredulous. "*You* created this beauty?"

"Even beasts need respite from plundering and pillaging," Khalid said dryly. "The silence is welcome after listening to the screams of tormented innocents."

Heather smiled, dazzling him. The man was actually quite charming at times. Perhaps, if they'd met under different circumstances. Another time, another place . . .

"The beauty of this place betrays the fact that this

castle was the scene of a great tragedy,'' Khalid said, stepping closer.

''What tragedy?''

''My home is called the Maiden's Castle,'' Khalid told her. ''And a restless soul haunts the battlement above us.''

''Spirits?'' Heather echoed, inching closer to him.

''Three hundred years ago, a Christian princess died there while pining for her Moslem suitor,'' Khalid said. ''Many of my men on the night watch claim to have seen her, forever waiting and pining for her Moslem lover.''

''Oh, my.'' Heather made the sign of the cross and leaned close to him.

Never one to lose an opportunity, Khalid turned her to face him and pulled her against his masculine frame. His face came closer and closer until his mouth covered hers—touching, tasting, exploring her sweetness in a gently persuasive kiss.

Unable to move, Heather fell under his spell as a languorous feeling overwhelmed her senses. Her arms crept up his chest to entwine his neck and pull him even closer.

With her seeming surrender, the tempo of the kiss changed, becoming ardent and demanding. Heather trembled with desire and met his thrusting tongue with her own.

Sanity returned in the form of a woman's moan of pleasure. *Hers!*

Heather jerked back. ''I'm no whore to be fondled at will,'' she said. ''My virginity belongs to my husband.'' With that, Heather fled his chamber.

Khalid stared after her. What terrible thing had he done? She enjoyed his kiss. He knew that for certain. So why was she upset? Did she believe that he would marry her?

Omar was waiting in the corridor outside the prince's chamber. "Why have you been dismissed so soon?" he cried as his charge marched past him.

"Which way to my chamber?" Heather asked without breaking stride.

"You have displeased the prince," Omar whined. "What did—?"

"Shut up," Heather snapped.

"But, our fortunes—"

Heather stopped short and rounded on the little man. "My honor is more valuable than your blasted fortune."

Omar shut his mouth. Gesturing Heather onward, he led her through the maze of corridors and stairs to her own chamber.

That night Khalid tossed and turned in his own bed without his beautiful captive beside him, though not quite alone. Faithful Argus snuggled comfortably against the length of his master's body. Meager consolation, to be sure.

Chapter 9

After a restless night of troubled sleep, Heather awakened early the next morning. She was alone. From the appearance of the bed and chamber, Heather knew Khalid had not slept beside her during the night. Perhaps he finally understood that she didn't want him near her. Or did she?

The image of the prince arose in her mind. Heather saw his handsome face coming closer and closer. She felt the warmth of his breath, his sensual lips pressed to hers. A delicious shiver shook through her body.

In the name of God! What was she thinking? Heather leaped out of bed and crossed the chamber to look out the window. Dawn was lighting the eastern horizon.

Heather realized with a start that she had to escape or lose her virtue. The unfamiliar feelings the arrogant prince stirred in her were too exciting, too tempting, too strong to resist.

Heather decided to leave as soon as possible and somehow find April. Together, they would return to England. Even if they had to walk across the breadth of Europe!

Because of the earliness of the hour, few people were about. Now would be the most propitious time to leave. Once Abdul arrived with the prince's men, escape would be extremely difficult, if not impossible.

How would she go? By land or by sea? Heather's gaze

drifted to the deserted beach. Those two dinghies still lay on the sand. By sea, it would be.

What kind of a disguise? Heather wondered. Traveling as a woman was dangerous, if not impossible. If only she had access to Turkish clothing! Well, there was nothing to be done for it. She would make do as an English stableboy. And May God, Allah, or Whoever protect her from discovery.

Heather raced across the chamber to her sea chest and pulled the top layers of gowns out. She dug deep and found the stableboy clothing she wore for riding. Her mother had forbidden her to take them to France so she'd hidden them at the bottom of her chest. Out came her threadbare breeches and shirt, followed by her cap and black leather boots.

Afraid of being caught in the act, Heather changed hurriedly, then pulled on the boots and tucked her fiery hair beneath the stableboy's cap. She picked up all her gowns, crumpled them into a ball, and carried them to the bed. Throwing them down, she formed them into what she hoped resembled a person and pulled the coverlet up.

Heather scurried across the chamber, pressed her ear to the door, and listened. No sound came from the corridor. Where were Khalid and Omar lurking? Taking a deep breath, she turned the knob. The door was unlocked. Omar would certainly catch hell for that.

Heather stepped into the dimly lit corridor. Hugging the wall, she tiptoed to the top of the stairs. Now, if she could just remember how to get out of this heap of stone . . .

After a sleepless night, Khalid had gone with Argus to the supposedly haunted wall walk that looked out over the bay. He needed to clear the cobwebs from his mind and hoped the salty smell of the sea and the glorious sight of the rising sun would help.

Khalid tried in vain to concentrate on who would want Murad dead. Vicious conspiracy or lone fanatic? Each time he tried to think about the assassination attempt, his mind conjured the vision of his flame-haired captive with her sultry looks, swaying hips, and dauntless spirit. Never had there been such a woman as she. If only they had met under different circumstances. Another time, another place.

In the name of Allah! What was he thinking? She was Fougere's betrothed and the instrument of his revenge.

As he gazed out to sea, Khalid caught a flash of furtive movement along the path leading to the beach. Stepping nearer to the edge of the battlement, Khalid fixed his gaze on the spot. Someone or something was hiding behind the boulders along the side of the path.

"*Inchallah,*" Khalid muttered aloud. His captive was escaping. Turning on his heels, Khalid bolted for the stairs. Argus followed behind.

At the beach, Heather hid in the reeds for a moment to catch her breath. Her heart pounded frantically, and she felt faint.

Heather forced herself to look up and down the deserted beach, then dashed for one of the two unattended dinghies. Huffing and puffing, she dragged it into the surf and jumped in, then started rowing toward freedom.

You will never see *his* face again. The thought popped into her mind. That fleeting thought troubled her for some unknown reason but was banished quickly.

Which way to Malik's villa? Heather wondered. Would she survive in this decrepit tub that posed as a boat? Or would she drown?

Heather hoped to reach Malik's villa by following the coastline. There she would somehow rescue April, and together, they would row back to England. If she drowned along the way, then so be it. She would gladly die a free woman instead of living as the prince's prisoner. Where was he anyway?

Heather glanced toward shore. As if her thoughts had conjured the man, Khalid stood there with his hands on his hips and watched her with a bemused smile on his face. Apparently, the prince had lost his mind. She was escaping, but he stood there smiling like a blinking idiot.

Khalid watched Heather struggling with the heavy oars. His wildflower was such a delicate blossom.

"Stay, Argus," Khalid ordered the dog. He pulled his boots off and rolled the legs of his pants up, then pushed the second dinghy into the surf and jumped in. Almost leisurely, he began rowing in the direction of his captive. After all, she was not going far in a boat that leaked.

Desperate to put distance between them, Heather rowed faster, but the prince's superior strength and long strokes outmatched hers. When his dinghy came abreast of hers, Heather knew the game was lost but chose to ignore that fact. She kept rowing and refused to spare him a glance. The prince made no move to capture her.

"Good morning, my lady," Khalid called.

Heather cast him a sidelong glance but said nothing. What new game was he playing?

Khalid cleared his throat. "I said, good morning."

"I heard you," Heather replied.

"Beautiful morning for a row, is it not?" Khalid asked.

"Quite invigorating," Heather answered, deciding to play along.

"Where are you going?" Khalid asked.

"Home."

"Your home is with me," he said.

"My home is in England."

"So, you are rowing to England? You will never make it."

Heather stared at him for a long moment. "I will if you leave me alone," she said in a pleading voice.

"If I did that, my beauty, you would certainly drown."

"I plan to hug the shoreline."

"In that case, you would do well to crawl on the sand," Khalid said. "That dinghy leaks."

"I don't believe you." Heather never faltered in her rowing.

"Look behind you."

Heather spared a quick glance at the horizon over her shoulder.

"Look down."

Heather stopped rowing long enough to check the bottom of the dinghy behind her back. Sure enough, water seeped in. She looked down at her feet. A puddle of seawater submerged her boots to the ankles.

Heather swore loudly in the most unladylike manner. In the next instant, she paled and looked at the prince, squeaking, "I can't swim."

Khalid positioned his boat against hers, then instructed her, "Climb in but do not upset us."

Very carefully, Heather stood up and climbed into the other boat. She sat down facing him. Their gazes met and fixed on each other for a long moment. Heather looked away first, and without a word, Khalid began rowing toward the shore.

At the beach, Khalid leaped out of the dinghy and dragged it onto the sand. None too gently, he lifted Heather out and set her down.

"Unspeakable dangers lurk outside my protection," Khalid warned, towering over her. "Consider yourself lucky that I saw you." He moved to take her arm, but Heather yanked it away and rounded on him.

"*Lucky?* You think me fortunate to be your prisoner?'' Heather asked. With her hands on her hips, she looked glorious in her fury. ''You left that leaking rubble there to trick me.''

''I would never wish to see you dead,'' Khalid said. ''Most women would feel honored to be my concubine.''

''C-c-concubine?'' Heather sputtered.

Preventing her intended tirade, Argus leaped at Heather. With his front paws resting on her shoulders, the dog licked her face.

''Get this mangy—''

It was then Heather learned an important lesson. Never speak while a dog is kissing you. Argus, in the process of licking her face, slipped his tongue into her open mouth.

''Yuch!''

''Sit, Argus,'' Khalid ordered. Then, ''That proves it.''

''What proves what?'' Heather asked, falling neatly into his trap.

''Since Argus is attracted to you, you must certainly be a bitch,'' Khalid said.

''I prefer his kisses to yours.''

In a flash of movement, Khalid yanked her against the long, masculine length of him. His lips hovered above hers, and he asked in a husky voice, ''Is that so?''

Though aroused by his nearness, Heather feigned indifference. ''Care to test it?''

''After you have rinsed your mouth,'' Khalid declined, loosening his grip on her. ''I saw Argus washing his backside this morning.''

''Oww!'' Wearing a sickened expression, Heather wiped her mouth furiously and glared at the dog. Argus wagged his tail.

Khalid grasped her forearm and dragged her up the

path toward the castle. Reaching her chamber, Khalid shoved Heather into the room and then rounded on the waiting eunuch.

"How did she get free?" the prince demanded, grabbing him by his shirt and lifting him high in the air.

"How?" Omar echoed, gulping nervously. "I do not understand."

"I walked out the door," Heather said.

"You left the door unlocked and unguarded?" Incredulous, Khalid flung the little man across the chamber and sent him crashing to the floor.

Heather ran to the eunuch's aid and dropped to her knees beside him. "Are you hurt?" she asked.

Trembling with fear, Omar shook his head.

"Omar is blameless," Heather said, rounding on the prince. "Attacking a much smaller person is unworthy, even for you."

"Silence," Khalid shouted.

Omar snapped his head from the prince to his captive and then back again. At this rate, there would be no strong sons, and his fortune would be lost before he even saw it. His reward for this thankless job appeared to be a sore neck.

"Consider this she-devil my prisoner and act accordingly," Khalid said to him.

"She-devil?" Heather cried.

Khalid turned cold blue eyes upon her, pinning her where she knelt. He started to leave but called over his shoulder, "Clean her up. And in the name of Allah, burn those disgusting clothes she is wearing." The door slammed shut behind him.

"Evil be to her who overtakes a man," Omar quoted from the Koran.

"You ingrate," Heather said, surprised. "I defended you against him."

"Women must show respect for the beard," Omar added.

"Up yours, you bloody bugger."

"But you are making me look bad," he whined. "And do not forget our fortunes."

"Leave me alone," Heather snapped. "And lock the door on the way out or the prince will be forced to kill you."

Omar rolled his eyes. The little heathen already gave orders like an imperial princess. Why wouldn't she surrender to the prince and become one in fact? Omar decided he would never understand women, especially this one. Allah be praised, a eunuch had no need to understand the gentler sex, only serve them.

That afternoon Khalid stood in the courtyard and waited to greet his men. Abdul and the others had just ridden in from Malik's villa and were dismounting.

Stepping forward, Khalid shook his man's hand and then dismissed his other warriors. "Your journey was swift and safe," he said in Turkish.

Abdul nodded. "And yours?"

"Stopping in Istanbul proved unproductive," Khalid told him. "A waste of my time."

"Why?"

"Mihrimah behaved in her usual contemptuous manner," Khalid said, unaware of the bitterness that crept into his voice when he spoke of his mother. "Murad has no idea who would profit from his death; Nur-U-Banu is convinced that Lyndar is guilty."

"Lyndar?" Abdul echoed.

"My uncle's newest *kadin*," Khalid said. "She recently delivered a son and named him Karim in honor of my brother."

"No mother wants to see her son destroyed," Abdul

remarked. "If something happened to Selim and Murad became sultan, the boy's life would be forfeit."

"The boy, born crippled, is imperfect and cannot challenge Murad's right to the sultanate," Khalid said. "No man will follow a cripple into civil war."

"Would this Lyndar champion a doomed cause?"

"With the possible exception of my mother, no woman is capable of masterminding such a plot."

"Any theories?" Abdul asked.

"Other matters have been foremost in my mind," Khalid admitted.

The hint of a smile appeared on Abdul's face. "Your captive, perhaps?"

Khalid glanced in the direction of Heather's chamber. "She tried to escape this morning. Fortunately, the dinghy she stole leaked."

Abdul smiled. "I'm relieved the little heathen did not slit your throat. Any news of the weasel's whereabouts?"

Khalid shook his head and would have spoken, but something caught his eye.

The keeper of the homing pigeons hurried across the courtyard toward them and stood nearby, waiting for the signal to approach. At the prince's nod, the man rushed forward, handed him a missive, and then retreated a few paces. The news was disturbing, and the wise servant had no intention of getting in the way of the prince's fabled wrath.

Khalid read the message and looked up. Fury made his expression a terrifying sight. The Sultan's Beast had returned.

"Bad news?" Abdul asked.

"Someone tried to assassinate Lyndar and her son."

"How? Where?" That a would-be assassin could gain entrance to Topkapi shocked Abdul.

"My mother's note is too brief. Tomorrow, we travel to Istanbul."

"I imagine this proves Lyndar's innocence," Abdul remarked.

"Mihrimah says there is evidence of Fougere's involvement," Khalid said.

"That weasel?"

"My lord," Omar called, distracting them. The rotund little man hurried across the courtyard and approached them without waiting for the prince's permission. "I have been searching for you."

"And so you have found me," Khalid said.

"Who is this?" Abdul asked, gazing down at the eunuch from his great height.

"My mother sent me Omar to care for my captive," Khalid replied. "Unfortunately, he leaves her door unlocked and unguarded."

Omar nodded at Abdul, then remembering his brush with death, cried, "She stabbed me."

"Who stabbed you?" Khalid asked. "And why are you not dead?"

"Bleeding, at least," Abdul added, a rumble of laughter welling up from his chest.

"It is no laughing matter," Omar snapped at the giant. He turned to the prince. "While your b-be-be—prisoner slept, I heard her moan. Naturally, I became concerned and hurried to nudge her awake. Calling for her father, she grabbed me with one hand and stabbed with the other."

"Are you injured?" Abdul asked.

"How did she get a knife?" Khalid demanded.

"Lucky for me, she was weaponless," Omar told them. "But if she had been armed, I would not be speaking to you now. Allah, she suffers from the fiercest of nightmares."

Khalid said nothing but looked in the direction of his captive's chamber. Heather, standing at the window, saw his gaze on her and stepped back.

Enough is enough, Khalid decided. Determined to purge her of her feelings of guilt, the prince turned on his heels and left his two men staring at his retreating back.

Heather whirled around at the sound of the door being unlocked. It swung open, and her captor filled the doorway.

"You are not responsible for your father's death," Khalid said, advancing on her.

"What?" Heather stared at him blankly.

"You will no longer dream about your father's death," Khalid ordered, pointing a finger at her. "That is my command."

"How dare—?"

"I dare when you disturb my household and frighten my servants."

"Frighten who?"

"Even now, Omar trembles because you stabbed him while you slept," Khalid told her. "Have you no memory of doing that?"

Heather paled. "Was he hurt?"

Khalid smiled. "You had no weapon."

"Then, what the bloody hell are you ranting and raving about?"

"You are the one ranting and raving," Khalid shot back. "Lower your voice when you speak to me."

"My thoughts and dreams belong to me," Heather insisted. "You cannot—"

"Your father's death was no fault of yours," Khalid interrupted, determined to exorcise her undeserved guilt. "Yes, you were disobedient, but it was your father's fate to die that day."

Trying to block his words out, Heather covered her ears with her hands.

"Listen to me." Khalid grabbed her hands and yanked them down, then gave her a rough shake. "A ten-year-old child, especially a female, is incapable of saving a man from assassins. You—"

Whack! Heather struck him with all her strength. "My father was kind, honest, just. A saint who loved me in spite of my faults, he called me his shadow because I followed him everywhere. The one and only time I disobeyed . . . Do not foul my father's memory by speaking of him!"

Khalid could only stare at Heather. Her powerful right and incredibly foolish audacity startled him. No man had ever struck him and lived.

She is distraught, Khalid told himself. She is unaware of what she is doing.

Oh, no? Khalid thought, waging an inner battle. This is the weasel's intended mate.

"Remove your loathsome self from my presence," Heather ordered. "I despise you."

"I do not desire your affection," Khalid said. Though hurt by her words, Khalid kept his face expressionless. He expected women to disdain him, and they always lived up to his expectations.

"You are the instrument of my revenge," Khalid said in an ominous voice, his piercing blue eyes pinning her where she stood. "Selling you at auction will draw the weasel out of his hole. You will go to the highest bidder, and your betrothed will meet his Maker."

Heather jerked back as if she'd been struck. She sank to her knees and covered her face with her hands.

Satisfied with her reaction, Khalid stormed out of the chamber. The door slammed shut and the lock clicked, sealing her fate.

Dear Lord! Sold at auction? Heather thought. What kind of monster could sell a woman? He'd kissed her and touched her so intimately. How could he do this to her?

The door was locked. What could she do?

Death would be her only escape. *Suicide is mortal sin,* whispered the religious teachings of a lifetime.

Heather vowed to meet her destiny bravely and hold back her tears. It didn't work. Her shoulders shook with her sobs, and a flood of tears coursed down her cheeks. She would escape somehow, and woe be to Savon Fougere if she ran into him before the prince did. For putting her in this horrifying position, Heather would kill him herself.

Early the next morning, Heather watched from the window as Khalid left with Abdul for Istanbul. She did not see him again. *Until that humiliating day . . .*

Chapter 10

"Seeing you again is a distinct pleasure, Prince Khalid."

"Is it?" Khalid replied, arching an eyebrow at the mustached Frenchman.

"Of course," the Duc de Sassari answered smoothly. "I never choose my words lightly." The duc glanced around the chamber, adding, "Quite a gathering."

Khalid scanned the private salon of Akbar the slave merchant. Istanbul's most prominent men filled the lavishly decorated chamber. At one end of the salon stood the dais where Heather would be auctioned.

The thirty-year-old Duc de Sassari cut an imposing figure. Tall and well built, the duc had dark hair and eyes, and wore the most ingratiating smile pasted on his face. Khalid neither liked nor trusted the man.

"How fares my sister?" the duc asked, breaking the silence between them.

"Your sister?"

"My half sister Lyndar is one of Sultan Selim's concubines."

"Lyndar is concubine no longer," Khalid told him. "She recently bore Selim's son."

"Excellent." This time the duc's smile was sincere.

Khalid scanned the chamber once more but failed to see the person for whom he looked. "Did you deliver my message to Fougere?" he asked.

"My cousin is a coward," the duc said. "You will not see him here today."

"Fougere does not care for his lovely betrothed?" Khalid asked, disappointed. A man who would sacrifice such a magnificent woman to ensure his own safety was no man at all. Should he cancel the auction and keep Heather for himself?

"Bidding for another is forbidden in this sale," Khalid warned.

"Savon would never accept a tarnished bride," the duc assured him. "He cares nothing for an English-woman he's never met."

"Legal tender is gold and must be paid in full before claiming ownership," Khalid said, ignoring the anger that was beginning to coil itself around his heart. But was it anger at having his plans thwarted? Or was he angry for Heather's sake?

"My pockets are heavy," the duc replied. "But why do you not keep the woman for yourself?"

Khalid ignored the question. Instead, he glanced around the chamber at the men speaking in hushed tones. Which one would bid the highest and take possession of his wildflower? Would that man have the patience to handle her stubbornness, or would he beat her? And which of them would hold her close when she cried out in the night?

Malik swaggered through the arched doorway into the salon. Without a word to the duc, Khalid turned on his heels and headed in that direction.

"I am glad to see you," Khalid said to his friend.

Malik nodded. "Any sign of Fougere?"

"The Duc de Sassari has come to bid," Khalid replied, gesturing across the room. "I wonder for whom."

"I told you the weasel would stay in hiding," Malik said. "Where is your wildflower?"

Khalid shrugged. "I assume Akbar is keeping her in a safe place."

"And soundproof too?" Malik asked. "Ah, yes. I had forgotten that Akbar sometimes drugs his merchandise."

"What?" That bit of information surprised Khalid.

"You did not know?" Malik asked. "Nothing to concern yourself about, though. Akbar only administers a mild relaxant to make his merchandise pliable enough for inspection. By the way, how did she take the news of her impending sale?"

Khalid kept his expression devoid of emotion and said nothing. In his mind's eyes, Khalid saw Heather as she'd appeared the last time he'd seen her. Visualizing her stricken expression wrenched his heart.

Distraught, Heather had lashed out at him with her only weapon—her words. Khalid knew he'd reacted in anger. In the name of Allah, he'd once vowed he'd never hurt another woman in anger. And now . . .

"My little bird went wild with joy when she learned I would be bringing her cousin home with me," Malik said, going in for the kill.

That statement certainly got a reaction out of the prince. "What did you say?" Khalid asked, rounding on his friend.

"Why, I intend to—"

"I heard you the first time," Khalid snapped. It irritated him that in a very few moments his own friend might possess the woman he desired.

A commotion at the door drew their attention. Six imperial bodyguards entered and scanned the crowd of men. Behind them walked Murad, followed by more bodyguards.

"I told you to remain inside Topkapi," Khalid said. His voice was low so that none but Malik could hear. "Strutting around Istanbul is too dangerous."

"I never strut," Murad said, then gave Malik a conspiratorial wink. "I came to see this barbarian of yours and, perhaps, add another exquisite jewel to the perfect setting of my harem."

"She is not worth the risk," Khalid said. "Excuse me while I instruct Akbar to begin the auction." With that, the prince stalked off.

"What do you think?" Malik asked.

"It appears my cousin does desire his captive."

"Oh, you should have seen them together," Malik said. "This wildflower inflames his senses and is, indeed, a fitting mate for the beast. We must help him realize his feelings for her before it is too late."

"Khalid does not stand a chance against the Lion of Istanbul and the Shark's Spawn," Murad replied.

"The Lion of Istanbul?" Malik echoed, suppressing a smile lest he offend the sultan's heir.

"I have decided that henceforth I will be known as the Lion of Istanbul," Murad told him.

Malik did smile then and dared to tease. "I thought you were the Stud of Istanbul."

Murad grinned. "I am that too, but the Lion of Istanbul is infinitely more dignified."

"What are you smiling at?" Khalid asked, returning to stand between them.

"We were discussing animals," Murad said.

"Would you care to stand closer to the dais?" Khalid asked his cousin.

"I am fine where I am," Murad replied.

Akbar entered the salon by way of a curtained doorway and stepped onto the dais. An expectant hush fell on the assembled men as they gave the slave dealer their full attention.

Expensively and colorfully dressed as befitting Istanbul's foremost slave dealer, Akbar smiled a welcome to the prominent men. His merchandise was always of the highest quality, and with this single sale, his fortune would be forever assured. Akbar turned and clapped his hands twice.

The curtain parted. Dressed in his finest, Omar appeared and led a white clad apparition toward the dais. Gauzy white silk covered Heather from head to toe. Only her drug-glazed emerald eyes showed.

As she stepped onto the dais, Heather stumbled, but Omar grabbed her arm and kept her from falling. He whispered something only she could hear and helped her onto the dais.

"The barbarian appears docile enough," Murad remarked.

"Akbar must have given her a large dose of . . ." Malik broke off when he glanced at his friend.

Apparently, Khalid was displeased. Anger tightened his sensual lips into a straight line, and the scar on his cheek whitened with his growing fury.

"Gentlemen, I beg your attention," Akbar called needlessly. "Prince Khalid graciously offers this exotic flower for sale. Her eunuch accompanies her free of charge. Legal tender is gold and must be paid in full before taking possession."

Akbar nodded at Omar who, with great ceremony, removed the veil covering Heather's face. The twenty men in the chamber gasped collectively at the startling beauty of her face.

Akbar smiled. "A virgin with the face of—"

"One hundred gold pieces," Malik called out.

Khalid snapped his head around to stare at his friend. Malik grinned broadly at him.

"One hundred and fifty gold pieces," a man near the dais bid.

Khalid craned his neck to see who dared to bid on his

wildflower. It didn't matter that whoever it was had been invited there to do just that. Murad and Malik exchanged knowing smiles.

"Who is that?" Khalid asked.

"Count Orcioni," Murad answered.

"Who is this Count Orcioni? I never heard of him."

Malik winked at Murad and added, "The famous whore-master of Pantelleria, a friend of the Duc de Sassari."

Akbar nodded at the eunuch. Omar whipped the white *yashmak* off his lady who stood clad in a ridiculously tiny bolero and pantaloons that left nothing to the imagination. Heather swayed on her feet.

"Allah," Khalid muttered. "What did the bastard give her to make her so unsteady?"

"Luxuriant hair the color of fiery sunset," Akbar went on.

"Two hundred gold pieces," a fat, ugly man called.

"Who is that?" Khalid asked. "I never invited him."

"Yagli Cirkin, a close friend of Akbar's," Murad replied.

"Yagli Cirkin?" Malik echoed, feigning appalled surprise. "Why, I heard he— Never mind."

"What did you hear?" Khalid asked.

"Yagli Cirkin is known for abusing his women," Murad told him.

Khalid growled low in his throat and started to move toward the fat man. Murad and Malik placed a restraining hand on his arms.

"Two hundred gold pieces," Akbar repeated. "Who will bid higher for this complexion as flawlessly soft as fine Bursa silk?"

"Three hundred gold pieces," the Duc de Sassari called.

"One thousand gold pieces," Murad said.

The men in the salon turned in unison to look at Murad. If the sultan's heir wanted the woman, they would bid no more.

Count Orcioni broke the silence, calling, "Fifteen hundred gold—"

"Two thousand!" Malik cut off the man's words.

"Three thousand gold pieces," Murad said.

Like a baited bear, Khalid snapped his head from his friend to his cousin. *The swines!*

Pleased with the way the auction was going, Akbar continued, "I have three thousand gold pieces from Istanbul's foremost connoisseur of womanflesh. Do I hear—"

"Four thousand," Yagli Cirkin bid, inching closer to the dais, within pinching reach of Heather.

"Five thousand," Malik shouted.

Murad nodded at Malik and called, "Six thousand gold pieces."

"Step closer, gentlemen," Akbar called. "Step closer to gaze upon the perfection of her exquisite breasts with their tempting, pink-tipped nipples." He gestured at Omar who remained motionless, then continued, "Step close to touch the woman's magnificent breasts, which Allah fashioned to satisfy the lustiest among us and to give suckle to any sons you may plant inside this virgin."

Akbar gestured again at Omar. The eunuch moved to remove his mistress's scanty bolero.

"No," Heather cried, elbowing him away.

Akbar reached for her. Heather swung at him.

"Stop!" Khalid shouted, and started forward.

The men watched dumbstruck as Khalid brushed past them and leaped onto the dais. He grabbed the *yashmak* out of Omar's hands and wrapped it around Heather, whose eyelids fluttered as she swooned. Khalid caught and lifted her into his arms.

"I have changed my mind," Khalid said. Standing in the rear of the salon, Murad and Malik exchanged victory smiles.

"You cannot change your mind," Akbar protested. "The auction has begun."

Khalid turned his fiercest scowl on the slave dealer. "I said, the sale is off."

"Foul," Count Orcioni dared to call.

"Unfair," Yagli Cirkin agreed.

"I have decided to keep my slave," Khalid told the assembled men. "At my own expense, I invite you to choose another piece of Akbar's fine merchandise."

"You will gift each man here with another slave of his choice?" Akbar asked, his dark eyes glowing with the thought of all the gold he would gain.

"Yes, except for Yagli Cirkin who was never invited to participate in this auction," Khalid said, leveling a deadly look on the slave dealer.

With Heather cradled against his chest, Khalid stepped off the dais. A path cleared for the unpredictable Sultan's Beast.

Reaching his cousin, Khalid paused. "Select as many virgins as you wish to deflower," he said.

"Though she is a beauty, I do prefer my virgins several years younger," Murad commented. "What will you do with her?"

"Need you ask such a question?" Malik teased.

It was then the Sultan's Beast gave the Lion of Istanbul and the Shark's Spawn the shock of their lives. "This virtuous noblewoman deserves an honorable marriage." Khalid announced, then turned to Malik. "Please escort Omar to my mother's house.'' With that, Khalid carried Heather through the arched doorway.

Early evening cast deep shadows across the deserted roadway outside Akbar's. Istanbul's faithful gathered at their prayers; Christian and Jewish infidels prepared for their evening meal.

Khalid paused for a long moment and gazed with love at his captive's face. Heather's eyelids fluttered open, and he found himself staring into her disarming green eyes.

''Khalid,'' Heather breathed like a sigh on a gentle breeze. Again, drugged sleep claimed her.

Holding her close, Khalid pressed his lips to hers. ''Forgive me, my precious wildflower,'' Khalid whispered. ''I will protect you always and never let you go.''

Abdul, with their horses in tow, materialized out of nowhere. ''Shall I fetch a litter?'' he asked. ''I am sure Akbar—''

''No.''

Abdul nodded and held out his arms to take Heather. Silently refusing to relinquish his treasure, Khalid shifted her in his arms and mounted his horse. Turning in the direction of Mihrimah's house, Khalid and Abdul rode slowly down the narrow roadway.

Unseen by them, a black-clad figure lurked in the alley beside Akbar's establishment and watched. As the prince rode past, the man pulled the black *kufiyah* away from his face and stared after them. His pinched expression resembled a weasel's, and anger curled his lips in a silent snarl.

The Sultan's Beast harbors tender feelings for the Englishwoman, the Comte de Beaulieu thought, fading into the shadows. My betrothed will be the instrument of the prince's downfall and death.

Reaching the courtyard of his mother's house, Khalid

slipped one leg over the side of his saddle and slid off his horse. Heather, cradled against his chest, slept undisturbed. Abdul took the reins and led their horses toward the stables.

Inside, Khalid strode past his mother's surprised servants, who scurried away to find their mistress and spread the gossip. Khalid headed for the chamber he occupied on rare visits to his mother, the one that had been his since boyhood.

Shifting Heather in his arms, Khalid opened the door and stepped inside, then shut it with his booted foot. He walked across the chamber to the bed and pulled the coverlet back. Ever so gently, Khalid set Heather down and began undressing her.

His breath caught raggedly in his throat at the sight of her unparalleled beauty, and the thought that he could have lost her dried his mouth with fear. The realization that he had a weakness, his love for his beautiful captive, almost felled him.

Khalid took a deep, calming breath. His wildflower belonged to him. She would be well protected so that no enemy could use his love for her against him.

Khalid shifted Heather so her head rested upon the pillow and pulled the coverlet up to her chin. Sitting on the edge of the bed, he reached out and traced a finger down the side of her silken cheek, then leaned close and planted a chaste kiss on her forehead.

"When I return, you will be mine forever," he promised.

"You love her and had not the heart to sell her?" sounded a voice beside him. "So much for revenge."

Khalid looked up at Mihrimah's disdainful expression. "Visiting you is always a pleasure, dear Mother," he said dryly.

Mihrimah leaned over and stared hard at the young

woman who had apparently captured her son's heart. "I suppose she's fair enough, except for those ugly freckles," Mihrimah remarked. "Does she carry my grandchild?"

Mihrimah reached to draw the coverlet back, but Khalid stayed her hand. Ignoring his mother's comment, he stood and started to leave. "She will sleep for hours, and I must go out. When Malik arrives with Omar, send the eunuch to watch over her."

Khalid opened the door and cocked a dark brow at his mother. "Let us leave her to sleep."

"Am I not allowed to look at her?" Mihrimah asked.

"I want her to sleep undisturbed," Khalid said. "When she awakens, you will meet her."

"Very well," Mihrimah acquiesced, crossing the chamber to precede him out. "But, I warn you, my curiosity will not be quiet until the morning."

"Tonight, Mother," Khalid agreed in a long-suffering voice. "You will meet her when I return." He turned away and started down the corridor, but his mother's voice stopped him.

"Where are you going?" Mihrimah demanded.

Khalid gave his mother an inscrutable smile. "To visit the *imam*."

"But, why?"

"To be married," Khalid called over his shoulder as he turned the corner and vanished from sight.

When he stepped into the courtyard, Khalid almost bumped into Abdul who was on his way inside. "My horse?" the prince asked.

"Down for the night."

Khalid looked irritated, but then his expression cleared. "Let us walk."

"Where?" Abdul asked.

"To the *imam*'s."

Abdul fell in step beside the prince, and the two men started off into the night. A short time later, they stood in front of the clergyman's residence. Without hesitation, Khalid banged on the door.

Several moments passed. The door swung open.

"The Sultan's Beast," a manservant cried, stepping back a few paces.

Uninvited, Khalid and Abdul brushed past the frightened servant just as his master came rushing into the foyer.

"Prince Khalid, how may I serve you?" the *imam* greeted them, the expression on his face mirroring his surprise.

"I want to get married," Khalid told him.

"Excellent!" The *imam* smiled. "If you give me the fortunate woman's name, my clerk—"

"Now," Khalid interrupted.

"I beg your pardon?"

"I wanted to get married tonight."

"This is an unusual request," the *imam* said. "The documents—"

"This is no request," Khalid said, leveling his fiercest scowl on the clergyman. "I *will* be married tonight."

"The marriage document can be prepared within the hour," the *imam* said. Thwarting the prince could be extremely unhealthy. "Whom do you wish to marry?"

"My slave, Heather—"

"Your slave?" The *imam* was shocked. "A prince does not marry his slave."

"He does if he so chooses," Khalid snapped, clearly irritated.

"You misunderstand," the *imam* explained. "Marrying a slave is illegal."

"Manumission," Abdul whispered to the prince.

"Compose documents of manumission and marriage,'' Khalid instructed. "I will sign the paper freeing my slave and then the other.''

"Well . . ." The *imam* hesitated.

"Of course, you will be generously rewarded,'' Khalid added.

"It can be done but will take a little time.''

"I will wait.''

The *imam* inclined his head. "Please, come into my salon and refresh yourself while you wait.''

Close to midnight, Khalid and Abdul emerged from the *imam*'s residence. The night was moonless and eerily silent, the narrow street deserted.

"I never imagined I would ever be a married man,'' Khalid remarked as they started for Mihrimah's.

Abdul cast his master a jaundiced look. "Try beating . . .''

Khalid halted abruptly and held his hand up in a gesture for silence. Footsteps behind them stopped. After exchanging glances, Khalid and Abdul began walking again. Footsteps scurried to keep up with them.

Khalid and Abdul slowed their gait. The footsteps slowed too.

Khalid stopped and silently gestured his man to walk without him; Abdul refused with a shake of his head. Khalid scowled, but Abdul merely gestured him to continue walking. This time it was Khalid who refused with a shake of his head.

A sudden rush of running feet made them whirl around. Two men, with daggers poised, flew at them. One man raced toward Abdul. The other, a giant of a man, caught Khalid off balance and pushed him to the ground. He raised his dagger to strike.

With lightning quick reflexes, Khalid kicked the man's groin, and the villain doubled over in pain. Khalid pushed him down and disarmed him. Before the man could regain his senses, Khalid pointed his own dagger at the assassin's throat.

"Allah have mercy," the villain begged, hearing his friend's death scream.

"Who sent you?" Khalid demanded.

"Fougere," the man rasped.

"Where is the weasel hiding?"

"I do not know. Allah curse him—"

It was the last word the hired assassin would ever speak. The Sultan's Beast slashed his throat from ear to ear.

Chapter 11

Where the bloody hell am I?

That was the first thought that popped into Heather's mind when she regained consciousness. She opened one eye and then the other. The chamber was dark, its only source of light a solitary candle burning on a table on the other side of the room.

And then Heather heard it—the disgusting sound of a snorting pig. She bolted up in the bed, ready to confront whatever was in the room with her.

It was only Omar, reclining against an enormous pillow and fast asleep, snoring. Apparently, whoever had purchased her had also bought the little man.

How could she escape with Omar guarding her? On the other hand, the little man was an incompetent jailor. She'd already proven that several times at Maiden's Castle. An outrageous idea came to her, and a smile flitted across her face.

Heedless of her nudity, Heather rose from the bed and silently searched the darkened chamber. In a few seconds, she found what she wanted—a chest.

Crouching down, Heather opened it and was relieved to see men's clothing. She pulled out black pants, shirt, *kufiyah,* and four sashes. Heather grabbed three of the sashes and tiptoed back to Omar, then dropped noiselessly to her knees. She used one of the sashes to tie the eunuch's ankles together. Clutching the other two, she hurried back to bed.

"Omar," Heather called weakly.

His snoring was her answer.

"Omar." A little louder.

In the midst of a dream about his guaranteed fortune, the eunuch began swimming up from the depths of sleep.

"Omar!" Heather shouted, then added in a whining voice, "I need you."

Awakening at the sound of her call, Omar leaped to his feet. "Wonderful news, my lady," the little man gushed as he started toward the bed. "The prince has—"

Boom! Omar hit the floor, face first. He lay motionless for several seconds and then moaned softly in a daze.

Heather leaped from the bed and raced across the chamber. She sat on the eunuch's back and used the second sash to bind his wrists together behind his back. She rolled him over and winced at the sight of his bleeding nose. Uncertain of what to do, Heather stared at him and hoped she hadn't seriously hurt the little man.

"I'm sorry if I've injured you," Heather apologized, peering into his face. Omar opened his mouth to tell her about the prince's change of heart, but she gagged him with the third sash.

Heather stood up and dashed across the chamber, then donned the pants and shirt. She tied the last sash around her waist to keep the pants from falling and then rolled the legs up. Next, Heather wove her thick mane of copper into one fat braid and tucked it beneath the back of her shirt. She wrapped the *kufiyah* around her head and pulled the front up to hide most of her face.

Heather hurried back to Omar and dropped to her knees, then whispered, "I need your boots."

Muffled squawks issued from behind the gag.

"I'm borrowing, not stealing," Heather added, recalling the severe punishment for theft. "I do intend to return them." Ignoring his outraged squawks, she yanked his boots off and pulled them onto her own feet.

Which way out? The chamber had two doors, one of which opened onto a garden. That could be her best bet.

"I thank you for all of your help," Heather said to the little man before turning away. "God be with you."

Heather scurried across the chamber, opened the glass door, and stepped into the garden. At least she'd made it outside. Intending to be far away by sunrise, she decided the fastest getaway would be on horseback. But, which way to the stables?

Heather started down one of the paths and then stopped short. Voices. Coming closer. Heather ducked behind the tall shrubs that lined both sides of the walkway.

"My son is a coward and an incompetent fool," a woman said in a scathing voice.

"Mother, you are wrong," a younger woman protested.

"Your son is the bravest, most intelligent man I have ever known." This came from a man.

"You are his friend and must say so," the older woman argued. "He was unable to kill—"

"Mother, we have offered our guest no refreshment," the younger woman interrupted as they passed by Heather's hiding place. "I'm certain Malik desires food and drink while he awaits Khalid's return."

Malik? Heather was shocked. It seemed she'd been purchased by the beast's own mother. If she was determined to escape before, Heather was even more determined now. She absolutely refused to slave for the hideous woman who'd given the world that monster.

But did the mother harbor no tender feelings for her own son? It was unnatural. And sad.

Don't borrow another's problems, Heather told herself. If the mother hated the son, that was his problem, not hers.

After the three had vanished from sight, Heather stood up and hurried down the walkway in the opposite direction. A short time later, she found the stables, more by accident than design.

Keeping herself well hidden, Heather stepped inside the deserted stables. In a stall on her right was Khalid's stallion. Heather had the powerful urge to thumb her nose at the prince by stealing his own horse, but thought better of it. She had no way to notify him beforehand that she was borrowing, not stealing, and a man who would sell a woman at auction would suffer no qualms about chopping a finger or two off that woman's hand.

Heather walked farther inside the stables. And then she saw the horse. The exquisitely beautiful mare appeared to be the color of rich mahogany and sported a pure white star on her forehead. They were meant for each other.

Grabbing one of the bridles that hung on the opposite wall, Heather never noticed the prince's insignia it bore. Quietly, she opened the gate and stepped inside the stall.

"There you are, my pretty," Heather crooned as the high-strung mare shied away nervously.

Heather reached out and stroked the mare's neck, whispering, "Beautiful lady, be kind to me and I will set you free." The horse calmed as Heather stroked her flank and whispered soothing words to her.

Ever so slowly, Heather slipped the bridle over the mare's head and adjusted it. Now for the blanket and saddle that hung over the gate. Heather carefully set the blanket across the mare's back and grabbed the saddle, then froze.

Footsteps.

Inside the stable.

Coming closer and closer.

An incredibly tall man walked by and stopped at the stall diagonally across from the mare's. Clutching the saddle, Heather tiptoed on silent feet to stand behind him. She tapped him lightly on the back, and when he whirled around, swung the saddle with all her might and bashed his face.

He never knew what hit him. Caught off guard, the man fell over backward and lay motionless. Heather peered down at his face. Malik's second-in-command, Rashid.

"So much for giants," she said with satisfaction.

Heather started to pick up the saddle, but changed her mind. At any moment, others could interrupt her escape. She didn't possess the strength to fight an army, only one giant at a time.

Heather walked back to the mare's stall and grabbed the reins. "Are you ready for your adventure, my beauty?" she whispered, then leaped onto the mare's back. As if in answer, the horse nickered and bolted out of the stall.

Crouched low over the mare's neck, Heather careened out of the stable and yard. Behind her, she heard the sounds of running feet and shouts of alarm. Too late. Heather disappeared into the night . . .

"Khalid, you promised me no kisses," Heather complained, and in her sleep, turned her face away.

The beast kissed her again, this time nipping her cheek wetly.

"Khalid . . ." Heather opened her eyes and found herself staring into the mare's doleful black eyes. "Good morning, my beauty."

The mare nuzzled her cheek again, then nudged her.

"We'll have none of that," Heather chided, standing slowly, every muscle aching in protest at the night she'd passed.

Was Khalid searching for her? If he found her, what would he do?

Kill me or worse, Heather thought. Slapping a prince is an unforgivable offense.

Better dead than slaving for his despicable mother, Heather reminded herself. That fact encouraged her to continue her journey, though she feared traveling alone.

Oh, why hadn't Khalid liked her the way she'd begun to like him?

Heather adjusted her clothing. Her cramped legs, parched throat, and empty stomach were a small price to pay for her freedom.

Somehow, Heather had found her way through the maze of Istanbul's narrow streets and left the city. Fearing she'd be caught in the dark, she'd passed the night behind the shelter of trees along the roadside.

Uncertain of what to do next, Heather looked around. Then she heard voices and the sounds of horses.

Peering through the trees, Heather saw a passing caravan. Should she follow it or not? Obviously, the caravan had a destination. Heather's hunger made her decision for her.

Heather adjusted her *kufiyah,* pulling it up to cover most of her face, and then leaped onto the mare's back. She guided the mare through the trees and fell in behind the caravan. Heather never wondered where the caravan was headed. Away from Istanbul was good enough for her.

Heather decided to follow the caravan as though she were part of it. When they reached the next village or town, she'd ask directions to Malik's villa where she'd beg sanctuary. At least, she'd be with her cousin.

Though disguised as a young man, Heather knew that her femininity might be discovered at any moment. What would she do if that happened? Heather banished that troubling thought and tried to be as inconspicuous as possible. Though she was unaware of it, her presence behind the caravan had been noted.

An hour passed. And then another.

Heather had just begun to feel relatively safe when a man from the front of the caravan rode toward her. Thanks to Omar, Heather did speak Turkish fairly well. Would these people believe her to be a native of this land? Heather prayed the approaching man would not confront her.

Apparently, the Lord either wasn't listening that day or was not in a particularly generous mood. Her prayer went unanswered.

The young man, perhaps in his early twenties, approached her but said nothing. He studied her and her horse for several, uncomfortably long moments. When his gaze fixed on her masked face, the man gave Heather a toothy smile. Turning his horse, he galloped back to the front of the caravan.

Several minutes later, an older man rode down the line toward Heather. He seemed to be the one in charge, and Heather was instantly on guard.

"Got a minute?" the man asked in Turkish.

Heather nodded but said nothing. She looked straight ahead at the road.

Through dark eyes that shone with shrewdness, the man studied this black-clad stranger as he rode beside her. He decided that Heather was too small to be a man and too delicate to be a boy. But, it was her hands that gave her away for sure. Without a doubt, Heather's hands were a woman's and quite obviously a stranger to hard labor.

Even more revealing, the horse she rode wore a bridle that bore Prince Khalid's insignia. Apparently, this concubine had stolen the horse and run away. If that was true, Prince Khalid would appreciate the return of his property.

"I am Koko Kasabian, head of the Kasabian family," Koko introduced himself. "We deal in finely woven carpets." He waited for her to speak.

Heather looked at him. Short and stocky, Koko had swarthy skin and black hair graying at the temples.

"And you are?" Koko prodded her.

"Malik, also known as the Desert Fox," Heather answered outrageously, lowering her voice in what she hoped was a good imitation of a man's voice.

More like a desert flower, Koko thought as he tried valiantly to swallow his laughter. "Why do you follow my caravan?" he asked.

"I am merely traveling in the same direction, not following," Heather replied.

"You carry no supplies. How far do you travel, Malik? Or would you prefer I call you Desert Fox?"

"Malik is fine, but my business is confidential."

"You are Prince Khalid's courier?" Koko asked casually.

Surprised, Heather gasped and snapped her gaze around to stare at him.

"The insignia on the bridle proclaims its owner," Koko said, gesturing toward it. "Why do you not use a saddle?"

"My message is urgent," Heather replied. "I had no time to saddle my horse."

"Yet you ride at a leisurely pace," Koko remarked.

"Prince Khalid's business is no concern of yours,"

she informed him. What else could she say? How could she reveal that she feared riding alone? That would be terribly unmanly.

The last time I rode alone my father . . . Heather forced the thought out of her mind. That way led to madness.

This runaway concubine is a quick thinker, Koko decided. Koko lifted a flask from his saddle and drank, then offered it to Heather.

Without hesitation, Heather accepted the flask, turned her face away, pulled the *kufiyah* down, and drank. Lord, she was thirsty. Now, if he would only offer her food!

At that moment, the young man rode back down the line toward them. He flashed Heather another toothy grin and then gave Koko his attention. The two of them made strange hand movements as if communicating with each other. Then, the younger man turned his horse around and galloped back to the front of the caravan.

"That is my oldest son, Petri," Koko said.

"What were you doing with your hands?" Heather asked.

"Talking."

"Wouldn't using your mouth be simpler?"

Koko smiled. "Simpler for me, but impossible for Petri. He has no tongue."

"I—I'm sorry." That shocked Heather. She'd never heard of anyone being born without a tongue.

"No need to be sorry," Koko said. "Though a good son, Petri had a bad habit of fabricating the truth. Unfortunately, he lied to the wrong person. The loss of his tongue was his punishment."

"The punishment in this land for stretching the truth is—?" Heather broke off, unable to voice such a gruesome thought.

"You serve Prince Khalid and yet remain ignorant of the law of this land?" Koko asked.

Heather stared straight ahead and refused to answer. *What a blockhead I am,* she thought, fearing she'd blown her disguise. What should she do now?

"The road is lonely and dangerous," Koko went on, casting her a sidelong glance. "Will you travel with us and share our meals?"

Heather hesitated. She had no wish for her true identity to be discovered. On the other hand, she and her horse needed sustenance.

"The honor would be ours," Koko said. "The Kasabian family will respect your privacy and secret business."

At that, Heather nodded her acceptance of his invitation. She was hungry and would be glad of the company as long as they kept their distance.

Two hours later, the Kasabian caravan stopped for their midday meal. At Koko's order, one of the men brought water and feed for her horse.

Wandering away lest the man try to engage her in conversation, Heather sat by herself in the shade of a tree. Talking with too many people could give away her identity. In spite of Heather's worry, the Kasabian women believed she was a man and kept their distance, and the men were busy caring for the horses.

Tired, hungry, and homesick, Heather closed her eyes. What had happened in Istanbul when her escape was discovered? Had Omar been punished for his incompetence? Of course he had.

In her mind's eye, Heather saw the little man's battered, lifeless body. Guilt coiled itself around her heart and made breathing difficult. How could she live with two deaths on her conscience? Why did she never consider the consequences of her actions?

And what of Khalid? Heather wondered, feeling un-accountably sad. He must have been wild in his fury when he learned that his mother's newest slave had out-witted him.

"Hello." A voice sounded in front of her.

Heather opened her eyes and saw a little girl smiling at her. "Good day to you," Heather said and smiled beneath her *kufiyah*.

The child pointed at Heather's masked face and asked bluntly, "What are you hiding beneath your—?"

"My youngest, Krista," Koko interrupted. He handed Heather a horn of milk and a rolled pastry. To Krista, he said, "Go back to your mother."

Krista jutted her jaw out in silent defiance.

"You shame me in front of my guest," Koko said sternly. "Now, go."

Krista turned on her heel and stalked off in the direction of the women.

"My only daughter is spoiled," Koko said with a sheepish smile. "It is her mother's fault. Why do you not eat? What *are* you hiding beneath your *kufiyah*?"

"I eat only in private because the scars on my face are too horrible for viewing," Heather lied, then swallowed nervously. She had a fondness for her tongue and would not want to lose it.

"I see." Thoroughly enjoying this game of cat and mouse, Koko studied her for a long moment. "We Armenians are a hardy lot and thrive under adversity. I will not lose my breakfast if you reveal your scars."

"I prefer to eat alone."

"As you will." Koko inclined his head and then turned to walk away. "We leave within the hour."

"What is this?" Heather called after him.

Koko cast her a puzzled look, then answered, "Armenian sweet crepe and goat's milk, of course."

Milk and pastry, Heather thought, to soothe a troubled disposition. She turned her back on the Kasabians, pulled the *kufiyah* away from her mouth, and devoured the pastry. Next, she gulped the milk and wiped her mouth on her sleeve.

The manners of a swine. That thought popped into Heather's mind. Perhaps Khalid was correct. Now, why did she think of him? She was free of the loathsome beast and should be happy. So, why did her heart feel heavy with loss?

Heather drew the *kufiyah* up and masked her face. She gave her head a shake and tried to banish the disturbing image of the prince's handsome face from her mind.

Heather felt as if she'd only rested a minute when she heard Koko's shout to mount their horses. She walked over to the mare, paused a moment to stroke its neck, and then leaped onto the horse's back.

"Got a minute?" Koko asked, materializing behind her.

Heather nodded.

"I wondered if you would care to ride with me at the head of the line."

"No, thank you." She'd rather eat dust than have the whole Kasabian tribe watching her.

"In that case, I will ride behind with you."

Heather shrugged, feigning indifference. She wanted to be alone to worry about what Khalid was doing to find her. Besides, she really wasn't very good at imitating a man. That a shrewd Armenian hadn't guessed her secret was a miracle. Yet refusing his company could arouse his suspicion.

The afternoon was nerve-racking for Heather. Koko badgered her with leading questions but gave up after a while. A *long* while. Heather felt certain the Armenian was trying hard to trip her up.

As the sun set in the west, the Kasabians reached their first destination. The caravansary where they would pass the night was a one-level inn surrounding a courtyard. Located every eighteen miles apart throughout most of the Ottoman empire, these caravansaries were a welcome respite for the weary traveler. A hearty meal and a safe resting place could be found here, and no one was turned away for lack of coin.

Heather dismounted. One of the Kasabian men was instantly at her side, gesturing to her that he would care for her horse. Apparently, Koko had issued orders that she should be treated as an important guest. Heather looked around, intent on setting Koko straight. After all, tending her own horse was the manly thing to do.

Koko and Petri stood a short distance away. Though silent, father and son seemed to be arguing as their hands worked furiously.

Glancing in her direction, Koko gave her a broad grin and dropped his hands to his sides. When Petri did the same, Heather had the uncomfortable feeling that she was the topic of their conversation.

Leaving his son, Koko walked inside with Heather. The Kasabians were the only caravansary guests on this night. Heather sat by herself on the floor of the common room and leaned against the wall.

Closing her eyes, Heather relaxed enough to doze off, but a boot lightly kicking her foot soon awakened her. Koko, with a plate in hand, stood in front of her.

"Eat now," Koko said, passing her the plate of minced meat.

"What is it?" Heather asked. Lord, but she was famished.

"Lamb."

"It looks raw."

"It is."

Heather set the plate down on the floor and then stood up. "I'm too tired to eat and need to check on my horse."

"You will return soon?" Koko asked.

"Yes."

Heather checked on the mare's welfare and then returned to the caravansary's common room. Petri passed her on his way out and flashed her another of his toothy grins. His smiling silence was beginning to grate on her frazzled nerves.

Wandering outside to the inn's courtyard, Heather sat down, leaned against the stone wall, and fell into a troubled sleep. Dreams about Khalid chopping her fingers off and cutting her tongue out kept Heather tossing and turning all night.

Before dawn, Koko nudged Heather awake. She felt groggy and drained, not to mention hungry. When the Armenian offered her a sweet crepe, Heather grabbed it out of his hand, turned her back on him, and stuffed it into her mouth.

Continuing on their journey, Koko chose to ride at the back of the line with Heather. They rode in silence until she noticed another young man led the caravan.

"Who is that in front?" Heather asked.

"My second son, Demetri," Koko answered.

"Where is Petri?"

"Doing his father's bidding."

It was midmorning when a loud, agonized wail from one of the wagons pierced the air. Koko was gone in an instant, riding hard to see what the problem was.

Now what? Heather wondered, wishing she had never met the Kasabians. She should have been farther away by now. The prince could catch up to them at any moment.

"A problem?" Heather asked when Koko returned.

"I mistakenly left some of my property behind," he said with a sheepish smile. "We must return to the caravansary at once."

"What?"

"I said—"

"I heard you the first time," Heather snapped. "Nothing is so valuable that we need to backtrack such a great distance."

"For myself, I would not care," Koko said apologetically. "But, my wife—such a sentimental woman—insists we return for Krista. After all, she *is* my only daughter."

Chapter 12

"You forgot your blasted daughter?" Heather shouted, without lowering her tone of voice to sound masculine.

Koko shrugged, unperturbed, and ignored the lapse in her disguise. "The unexpected happens sometimes, but we Armenians are a hardy lot and—"

"Thrive under adversity," Heather finished, thoroughly disgusted with him and every other Armenian.

Koko nodded. "Precisely."

"Send Petri to fetch Krista," Heather suggested. "We will wait for them here."

"Petri is unavailable."

"Demetri, then?"

"We return to the caravansary," Koko insisted, "and will remain there for the night. In the morning we will begin our journey again. What have we lost but a day?"

"Meeting you was a distinct pleasure," Heather said, turning her horse. "I will be on my way."

"Alone?" Koko sounded appalled. He reached out and grasped her reins. "I beg you to reconsider."

"Why?"

"Traveling alone is dangerous," Koko said. "Brigands could murder you and steal your possessions."

"I have no possessions," Heather replied, tugging her reins out of his grasp.

"What about your horse?"

Heather hesitated. She hadn't thought of that.

"And, if you were a woman, your fate would be even worse," Koko added slyly.

Heather was beginning to feel apprehensive. "In what way?"

"Those dirty vermin would abuse a woman's body in every disgusting way possible," Koko said. "First they would—"

Heather was frightened but determined. "I go my own way."

"So be it." Koko shrugged and smiled at her. "Each man must follow his own fate—*kismet*."

Koko shouted an order in his unfamiliar Armenian language. The caravan began moving, making a U-turn until they were headed back in the direction of the caravansary.

Koko lingered for a minute. "Good-bye, Malik," he said. "May Allah protect you." With that, the Armenian whirled his horse around and rode after his caravan.

For a brief moment, Heather watched them and then gazed at the road ahead. She felt alone and vulnerable.

The world was a big place, Heather thought. There was no reason to believe that Khalid was searching for her in this direction. Disguised as a man, she'd managed to fool the whole Kasabian tribe. Or had she? Even if the Armenian suspected otherwise, he'd respected her privacy and hadn't mentioned it. Besides, traveling alone terrified her. Oh, why had she run away? What should she do?

"Wait for me," Heather called, spurring her horse after the caravan.

Four hours later, they sighted the caravansary, and Heather had her first inkling that something was amiss. Too many men and horses were milling about. Early afternoon was the wrong time for travelers to stop for the night.

Playing it safe, Heather stayed hidden behind the Kasabians. She touched the *kufiyah* masking her face and then dismounted.

With this many people, how could she possibly retain her disguise? Heather wondered, stroking the mare's neck. If anyone guessed her true identity . . . Heather refused to even think about that possibility.

It was then Heather suffered the first of several shocks she would get that day. Holding little Krista Kasabian's hand, Khalid emerged from the caravansary. Behind him walked Petri.

It appeared the world was smaller than she had thought.

She should have known better than return with the Kasabians, Heather berated herself, unaware this whole scene had been engineered by Koko. Perhaps if she faded into the background, she might get away with no one the wiser.

Heather stood motionless, rooted to that spot, the familiar sight of Khalid mesmerizing her senses. In spite of what he'd done to her, every nerve in her body tingled with the excitement of seeing him again, and she suffered the nearly overwhelming urge to fly into his arms and surrender herself to him.

My hunger makes me weak, Heather told herself as she watched Koko embrace his daughter. At least, the prince had fed her, which was more than the Kasabians had done. A woman could not survive on sweet crepes alone.

Koko sent Krista to her mother who clung to the little girl as if she would never let her go. Watching this touching reunion, Heather forgot her own worries and felt an insistent tugging upon her heartstrings. How wonderful it must be to hold your own child in your arms, she thought. Too bad the babe came with a father. From what she'd heard of the weasel and seen of the Sultan's Beast, having a husband was somewhat less than desirable.

"My prince, I thank you for protecting my daughter in my absence," Koko said loudly, drawing Heather's attention.

"Take better care of your prized possessions, my friend," Khalid said, "else you risk losing them."

Koko nodded. "Your Desert Fox travels with us and will want to report to you."

Khalid arched a dark brow at the Armenian.

"Malik," Koko said, gesturing toward Heather.

Bloody bugger, Heather thought. She was caught.

Khalid turned his intense blue-eyed gaze upon Heather and stared at her. He knew he had her trapped and was not in any rush.

"Ah, yes. My brave but foolish Desert Fox," Khalid said. At that, he sauntered toward her.

Heather tried to jump onto her horse, but Abdul, having positioned himself near her lest she flee, reached out to grab her arm. Reacting instinctively, Heather landed a vicious kick to his shin and escaped him.

In a flash of movement, Heather leaped onto the mare and bolted. Khalid jumped onto his own stallion and, leaving a storm of dust in his wake, chased his quarry.

Becoming one with her horse, Heather crouched low over the mare's neck and begged her to run even faster. Khalid, gaining on the distance that separated them, smiled with admiration at the expert way Heather handled her mount.

Closer and closer rode Khalid.

Heather could almost feel the beast's breath on her back and spurred her horse on. Unfortunately, the mare was no match for the stallion.

Diagonally behind the mare, Khalid leaped from his saddle and tackled Heather. As they flew through the air toward the ground, Khalid held her tightly and turned his body to take the brunt of their impact. They slammed, full force, onto the hard earth. Silence reigned for several minutes, the only sound being their labored breathing.

Their thoughts, however, were not as still as their tongues. Khalid felt relieved that he had found his Wildflower alive and unharmed, but irritated at the trouble she had caused him. Heather felt angry to have been so easily caught, not to mention almost killed in the catching, yet her senses were alive to her captor's presence.

"Are you injured?" Khalid broke the silence.

"No. And you?" Heather asked.

"Unfortunately for you, I am fine." Khalid pushed Heather onto her back and stared down at her masked face, asking, "The Desert Fox, I presume?"

"Very funny."

Khalid pulled the *kufiyah* away from her face. "You were trying to escape, my wildflower."

"I *did* escape," Heather corrected him. "If not for that blinking idiot—"

"If not for the Armenian, you would be dead," Khalid interrupted her. "Be thankful Kasabian recognized your worth to me."

"You mean he knew all along that I was . . ."

Khalid laughed in her face. "You actually believed you could hide your womanhood?"

"I would have made it," Heather said.

Khalid kissed the tip of her upturned nose and then stared into her disarming green eyes. "Where were you going?"

"Home."

Khalid laughed in her face again.

"What is so amusing?" Heather asked.

"The Kasabians travel east to Armenia," Khalid told her. "England lies far to the west."

"I still would have made it."

Khalid cocked a dark brow at her.

"The world is round," Heather told him. "By traveling east, I can eventually reach the west."

"Perhaps, my love, but you would arrive home an old gray-haired woman."

My love? His endearment shocked Heather. How could he sell her into slavery and then call her his love? Confused by his words, she changed the subject. "How fares Omar?"

"As well as can be expected."

"And what was his punishment for incompetence? The loss of a couple of limbs?" Heather asked, masking her feelings of guilt with anger. Whatever the little man had suffered was her fault.

"Thanks to Petri Kasabian's timely arrival in Istanbul, I spared Omar's life," Khalid told her. "Except for the broken nose and the two black eyes *you* inflicted on him, Omar is well and awaits you at my mother's residence."

"I refuse to slave for your mother," Heather said.

"Is that so?" Khalid asked, his lips hovering above hers.

"Yes, and another thing—"

Taking advantage of her open mouth, Khalid's lips captured hers in a long, smoldering kiss. As his mouth slashed across hers, his tongue slipped past her rosebud lips and explored the sweetness beyond them. Khalid poured all his passion into that single, stirring kiss. Overwhelmed by his intimate touch and his clean masculine scent, Heather surrendered and returned his kiss in kind. And then some.

It was Khalid who finally broke the kiss. He stared

down at her dazed expression and brushed his fingertips against the silken skin of her cheek.

I love him, Heather thought. Masking her shame at her response to his kiss, she said, "Am I a serpent to mate in the dusty road?"

"You are as tempting as Eve in the Garden of Eden," Khalid said.

"Pagans like you know nothing of paradise."

"Do we not?" Khalid slid his hand down her body to the valley between her thighs and caressed her. "Paradise lies here, my princess."

"I am no princess," Heather said, her complexion a vibrant scarlet.

Khalid stood up. Reaching down, he helped her to her feet and then whistled to summon his horse. The stallion returned from where he'd been grazing. Behind him trotted the mare.

"As the mare follows the stallion, you will follow my lead," Khalid said in a husky voice.

If possible, Heather's complexion reddened even more, and she dropped her gaze. His words caused a melting feeling in the pit of her stomach.

"Did you enjoy your adventure, my beauty?" Heather whispered as she stroked the mare's neck. "What is she called?"

"I named her for you," Khalid said, a smile touching his lips. He drew the *kufiyah* up to mask Heather's face, then gazed deeply, longingly into her eyes. "Foolish Pleasure."

Before Heather could open her mouth to reply, Khalid lifted her onto his saddle and mounted behind her. With the mare in tow, they rode in silence back to the caravansary.

The prince's men and the Kasabians were still milling about when they returned. As two of the prince's men rushed forward to take their horses, Khalid pulled Heather off his stallion, and keeping a tight grasp on her arm, advanced on Koko.

"I thank you for your assistance," Khalid said to the Armenian. "Bring your carpets to Maiden's Castle when you journey to Istanbul again."

"You are too generous, Prince Khalid," Koko said, mentally rubbing his hands together at the prospect of making a great deal of coin. "Will you chop her fingers off now?"

"You bloody bugger," Heather cried, yanking the *kufiyah* off her face.

Calmly and deliberately, Khalid drew the *kufiyah* up to hide most of her face. "Why would I do that?" he asked.

"The woman stole your horse."

"The woman is my wife, and the horse was a wedding gift to her," Khalid announced, shocking everyone but Abdul. "She stole nothing."

"Your wife!" Koko exclaimed.

"Your wife?" Heather echoed, yanking the *kufiyah* down to stare at him.

"No one must gaze upon the face of a prince's wife," Khalid said, pulling the *kufiyah* up again. To Koko, he said, "The Kasabian family is most welcome to attend my wedding celebration tonight."

"The honor is ours, my prince," Koko replied.

Khalid inclined his head in a gesture of dismissal, and with Heather in tow, turned to enter the caravansary. Heather tugged on his sleeve and refused to budge.

"If I am truly your wife, duty demands that you protect me," Heather said when he looked down at her. "Doesn't it?"

Khalid nodded once.

Heather pulled the *kufiyah* down and pointed at Koko,

saying accusingly, "That man tried to starve me. I demand satisfaction."

Khalid yanked the *kufiyah* up and growled, "Keep your face covered." He ushered Heather toward the caravansary door. How many years would it take her to learn to keep her face covered?

Khalid paused in the common room to speak with the innkeeper. "Is everything as I ordered?" he asked.

"Yes, my prince."

"The bath?"

"Scented, steaming, and set up inside your tent," the other man answered.

"Good." Khalid produced a small pouch filled with coins and handed it to the innkeeper. "Have my man bring food for my wife, and spare nothing for tonight's celebration."

"Yes, my prince," the innkeeper said and bowed his head.

Khalid led Heather into the courtyard where she'd slept the previous night. One short day had changed its look completely. Now the prince's palatial tent seemed to fill it. His guards stood here and there, insuring their privacy from would-be intruders.

"My dear," Khalid said, parting the tent flap and gesturing her inside.

"Why did you lie?" Heather asked as soon as they were alone. "You needn't actually have cut my—"

"I spoke no lies," Khalid interrupted. "Get out of those clothes. You stink."

Heather ignored the insult. "You said we were married."

"We are."

"I cannot recall attending our wedding and do not believe you."

"Your presence was unnecessary. I only needed your

guardian's permission," Khalid told her. "Now, get out of those stinking clothes and into the tub."

"My guardian?"

Khalid gave her a wolfish grin. "I was your guardian and gave myself permission to marry you."

"I spoke no vows."

"As I said, that was unnecessary."

"I cannot credit that." Heather had never heard of anything so ridiculous.

Khalid sighed in exasperation and produced a document. Handing it to her, he said, "This is our certificate of marriage."

"I can't read this," Heather said, thrusting the document back at him. "Besides, why would you want to marry me? You don't even like me."

I love you, Khalid thought but said, "Disrobe and get into the tub before the water cools. In Omar's absence, I will play the eunuch."

"I certainly hope so," Heather said, bringing the hint of a smile to his lips.

If she hadn't been so dirty and tired and hungry, Heather would have fought him; but, all she wanted at the moment was to fill her empty stomach, submerge her body in the steaming water, and sleep for a month or two. She would deal with the arrogant prince later.

Without argument or modesty, Heather stripped and climbed into the tub. The scented, steaming water made her groan in pleasure.

"Soap," she said. "I need soap."

Khalid rolled his sleeves up and then produced the desired soap. Aware that she was feeling poorly because of her two-day ordeal, he washed her without trying to seduce her. Though he felt his arousal keenly, Khalid was a patient man. He would take her when she was clean, fed, and rested. The gift of his bride's virginity demanded moonlight and whispered words of love, not a quick tumble on the carpet.

Groggy from sleepless anxiety and the hot bath, Heather let Khalid dry her, wrap her in a caftan, and gently comb the snarls from her wet hair. Then he led her to his couch.

Khalid pulled the coverlet back and helped her down. Abdul walked in, handed the prince a plate, and then started to leave.

"Wait," Heather called to the warrior.

Abdul turned around and looked at Khalid who nodded for him to stay.

"Show him that paper," Heather said.

Khalid produced the certificate of marriage and handed it to Abdul. "Tell her what is written," he ordered his man.

Abdul looked at the document and then returned it to the prince. Without gazing upon Heather's face, he said, "You are the prince's wife. Unfortunately." Abdul flicked a glance at Khalid, adding, "Beating her would work."

"His impertinence should be punished," Heather said when they were alone again.

"And what about yours?" Khalid asked.

"Princesses are expected to be impertinent," Heather told him.

"But not to the prince."

"I must work harder on that, I suppose," Heather said. Would she ever see England again? How could she avoid losing her Englishness in a land so different from her own? Given a choice, could she leave this man who had captured her heart?

"What about Fougere?" Heather asked. "Have you given up your revenge?" *Or is this marriage part of it?*

Khalid stared at her for a long moment, then answered, "My revenge is postponed for a few days, never canceled."

Sitting on the edge of the bed, Khalid fed Heather sizzling chunks of mutton grilled on a spit. When the plate was empty, Khalid gently pushed her back on the bed and then stood.

"We will sup together tonight," he said. "Now I must greet our guests and see to their entertainment."

"Isn't the bride invited to the festivities?" she asked.

"Men and women do not celebrate together."

"How civilized."

"I order you to sleep without worry," Khalid said. "And know as you do, I am keeping you safe."

"But I'm not tired," Heather protested, then ruined her words by yawning.

"Why do you wear dark circles of fatigue beneath your eyes?" Khalid asked.

"Decoration."

"I think not."

"Perhaps the days in your company have aged me."

"I believe the days *without my company* have aged you," Khalid said, then sat down on the edge of the couch again. "Close your eyes." He sat where he was until her breathing evened and he knew that she slept. Then he leaned over and brushed his lips against hers.

"Tonight, my wildflower, you will truly be mine," Khalid whispered. He stood then and left his tent.

When she awakened later, Heather lay with her eyes closed and considered her new position in life. Two short days had changed her life completely. She'd gone from runaway slave to prince's wife, though she didn't actually feel comfortable with either title. One was too low and the other much too exalted.

That Khalid had married her by proxy without her permission bothered Heather not at all. She had never entertained the notion of choosing her own husband. That wasn't the way of the world. She'd been bred to accept the fact that she would wed where she was told.

Fortunately for her, Khalid was young, virile, handsome, and carried royal blood in his veins. Though he wasn't the man the queen had chosen, Khalid was more than suitable.

What Heather was unable to fathom was why *he* wanted to marry her. Certainly, the youngest daughter of a foreign earl was a step down for the prince.

The sounds of sloshing water penetrated Heather's thoughts, and she opened her eyes. Two candles burning on the table bathed the tent's inner chamber in a soft glow.

Her gaze focused on Khalid. With his back toward her, he sat in the wooden tub. A large man sitting in so small a tub made an incongruous picture, and Heather stifled a giggle. Instead, she seized the opportunity to study him without being observed.

The flickering light of the candles danced sensuously across the broad expanse of his shoulders and upper back. When he stood suddenly and climbed out, Heather stared in awe at the magnificent sight of his broad shoulders tapering to a narrow waist. His buttocks were perfectly, wonderfully rounded and his thighs well muscled.

A modern-day Adonis, Heather thought, and nearly swooned.

She had never seen a man such as this, nor had she seen any naked man. Thinking of what would happen between them that night made Heather blush. She knew her duty as a wife, but was enjoying that duty acceptable? Khalid was even more handsome and manly than her brothers-in-law. Heather just knew she was going to enjoy her duty, and somehow, that seemed sinful.

Khalid finished drying himself and tossed the towel

aside. He grabbed his shirt and pants, and then turned around.

Heather snapped her eyes shut.

With clothing in hand, Khalid padded on bare feet across the tent and stared down at his exquisitely beautiful bride. Noting her heightened color, he knew she had awakened. In silence, Khalid stood there and watched her feigning sleep.

Unaware of his presence beside her, Heather opened her eyes and found herself looking at the dark mat of hair covering his chest. Her gaze dropped to the masculine appendage lying at his groin. It grew beneath her wide-eyed stare. With an inarticulate squeak, Heather snapped her eyes shut.

"I know you are awake," Khalid said, a smile lurking in his voice.

Heather refused to answer.

"Open your eyes, Wildflower," he coaxed. "See what your husband brings to your marriage bed."

"C-c-cover yourself," Heather managed to choke out. "Please."

Khalid pulled his pants on. It appeared his fearless wildflower would require a great amount of patient coaxing. There would be time enough for that later.

"I am decent," he announced.

Heather opened one eye, and seeing his naked chest, snapped it shut again. "Liar."

"Such blushing modesty over a man's chest?" Khalid asked. "I assure you my jewels are covered."

Still wary, Heather opened one eye first, then the other, and sat up. Khalid sat down on the edge of the couch. He leaned close and planted a chaste kiss on her lips. Heather froze.

"Relax," Khalid said, one of his powerful hands gliding up and down the length of her right arm. "Stop worrying about your wedding night."

"How do you—?"

"Fearing the unknown is natural, my blushing bride," Khalid said. "Though you will never believe me, I say there is nothing to fear. Pleasure beyond your wildest imaginings awaits you in my bed."

Heather reddened at his words. Lord, but it was suddenly hot inside the tent, and she felt faint. Perhaps, she was becoming ill.

Khalid stood up abruptly. He pulled his white linen shirt over his head and tucked the bottom edge into his pants. "For the moment, I will play the eunuch and brush that glorious mane of silken fire."

He walked over to his chest and produced a brush, then went back to the couch and sat down. "Turn around," he ordered.

Heather did not know what to make of him. It appeared that marriage had changed the prince's whole disposition. Gone was the ruthless Sultan's Beast, replaced by a considerate husband.

"Please, turn around," he repeated.

Please? Heather did as she was asked.

Khalid brushed her hair until it crackled like the flames it resembled. Setting the brush aside, he lightly nuzzled the side of her neck, sending a delicious shiver dancing down her spine.

"Are you hungry, my beauty?" Khalid breathed against her ear.

Oh, Lord! Heather thought, flustered by his disturbing nearness and touch. First he made her sweat and then he made her shiver.

"My sweet?"

Heather had no idea what he was asking her.

"Come," Khalid said, offering her his hand.

Caught by the intensity of his piercing blue-eyed gaze, Heather could only stare at him. He gave her an encouraging smile, and she placed her hand in his.

Khalid escorted her to the table and helped her sit down on one of the enormous pillows. After pouring her a goblet of rosewater, Khalid rang a tiny bell to alert his waiting servants that he was ready for supper. The sound of music, laughter, and men's voices drifted in from the caravansary.

"What's happening out there?" Heather asked in a whisper.

"My men and the Kasabians are celebrating our marriage."

"Then, it's true. We really are married?"

"Marriage is too serious a matter to lie about," Khalid replied. "Do you dislike the idea of being the pampered wife of an Eastern prince?"

"No, but I still do not understand how the priest—"

"Here is our supper," Khalid said, interrupting her. The operative word was *priest,* and Khalid had no intention of correcting her wrong assumption that a Christian man of the cloth had married them. At least, he'd wait until morning.

Beneath Abdul's supervision, two men entered and set plates of food on the table. There were green beans in oil, a warm salad of fried carrots and yogurt, a roasted chicken with rice and apricot stuffing, and flatbread.

"How is Abdul feeling?" Heather whispered. "I hope I didn't injure him?"

"No permanent damage, merely his pride."

"Should I apologize?" she asked.

"A princess never apologizes," Khalid said.

"Not even to her prince?"

"She would never behave toward the prince in a manner that required an apology," Khalid said, his voice stern.

Heather arched a perfectly shaped copper brow at him.
"I find that difficult to believe."

"I swear it is true," he lied.

"But, if the princess in question did do something?"

"Unfortunately, even a princess is not above punishment," Khalid replied.

"What about the prince?"

"What about me?"

"What if you did something that required an apology to the princess?" Heather asked.

Khalid gave her a devilish grin. "A prince enjoys more freedom of action than a princess."

"That's unfair."

"That is the way of the world. Remember it."

Heather was silent for a long moment, then said, "May I ask you a personal question?"

"You are my wife and may ask me anything you want," Khalid told her.

"Why did you marry me?" Heather asked. "You don't even like me."

With a gentle expression on his face, Khalid studied her and then gestured her to sit beside him.

Heather stood and walked around the table, then plopped down beside him. She gazed at him expectantly, her face merely inches from his.

Khalid placed his arm around her shoulder and pulled her close. He planted a chaste kiss on her lips and then stared into her disarming green eyes.

"I want you." His voice was husky with long-denied need.

"I—I don't understand."

I love you, Khalid thought. However, he refused to let her rule him through his love, as his grandmother Khurrem had ruled his grandfather Suleiman.

Khalid kissed her again, then whispered against her lips, "I married because I desire you in my bed."

That answer didn't sit well with Heather. "How many women have you married because you desired them in your bed?" she asked. The thought of another woman sharing his life made her unaccountably angry.

"What do you mean?"

"April told me a man in this heathen land can marry four women and keep countless concubines," Heather said, her voice rising. "I am English and cannot approve of that custom."

So that was the problem. His blushing bride suffered from jealousy. It was definitely a good beginning. Khalid arched a dark brow at her and said, "This is not England."

"I can adjust myself to a great many things," Heather told him, "but I will never accept sharing my husband with . . ."

Khalid pulled her close. "As you already know, I do not keep a harem. Besides, speaking of other women is an unsuitable topic for newlyweds."

"But—"

"*Ahem!*" Abdul cleared his throat as he held the tent flap aside for the two servants who cleared their plates away. Chewing on mint leaves, Khalid and Heather washed their hands in the bowls of warm water left for them and then shared a towel.

"Let us walk outside and enjoy the evening," Khalid suggested, noting the apprehension shadowing his wife's expression.

Heather was quick to nod her agreement. At that precise moment, she would have agreed to almost anything in order to delay the inevitable.

Khalid and Heather stepped into a sensual night created for romance. A crescent moon hung overhead, accompanied by a thousand glittering stars enhanced in the perfect setting of a deep indigo sky. The intoxicating fragrance of flowers pervaded the air, and the muted sounds of a stringed instrument drifted to them from inside the caravansary.

The guards that Heather had earlier seen were gone. Only Abdul sat near the entrance to the caravansary to ensure their privacy.

With her arm entwined with her husband's, Heather breathed deeply of the perfumed air and stole a shy peek at the man. Though he'd taken her captive and tried to enslave her, Heather was willing to forgive his trespasses. Khalid had married her, and that made her feel valued and cherished. He was a warrior to be admired and an incredibly handsome prince.

What more could she want?

Love.

One step at a time, Heather told herself. Those who run too fast usually trip and fall.

"Though the brilliance of the sun does illuminate your beauty, the mystery of the night suits you even more," Khalid said, flattering her outrageously.

Heather blushed at his words. "You are beautiful too."

"I am a 'scar-faced beast,' " Khalid reminded her. "That is what you said."

"I do admit I was wrong."

"Do my ears deceive me?" Khalid asked. "I thought I heard you—"

Silencing him, Heather reached up and placed a finger across his lips. She caressed his scarred cheek and then shocked him even more when she planted a kiss on it. "It is a beautiful scar and gives you character."

"No other woman in this world would described my

scar as beautiful," Khalid said, leaning close to kiss her.

Heather stepped back a pace. "Tell me about yourself."

"What would you like to know?"

"Something about your family."

"Our journey to Istanbul will be long and dull," Khalid said, aware that she was stalling. "I will amuse you with tales of my family then."

"What about children?"

"I have none."

"I mean, do you like them?"

Khalid pulled her into his embrace. "We will make dozens of children," he promised, his lips hovering above hers.

"I—I don't believe I'm capable of handling that many," she whispered.

"As many as you desire. And I will love each one as though he was the first." His mouth captured hers in a lingering kiss.

Without warning, Khalid scooped her up. Heather entwined her arms around his neck.

"I have waited for you forever," Khalid said, his voice hoarse with emotion. With that, he carried her back to the tent, and once inside, gently placed her on their marriage bed.

Fully clothed, Khalid lay down beside Heather and gathered her into his embrace. His lips sought hers in a slow, soul-stealing kiss that seemed to last forever. Swept away by his passion, Heather returned his kiss with equal ardor. His lips left hers and sprinkled dozens of feather-light kisses on her temples, eyelids, throat, and especially the bridge of her upturned nose.

Heather giggled at the tickling sensation he was creating. "What are you doing?" she whispered.

"I am kissing each one of your freckles," he answered.

"Do we have that much time?"

"Forever."

Khalid held her tightly as if he would never let her go. His mouth captured hers, and they kissed for an eternity.

"Shouldn't we remove our clothing?" Heather asked, eager to feel the muscular planes of his body beneath her hands.

"I suppose, if that is what you want," Khalid teased her. "Do you?"

Mesmerized by the intensity of his smoldering gaze, Heather stared in a daze at him. In a voice no louder than a whisper, she answered, "Yes."

Pleased by her willingness, Khalid kissed her lightly and then asked, "Are you afraid, my love?"

"Yes."

Khalid smiled at her honesty and held her close. He brushed his lips across her forehead and promised, "There is nothing to fear. Trust me."

Khalid planted a kiss on her lips and then rose from the couch. Giving her no time to reconsider, he removed the caftan from her trembling body and dropped it on the floor. Staring down at her beauty, Khalid suffered the powerful urge to suckle her pink-tipped nipples, but held himself in check. It was too soon; he would frighten her. Instead, Khalid reached out and caressed her from the column of her throat to the juncture of her thighs.

"Exquisite," he whispered, then pulled his shirt over his head and tossed it aside. When he reached for the top of his pants, her voice stopped him.

"I—I've changed my mind," Heather said. "About the clothing, I mean. I prefer to stay dressed."

"Too late, Princess." Khalid let his pants drop to the

floor and stepped out of them, then lay down beside her again.

Panicking, Heather turned away from him. Khalid reached out and touched her arm.

"Come to me," he said. "I yearn to hold my wife in my arms."

Irresistibly drawn by his presence and his softly spoken words, Heather turned into his embrace. For the first time in her young life, she experienced the incredible sensation of masculine hardness touching her female softness.

Khalid claimed her lips and kissed her thoroughly, stealing her breath away. Gently, his hands caressed while his lips moved down the column of her throat and beyond.

"Please," Heather begged as his mouth captured one of her rosebud nipples. By the time he began teasing its mate with his tongue, Heather had forgotten for what she'd been pleading. The heat that ignited between her thighs banished all coherent thought from her mind. She burned to be possessed by this man—her husband.

"I want you," Heather breathed.

"Spread your legs for me," Khalid ordered, his lips returning to hers.

Without hesitation, Heather did as she was told. Khalid kissed her and slowly inserted one long finger inside her. Shocked, Heather tried to get away, and in the movement, impaled herself on his finger.

"Be easy, my love," Khalid whispered, gently pushing her back on the bed. "Please, relax. Relax and there will be no pain."

Khalid kissed her again and then inserted a second finger inside her, saying, "Be still, my love. Accustom yourself to the feel of it. You are so wonderfully tight. I want to make you ready to receive me."

He dipped his head to her breasts and suckled her

aroused nipples. His fingers began to move rhythmically, seductively inside her.

Gradually, Heather relaxed. Catching his rhythm, she began moving her hips, enticing his fingers deeper inside her writhing body.

"Created for passion," Khalid said. "You were made for me to love."

Heather moaned throatily. His words and fingers inflamed her senses. Her hips moved faster, and then his fingers were gone.

"No," she protested their desertion.

Khalid knelt between her thighs. The ruby knob of his engorged manhood teased the pearl of her womanhood, making her moan again.

"Look at me, my love," he ordered, his manhood poised to pierce.

Heather opened her eyes and stared in a daze at him.

"I would spare you the virgin's pain if I could," Khalid said. "Do you believe me?"

"Yes."

"Tell me what you need," he coaxed. "Tell me and I will give it to you."

"I need you," she whispered, delirious with desire.

Khalid pushed himself inside her with one powerful but kind thrust and buried his masculine sword to the hilt. Clutching him, Heather cried out in surprised pain as he broke through her virgin's barrier.

Khalid lay perfectly still for several long moments, letting her become accustomed to the feel of him inside her. Then he began to move seductively, enticing her to move with him.

Caught in the midst of swirling passion, Heather wrapped her legs around his waist. She moved with him and met each of his powerful thrusts with her own.

Suddenly, unexpectedly, Heather exploded as wave

after wave of exquisite sensation carried her to paradise. Knowing his bride had found her fulfillment, Khalid groaned and shuddered and poured his seed deep inside her body.

They lay still for long moments. The only sound in the tent was their labored breathing. Finally, Khalid rolled off her, pulled her into his embrace, and planted a kiss on her cheek.

"Are you all right?" he asked.

"I think so," she answered. "Are you?"

"I am *more* than all right," he said. "Now, sleep without worry."

Resting her head against his chest, Heather closed her eyes. Soon her breathing evened and he knew she slept.

Unfortunately, Khalid was unable to sleep without worry like his bride. His enemies would stop at nothing to get to him, and the realization that he now had a soft spot troubled him greatly.

Khalid knew he had done the unthinkable. He had married his weakness.

Chapter 13

The next morning Heather awakened with the feeling that her life had changed, something wonderful had happened. And then she remembered. Her prince had made her his princess.

Heather yawned, stretched, and rolled over. Her husband wasn't there. She was alone in the tent.

The sound of her husband's voice, issuing orders to his men, drifted in from outside. Content with her new position in life, Heather lay back on the pillows. She smiled and closed her eyes.

Her thoughts wandered to what had happened between them the previous night. She could almost feel his lips on hers, his hand caressing her body intimately, the weight of him as he covered her and shared his love.

Heather flushed hotly. Again, his warm, insistent lips claimed hers. It felt so real.

"Awaken, my sleeping beauty," Khalid said, his lips hovering above hers.

Daydreams do not speak out loud, Heather thought. She opened her eyes and smiled at her husband.

"Why are your cheeks stained pink?" Khalid asked. "What are you thinking? Or do your thoughts belong only to yourself as you once insisted?"

Heather sat up and let the coverlet drop to her waist, baring her breasts to his gaze. "I—I want . . . " She broke off, too embarrassed to continue.

"What do you want? Tell me and it is yours."

Leaning close, Heather kissed his scarred cheek, and her hand dropped to his groin. "I want to shiver with the heat again," she said, remembering her cousin's words on lovemaking.

"You enjoyed your wedding night?" Khalid pulled her close, and his lips captured hers in a lingering kiss. Then, he drew back and said, "More than anything else, I would love to crawl into bed with you, but we have no time to linger. My men grow impatient to be gone. Once we reach Istanbul, we will have forever to revel in each other."

Khalid almost smiled at her disappointed expression. Instead, he planted a kiss on each of her perfectly formed breasts. "There is food on the table, a pan of warmed water for washing, and fresh clothing," he said. "If you require anything else, look in my bag or chest." With that, he gave her a quick kiss and left.

Heather rose, washed, and drew the fresh caftan over her head. A black *yashmak* had been left for her, but she ignored it. She would delay putting that on as long as possible. Heather pulled the boots on that she'd "borrowed" from Omar and then wove her hair into one thick braid.

Crossing the chamber, Heather plopped down on one of the pillows beside the table and looked over the morning's fare. There were olives, flatbread, goat cheese, and hard-cooked eggs.

Heather peeled the shell from two of the eggs and sliced them open, then ate the yolk and pushed the whites aside. There were very few things she detested more than egg whites. As she ate the flatbread and cheese, Heather found joy in her husband's voice, calling instructions to his men outside the tent.

Finished with her meal, Heather returned to sit on the

couch, but blushed at the tiny bloodstains there. Her virgin's blood. Soon, she became tired of waiting and decided to write a letter to her mother. That way, it could be sent as soon as they reached Istanbul.

Heather searched her husband's bag and then his chest where she found paper and quill. Sitting at the table, she wrote a note and explained what had happened to April and her since leaving England.

Fabricating the part about being rescued from abductors by an Ottoman prince, Heather wrote that she'd promptly fallen in love and married him. She was content with her husband and intended to remain where she was. Prince Khalid was very stern, very arrogant, and very handsome. Beneath his fierce exterior hid a gentle heart. *And he loved her.* At least, he'd called her "my love"!

She ended by promising a more detailed letter after she had settled into her husband's home.

Heather stood up. In a hurry to give the note to her husband for safekeeping, she stepped outside the tent into the courtyard. Gone was the quiet, almost magical sensuality of the previous evening.

Standing near the tent, one of the prince's warriors noticed her and nudged his friend. Others noted her appearance and turned to stare at her.

Oblivious to their surprised expressions at seeing the prince's wife unveiled, Heather smiled at the first two warriors. Startling them with her knowledge of their language, she asked in Turkish, "Where is my husband, please?" She definitely liked the sound of the word *husband.*

Horrified that she would actually speak to them, those two hardened warriors of many fierce battles backed away fearfully.

What rude men, Heather thought. And then she saw

her husband. Heather lost her smile of greeting when she saw his forbidding expression directed at her.

"Cover your face," Khalid shouted, advancing on her.

With her rosy lips forming a perfect O, Heather whirled around and ran inside the tent. From outside, she heard the humiliating sounds of masculine laughter.

Khalid watched her disappear. His wife was much too free with her person. She needed to understand what was expected of a prince's wife. It was time to lay the law down.

"Try beating her," Abdul called.

With a muttered oath, Khalid stepped inside the tent.

Heather shook with humiliated rage as she paced back and forth inside the tent's inner chamber. How dare he speak to her in that demeaning tone of voice in front of the servants! Her father had never used that tone of voice on her mother.

The tent flap parted. Khalid walked in.

"You insufferable oaf. You're a toad, not a prince," Heather said. "Is it my fault I was in such a hurry to see you that I forgot the damned veil? Why would I purposefully wish to anger you?"

Heather stood there, glorious in her fury, daring to outface him. A fact that was not unappreciated by her husband.

Khalid decided to be reasonable. Being his princess was new to her. "A prince's wife must keep her face covered in the company of strangers, especially men," he explained, advancing on her. "To do otherwise is considered unseemly."

"I didn't realize your servants weren't allowed to see me unveiled," Heather said.

More foolishness, Khalid thought. Allah grant me patience.

"Those men outside are warriors, not servants," he told her. "Now, what must I do?" Khalid went on as if thinking out loud. "I suppose I must blind those faithful warriors who dared to gaze upon my wife's face?"

"Spare your men," Heather cried, grabbing his arm. "The blame lies with me. I swear I will adjust myself to your customs. Please . . ."

After several long moments of consideration, Khalid nodded. "What was it you wanted?"

Heather held the letter up. "I would like this sent as soon as we reach Istanbul."

Khalid gave her a puzzled look and held out his hand. Without permission, he opened the letter but was unable to read the English. He walked to the table and lit a candle. It was then Khalid spied the discarded egg whites from his wife's breakfast.

"What is this?" he asked.

"A letter to my mother."

"No, this."

Heather walked to the table, stood beside him, and looked down at the egg whites. "What do you think it is?"

"You tell me," he said.

Heather peered closely at the remains of her breakfast. "Why, they appear to be the whites of hard-cooked eggs."

"I know what they are."

"Then, why did you ask?"

"I meant, what are they doing here?"

"What do you mean?"

"Do not answer my questions with questions," Khalid ordered. "Why are these egg whites not in your stomach?"

"I hate egg whites," Heather told him. "I do adore the yolks though."

"You eat the yolk and discard the white?" Khalid

asked, surprised. "You are wasting Allah's bounty. Either eat the yolk and the white or eat nothing. Do you realize there are poor people—"

"—in Armenia who are starving and would kill for the white of an egg," Heather interrupted.

Khalid's lips twitched. "I was going to say Azerbaijan."

Heather had never heard of that place. "Are there no starving people in Armenia?"

"Of course, but the Armenians are not Moslems and so are of no account."

"How compassionate of you."

"Find someone who eats only the whites or refrain from eating eggs." With that, Khalid touched the letter to the candle's flame.

"What are you doing?" Heather cried, trying in vain to save it.

"No letters to England," Khalid said, holding her at bay with his free hand. "Forget about your past life."

"Forget about my mother?" Heather cried. "My family?"

"Listen to me," Khalid said, grabbing her shoulders. "Once the letter is sent, the English will petition the sultan for your release. It would matter little that you are my wife."

"But my mother—"

"Your mother already grieves for you," he said. "Why ease her mind when you cannot return to her arms? Her hopes would be raised for nothing. Now, my men are waiting to take the tent down. Put the *yashmak* on and come outside."

"The sun is warm," Heather said. "I will suffer from the heat. Is there nothing lightweight I can wear?"

"You cannot travel without the *yashmak*," Khalid ordered. "I forbid it."

"You refuse to allow it?" Heather echoed. Why, of all the arrogant pigheadedness!

Khalid knew arguing with her was useless. His wife's stubbornness required action, not persuasion.

Khalid grabbed the *yashmak* and dressed her in it, though she refrained from struggling. When the veil covered her face, he threatened, "Remove it, and I will throw you across my knee and spank you."

Behind the veil, Heather muttered something unintelligible.

"What did you say?" he asked.

Heather lifted the veil. "I said, this sucks the hind teat." She let the veil drop into place.

Khalid grasped her arm and escorted her outside. He suffered the dreadful feeling that his willful bride required constant supervision, and Omar was useless as a guard.

The prince's men had the tent emptied and down in a few short minutes, and the courtyard looked as if they had never been there. With that completed, Khalid led Heather through the caravansary to their waiting horses. The place was deserted, the Kasabians having begun their journey earlier.

"My mare?" Heather asked, looking around.

"Abdul will care for the mare," Khalid said. "You, my princess, will ride with me."

"You don't trust me?" Heather smiled impishly behind the veil, a smile that lit her eyes and made them sparkle like emeralds.

"Your recent behavior does not encourage trust," Khalid said.

"Between husband and wife should dwell trust," Heather said. "You must work harder on that, my lord."

"And you, Princess?"

"I trust you."

Khalid said nothing. Instead, he lifted her onto the saddle and mounted behind her. They rode in silence for two hours. Sitting so close their bodies touched, each was alone with troubled thoughts.

Khalid dreaded introducing to each other his recalcitrant wife and his disdainful mother who had been born in a foul mood. If they ever joined forces, he would be marked for certain death. No chance of that happening, though. They would probably kill each other off with their tongues . . .

My husband fears the English will take me, Heather thought. He cares too much for me to risk being parted. With luck, I should be able to convince him that the queen would welcome our union. Trade between our two countries could begin. That would satisfy my countrymen.

Gradually, Heather relaxed and let go of her anger. When she leaned against his chest, Khalid knew her sulking was finished. Perhaps he'd won this battle between them.

"Tell me about your family," Heather said.

Pleased with her interest, Khalid dropped a kiss on the top of her head. "About three hundred years ago," he began.

Heather giggled. "Khalid, I am unable to follow three hundred years of who begat whom. Start with your immediate family, and I can learn the rest a little at a time."

"I like the sound of my name on your tongue," he said, smiling down at the top of her head.

"Good. Then, you'll never be tempted to cut it out," she said.

Khalid began his tale again. "My father, now deceased, was Rustem Pasha, one of my grandfather's grand viziers. Mihrimah, my mother, is the daughter of

Suleiman, the greatest of all sultans, and his beloved Khurrem. My sister Birtryce and my brother Karim are dead. I have one younger sister Tynna. Sultan Selim is my mother's brother, and my cousin Murad is his heir.''

''That only tells me their names and relationships to you,'' Heather said. ''Tell me more.''

Khalid's voice dropped so that none but she could hear him. ''Sultan Selim devotes himself to wine, though the Koran forbids the consumption of alcohol. Murad loves women and gold. My sister is the sweetest of the sweet, quite the opposite of my mother. Mihrimah is a conniving bitch who would have made a great sultan had she been born a man.''

''It appears that every family has its flaws,'' Heather said. ''How did you become friends with Malik?''

''The Shark's Spawn or the Desert Fox?''

Heather giggled. ''The Shark's Spawn.''

''Malik is the grandson of the renowned Khair ed-din, Barbarossa to your Europeans,'' Khalid told her. ''Malik attended the prince's school with Murad, Karim, and me.''

''Where did you get your blue eyes?''

''I inherited my blue eyes from my great-grandmother whom my great-grandfather stole from her family while conducting one of his campaigns.''

''Abducting and enslaving young innocents appears to be a family tradition,'' Heather remarked.

Heedless of his watching men, Khalid nuzzled her neck and whispered against her ear, ''We abduct only the finest.''

''Would it be possible for the priest who married us to visit Maiden's Castle and celebrate the mass for me?'' Heather asked.

''I am a Moslem,'' Khalid answered.

"You needn't attend."

Khalid knew the time had arrived to reveal the whole truth. "The *imam* married us."

"*Imam?*" Heather echoed. "Is that your word for priest?"

"In a manner of speaking," Khalid answered. "The *imam* is a Moslem clergyman."

Several seconds passed before Heather realized what he meant. "A Moslem priest married us?"

"Correct."

"That can't be," Heather cried, her voice rising in direct proportion to her agitation. "I need a real priest."

"The *imam* is a real holy man," Khalid said, his voice stern. "Lower your voice when you speak to me."

"I will not lower my—"

With one hand, Khalid reached around and covered her mouth. Heather tried to speak but merely got a mouthful of black veil. Khalid held his hand up and signaled the others to stop for a rest. He dismounted, pulled his wife off the stallion, and practically dragged her a fair distance away where they could argue privately.

"Whatever happens, you must behave like a proper Turkish lady," Khalid warned, towering over her.

"I am English," Heather said, undaunted by his menacing stance.

"I am a Moslem and needed to be married by the *imam*," Khalid tried to explain.

"As a Christian, I cannot accept this heathen union," Heather replied.

"Heather . . ." His voice held a warning note.

"You stole my virginity," she accused, pointing a finger at him. "You—"

"I stole nothing," he said. "You willingly spread your legs for me."

"Oh, Lord! I am a fallen woman," Heather wailed. "Who will marry me now?"

"Women in my country are allowed only one husband," Khalid said. "I am yours."

"I cannot accept this marriage without benefit of a priest," Heather told him. "Find a priest and repeat your vows in front of him."

"No. I am the sultan's nephew and would create a scandal if I participated in a Christian ceremony," Khalid said.

"I demand my release." Heather stamped her foot for emphasis. "Send me home to England."

"Your home is with me," Khalid said. "If you try to escape again, I will kill you."

Heather looked him straight in the eye and said, "Then, I die a martyr to my faith."

Khalid laughed in her face. His wife certainly had a flair for the dramatic. He unfastened her veil, saying, "Allah protects children and fools."

"Are you implying that I'm a fool?" Heather asked, ready for battle.

"You proved your womanhood last night, Princess. You are definitely no child." Khalid yanked Heather into his embrace and kissed her into a daze. Then, he covered her face and led her back to the horses.

They continued their journey. Heather fumed in silence but was uncertain of what upset her most. Was it the infidel's pigheadedness or her easy surrender to his kiss? The religious teachings of a lifetime kept whispering that she needed a priest's blessing or suffer a hideous punishment in the hereafter. On the other hand, she did love him, and he believed they were well and truly married. It seemed to Heather that a virgin's life had been so much simpler.

Afternoon aged into tall shadows cast by the sun moving across the western sky. The long, tedious hours in the saddle wearied Heather and eased the urgency of her anger.

Since Khalid had cared enough to marry her in the first place, Heather told herself, he would ultimately agree to participate in a Christian ceremony. The prince needed time to accustom himself to the prospect of speaking vows in front of a priest.

Heather cared little if the ceremony was performed at midnight with no witnesses. As long as she felt well and truly married, she could be content.

As Heather saw it, there was only problem. How best to change his mind? The use of logic? No, the prince was undoubtedly an illogical man. Why else would a man marry an unwilling woman? That left her own behavior. Would he be swayed by vinegar or sugar on her tongue? Sugar, most definitely. Although, she wasn't certain even that would work. The prince was so damn inflexible.

Unable to decide upon the most propitious course of action, Heather grew tired of thinking and riding. She sighed deeply and relaxed against her husband's chest.

Khalid decided that the woman in his arms needed time to accustom herself to the position of obedient wife. Given time, she would adjust and settle in. As wild and free as the wind, Heather was different from any woman he'd ever known, but it was imperative that she obey. How best to ease the difficult transition from her former spoiled life to the obedient new without breaking her spirit? He refused to waste his life in argument. His wife was as sexy as Eve in paradise, and he intended to enjoy her. Thoroughly.

Why, Heather had begun to change already. No longer did she fight him at every turn. *Every other turn,* Khalid thought wryly. She'd even managed to learn his language, though she did speak with a heavy accent.

Apparently, his flexibility in dealing with her had helped matters along, Khalid decided.

Rumor had already spread throughout Istanbul that the Sultan's Beast had mated with a wild, flame-haired pagan from the far West. As the prince's entourage wended its way through the city's bustling streets, the general populace stared openly at them. Most directed their attention on the black-clad woman.

Oblivious to the speculative furor she was creating, Heather sat cuddled against her husband's chest. She appeared more like a helpless kitten than the cunning tigress who, rumor had it, disguised herself as a boy and escaped the Sultan's Beast.

Khalid nudged her gently. "Princess, we have arrived."

Heather sat up straight and looked around. Khalid dismounted and then lifted her off his stallion. One of his men rushed forward and led the stallion away. As Abdul walked past leading the mare, Heather stopped him.

"Thank you for our adventure, Foolish Pleasure," Heather whispered, stroking the mare's neck. She turned to Khalid, asking, "May I visit her?"

"Yes, with a proper escort."

"Ahem," sounded a voice near them.

Khalid and Heather turned around. Omar stood there. The sight of his two blackened eyes and bandaged nose shocked Heather.

"I am sorry," Heather apologized, taking the little man's hand in hers. "I never meant to harm you."

Omar nodded, silently accepting her apology, then turned to Khalid and said, "Greetings, my prince. Mihrimah awaits you in her salon and begs both of you to see her before you retire to your chamber."

"My mother never begged in her life, little man," Khalid said, cocking a dark brow at the eunuch. "Those who fabricate the truth lose their tongues."

His wife's giggle drew his attention. "What do you find so amusing?" he asked.

Her eyes sparkled with laughter. "You."

Khalid pulled her close, lowered her veil, and planted a kiss on her lips. Then he fastened the veil and admonished, "Laughing at your husband's expense is strictly forbidden in this land."

"Remember the punishment for fabricating the truth, my lord," she warned. "Husbands without tongues cannot order their wives about."

"You would like that, would you not?"

Seeing their playfulness, Omar filled with hope. Somehow, the beast had tamed his mate. Perhaps, his fortune was again guaranteed. Allah be praised!

Followed by the eunuch, Khalid escorted Heather inside. He dreaded introducing his mother and his wife, but knew that the time had arrived. Delay was impossible.

"Interrupt us in thirty minutes," Khalid instructed Omar when they stood outside his mother's salon. "Your mistress requires a bath and a light supper in our chamber."

Khalid knocked on the salon door and then walked in. Beside him, Heather stared at her husband's mother.

Like a queen granting an audience, Mihrimah sat on a pillow beside a table and waited for them to approach. She looked intimidating, to say the least.

An attractive woman in her mid-forties, Mihrimah exuded an air of arrogance. Her hair was light brown shot throughout with threads of silver and her eyes were hazel. The rest of her features were those of her son.

So this is the unnatural woman who spoke with such

contempt of her only son, Heather thought. A protective streak arose in Heather, along with dangerously hostile feelings toward the older woman.

Khalid and Heather sat down across the table from Mihrimah. "Mother, I present my wife," Khalid began to introduce them.

"Does she speak our language?" Mihrimah asked her son.

"She does," Heather answered.

"Heather, I present Mihrimah," Khalid finished the introduction.

Without a smile of greeting or a cordial word, Mihrimah reached across the table and tried to pull the veil from her daughter-in-law's face. However, Heather was faster. She grabbed and stayed her mother-in-law's offending hand.

"You may not touch me without my husband's permission," Heather said in a soft voice.

Surprised, Mihrimah dropped her hand. Being thwarted for the first time in her forty-odd years left the woman speechless.

How like her foolish son to choose an unsuitable bride, Mihrimah thought. Didn't the little barbarian know how important she was? As the sultan's sister, Mihrimah had great power. One word from her, and the little barbarian's life would be less than worthless. She possessed the power to make this disrespectful upstart wish for death.

Khalid wondered why he had worried about these two joining forces against him. His wife—*Allah bless her!*—had too much spirit to submit to his mother's will.

In spite of her differences with her husband, Heather assumed the role of loving wife in front of his despicable mother. After all, someone needed to take his side in this unnatural family. If not his own wife, then who?

"Forgive my rudeness," Mihrimah said, recovering her composure. "Naturally, I am anxious to meet my new daughter."

"My mother lives in England," Heather said in a sweet voice. She turned to Khalid, asking, "Husband, may I remove my veil?"

Surprised by her display of meekness toward him, Khalid wondered what game his wife was playing and decided to play along with her. Indeed, the rare sight of his mother rendered speechless was worth it.

"Allow me, my wildflower," Khalid said, unfastening her veil.

Mihrimah stared hard at Heather who boldly returned the stare. In those first seconds, each tried to gauge the other.

"How lovely you are, my dear," Mihrimah said smoothly. "I see why my son married you."

Heather smiled politely. She willed herself to blush and succeeded.

Mihrimah realized that flattery would be useless. Apparently, the girl was as intelligent as she was beautiful. Mihrimah lifted a tiny bell from the table and rang it.

A serving girl entered so quickly that Heather wondered if she'd been listening outside the door. The girl set a tray on the table and left at a gesture from Mihrimah.

On the tray were gazelle horns, a curved pastry made from flour, ground nuts, and honey. Tiny cups filled with Turkish coffee accompanied the pastry.

Heather raised the cup to her lips and swallowed a gulp of coffee. Her eyes widened in surprise at the brew's bitterness. She choked on the foul taste and wished she could rinse her mouth.

Khalid slapped her back lightly. "One must acquire a taste for this particular poison," he said.

"P-poison?" she croaked.

"Merely a phrase, my love."

"Oh." Heather gifted him with one of her most dazzling smiles.

The beast has lost his growl, Mihrimah thought in surprise, watching this interesting byplay. Could that be budding love shining from her daughter-in-law's eyes? No, that was impossible. Wasn't it? No sane woman could love her son, scarred beast that he was.

That was it. The woman from the West was insane. Most young ladies had the sense to cower before the powerful daughter of Suleiman and Khurrem, but this one cowered before no one.

Realizing she had badly miscalculated, Mihrimah chided herself. She'd thought to use the girl's disdain for her son and set her up as a spy in his household, but this slip of a girl had a mind of her own. Any woman with the courage to dress as a man and travel the road on her own would be impossible to control.

Khalid and Heather appeared to be a loving couple. Were they as loving as this behind closed doors? Or was this display of unity for her benefit? Perhaps there was a chance to wedge them apart.

"I am surprised you have tamed her so quickly," Mihrimah said to her son.

"I am no animal to be tamed," Heather said, her anger rising. "Nor am I a deaf slave to be discussed in my own presence."

"Assuming that rude tone of voice is disrespectful," Mihrimah said.

"Forgive me, but you have been misinformed," Heather said. "My husband and I are in perfect accord, have been in perfect accord since our first meeting, and always will be in perfect accord."

Khalid stared at his wife. It seemed his wife had forgotten the punishment for fabricating the truth.

"Then, why did you escape?" Mihrimah asked.

"A minor misunderstanding," Heather snapped, losing patience with the probing questions. She was tired, and the stress of this interview made her head ache.

Mihrimah gasped. No one had ever spoken so disrespectfully to her.

Smiling inwardly, Khalid kept his face expressionless. He knew he should correct his wife's manners but remained silent anyway. Never had he seen anyone, man or woman, get the better of his mother.

"It appears you have chosen poorly, my son," Mihrimah said, casting a sidelong glance at the viper sitting next to him. "Divorce her at once. I will call for witnesses."

"No," Khalid refused, his expression darkening at her odious suggestion.

Mihrimah tried a different approach. "She traveled the road alone for two days. At least, have the physician verify her virginity."

It was Heather's turn to gasp. Her face mottled with barely suppressed rage, and she had a difficult time controlling the powerful urge to leap across the table and throttle the woman.

Khalid put his arm around his wife's shoulder and drew her close, feeling her trembling anger. "My bride was a virgin," he said.

"Visiting Topkapi is out of the question until she learns manners," Mihrimah went on, determined to create discord between them. "Would you like me to train her to be a proper wife?"

"Where is Tynna?" Khalid asked, changing the subject to avoid an all-out brawl.

"Visiting your cousin Shasha," Mihrimah answered. "Praise be to Allah, I sent her to Topkapi for the night. This one's manners will be a bad influence on your impressionable sister. By the way, have you discovered the weasel's whereabouts?''

Heather gazed at Khalid who cast his mother an admonishing look, warning her off that subject. In the end, it was Malik who saved the prince from answering.

The door burst open, and Malik swaggered in. ''What a touching scene,'' he said, noting their dark expressions, and then plopped down on a pillow. ''Such an intimate family gathering warms my heart.''

Heather reached for her veil, but Khalid stopped her. ''Malik is family to us,'' he said. ''You may leave your face uncovered in front of him.''

Malik smiled and nodded at Heather.

''How is my cousin?'' Heather asked.

''April is well and nags me constantly to bring her to Istanbul for a visit,'' Malik told her. To Khalid, he said, ''You owe me twenty-five thousand gold pieces.''

''For what?''

''I paid Akbar the monies due him.''

''Twenty-five thousand gold pieces?'' Khalid exclaimed.

Malik grinned and shrugged his shoulders. ''Determined to pauper you, Murad purchased ten virgins of the highest quality. You did bid him choose whatever he wanted.'' He turned to Heather, adding, ''You cost your husband a small fortune.''

Confused by their conversation, Heather looked at her husband. ''What does he mean?''

''I will explain everything later,'' Khalid said.

''A waste of gold, if you ask me,'' Mihrimah grumbled.

''Nobody asked you,'' Heather muttered in English.

Malik struggled against a smile. It appeared this loving family was now complete.

"What did you say?" Khalid asked, thinking he'd better correct her deplorable manners now.

Heather looked at him and smiled as winsomely as she could. "I said, I feel so tired."

"She lies," Mihrimah accused, though she was ignorant of English.

Someone knocked lightly on the door. "Enter," Khalid called.

Omar walked in. "As instructed, I have come to escort my lady to the baths."

"Go with Omar," Khalid said to Heather. "I will sup with you later."

As soon as the door closed behind Heather, Mihrimah said, "That one is bad tempered and rude. A fitting mate for a beast though."

"She appears to possess some of your finer qualities," Malik teased her.

In spite of her foul mood, Mihrimah smiled and then looked at her son. "When are you taking her to Maiden's Castle?" she asked. "Soon, I hope."

"Soon is a relative thing, Mother," Khalid replied, then turned to Malik. "It is time for Fougere to die."

"Past time, if you ask me," Mihrimah said.

"Nobody asked, you," Khalid snapped, irritated by her insulting attitude.

Malik swallowed his laughter. Allah, the husband sounded a lot like the wife.

"You do not even know where the weasel is hiding," Mihrimah said.

"We will visit the Duc de Sassari in the morning," Khalid said to his friend. "His ship still lies in the harbor?"

Malik nodded.

Khalid turned to his mother. "You must protect my wife until Fougere is dead."

"Shelter that viper?" Mihrimah cried.

"Guard my wife, or I will take her to Maiden's Castle and postpone our revenge on Fougere," Khalid said. When had his wife become more important than his revenge?

"I suppose I can tolerate her for a few days," Mihrimah acquiesced.

As the three in the salon discussed several wonderfully gruesome methods of dispatching Savon Fougere, Heather followed Omar through a maze of corridors to the baths. Mihrimah's house was quite modern, unlike the ancient stronghold of Maiden's Castle. Even the corridors were considerably bright and airy because of the mullioned windows that opened on an inside courtyard.

Heather stared hard at the eunuch's back, but he refused to meet her gaze. The little man acted uncharacteristically formal and coolly polite. Apparently, his feelings had been hurt, and that made Heather feel even guiltier about causing his injuries.

When they entered the baths, two young women rushed forward to serve them. Omar remembered his mistress's reluctance to bathe in front of an audience and stopped them.

"Leave," he ordered, gesturing them away. "I will attend the princess."

"You already wear the marks of her displeasure," one of the women teased him, making her friend giggle. "Let us protect you."

Omar crimsoned at the insult. But what could he say? The whole household knew he was incompetent.

"You will not speak to the prince's most valued and trusted servant in that rude manner," Heather said in an arrogant voice, coming to the eunuch's defense.

Both women paled. "I am sorry," the first one said, bowing her head.

"You will be even sorrier if you make the same mistake again," Heather added, "for I will have your tongue cut out. Do you understand?"

"Y-yes, Princess."

"Apologize to Omar at once."

Both bathing attendants bowed formally to the eunuch.

"Forgive us, Omar," the first one offered.

"We meant no disrespect," the second added.

Omar puffed his chest out with self-importance. "Apology accepted, slave. Run along and refrain from further silliness."

"Thank you for defending me," Omar said as he applied the almond paste that would remove her body hair.

"You're very welcome," Heather said. "Though I do believe it was the least I could do. I am sorry for causing trouble."

Omar nodded and gave her a little smile, the first one he'd given her since she'd arrived at Mihrimah's. Working without talking, the eunuch wiped the paste off, paused a moment to inspect her, and led her to the small tub. First, Omar washed and rinsed her mane of copper and then her body. Afterward he escorted her to the in-ground pool where she would soak in the heated water.

"My lady, I would tell you what to expect tonight," Omar said, taking pity on her innocence.

"Tonight?" Heather echoed, puzzled.

"Your wedding night."

"That was last night."

Omar decided the prince's lovemaking had gentled her disposition, but an upsetting thought popped into the eunuch's mind.

"May I ask who prepared you to receive the prince?" Omar said, helping her out of the pool and across the chamber to a marble bench.

"The prince played the eunuch. At least, for a few minutes."

Omar chuckled. Relief that he had no rival for his job fully restored his good humor.

"Does it hurt?" Heather asked abruptly.

"A little, especially when I sneeze."

"Injuring you was never my intent," she apologized.

"Lie back on the bench, and I will massage you with the aloe lotion," Omar said.

Heather lay down on her stomach. Omar warmed the aloe in his hands and began kneading the stress from the muscles in her upper back and shoulders.

"You feel tense," he said.

"That's Mihrimah's fault," she replied. His strong hands felt good to her.

"A nasty woman if I ever met one," Omar remarked.

"Nastier than I am?"

"Nastiness is no flaw of yours," he told her. "You were merely unaccustomed to our culture."

"Perhaps," Heather murmured. Then she asked, "Malik said I cost Khalid a fortune. What does he mean?"

"The prince paid a fortune to keep you, and what a sight it was to behold," Omar gushed. "The invited guests at the auction were bidding extravagantly for your beauty. With each higher bid, the prince's expression darkened and became more frightening. As you swooned, Prince Khalid leaped onto the dais, covered you with the *yashmak,* and scooped you into his arms. Then he faced those assembled men and announced that the sale was off. They grumbled about their loss, but he invited each one of them to choose another woman. At the prince's own expense, of course. Prince Khalid carried you here and saw to your comfort, then went to the *imam*'s and made you his princess that very night. What do you think of that?"

"Why did he bother to marry me?" Heather asked. "He'd already made me his slave."

"The prince adores you," Omar said.

"That is too fantastic for belief," Heather scoffed. "I need your advice on a matter."

"Advising you is one of my duties," Omar told her.

"What is the best way to manage the prince? Vinegar or sugar on my tongue?"

"Sugar on your tongue," the eunuch answered without hesitation. His duties also included keeping domestic peace in the prince's household. "Turn, please."

Heather rolled over and lay on her back. Omar warmed more of the aloe lotion in his hands and began massaging her thighs, belly, and breasts. Apparently, his mistress had adjusted to her new life, though she was probably unaware of it. A month earlier, her European modesty would have prevented him from massaging her so intimately.

"Do you know any Catholic priests?" Heather asked.

"Priests?" Omar echoed. "No, why?"

"Never mind," Heather said. "Tell me why women must be veiled."

"An unveiled woman is unseemly," Omar informed her, repeating her husband's words. "The sight of a woman's face tempts a man to covet another's property."

"What property?"

"The wife is the man's property," Omar told her. "You belong to the prince. Without his permission, no man may gaze upon your face. Your beauty is meant for the prince's pleasure."

"What about the prince's beauty belonging to me?" Heather asked.

"You believe the prince is beautiful?" Omar asked, surprised.

Heather opened her eyes and stared at him. "Don't you?"

"In spite of his scar, Prince Khalid is quite handsome," he allowed.

"His scar is beautiful and gives him character," Heather said.

Omar grinned, pleased that she cared for the prince. Soon his mistress would have the royal seed planted in her belly; then his own fortune would be guaranteed.

Omar helped her stand and then dressed her in a fresh caftan. Instead of returning her to Mihrimah's salon, the eunuch escorted her to her husband's chamber.

Warding off autumn's evening chill, the bronze brazier had already been lit, and several candles placed in various sections of the chamber cast dancing shadows on the walls.

On the table sat dishes with olives, nuts, goat cheese, flatbread, and a decanter of rosewater. The sight of the food made Heather hungry. Except for the pastry, she hadn't eaten since breakfast.

"This measly offering is our supper?" she asked.

"I will bring the hot food when the prince arrives," Omar told her.

"Do you like egg whites?" she asked, gifting him with a mischievous smile.

"Egg whites?" Her question puzzled him.

"Yes, do you eat them?" she repeated.

Before Omar could reply, the door swung open. Fresh from the baths, the prince walked in, and Omar left to fetch their supper.

"Let us walk in the garden until supper arrives," Khalid suggested.

Heather accepted his offered hand and rose from the pillows. Hand in hand, they stepped outside into the torch-lit garden and started down one of the paths. The evening air chilled Heather, making her shiver. As they walked, Khalid put his arm around her, pulled her against the side of his body, and shared his heat.

Heather inhaled deeply of the perfumed air, saying, "The flowers' scents mingle together beautifully."

"Like we do," he said.

Heather blushed at his words.

"I will give you a tour of my garden when we return to Maiden's Castle," Khalid said. "My garden is even more beautiful than this because I am its gardener."

"Modest, aren't you?" Heather teased.

Khalid shrugged, then stopped walking and pointed at a purple and gold star-shaped flower. "This aster keeps evil spirits away, or so the ancient Greeks believed."

"What is this?" Heather asked, pointing at a nodding violet blossom.

"Venus looking glass," Khalid answered. "Legend says that Venus owned a magical mirror that reflected beauty to whoever looked at it. One day she misplaced her mirror. A poor shepherd boy found the mirror but refused to return it. When Cupid tried to retrieve it, the mirror shattered. Wherever a piece of the magical glass landed, this flower grew."

"How lovely," Heather said, enchanted by the story and the man.

Khalid pointed at another flower. "This deep blue blossom is Cupid's dart or compulsion and is used in love potions."

Heather smiled at that.

They started back down the path toward their chamber. Standing on the terrace near the door, Khalid and Heather paused to admire the sight and scent of the exotic night.

"What makes your mother so nasty?" Heather asked.

Khalid smiled. "From where does this question come?"

"I am merely curious."

"In spite of her opulent life, my mother is an unhappy woman," Khalid said. "More cunning and ambitious than Selim, Mihrimah would have been sultan had she been born a man. Instead, she has lived a frustrated life behind the veil."

"Would you see the same thing happen to me?" Heather asked.

"You, little one, are as different from my mother as day is from night," Khalid said. "Her unquenchable thirst for power is noticeably absent in you. Mihrimah has a man's spirit trapped inside a woman's body, and where I am concerned, suffers from a lack of maternal instinct. Besides that, death has already claimed her husband, son, and daughter."

"How did your father die?" Heather asked.

"Executed by the sultan's order."

That shocked Heather. "Your uncle ordered his own brother-in-law's death?"

"No, my grandfather ordered his son-in-law's death."

"Oh, my."

"This startles you?" Khalid asked. "Are there no such political maneuverings in your England?"

"During my lifetime, no."

"At seventeen years, you are still a babe," Khalid said. "Even worse than the death of my father, my brother and sister lie in early graves because of Fougere."

"Are you really going to kill him?"

Khalid turned her in his arms to face him. "Does that bother you?"

"If Fougere is guilty, he deserves to die," Heather said.

Khalid felt relieved by her answer, not that it really mattered what she thought. "You approve of revenge?"

"I would avenge my own father's death if I could," she admitted.

Khalid did not want her thinking about her father's death. Those thoughts led to troubled sleep. "Why were you hostile to my mother?" he asked.

"She was hostile to me," Heather said.

"No, Wildflower. You set yourself against her from the first moment you saw her," Khalid said. "I would like to know what is in your heart."

"I—I don't want to hurt your feelings," she replied.

Khalid pulled her close and planted a kiss on her forehead. With their bodies pressed together, he stared at her beautiful upturned face. A man could drown in those fathomless pools of green that were her eyes. "You care for my feelings?" he asked in a husky voice.

"I just said so."

"Where my mother is concerned, my feelings will remain uninjured," he said. "I promise."

"That night I escaped, I came through the garden door," Heather told him. "Hearing voices, I hid behind the shrubs over there. As she passed by, your mother made disparaging comments about you."

"Such as?"

"Never mind about that. Every child needs a mother to love him unconditionally. I cannot respect a woman who does not speak well of her own son."

Touched by her concern, Khalid lowered his mouth to hers. His lips claimed hers in a lingering kiss that melted into another. And then another . . .

Carrying their supper tray, Omar returned but found the chamber empty. He set the tray on the table and crossed to the door, intending to call them inside to eat.

What Omar saw filled his heart with joy. The prince and his lady were locked in a passionate embrace.

Omar grinned from ear to ear and backed away noiselessly. He glanced at the tray on the table but decided to leave it. A satisfied man was a hungry man. That the food was cold mattered little.

Thank you, Allah! Omar sent up the silent prayer as he left the chamber.

Chapter 14

The sun was high in a cloudless sky on that Wednesday, a business day for Moslems, Christians, and Jews. Istanbul, city of many faces, had been awake for hours. Restless crowds filled the twisting cobbled streets; cries of vendors, selling everything from vegetables to yogurt to drinking water, rose above the din.

Khalid and Malik rode in companionable silence as they picked their way carefully through the crowded streets toward Beyoglu, the base for European merchants. Behind them rode Abdul, Rashid, and a contingent of ten warriors in the prince's service.

Men, women, and children gawked at the prince's entourage as it passed by. Seeing the beast who'd ordered the slaughter of hundreds of innocents, most adults made a sign to ward off evil. Christians crossed themselves; Jews turned their heads and sent up a silent prayer to Yahweh; Moslems fingered their *masallahs*, necklaces of blue beads that warded off the evil eye. Mothers, regardless of religious persuasion, whispered dire warnings to their wayward children and pointed at the Sultan's Beast.

"You are creating your usual stir among Istanbul's populace," Malik remarked.

Khalid shrugged his shoulders and stared straight ahead.

"Scowl less, and the people will not fear you," Malik suggested.

"Fear can be a useful thing," Khalid said, glancing sidelong at his friend. "They hear the legend, see the scar, and fear the beast."

"Your wildflower never feared the beast."

Khalid said nothing, but his expression darkened even more.

"Do I detect trouble in paradise?" Malik asked. "Have you passed a sleepless night listening to your mother and wife fight?"

"Be quiet," Khalid growled.

"You do seem tired and cranky."

"If you must know, my wife has been nagging me," Khalid said in a long-suffering voice.

Malik chuckled. "The Sultan's Beast, the most feared man in the empire, hounded to distraction by that slip of a girl?"

"She insists I repeat my marriage vows in front of a Christian priest," Khalid complained. "Last night, she found fulfillment in my bed but wept afterward. She says she cannot feel properly married without benefit of a priest, and our bedsport makes her a whore."

"That problem is easily solved," Malik said. "Send for a priest and have done with it."

"The sultan's nephew participating in a Christian ritual? That would cause a scandal."

"No one needs to know," Malik said. "It can be done in secrecy."

"*I* would know," Khalid replied. "Besides, that would not give me a peaceful night's sleep. My wife's nightmares about her father's murder awakened me in the middle of the night."

"Perhaps a visit from April would help."

"I doubt it. Seeing the cousin would only remind her of England."

Malik nodded. "Then, pass the night in another chamber."

"Who would soothe her fears when she cries out in the night? Omar? That one is useless for anything beyond massages."

Malik smiled. Apparently, the prince had been stuck by Cupid's dart.

"I never realized that marriage was so irritating," Khalid said. "My wife refuses to eat the white of an egg but does adore the yolk. This morning I had to eat her discarded egg whites."

Malik laughed.

"If she wastes Allah's bounty again, she will be sorry," Khalid added.

"I guess what they say about midwives is true," Malik remarked.

"What is that?"

"Midwives slap a newborn's ass to knock the balls off the stupid ones," Malik said with a straight face.

Khalid bit his bottom lip to keep from laughing. It wouldn't do for Istanbul's populace to see the Sultan's Beast laugh. That would ruin his fearsome image.

"Here we are," Malik said.

Several sailors and a longboat from Malik's ship awaited them. Khalid, Malik, Abdul, and Rashid climbed into the longboat, and the sailors began rowing in the direction of the Duc de Sassari's ship. The prince's contingent of warriors remained with their horses on shore.

Malik stood up in the longboat when they reached the duc's ship and called, "Prince Khalid requests permission to come aboard."

Five minutes passed. Finally, the ship's captain appeared and ordered his men to lower the rope ladder. Then, he gestured him up.

Khalid, Malik, Abdul, and Rashid climbed the ladder to the deck. The rest of the sailors stayed in the longboat.

"I am Captain Molinari," the man introduced himself. "Please, follow me."

Khalid, Malik, and Abdul went below with the captain. At the prince's instruction, Rashid remained on deck.

Captain Molinari knocked on the duc's door and then opened it. Khalid and Malik entered the cabin, but Abdul and the captain stayed outside.

Seated at a table and drinking wine with Count Orcioni, the Duc de Sassari stood up when they walked in. "Prince Khalid, this is a pleasant surprise," the duc greeted him, an insincere smile pasted on his face.

Khalid returned the duc's smile, equally insincerely. "Pleasant?"

"Seeing you is always a pleasure." The duc fingered his black mustache nervously. "Please, be seated."

"I prefer to stand."

"A glass of wine, perhaps."

"My religion forbids the consumption of alcohol," Khalid said.

"Of course, I forgot," the duc replied. "May I present Count Orcioni, a distant cousin of mine from Pantelleria."

Khalid nodded stonily at the count, the man who would have made his sweet wildflower an uncherished whore. "You are already acquainted with my friend, Malik ed-din."

"Who has not heard the rousing tales of the Shark's Spawn?" the duc replied.

Malik nodded in acknowledgment, then turned his attention on the count. "So, how goes the pandering business, Orcioni?"

Count Orcioni choked on his wine.

"No offense intended," Malik said.

"None taken," the count replied.

"Why have you lingered in Istanbul?" Khalid asked the Duc de Sassari.

"You rowed out here to ask me that?"

"Could your lingering have anything to do with Fougere?" Khalid asked. "He is somewhere in Istanbul."

"Savon in Istanbul?" The Duc de Sassari laughed. "With all due respect, Prince Khalid, you are mistaken. Savon is too much a coward to journey to Istanbul."

"Fougere is a coward, but he is hiding somewhere near," Khalid said. "That much I learned from the assassin."

The Duc de Sassari fixed a suitably shocked expression on his face. "My cousin hired an assassin to attack you?"

"You had no knowledge of that?" Khalid asked, arching a dark brow at the other man.

"I can assure—"

"You are lying," Malik blurted out.

"I swear I am ignorant of this crime and relieved you survived such a dastardly attack," the duc said to Khalid. "Seeking an audience with Lyndar has kept me in Istanbul. Though she is my halfsister, I need the sultan's permission for such a visit."

"In that case, allow me to expedite matters for you," Khalid offered.

"I would be most appreciative."

"Consider it done." Khalid smiled, but his blue eyes remained cold. "If Fougere does contact you, tell him I have married his betrothed."

"I doubt Savon will—"

"And tell Fougere that he is a walking dead man," Khalid added.

"What will your wife say when you arrive home with a beautiful slave from Akbar's?" Malik asked the duc.

Count Orcioni entered the conversation, saying, "Actually, the duc generously gave me his pick. I chose a set of young blond Circassian twins who are identical in every way except for a tiny beauty mark one carries above her upper lip. I thought my patrons would appreciate their novelty."

"I refuse to spend my gold on a gift for a friend of Fougere's," Khalid said, turning his stony gaze upon the whore-master of Pantelleria. "I demand the immediate return of those women."

"It's too late," Orcioni protested.

"I paid for them," Khalid reminded the other man.

"The women are of no importance," the duc said to the prince.

"My uncle is the sultan," Khalid warned. "At any moment, he could impound your ship, and unraveling any misunderstanding between us could take a very long time."

"Molinari!" the duc shouted. When the captain answered his call, he ordered, "Bring those slave girls here."

Several long minutes passed in silence. The captain returned with the two veiled slave girls.

"The ladies will not be staying," Khalid said to Abdul. "Escort them above deck and guard them." He looked at the duc, saying, "You will visit your sister within the week. Be ready for the summons."

"My thanks, Prince Khalid," the duc replied.

"Do not forget to tell Fougere that he is a dead man," Khalid said, then left the cabin with Malik.

Without a word, the Duc de Sassari stared out the porthole. First, he saw two giant warriors carry the women down the ropes and hand them into the longboat.

Next came Khalid and Malik. The sailors shoved away from the ship and began rowing toward shore.

The Duc de Sassari marched across the cabin and said to his sea chest, "Come out."

The lid opened slowly, and the face of a human weasel appeared. Savon Fougere, the Comte de Beaulieu, climbed out of his hole. "You named me a coward," he whined.

"Shut up, Savon," the duc said.

"But you—"

"Any man who hides in a sea chest is no man at all," Count Orcioni spoke up.

"Mind your own business, flesh peddler," Fougere snapped.

Insulted, Count Orcioni stood up and started toward the other man.

"Gentlemen, please," the duc shouted.

"My apologies," Fougere said, backing away from confrontation. He stared out the porthole and watched the longboat. "I swear I will kill him."

"What caused this vendetta with the prince?" Count Orcioni asked.

"I killed his sister," Fougere answered, staring out the porthole.

"Why in God's name did you—?"

"Several years ago, Savon ordered his fleet to attack a lone ship of theirs," the duc explained. "He thought to steal whatever valuables it carried. Unfortunately, the ship sank during the ensuing battle."

"How was I to know the ship carried an Ottoman princess?" Fougere asked, whirling around. "Afterward, I couldn't very well sail into Istanbul and apologize for my mistake. As long as that beast breathes, I live in constant fear for my safety."

"Forget the prince and the Englishwoman," the duc advised. "Go home to Beaulieu."

"When the time is ripe," Fougere vowed, "I will use the bitch to lure that scarred beast to his death."

When the longboat reached shore, Abdul and Rashid jumped out first and helped the two women. At the prince's order, each took a girl on the horse in front of him.

"Will you make them servants in your mother's household?" Malik asked.

"These two appear much too fine for that," Khalid said.

"Starting your own harem?" Malik asked.

"My wildflower would never accept that."

"Then will you return them to Akbar's?"

Khalid gave his friend an inscrutable smile. "Follow my lead, and you will see."

Khalid led them back through Istanbul's crowded streets in the direction of his mother's house. As they neared the *imam*'s residence, he gestured for them to halt and then dismounted.

"Bring the women here," Khalid ordered. When they stood before him, he lowered their veils. The two girls appeared to be about seventeen, give or take a year.

"What are your names?" Khalid asked.

"I am Cyra," the one with the beauty mark answered, her gaze glued to the ground.

"And I am Lana," her sister said, her gaze also downcast.

"Abdul, escort Lana," Khalid said as he fastened their veils. "Rashid, you accompany Cyra."

Without another word, Khalid headed toward the *imam*'s residence. He banged loudly on the door.

Several moments passed. The door swung open.

"The Sultan's Beast," the *imam*'s manservant cried and stepped back.

Khalid, followed by the others, brushed past the man.

Hearing his manservant's cry, the *imam* rushed into the foyer.

"Prince Khalid, an unexpected pleasure," the clergyman said. "What brings you?" Seeing the two veiled women, the *imam* stared at them for a long moment and then turned back to the prince.

"You wish to marry again?" the *imam* asked, incredulous.

"Once is more than enough." Khalid pointed at Abdul and Rashid, saying, "They do."

"What?" Abdul and Rashid exclaimed simultaneously.

Malik chuckled. The two young women giggled.

"It is past time you took wives, and it is my wish that you marry," Khalid said. "Almost identical, these sisters would languish if separated. This way, whenever Malik travels to Istanbul, the one sister can visit the other."

Khalid looked at the sisters. "You would like that, would you not?"

The two women nodded.

"Do you swear to be obedient wives?"

Again, they nodded.

Khalid turned his gaze on the two warriors. "Tell the *imam* you wish to marry immediately."

"I do," Abdul and Rashid chorused together.

"Wonderful," the *imam* said, clapping his hands together. "Come with me. There is time before prayers to write the documents."

The two warriors followed the *imam,* but Malik held back. "Where will they pass their wedding night?" he asked the prince.

"Mihrimah's?"

Malik shook his head. "I will see them ensconced at my house and then return to my ship. I find I miss my little bird and want to go home to my villa in the morning. Unless you need me in Istanbul?''

''When I discover the weasel's hole, I will send you a message,'' Khalid said. ''You wish to be in on the kill?''

Malik grinned. ''There is nothing I want more.''

In the meantime, Heather had been left under Omar's incompetent supervision. Hoping to avoid her mother-in-law, Heather remained closeted with Omar in her chamber. Mihrimah had the same idea and avoided her daughter-in-law by going out to visit a friend.

By noon, Heather felt her self-imposed confinement. She was restless and bored. What she needed was a long walk in the garden.

Without a word to the eunuch, Heather headed for the garden door. Omar was one step behind her.

Exasperated, Heather whirled around and said, ''With all due respect, will you please leave me alone?''

''Alone?'' Omar echoed.

''I do desire a few moments of privacy.''

''You do not know the way,'' he argued.

''Becoming lost in an enclosed garden is impossible,'' she replied.

Omar hesitated. ''Well . . .''

''I swear I am not considering escape,'' Heather said, realizing the cause for his concern. ''I merely have a need to be alone with my thoughts.''

Omar's expression mirrored his disbelief.

''Please, let me sit alone in the garden,'' Heather pleaded. ''Thirty minutes is all that I ask.''

''Very well,'' Omar agreed reluctantly.

Heather paused. ''Beginning tomorrow morning, you will serve me two egg yolks with my breakfast. Only the yolks.''

''What will I do with the rest of the egg?'' Omar asked.

"Discard the shells and eat the whites."

"As you wish."

Heather smiled at the little man and then stepped outside into a glorious late-autumn day. The sky was blue with nary a single cloud to mar its perfection, and the air was crisply clean.

Heather inhaled deeply of the mingling scents of the myriad flowers and started down one of the paths. She stopped when she saw the star-shaped asters and picked one of the flowers, then tucked it behind an ear. If the blossom really kept evil spirits at bay, then she need not concern herself with meeting her mother-in-law here.

Seeing the Venus looking glass and Cupid's dart, Heather thought of Khalid and their lovemaking of the previous night. The prince held a strange power over her. His kiss made her forget herself and all she held dear. If only she could convince him to repeat his vows in front of a priest!

Continuing down the path, Heather spied a marble bench near a fruit tree. She sat down, and resting her chin in her hands, pondered how to broach the subject of the priest with her husband.

"Hello," a voice sounded near her.

Startled, Heather looked up. Standing there was a girl, perhaps a year or two younger than herself.

Of average height and slender, the girl had brown hair and gold-flecked hazel eyes. Her smile was gentle, and when she spoke, her voice soothed the listener's ear.

"Are you the one?" the young woman asked.

"What one?"

"The woman my brother married."

"Are you Tynna?" Heather asked.

"Yes," she answered.

"Then I'm the one. My name is Heather."

Tynna inclined her head, saying, "I am pleased to make your acquaintance."

"You are?" Heather asked, surprised.

Tynna smiled. "I am *very* pleased to meet you."

Tynna sat down and said, "We despaired of Khalid ever deciding upon a wife. Why are you wearing that flower in your hair?"

"To keep evil spirits away," Heather replied. "Why did you despair of Khalid ever marrying?"

"Mother says his scar frightens people, especially women."

"My husband is a warrior, and his scar is a badge of courage that gives him character," Heather announced. "I will not suffer another word against him."

"I love my brother," Tynna said.

Heather smiled. "In that case, would you like to be friends?"

Tynna returned her smile and said, "Any woman who loves my brother is already a friend."

Love? Heather opened her mouth to correct the other girl's wrong assumption, but Tynna went on.

"Your hair is the color of a fiery sunset, and your face reminds me of a mischievous angel," she said. "You are very beautiful. I see why my brother married you."

Heather covered her nose with one hand and mumbled, "Except for my freckles."

"What did you say?"

Heather removed her hand. "You may as well know, I suffer from freckles."

"Like a sprinkling of gold dust, your freckles enhance your exotic beauty," Tynna complimented her.

Heather smiled. "Why, I never thought of my freckles quite like that."

"From where do you come?" Tynna asked.

"England," Heather answered, her tone of voice making it sound like heaven on earth. "England is—I mean, was—my home and lies far to the west of here."

"The sultan has arranged for me to marry next summer," Tynna told her. "My husband-to-be is a Moscovite prince from my great-grandmother's homeland."

"What is a Moscovite prince?"

"Prince Nelos comes from Moscow where the winters are bitterly cold," Tynna said. "What does being a man's wife feel like?"

"Forget every rumor you've ever heard," Heather advised, feeling superior in spite of her limited knowledge. "The woman trains the man, not the other way around. Of course, I am no expert, but as I experience married life, I will tell you everything. By the way, what kind of fruit is that?"

"Peaches," Tynna answered. "You have never eaten one?"

"No."

"Peaches are wonderfully juicy and sweet."

"I think I'll try one," Heather said, standing up. "Would you like one?"

Tynna also stood. "We have some inside."

"Going inside is unnecessary," Heather said with an impish grin. "Watch me."

Amazing her young sister-in-law, Heather climbed the peach tree. She reached out and touched a peach, then called, "It's fuzzy."

"The ripest fruit is higher up," Tynna said.

Heather climbed higher. She picked two peaches and dropped them to Tynna who waited for her to descend before eating. Heather looked down and hesitated. The ground seemed awfully far away, especially since she'd never cared for heights.

Drawing their attention, an angry voice came down

the path toward them. Heather wondered if climbing trees was also against the rules here. There were so many new rules to remember.

"If you value your worthless life, where is she?" The angry voice belonged to Khalid.

"She pleaded for privacy," Omar whined his explanation.

"You let her outside unsupervised?"

"She swore to me that—"

"You will regret it if she's gone, little man."

Khalid and Omar saw Tynna and hurried toward her. The strange sight of her brother confounded by a woman made Tynna laugh.

"Have you seen—?" Khalid started to question his sister.

"I am here," Heather called.

Khalid whirled around but saw nothing.

"Up here!"

Khalid looked up. "What are you doing?"

"Picking peaches," Heather said.

"Come down."

"No."

"First egg whites and now peaches," Khalid grumbled.

"Becoming upset never helps, my lord," Heather called.

"I said, come down," Khalid shouted.

"I would if I could," Heather tried to explain, "but I can't so I won't. Understand?"

Khalid counted to ten and then asked, "Why can you not come down?"

"I'm stuck."

"On the branch?"

"No, on my fear," she confessed.

"*Inchallah*," Khalid muttered. He removed his dagger from his belt and handed it to Omar, then climbed the tree until he stood two branches below her.

Heather gifted him with a dazzling smile. "Hello, my lord. Would you care for a peach?"

"No," he snapped.

"I am merely being polite."

"Forget polite," Khalid said. "Place your left foot here."

"I'm afraid."

"Do it."

Slowly but surely, Khalid guided her descent, ready to catch her if she slipped. Finally, Heather stood on a lower limb, and Khalid stood on the ground.

"Jump," he ordered.

Heather shook her head.

"You cannot live your life in the tree," Khalid tried to reason with her. "I will catch you. Trust me."

Heather closed her eyes and leaped into her husband's waiting arms. Knocked off balance, Khalid fell over backward with Heather on top of him.

"Are you injured?" he asked.

Heather shook her head. "Thank you for rescuing me."

Regardless of their audience, Khalid rolled Heather onto her back. Nose to nose with her, he said, "So, my intrepid wildflower does harbor a few fears."

"Shame on you," Omar scolded. "Proper Turkish ladies do not climb trees."

The prince turned his head to look at the eunuch and said, "Shut up, Omar."

Khalid looked down at his wife who smiled at him. Her lips were so temptingly close and inviting. He lowered his head. His mouth captured hers in a lingering kiss.

"How touching," a woman's voice sneered. "The beast and his mate coupling in the dirt."

"Mother!" That cry of surprise came from Tynna.

With their bodies still pressed together, Khalid and Heather looked up at Mihrimah.

"If your son is a beast," Heather said, "what exactly does that make you?"

"Mind your manners," Khalid said. "Proper Turkish ladies respect the elderly, no matter how cranky the old person is."

Heather giggled. "Well said, my lord husband. You are learning."

"I fail to see the humor in an Ottoman prince toiling with his princess in the dirt," Mihrimah said. "I came home early to give instructions for a family supper for the four of us. And this is the abuse I get for my kind consideration?"

Ignoring his mother, Khalid stood and helped his wife up. They took a moment to brush the dirt from their clothing.

Heather turned to her mother-in-law, saying, "I am heartily sick of eating grilled mutton."

"What would you like, my dear?" Mihrimah asked, clearly irritated.

"Since leaving England, I haven't eaten roasted pork, and it is a particular favorite of mine."

Everyone but Khalid gasped audibly. Their hands flew to cover their mouths. They were either startled or nauseous.

"Why is roasted pork so startling?" Heather asked. "This land has pigs, doesn't it?"

"The Koran forbids the consumption of pork," Khalid told her.

"I am no Moslem," Heather reminded him.

"You are a Moslem's wife," Khalid said.

"Are you implying that I can never eat pork again?" she asked.

"I am saying it, not implying."

"I demand pork."

"Stop saying that word, or you will make everyone sick."

"Pork," Heather said with a smile, unable to resist his challenge. "If I cannot eat pork, I refuse to eat anything. Ever." With that, she marched down the path in the direction of her chamber.

"We serve pork only on Fridays," Khalid called after her. "Too bad, Christians like you are forbidden meat on that day."

Watching his wife's pace quicken, Khalid chuckled at her expense. He knew only too well her hearty appetite and fondness for food. She would never starve herself.

His good humor earned Khalid surprised looks from his mother and sister. It seemed to them that he hadn't smiled in years. The woman from the West had changed him.

Heather remained in her chamber for the rest of the afternoon. What she did most was pace back and forth like a caged tigress, and watching her from his pillow, Omar grew tired. Occasionally, Heather wandered to the garden door and gazed out at the world outside her prison.

What exactly do ladies in this land do to fill the day's endless hours? Heather wondered. She was accustomed to coming and going as she pleased.

As long as they were Mihrimah's guests, Heather knew she would have no duties to keep her occupied. But, what would happen when they returned to Maiden's Castle? Would she have duties then? Heather certainly hoped so.

Did the harem ladies lounge idly about? Perish the thought. Heather knew she would go mad within a week if that was the life that awaited her.

And where was Khalid? She'd expected one of his lectures hours earlier.

There was a knock on the door. Omar rose slowly from his pillow and padded across the chamber. When he opened the door, a small army of Mihrimah's servants marched in. Their arms were laden with clothing. Without a word, they set their bundles on the bed and then left.

"Look, my lady," Omar cried. "The prince sends you gifts."

Heather walked to the bed and stared at the clothing. There were caftans, harem pants, tunics, boleros, sashes, and slippers. All had been created from the finest fabrics that money could buy.

Hiding her excitement, Heather fingered each garment. No man had ever given her a gift, and she wondered about the prince's feelings for her. Heather knew the mountain of clothing on her bed had cost many gold coins.

"The prince adores you," Omar gushed.

Heather glanced sidelong at the little man, saying, "This has the look of bribery to me."

"Give the prince a son, and he will give you the world," Omar told her. "The Koran says that paradise lies at a mother's feet."

"I'd rather give him a daughter," Heather replied. "Yes, a house filled with little girls to pester him."

"Bite your tongue," Omar said.

A deep masculine chuckle sounded from the doorway. Lady and eunuch whirled around. With a tray in his hands, Khalid stood there. Omar beamed at the amazing sight of the prince serving his wife supper.

"Omar, wipe that stupid grin off your face," Khalid ordered, sauntering into the room. "Put the clothing away and then leave." Khalid turned to Heather and said, "I like little girls, and do hope each one resembles you."

Heather stared at him in surprise. Why was he so complimentary? What was his game?

"Come, mother of my daughters," Khalid said. "Let us sup together."

"Hunger eludes me," Heather lied.

"Sit here while I eat."

Heather decided she couldn't refuse him after he'd given her those gifts. She crossed the chamber and sat on a pillow beside the table.

On the tray were lamb rolls stuffed with nuts, a yogurt and cucumber salad, and saffroned rice pilaf. There was shredded pastry with nuts for desert and a decanter of rosewater.

Khalid filled his plate and ate with obvious gusto. Heather watched him in silence, afraid to speak lest she drool. She hadn't eaten since breakfast and was uncertain of how much longer she could go without food.

Khalid raised his eyebrows at her. Ignoring him, Heather started to get up.

"Sit there until I am finished," he ordered.

"I have a cramp in my leg," she lied.

"I do not believe you," Khalid said. "You are hungry. Eat."

"I cannot live without pork," Heather announced dramatically.

Khalid choked on a piece of lamb. He grabbed his goblet of rosewater and drank, then studied her for a long moment. "Pork will never be served in my household; however, when the danger from Fougere has passed, I will allow Omar to take you to the Christian's market. There you may eat pork until you burst."

"You would do that for me?" Heather asked.

"Only on Fridays."

Heather scowled at that.

"I am teasing you," Khalid said. "Please, eat before you expire."

Heather eyes him skeptically. "Do you swear to it?"

"You doubt my word?" Khalid countered, irritated.

"If you say it, I believe you," Heather quickly amended lest she lose what she had gained. She reached for the lamb and started to eat.

"If you let me eat pork," Heather asked in between bites, "why won't you repeat your vows in front of a priest?"

"A world of difference lies between religious tolerance and participation," Khalid told her.

Heather dropped the subject. If she nagged him constantly, he would never agree to a priest. She would find another way to change his mind.

"Why did you serve me supper here?" she asked.

"Supping with my mother would have given you indigestion," he replied.

"What about you?"

"Me, too."

"When are we returning to Maiden's Castle?" Heather asked.

"As soon as I find and kill Fougere." Khalid watched her closely.

There was no reaction to his words. Heather reached for another lamb roll. "Will I have duties at your home?" she asked.

"*Our* home," Khalid corrected her.

"What will I do all day?"

"The usual tasks women do."

"What are the usual tasks that women in this land do?" Heather asked.

Khalid shrugged. "I will ask my mother. Sewing, perhaps."

Heather grimaced. "I'm afraid I'm not very good at sewing."

"Then what can you do?" Khalid asked with a smile.

"After my father died, I took weaponry lessons with my brother," Heather told him, clearly proud of herself. "I can shoot an arrow straight and sure, handle a dagger with deadly expertise, and ride a horse like the wind rides the sea."

"Your mother approved?" Khalid asked, surprised.

"Because of my nightmares, my mother usually gave her permission for anything that would make me happy," Heather said, then leaned closer to him. "I confess I have been spoiled."

"I would never have guessed," Khalid said dryly. "You need to cultivate a lady's activities."

"Such as?"

"How would I know that?" Khalid said. "In case you have not noticed, I am no lady."

Heather giggled.

"Ask my mother what daily tasks a lady performs," Khalid called to Omar who was on his way out. The eunuch nodded and left. Khalid turned back to Heather, saying, "And no more climbing trees. Understand?"

Heather smiled and nodded.

With supper finished, Khalid stood and helped Heather up. While he went to his chest and rummaged through it, Heather gazed out the garden door at the beauty of twilight.

"I have another gift for you," Khalid said, standing behind her.

Heather turned around. In his hands was a necklace fit for a queen. It was crafted of heavy gold, and set inside its woven links, emeralds and sapphires glittered.

Speechless, Heather stared at it.

"Turn around." When she did, Khalid set it around

her neck and fastened its clasp. He drew her back against the muscular planes of his body and nuzzled the side of her neck. His hands cupped her breasts.

"About the priest . . ." Heather said, disturbed by his nearness.

Khalid ignored her words. He unfastened the front of her caftan and slid it off her shoulders, then turned her to face him.

In naked glory, Heather stood before him. Her only attire was the luxurious mane of copper hair that fell to her hips and the jeweled necklace.

Khalid stepped back a pace to admire her. "You are a pagan goddess," he said, his voice hoarse, desire gleaming from his blue eyes.

"It isn't dark yet," she said, recognizing *that* look.

"Darkness is unnecessary for lovemaking," he told her, stepping closer.

Khalid pulled her into his arms and kissed her shyness away. All thoughts of the priest fled her mind. Heather wrapped her arms around his neck, pressed herself against him, and returned his kiss with equal ardor.

Leaving her lips, Khalid rained wet, feathery kisses down the column of her throat. Lower and lower dropped his lips, and he suckled her aroused nipples. Heather moaned at the incredible sensation he was creating.

Unexpectedly, Khalid knelt in front of her. His tongue slashed her moist female's crevice.

Heather gasped in shock and tried to pull away. His hands cupped her buttocks and held her captive to his exploring, tormenting tongue.

"I want to taste each delicious inch of your sweet flesh," he whispered against her cleft, his seductive words making her squirm with hot desire.

Up and down, Khalid flicked his tongue in a gentle

assault on her womanhood. He licked and nipped her tiny female button while his fingers tugged and taunted her hardened nipples.

Surrendering, Heather melted against his tongue. She cried out as wave after wave of throbbing pleasure washed over her.

Khalid pulled her down on the carpet in front of him and kissed her thoroughly. Too impatient to carry her to bed, he turned her onto her belly and planted a kiss on each of her buttocks.

"Get on your knees," Khalid whispered, freeing his engorged manhood from the confinement of his pants.

Holding her steady, Khalid mounted her from behind and rode her hard until she shrieked with pleasure. Then he surrendered to her, shuddering and spilling his seed deep within her body.

Lying on the carpet, Khalid cradled Heather in his arms. He caressed her face. Her *wet* face. There were tears on her cheeks.

"Did I hurt you?" he asked.

"No, but without benefit of a priest . . ."

Khalid rolled her onto her back and pressed his body into hers. Nose to nose with her, he insisted, "You are my wife."

Khalid spread her legs and entered her again. His manhood grew inside her body, and then he began to taunt her without mercy. Ever so slowly, Khalid pierced her softness and then withdrew until Heather panted and moaned with need.

"Say you are my wife," he ordered, "and I will give you what you crave."

Heather stared up at him, her startling green eyes glazed with passion. "I am your wife," she breathed.

Khalid thrust inside her. Again and again, he ground himself into her throbbing womanhood. Like a wild creature, Heather met each of his powerful thrusts with her own.

With mingling cries, they exploded together and then lay still. Khalid moved to one side and pulled Heather with him. Cradled in each other's arms, they fell into a sated sleep on the carpet.

Chapter 15

"Wake up."

Ignoring the voice, Khalid rolled onto his stomach.

"Wake up, I said." The shrew's voice grew louder.

Verging between consciousness and sleep, Khalid was caught in a horrifying nightmare. His wife had somehow been transformed into his mother. Almost as bad, his bed was as hard as the floor.

"Wake up, you ugly beast." With her foot, Mihrimah nudged her naked son.

Startled, Khalid sat up and looked around in confusion. Then he remembered the previous evening's love-making with his wife. Allah be praised, he'd only imagined his wife had become as shrewish as his mother.

"Why do you sleep on the floor?" Mihrimah asked.

"You woke me up to ask me that?" Khalid asked, then realized he was quite naked and his manhood erect. Masking his shame, he snapped, "What do you want?"

Mihrimah chuckled at his embarrassment. "Where is your wife?"

Khalid studied his mother's disapproving expression. Apparently, she knew what he did not.

"If this is a game, I give up," he said. "Where is she?"

"The fearsome Sultan's Beast cannot control his own wife," Mihrimah sneered.

"I am in no mood to listen to your insults," Khalid said. "Say whatever you came to say and then leave."

"The little barbarian is teaching you her disrespectful habits," Mihrimah scolded him.

"Mother." Khalid's voice held a warning tone.

"Your wife and your sister are on their way to the stables," Mihrimah told him. "I tried to stop—"

Heedless of his nudity, Khalid leaped up. He pulled his pants and boots on, then grabbed his shirt and headed for the door.

"If your wife were where she should be," Mihrimah said two steps behind him, "that morning cock of yours could rest in peace."

Khalid's complexion reddened even more. "Allah save me from old, foolish women," he muttered, leaving the chamber.

Mihrimah was close on his heels. She wasn't about to forgo the sight of her son reprimanding the English viper. With any luck, he'd beat her into submission.

"Heather," Khalid shouted, marching into the stables.

Standing in front of a stall, Heather and Tynna turned at the sound of his voice. Their smiles of greeting died when they saw his forbidding expression. Heather looked past him. Wearing a triumphant smile, Mihrimah stood just behind him.

Seeing her mother-in-law's expression, Heather said, "Whatever she told you is a lie."

Khalid grabbed his wife's arm in a tight, punishing grip and gave her a shake. "I gave no permission to ride. Where were you going?"

Ready for battle, Heather shrugged off his hold and rounded on him. "I wasn't going anywhere."

"Then what are you doing here?" Khalid asked.

"I brought your sister to see Foolish Pleasure," Heather said.

"You are lying," Khalid accused.

"She speaks the truth," Tynna interjected. "I assured her you would not become angry."

Mihrimah gasped. "If you ask me, the little barbarian should be beaten for her waywardness," she spoke up.

"Nobody asked you," Khalid said.

Turning back to his wife, Khalid gentled his voice. "Riding is unfeminine," he tried to explain.

"Riding is neither feminine nor masculine," Heather informed him. "You said I could visit Foolish Pleasure."

"I said you could visit when accompanied by a proper escort, and my sister hardly qualifies," Khalid said. "Even worse, your face is uncovered. When will you understand that a prince's wife must be veiled?"

Heather held up her discarded veil. "I did cover my face before leaving our chamber."

Silencing her, Khalid reached out and gently placed the palm of his hand against her cheek. "I need you in the morning," he said in a husky voice.

"Why?"

"To soothe his morning cock," Mihrimah answered for her son.

Heather blushed scarlet.

Khalid caressed her burning cheek.

"What is that?" Tynna asked.

"Never mind," Mihrimah snapped at her daughter.

"I am no whore to be at your beck and call," Heather said, slapping his hand away, her face aflame with shame. How could he mention *that* in front of his mother and sister?

"Where is Omar?" Khalid growled, irritated that his mother should witness his wife's insolence toward him. "If that incompetent fool had been doing his job, this situation would never have arisen."

"Leave Omar out of this," Heather said.

Resisting the urge to throttle her, Khalid counted to twenty. Arguing with his wife would solve nothing. Only his mother would be satisfied. When he got his wife alone, he intended to lay down the law. Again.

"Let us return to our chamber and breakfast," Khalid said in an effort to make peace. "We can discuss this gently."

"I've already eaten," Heather told him, covering her face with the veil. She lifted her upturned nose in the air, dismissing him.

"You will keep me company while I eat," Khalid said.

Irritated to be ordered in the presence of his mother, Heather stared at him. "Very well," she agreed. Once alone with her husband, she intended to lay down the law. Again.

Brushing past him, Heather marched out of the stables. Khalid admired the angry sway of her hips. Mihrimah and Tynna followed behind them. The sound of Mihrimah's laughter irritated both the prince and his princess.

"Mother, please," Tynna pleaded.

"Do not dare tell your mother what to do," Mihrimah scolded. In a loud voice, she added. "That one is a powerfully bad influence on you."

As they neared the house, a servant stopped Heather. "Omar begs to be released from his duties today," the girl said. "The poor man lies on his death bed."

Yanking the veil off her face, Heather raced to the eunuch's small chamber. Khalid, followed by Mihrimah and Tynna, ran after her.

Groaning in apparent agony, Omar lay on his bed. His eyelids were swollen; hideous red welts marked his face, throat, and hands.

"The plague," Mihrimah cried, holding her daughter back.

Unafraid, Heather reached out and turned the little man's face this way and that. After a close inspection, she announced, "Omar suffers from hives, which are neither contagious nor fatal."

"How do you know?" Khalid asked.

"My brother suffers from this same malady whenever he eats berries."

Unconvinced, Khalid turned to the eunuch. "Did you eat berries?"

"No, egg whites." Omar moaned dramatically.

Khalid turned toward his wife slowly. His expression mirrored his anger.

"I swear I did not know," Heather said, backing away from his forbidding expression.

"I warned you about wasting Allah's bounty," Khalid said, taking a step toward her.

Heather eluded his reach. With a horrified giggle, she dashed out of the chamber.

"Halt," Khalid ordered, but was ignored. Then, he gave chase.

Racing blindly around a corner, Heather slammed full force into Abdul. She fell backward and landed with a heavy thud on the floor.

Khalid knelt beside her and asked, "Are you hurt?"

"Why is this bloody bugger always in my way?" Heather asked as her husband helped her up.

"What is 'bloody bugger'?" Khalid asked.

"I'll tell you later," she said.

Khalid looked at his man. With Abdul was an imperial messenger who handed him a missive.

Khalid read the message and then looked up. The Sultan's Beast had returned. "There has been another attempt on Murad's life," he said.

Arriving in time to hear that, Mihrimah said in a scathing voice, "If you had been searching for the assassin instead of nestling between the barbarian's legs, your cousin's life would be in no danger."

Thinking his mother correct, Khalid stared hard at Heather. He was in a quandary about what to do. On the one hand, he needed to visit Topkapi. But with Omar ill, there was no one to guard Heather. Though Khalid knew she would not run away, his wife's restless spirit could very well get her into trouble.

"Why are you staring at me?" Heather cried. "I didn't do it."

"Go to Topkapi, my son," Mihrimah spoke up, understanding his dilemma. "I will take Tynna and this one to visit the bazaars. She will cause no trouble."

"Cause trouble?" Heather echoed, insulted.

Khalid nodded at his mother and then turned to his wife, saying, "Obey my mother in all things. Do you understand?"

Clearly unhappy, Heather glanced at her mother-in-law and then met her husband's concerned gaze. "I understand," she said. "Do not worry about me."

Khalid nodded once and then ordered Abdul, "Fetch a pouch of gold from my chamber. Visiting the bazaars without gold to spend is a waste of time."

Heather gifted her husband with a dazzling smile, beguiling him. She'd never owned her own money before. Apparently, the prince did care for her.

"Give me the pouch," Mihrimah insisted when Abdul returned. "This one will lose it."

"My wife will carry her own gold and spend it on whatever she chooses," Khalid said, handing the pouch to Heather. With that, he walked away.

A couple of hours later, three curtained litters, carried by Mihrimah's slaves and protected by eight bodyguards on horseback, stopped on a quiet street near the bazaars. Wearing diaphanous, muslin *yashmaks* and tasseled, silk cloaks, Mihrimah and Tynna emerged from two of the litters.

Heather, shrouded in a heavy black *feridye,* stepped from the third litter. Not even her eyes showed. In her hands, she clutched the pouch of gold coins as if it were the crown of England.

Mihrimah had ordered Heather to wear the *feridye.* A heated debate had followed, and Mihrimah had emerged victorious. That anyone should gaze into the eyes of her son's wife was unseemly. Furthermore, the black shrouding would prevent Heather from raising her eyes to any man. At least, if she committed that breach of etiquette through ignorance, no one would know.

"I feel like a walking corpse," Heather complained. "I still do not understand why—"

"Custom requires you wear the *feridye,*" Mihrimah told her. Allah grant her patience, she was weary of this one's complaints.

"Silly custom if you ask me," Heather muttered.

"Nobody asked you," Mihrimah drawled.

Heather snapped her head around to her mother-in-law, Mihrimah raised her eyebrows at her, and Tynna giggled. Unseen by them, Heather's lips turned up at the corners. It was the first *almost* cordial moment that had passed between the two of them.

"Why don't Tynna and you wear this . . . this—?"

"*Feridye,*" Tynna supplied.

"Whatever."

"Shall we shop?" Mihrimah asked. "Or would you prefer to argue?"

"Shop," Heather answered, giving in.

Surrounded by their bodyguards, Mihrimah led the

way. They proceeded down the street toward the *bede-stans*, covered bazaars.

Getting her first glimpse of the marketplace, Heather stopped short and sucked in her breath at the incredible sight and cacophony of sounds that greeted her. Hundreds of talking people crowded the narrow street. Except for the black or white-shrouded women, a rainbow's variety of colors dazzled the eye. Having passed her entire life at Basildon Castle, Heather had never seen so many people gathered together. The thought of stepping into that throng excited yet frightened her.

Seeing her daughter-in-law's hesitation, Mihrimah smiled behind her *yashmak* and gestured Tynna to walk on the other side of Heather. Mother or not, Khalid would never forgive her if she misplaced his wife.

As they walked down the street, the mob seemed to part for them. Recognizing the imperial insignia on their bodyguards' livery, the vendors and common people turned to stare.

Heather, the cunning tigress who had mated with the Sultan's Beast, became the bazaar's main attraction. Feeling the myriad gazes upon her, Heather was relieved that the *feridye* shrouded her and none could see her face.

"Why are they staring at us?" Heather whispered to Mihrimah.

"They are curious about you."

"How do they know about me?"

"How little you understand," Mihrimah said, though not unkindly.

"Enlighten me."

"You are the foreign bride of a prince, one of the most powerful and feared men in the empire," Mihrimah explained. "Do not the common people of England stare at their princes and princesses?"

"I suppose so," Heather replied. "I don't really know."

"Why not?" Tynna asked.

"I never traveled to London," Heather admitted. "That's where the queen holds court."

"Are you not a nobleman's daughter?" Mihrimah asked.

"Yes, but I never left my father's estate."

"Keeping you secluded from polite society was a wise decision," Mihrimah remarked.

"And what does that mean?" Heather asked, her voice rising in anger at the perceived insult.

Mihrimah glanced around. The ears of a hundred people strained to hear this heated exchange between the beast's mother and wife.

"What purchase interests you first?" Mihrimah asked, changing the subject.

Heather thought a moment. "I'd like a satchel in which to place all of my other purchases."

Mihrimah chuckled. "You are not as unintelligent as you appear."

"Now, see here, you old—"

"Remember where we are, my dear," Mihrimah warned.

Heather glanced at their attentive audience and then nodded. She would set her mother-in-law straight when they were alone.

Their first stop was at the vendor of satchels. Bags in all shapes and sizes covered the walls and table of his stall. These bags had been fashioned in leather, tapestry, canvas, and every other fabric imaginable.

Heather pointed at a black leather satchel, and the vendor handed it to her for her inspection. Deciding the satchel would do but ignorant of its value, Heather withdrew a handful of gold coins from her pouch and displayed them in the palm of her hand.

"How many of these do you want for the bag?" she asked.

The vendor reached to claim the small fortune, but Mihrimah's hand was faster. She covered her daughter-in-law's palm, shielding the gold from the man.

"This piece of black hide is worth two gold pieces," Mihrimah said. "If that much."

"Two gold pieces," the vendor cried. "Why, this finely crafted leather is worth at least ten."

"Ten!" Mihrimah exclaimed. "You shameless old cheat—"

"Ten gold pieces and a bargain at that," the vendor insisted.

"No bargain at all," Mihrimah muttered. She turned to Heather, saying, "Put your coins away, dear daughter. There are many skilled and less expensive craftsmen in the marketplace."

Heather placed the coins back in her pouch. The three women turned and started walking away.

"Wait," the vendor called.

Mihrimah stopped, turned around, and eyed the man coldly.

"I offer a special price for the family of Prince Khalid," the vendor said.

That piqued Mihrimah's interest. Followed by Heather and Tynna, she walked back to the vendor, and the haggling began in earnest.

Soon, Heather had purchased the black leather satchel for only four gold coins. She had also altered her opinion of her mother-in-law. Apparently, there were things she could learn from Mihrimah.

After browsing in the crowd for a while, they decided to rest and refresh themselves at the beverage vendor's.

"I want rose petal sherbet," Tynna said.

"What flavor would you like?" Mihrimah asked Heather.

"None."

"Are you not thirsty?" Tynna asked.

"I have an aversion to that drink," Heather replied.

"Why?"

"Each time I drink sherbet, I find it's drugged."

Mihrimah smiled behind her *yashmak.* "The vendor is an honest man and would not do that."

"Still, I do not care for it."

"Then, I will order you a lemonade."

"What's that?"

"A drink made from lemons. It's taste is tart," Mihrimah told her.

"It will make your lips pucker," Tynna added.

"May I remove the veil to drink it?" Heather asked.

"Simply lift the veil's bottom edge and raise the cup beneath it," Mihrimah said.

After the three had refreshed themselves, they thanked the vendor who had refused to accept payment. Mihrimah led them away.

Heather spied a stall where an old woman sat alone and insisted on stopping there. "What are you selling?" she asked.

"Potions," the woman answered in a heavily accented voice. "Give this paste to your husband, and his tool will never tire."

Blissfully ignorant, Heather turned to her mother-in-law, asking, "What tool?"

"My son needs no potency paste, *jadis,*" Mihrimah said to the woman, pulling her daughter-in-law away from the stall. "Come along, my dear."

"What's *jadis?*" Heather asked.

"A witch," Tynna answered.

Heather glanced back at the old woman. Then she made a protective sign of the cross just to be sure.

Mihrimah reached out and slapped her hand, warning, "Never do that in public."

Too late. Mihrimah noticed many in the crowd staring at Heather and then whispering to each other. Rumor quickly spread throughout the watching throng of people that the Sultan's Beast had mated with an infidel Christian.

Their next stop was the pastry vendor's stall. Having missed lunch, Heather and Tynna stuffed themselves with several pastries including "lips of the beauty," a sickeningly sweet dessert. Watching them, Mihrimah felt nauseous.

"Mother, take us to see the goldsmiths," Tynna said, licking her fingers. "Let us show Heather the fabulous jewels there."

"I'd like that," Heather said.

"You are not tired?" Mihrimah asked, hoping to entice them home.

"No," Tynna and Heather chorused together.

Surrounded by their guards, Mihrimah escorted them away from the crowds toward a much quieter lane. Here the merchandise was displayed inside shops. They browsed through two shops where the merchants seemed acquainted with Mihrimah.

Entering a third shop, Heather stopped short. Attached to a heavy gold chain, a unique piece of jewelry shaped like a strange beast caught her eye. The pendant was a blaze of gold with sapphires and emeralds, lit by two hundred diamonds, and two ruby eyes.

"What is this?" Heather asked the goldsmith.

"A griffon."

"I do not understand."

"The griffon is a mythical creature," the goldsmith explained. "See. It has the head, forepart, and wings of an eagle but the body, hind legs, and tail of a lion."

A mythical beast, Heather thought. *Like Khalid.* She reached out and touched it with her fingertips. "I want it."

"This piece is much too heavy and more suited for a man," Mihrimah advised. "Choose something else."

"The griffon is not for me," Heather said.

"Then, who?" Mihrimah asked.

"A wedding gift for my husband."

Their reactions were not what Heather would have expected. Tynna giggled. The goldsmith stared at her as if she'd grown another head. Mihrimah smiled at her daughter-in-law's ignorance.

"The man purchases gifts for his wife's favors," Mihrimah explained. "Not the other way around."

"I want that griffon," Heather insisted, her expression becoming mulish though none could see it. "My husband said I could purchase whatever I liked. Did he not?"

"Very well," Mihrimah said, then nodded at the goldsmith to wrap the pendant and chain.

The griffon actually cost more than Heather had. Seeing the chance to ingratiate himself with the imperial family, the goldsmith took the gold coins Heather offered in the palm of her hand. Lifting the last gold coin, the goldsmith heard her tiny groan of disappointment that all of her coins were spent.

"Let me see," the man said, making a show of counting them. Finally, he returned two gold pieces to her and said, "You have offered me too much."

"Are you certain?" Heather asked, slipping the wrapped griffon and two gold coins into her satchel.

The goldsmith smiled. "Yes, Princess."

Mihrimah knew the griffon's worth but held her tongue. If the stupid man wanted to cheat himself, then so be it.

"Can we go home now?" Heather asked. "I want to give Khalid my gift."

"You still have two coins," Mihrimah said. "Wouldn't you like to purchase something for yourself? A yard of silk, perhaps?"

"No, I'm saving my gold."

Tynna giggled. "For what?"

"For nothing," Heather replied. "I never owned gold before and want to keep it as a memory."

"What the gold buys is important," Mihrimah told her. "The gold itself means nothing."

"Nevertheless, I'm saving my coins," Heather said.

Mihrimah shook her head disapprovingly. If the lovely young bride squandered all her coins, the rich, adoring husband would gift her with more. That was the way of the world. Apparently, her young daughter-in-law had many lessons to learn, and Mihrimah did not want her grandchildren infected by this one's strange European ideas.

As they backtracked through the marketplace, a sudden uproar drew their attention. Careening at breakneck speed down the narrow, crowded street came a masked man on horseback. Shrieking people scrambled to get out of his way, and instinctively, several of their bodyguards rushed to assist old people and children.

From the corner of her eye, Heather saw another masked figure break through the loose ring of their distracted bodyguards. Clutching a gleaming object, he dashed toward Mihrimah.

"*No!*" Heather screamed and pushed Mihrimah out of his path. She tried to halt the death blow with her hand. And stop it she did. So deeply did the dagger pierce the center of her palm, its tip jutted out from the back of her hand.

The would-be assassin turned to flee. With his scimitar, one of their bodyguards felled the villain.

"You fool," Mihrimah shouted. "Dead men do not speak. How can we discover who sent him?"

Tynna, staring at her bleeding sister-in-law, wept loudly. Mihrimah slapped her hard, shocking the hysteria out of her.

Next, Mihrimah knelt beside her daughter-in-law to offer comfort. Still clutching her bag of purchases, Heather lay on the street. The dagger protruded from the back of her right hand.

"I don't want to die," Heather said, looking at her through a haze of pain.

"You will not die." Mihrimah whipped the gauzy *yashmak* off her face and wrapped Heather's injured hand. "Keep your eyes averted until we can get you home."

Mihrimah's slaves arrived with their litters then. Two of their bodyguards lifted Heather into their mistress's litter and then Mihrimah climbed in. She cradled her young daughter-in-law in her arms during the short journey home.

Khalid and Abdul rode into the courtyard at the same time that his mother's entourage arrived. Answering the bodyguard's shouts, Khalid leaped off his horse and ran toward his mother's litter.

As his mother began the tale of what had transpired at the bazaar, Khalid removed his wife's veil and gazed at her dazed expression. Worry etched itself across his features. He lifted her into his arms and carried her inside to their chamber where he gingerly laid her on the bed.

What should he do? Remove the dagger at once, or wait for the physician?

Through a daze of pain, Heather opened her eyes and whispered, "I got stuck."

"You will be fine," Khalid assured her, unwrapping her hand.

For the first time, Heather dared to look at her hand. "Oh, Lord," she mumbled, and lost consciousness.

"Praise Allah, she fainted," Khalid said to his mother. "Hold her hand steady."

Mihrimah grasped her daughter-in-law's hand while Khalid carefully pulled the dagger out. Blood gushed heavily from the two wounds.

Khalid bandaged his wife's hand with a piece of white linen, but a telltale spot of red appeared and grew larger with each passing second. Where was the damned Moor?

"She stopped the dagger meant for me," Mihrimah said. With the immediate danger past, she began trembling with the fear she'd suppressed.

Khalid said nothing. He held his unconscious wife in his arms and cursed himself for being a fool. Never should he have allowed that visit to the bazaars. Fougere lurked somewhere in Istanbul.

The door burst open, and the physician hurried into the chamber. The Moor cleansed and stitched the two wounds, then bandaged Heather's hand.

"The princess's injury is not life-threatening," the Moor assured the prince. "Her scars will be minor."

At that, Khalid nodded and left. He needed to question the witnesses and learn whatever he could about the assassination attempt.

Before leaving his patient, the Moorish physician turned to Mihrimah and handed her a packet. "When the princess awakens, give her this pain-numbing powder."

Mihrimah kept a lonely vigil beside her daughter-in-law's bed. The little barbarian had saved her life and, apparently, loved her scarred son. Perhaps there was more to Heather than what the eye perceived.

"Will I live?" Heather whispered, opening her eyes after what seemed to Mihrimah like hours.

"The physician sewed the wounds and bandaged your hand," Mihrimah told her. "You will recover with only two tiny scars."

Her throbbing hand awakened Heather fully, and she grimaced with the pain. Noting her expression, Mihrimah walked to the door and ordered a slave to bring a goblet of sherbet.

"Where is Khalid?" Heather asked.

"Trying to discover who would attack me," Mihrimah answered. "I applaud your courage and thank you for saving my life."

"If I'd realized the assassin was after you, I wouldn't have stopped him," Heather replied. Christ, but her hand hurt!

"That is a lie."

"I hope this doesn't mean you like me now," Heather said.

"No, it means I can tolerate you better," Mihrimah shot back.

Heather cast her an unamused look and asked, "How is Omar?"

"The little man will be up and about in the morning," Mihrimah replied. "The physician examined him too."

A slave girl entered, handed the goblet of sherbet to her mistress, and then left. Mihrimah added a dose of the medicinal powder, stirred the mixture with her finger, and offered it to the patient. Heather refused it with a negative shake of her head.

"Drink the sherbet to ease the pain," Mihrimah ordered.

"Will I sleep?" Heather asked.

"Yes."

"Sleeping gives me nightmares."

"About what?"

"Nothing that concerns you," Heather shot back, instantly on guard. "Tell me why you despise your own son."

Genuinely surprised, Mihrimah stared at her for a long moment. "Though he does have his faults, I do love my son."

"Liars have their tongues cut out," Heather said.

"Why do you believe I dislike my only son?" Mihrimah asked.

"I heard you blame him for the deaths of your children," Heather answered.

"When?"

"Never mind when," Heather said. "I heard it from your own lips."

"At times bitterness and loss rule my tongue," Mihrimah admitted. "Because of his deformity, Khalid must be prepared for the inevitable rejection of others, especially women."

"What deformity?"

"His scar."

Heather looked her mother-in-law straight in the eye and asked again, "What deformity?"

Mihrimah leveled an admonishing look on her.

"My husband is a warrior," Heather said. "His beautiful scar gives him character."

"I am glad to hear that," Mihrimah said. "Perhaps Allah intended you to be his true mate. Too bad He sent a barbarian."

"*Barbarian!*" Heather tried to sit up but was too weak. She fell back on the pillows. Angry frustration and her throbbing hand made tears well up in her eyes.

At that moment, the door swung open. Khalid walked in.

"Your mother is upsetting me," Heather said, "and my hand hurts horribly."

Khalid turned a forbidding expression on his mother. Mihrimah's eyes narrowed on her outrageous daughter-in-law.

"I offer her comfort," Mihrimah defended herself.

"Comforting anyone is beyond your capability," Khalid said.

Insulted, Mihrimah stood and headed for the door. "If the stubborn chit would drink the sherbet the physician ordered, her hand would hurt less."

Now Khalid scowled at his wife.

"You wagging-tongued witch," Heather cried.

"I will visit you tomorrow, my dear," Mihrimah said with an infuriating smile.

"To be certain I'm not feeling better?" Heather asked.

"Precisely." Mihrimah started out the door.

"Wait," Heather called.

Mihrimah paused and turned around.

"Will you teach me how to cheat the vendors?" Heather asked.

Mihrimah's expression mirrored her confusion. "I do not understand."

"I want to learn how to cheat the vendors like you did today."

Khalid chuckled.

"Haggling is not cheating," Mihrimah informed her. "The vendors expect it."

"Can you teach me?" Heather asked.

Mihrimah paused for a moment as if thinking, then said, "If you drink the sherbet, I will consider it."

"Very well," Heather gave in.

Khalid handed her the goblet of sherbet. Heather took a small sip and tried to give it back to him.

"All of it," Mihrimah ordered in a stern voice.

"*Jadis*," Heather muttered, making her husband smile.

When Heather had drunk every drop of the sherbet, Mihrimah cast her a satisfied smile and left. Khalid set the goblet aside and eased onto the edge of the bed.

"Your pain is my fault," he said. "I should never have allowed you to go out while Fougere is in Istanbul."

"What has that weasel to do with this?"

"Most likely he is the one who ordered the attack."

"That dagger was aimed at your mother, not me," Heather reminded him.

"What does it matter for whom the dagger was meant?" Khalid asked.

"Fougere has no reason to kill your mother," Heather said. "I doubt he is behind this."

"There is no one else."

"Why would he try to kill your cousin?"

"Fougere fears my family," Khalid said.

"That is no good reason to murder your cousin or mother," Heather said, stifling a yawn. "Villains are usually people you least expect. In this case, probably a woman."

Khalid smiled condescendingly at her.

"And what is so amusing?" Heather asked.

"You are adorable when you try to reason," Khalid said, a smile lingering in his voice.

"*Try* to reason?" she cried. "Women can do anything men can do, only better."

"Women do not kill."

"Oh, no? If a woman can save a life as I did today, a woman can take a life."

"A woman is capable of murder only when her child is in . . ." Khalid broke off and stared open-mouthed at her. Finally, his face split into a wide grin. He leaned close and planted a smacking, wet kiss on her lips.

"Another punishment?" Heather asked. "For what?"

"There is a woman whose child Murad threatens," Khalid told her, "but executing treason like this requires a man's counsel."

"You're welcome, my lord," Heather said pertly.

Puzzled by her words, Khalid stared at her blankly.

"You did thank me for opening that closed mind of yours a crack, did you not?" she said.

Khalid tapped the tip of her upturned nose. "You are much too intelligent to be a woman."

Heather yawned, too tired to rise to his baiting. "Where is my bag?" she asked.

"Forget the bag," Khalid ordered. "You need sleep."

"I want my bag," she insisted.

Muttering about the foolishness of women, Khalid got up and fetched the bag. He sat down on the edge of the bed again and handed it to her.

Heather opened the satchel and peered inside, then withdrew something wrapped in a cloth. She handed it to him, saying, "Open it."

Khalid unwrapped the griffon pendant and gold chain. Holding it flat in the palm of his hand, he noted its sapphires, emeralds, diamonds, and rubies. All women were alike in one thing, their love of fine jewelry.

"The griffon is beautiful but too heavy a piece for such a petite woman like you," Khalid said.

"I bought it for you."

Her softly spoken words caught him by surprise. Having never received a gift from a woman, including his mother, Khalid stared at her blankly. Finally, a smile stole across his handsome features, and he reminded Heather of nothing more than a young boy at Christmas.

"I—I do not know what to say," Khalid said, placing the gold chain over his head. The griffon pendant fell into place against his chest and sparkled against the whiteness of his shirt.

"Say 'thank you,' " Heather suggested.

Khalid leaned close and pressed his lips to hers. Then, in a voice hoarse with emotion, he said, "I will always wear it next to my heart."

"It reminded me of you."

"I look like this?" Khalid asked, feigning horrified dismay.

Heather giggled. "Both the griffon and you are mysterious mythical creatures."

"Since you wasted all your gold on me, I suppose you will be begging for more," he said.

Heather shook her head. "My gold wasn't wasted, and I still have two pieces left. I'm saving them."

"For what?"

"I like owning money."

Khalid smiled. He pulled his boots off, lay down beside her on the bed, and drew her into his embrace. Lowering his head, Khalid kissed her lingeringly, but Heather ruined the moment by yawning against his lips.

"Yawning in my mouth while I kiss you is insulting," he teased her.

"Don't you regret forcing that sherbet down my throat?" Heather asked.

"You will never know how much."

"A wise man listens to his wife."

Khalid kissed the tip of her upturned nose. "Relax, and I will guard you while you sleep."

Heather snuggled into his arms, rested her head against his chest, and looked up at him with her disarming green eyes. Perhaps sympathy would gain her what she desired most.

"My hand hurts," Heather whispered.

"Close your eyes and sleep," Khalid said. "You will feel better in the morning."

Heather closed her eyes and sighed. "About the priest," she said.

"Forget about the priest."

"But my hand hurts."

"What has the priest to do with your hand?"

"If you repeat your vows in front of a priest, my hand will feel much better."

Khalid's lips quirked as he struggled against a smile. "Go to sleep," he ordered.

Heather relaxed in his arms. It felt good to be protected. This was a strange land, filled with strange people and even stranger customs.

When her breathing evened, Khalid knew she slept and planted a light kiss on the top of her head. His negligence had almost cost him her life, he thought. Until Fougere was dead, he needed to be cautious. Plead as they would for freedom, his family would remain inside these walls. Though his mother and his wife were sure to complain, they would no longer be allowed to traipse around Istanbul unless he guarded them himself. Fougere, cowardly weasel that he was, dare attempt nothing while the Sultan's Beast was near.

Chapter 16

"Do not speak unless spoken to," Khalid instructed.

"Raise your eyes to no man," Mihrimah said in a stern voice.

"Can I breathe?" Heather asked, annoyed by their badgering.

"Keep your temper under control," Khalid ordered.

"Watch your manners," Mihrimah added. "Show proper respect, and call no woman a *jadis.*"

Standing like a child between the mother and the son, Heather felt like screaming. Both had been hovering over her and giving her instructions for five days. If she vented her anger, Khalid would refuse to let her accompany them to Topkapi Palace, and Heather was heartily sick of being held prisoner at Mihrimah's. Instead of giving them a large piece of her mind as she wanted, Heather rubbed her bandaged hand nervously.

"Do not play with your bandage," Khalid ordered, slapping her uninjured hand.

"I itch," Heather protested.

"Fingering your bandage looks unseemly," Khalid said.

"*Unseemly.*" Heather's temper exploded. "I am sick unto death of that word."

"Lower your voice when you speak to me, or you will wish for death," Khalid warned.

"What will you do?" Heather asked him. "Threaten me to death?"

Standing near them, Tynna giggled. Mihrimah shook her head in disapproval. She feared her daughter-in-law would behave badly and embarrass them in front of the sultan and his women.

"Do you wish to accompany us?" Khalid asked his wife.

"Yes."

"Behave appropriately or stay behind." Khalid turned away to reach for the *feridye* that Omar held.

Heather curled her lip at his back, making Tynna giggle again. Khalid whirled around and eyed his wife suspiciously.

Two weeks had passed since the incident at the bazaar. Though sorely vexed at times, Mihrimah was still solicitous of her daughter-in-law, and her criticisms of her son had lessened somewhat. Tynna visited her bed-ridden sister-in-law each day and tried to keep her entertained. At night, Khalid held her close and comforted her.

Each passing day saw Heather heal, but her boredom grew by leaps and bounds. Heather wanted to feel the sun and the wind on her face. A sedate stroll in the garden was less than satisfying.

Learning that Heather had saved his aunt's life, Prince Murad insisted that Khalid bring her to Topkapi Palace. His mother, his sister, and his own wife were intrigued by the tale of this courageous European woman, as were all the other ladies of his father's harem.

"Do not drop the veil until we are inside Topkapi," Khalid ordered, lowering the *feridye* into place.

"And do not peek out of the litter's curtain," Mihrimah warned. "I know that you did so when we traveled to the bazaar."

"Anything else?" Heather asked, irritated.

"Do not climb any trees," Tynna added.

Heather giggled, and Tynna joined in. Unamused, Mihrimah pursed her lips. Khalid seemed to have developed a nervous twitch in his scarred cheek.

Heather smiled inwardly. Serves them right, she thought, for making her feel ignorant. Was she not the cousin of Queen Elizabeth? How dare they imply that she was a barbarian!

Khalid, astride his magnificent black stallion, supervised their security as their entourage wended its way slowly through Istanbul's crowded streets toward the waterfront. The ladies sat hidden inside the curtained litters and were carried by Mihrimah's slaves. Arriving at the quay, Khalid escorted them onto an imperial barge that traveled down the Bosporus to Topkapi Palace.

When they stepped ashore, the *agha kislar* stood there to greet their party and escorted them past the sultan's fierce halberdiers. The entrance to the harem was through the carriage house with its carved double doors inlaid with mother-of-pearl. A corps of eunuchs stood guard just inside the door.

Heather was grateful for the black veil that enabled her to see without being seen. Were the myriad guards there to keep the uninvited outside or the ladies inside? Escaping Topkapi would be virtually impossible.

The *agha kislar* led them through the *meskane* and the courtyard of the *kadins*. He left them at Nur-U-Banu's apartments.

The *bas kadin*'s salon was the most opulent chamber Heather had ever seen. Lavishly tiled and carpeted, the salon featured an enormous bronze brazier, opaque colored glazes upon the walls, and Ottoman mullioned windows that looked out upon a private garden.

Seated on pillows around a table were two women

and a handsome, young man. The older of the two women, Murad's mother, smiled when they entered.

"Welcome, my husband's family." With her gaze fixed on Heather, Nur-U-Banu said to Khalid, "Is this she?"

"Yes, unfortunately," Mihrimah answered in a waspish voice.

Heather snapped her head around to glare at her mother-in-law.

Khalid grasped his wife's arm and drew her forward, saying, "I present Heather, my wildflower. Heather, this is Nur-U-Banu." He turned to the handsome man with the red-gold hair and dark eyes. "Prince Murad, my cousin."

"Let us see her face," Murad said.

With her husband's help, Heather removed the black veil.

"We meet again," Murad said with a smile. "I admired your beauty at the auction."

Mortified that he had witnessed her shame, Heather crimsoned and stared at the carpet.

"Modesty enhances your beauty," Murad said smoothly, then turned to the lovely dark-haired woman sitting beside his mother. "My *kadin,* Safiye."

Heather nodded at the woman, then whispered to Khalid, "What's *kadin?*"

"Safiye is the mother of my oldest son," Murad explained.

"Nephew, your wildflower is nothing like you described," Nur-U-Banu said.

Mihrimah chuckled. Puzzled, Heather looked from her mother-in-law to her frowning husband.

"Khalid insisted your hair resembled the color of a withered orange," Murad teased. "He said—"

"Let us sit and become acquainted," Khalid interrupted, thinking his relatives were idiots. Albeit royal idiots.

"Except for Heather, we are already acquainted," Nur-U-Banu said. "Please, make yourselves comfortable."

They sat on the enormous pillows that had been set around the table. Nearby, the bronze brazier chased away autumn's chill. Nur-U-Banu rang a tiny bell, and several slaves entered with golden platters filled with grapes, dates, flaky pastries, and goblets of rosewater.

"Where is Shasha?" Tynna asked.

Murad replied, "My exceedingly spoiled sister will be along any . . ."

The door burst open. A whirlwind of a woman rushed in. Of an age with Tynna, she had light brown hair, aqua eyes, rosy cheeks, and a small nose.

"This must be she," Shasha said, looking at Heather.

Feeling exceedingly conspicuous, Heather stared hard at a grape. Her husband dared to lecture her on proper manners and then delivered her into this den of rudeness. Was she the only one required to be polite?

"Heather, this is Murad's sister, Shasha," Khalid introduced them.

"What marvelous flaming hair," Shasha said. "It resembles a fiery sunset."

"Better a sunset than a withered orange," Heather said dryly.

"Do you like being married to the Sultan's Beast?" Shasha asked, plopping herself down between Mihrimah and Heather.

"Remember your manners," Nur-U-Banu scolded.

"Tell us how you saved my aunt's life," Shasha said, ignoring her mother. "Let me see your hand."

Heather held her bandaged hand up, saying, "It was nothing."

"Please, tell us the story," Safiye urged.

"Heather accompanied my mother and sister to the bazaars," Khalid spoke up. "Seeing the villain break through the ring of their guards, she pushed my mother out of harm's way and stopped the death blow with her hand."

"Heather is the most courageous of women," Tynna added. "In fact, she only fears trees."

Mihrimah chuckled. Khalid smiled at the memory of his wife stranded in the peach tree.

"I would hear this story," Murad said.

"Heather climbed the tree to pick peaches," Tynna said. "Looking down from the branch's great height, she got stuck on her fear. Fortunately, Khalid happened by and rescued her."

Everyone but Heather laughed.

"Pork is one of this Christian's favorite foods," Mihrimah told them. "Khalid said she could eat it on Fridays."

Again, everyone laughed at Heather's expense. She colored beet red and struggled to control her rising temper.

"Why so silent?" Murad asked her. "Does shyness hold your tongue?"

Heather glanced at her husband's warning frown, then dropped her gaze, feigning shyness. "I am trying to learn your customs but do make many mistakes. My husband instructed me to keep my mouth shut."

Murad smiled. "What other instructions have you been given?"

"Do not raise my eyes to a man," Heather said, peeking up at him. "Do not lose control of my temper. Do not call anyone a *jadis,* and do not scratch myself."

"You forgot 'do not climb trees,' " Tynna added.

Everyone but Khalid laughed. He was too busy scowling.

"Your pendant is unusual," Murad said, noting his cousin's darkening expression. "A beast wearing a beast."

"My wife gave me this griffon," Khalid said.

"Your wife does harbor warm feelings for you," Murad remarked.

"My feelings would be ever so much warmer if he'd call for a priest," Heather said, without thinking. "Until then, we are not really married."

"Be silent," Khalid growled.

"Do not scold her," Safiye said, recalling her own difficult transition from Venetian noblewoman to prince's concubine. "She is refreshingly honest, a quality short of supply within these walls. Setting aside a lifetime of beliefs and embracing Allah can be difficult. I know this from experience."

"It seems we are in accord about one thing," Nur-U-Banu said to her daughter-in-law.

"Mothers and wives will always bicker," Murad said to Khalid. "That is the way of the world."

Nur-U-Banu rose from her pillow. "We will give Heather a tour of the grounds while you meet with the sultan."

"Come, cousin," Shasha said, yanking Heather's uninjured hand. "Some of the women are playing games outside."

Shasha and Tynna pulled Heather out the door. Nur-U-Banu, Mihrimah, and Safiye followed at a more sedate pace.

Surrounded by cypresses, the sultan's garden was a picture of perfect serenity. The intoxicating scents of roses, jasmine, and verbena pervaded the air. Footpaths led to tiny ponds that exotic fish and floating water lilies called home. Gilded gazebos and kiosks provided shade, and bubbling fountains of water gurgled rhythmically.

"Why are there so many fountains?" Heather asked.

Tynna and Shasha looked at each other and then shrugged. The fountains had always been there, and the two girls had never questioned their existence.

"Running water shrouds the words of private conversations," Nur-U-Banu explained. "The noise of the water reduces the chance of eavesdroppers hearing . . ."

From a distance sounded the whoop and laughter of frolicking women.

"Come," Shasha cried, grabbing their hands. "The ladies are playing 'Istanbul Gentlemen.' "

Shasha dragged Heather and Tynna through a cluster of trees toward a clearing of manicured lawn. Guarded by eunuchs, ten young women were enjoying the morning. Nine of them wore white muslin pantaloons, brightly colored tunics, satin cloaks, and velvet slippers. Gold cloth caps sat on the crowns of their heads. But, it was the tenth woman who captured their attention.

Dressed as a man, the woman had her eyebrows thickened with kohl and a mustache painted above her upper lip. She wore a fur coat turned inside out, and upon her head was a carved watermelon. The woman sat facing backward on a donkey. In one hand she clutched the donkey's tail and in the other prayer beads made from garlic cloves.

Someone kicked the donkey and off she went, trying hard to maintain her precarious perch upon the beast's back. Unfortunately, the more the woman giggled, the more she swayed this way and that. In a few short minutes, she fell off the donkey.

"Let me try," Heather said.

"But, your hand," Tynna protested.

"I don't need my right hand," Heather boasted. "I'll use my left."

Nur-U-Banu looked at Mihrimah who nodded permission. "Let Heather have a turn," the sultan's *bas kadin* ordered.

Heather shrugged her cloak off. She donned the inside-out fur and set the watermelon on top of her head.

"I bet you can ride that dumb donkey forever," Shasha said, painting Heather's eyebrows and mustache with the kohl.

One of the eunuchs lifted her onto the donkey. Heather grasped the creature's tail with her left hand and clutched the string of garlic cloves in her bandaged hand. Someone kicked the donkey and off she went. Heather swayed this way and that but in spite of her laughter managed to stay seated.

The donkey started down one of the footpaths. Before the eunuch could herd the poor creature in the right direction, someone grabbed the donkey's bridle and jerked it to a halt. Heather toppled forward, but strong hands grabbed her by the waist and set her on her feet.

"Heather," said a familiar, obviously irritated voice.

The strong hands whirled her around. Khalid stood there with Murad.

"What do you think you are doing?" Khalid demanded.

The watching young women shrank back at the sound of the beast's snarl.

"I'm escaping," Heather replied, unafraid. "Do you think I'll get far in my disguise?"

The nervous twitch returned to Khalid's cheek. Murad chuckled at his cousin's expense.

The horrified women stared at Heather. Never had they seen a woman behave so disrespectfully to a man. And this was no ordinary man. He was the Sultan's Beast.

Khalid made a growling noise low in his throat.

"I'm sorry for my disrespect," Heather apologized,

stepping back a pace. "Your mother gave me permission to play."

Khalid turned his blackest scowl on his mother. "How could you allow her to do this?"

" 'Istanbul Gentlemen' is a harmless game," Mihrimah answered.

"Harmless? What if she carries my child and falls off the donkey?"

"I had not considered that," Mihrimah admitted.

"Carries your child?" Heather echoed. The thought of being someone's mother hit her like a ton of bricks.

Khalid looked at her. "Begetting children is the natural byproduct of—"

"Any of these beauties could carry my father's seed," Murad interrupted, "yet he does not forbid them their meager pleasure."

"With all due respect, none of these beauties is my wife," Khalid said. "Besides, the sultan already has two sons."

Murad nodded. "Choose another game to play while Prince Khalid's wife visits us," he called to the ladies.

"How about water tag?" Shasha suggested.

"No," Khalid and Heather said together.

"Because of your hand?" Shasha asked.

"My intrepid wife fears the water," Khalid said. "She cannot swim."

Heather blushed in embarrassment and stared at the ground.

"How about land tag?" one girl suggested.

"Or beauty and ugly poses," said another.

"I believe we should take our guests to the baths before we serve them dinner," Nur-U-Banu said.

Without argument, the group of women headed inside. Heather walked with Tynna, Shasha, and Safiye. Nur-U-Banu and Mihrimah lingered behind.

"Your meeting with the sultan has ended?" Nur-U-Banu asked.

Murad shook his head. "Postponed until he leaves Lyndar's apartments."

Nur-U-Banu nodded and then turned to Khalid, saying, "Worry no more about your wildflower. We will care for her properly." With that, Nur-U-Banu and Mihrimah followed the others inside.

Topkapi Palace's harem bath was like nothing Heather had ever seen or even imagined. Created completely in white marble, it featured tall, narrow columns and a skylight. Its floors and walls were inlaid with opulent faience tiles. Scattered throughout were marble sinks adorned with brass faucets.

Swirling steam, subdued conversations, and muted laughter mingled in the humid air. One hundred exquisitely beautiful women, accompanied by their slaves, lounged in the baths. Some women were naked; others were partially dressed in fine linen so saturated with mist that it revealed the whole body. Oblivious to their nudity, these myriad beauties laughed and chatted and refreshed themselves. Busy slaves, naked from the waist up, walked back and forth.

Heather had never seen so much skin in her life. When a slave girl stepped forward to help her discard the heavy bathing robe, Heather clutched it to her breast and shoved the girl away.

"Take it off," Mihrimah ordered, shrugging her own robe off. "You are rude."

"No," Heather refused, turning to Mihrimah. Her eyes nearly popped out of her head when she saw that her mother-in-law was naked.

Nur-U-Banu suppressed a laugh, then explained in a gently persuasive voice as if to a child, "We are all friends here. You expose nothing that I do not also have."

Reluctantly, Heather shrugged the robe off.

Mihrimah looked her up and down, then snorted and said, "I doubt you carry my son's seed."

Heather crimsoned, but before she could open her mouth to reply, Tynna and Shasha pulled her toward a corner of the bath where slaves scrubbed them. Shasha, who kept up a steady stream of chatter, saved Heather from the impossible task of making polite conversation among all those naked bodies. Soon, Heather sat on the edge of the heated pool while Shasha and Tynna soaked in the water.

"Those women over there are painting kohl around their eyes to keep the evil eye away," Safiye explained, sitting down beside her. "The women beside them are washing their hair with egg yolks."

"Isn't that wasting Allah's bounty?" Heather asked, repeating her husband's words to her.

Safiye shook her head. "They use the egg whites to discourage the crow's feet around the eyes."

That piqued Heather's interest. "So, one may eat an egg yolk but save the white to apply to the eye area?" she asked.

"Yes."

"And what are those women doing over there?" Heather asked.

"Using almond and jasmine paste to whiten their skin," Safiye answered.

"Could this paste remove my freckles?"

"Prince Khalid does not like your freckles?" Safiye asked with a smile.

Heather shrugged. "I wasn't thinking of what he liked."

"Then, who?" Safiye asked, looking at her curiously.

"*I* wish to be rid of my freckles," Heather said. "Will the paste help?"

Safiye shrugged. "I think not, but you could try. Perhaps, with repeated applications, they will fade."

After they had steamed, Nur-U-Banu and Mihrimah led them through a vestibule and a series of warm rooms where the women were pumiced, scraped of all body hair, and massaged. Then they went to the *tepidarium,* a resting room. Gilded hangings, encrusted with pearls, decorated the walls. Persian rugs covered the floor. Low sofas, piled high with soft pillows, offered them comfort.

Wrapped in warm robes, they rested for an hour and then dressed. Nur-U-Banu ushered them into the harem's common room where they would dine. As the sultan's *bas kadin,* she enjoyed her own luxurious apartments but knew the *odalisques,* the sultan's concubines, were curious about her nephew's wife.

Luncheon consisted of a lamb dish, pilaf, a vegetable medley in olive oil, and eggplant. Instead of the usual rosewater, they drank *boza*—a sour, fermented barley drink sprinkled with cinnamon. The delicacies arrived on silver trays, around which lay embroidered silk napkins wrapped in rings made of mother-of-pearl.

With her usual gusto for eating, Heather reached for a slice of eggplant but noticed a small food stain on her bandage. She started to reach with her uninjured hand, then remembered the rule against using her left hand for anything but "unclean" tasks.

Heather looked around. Even the youngest among them utilized only three fingers of their right hands. They ate with delicacy and grace, not gusto. Each of their movements was skilled and precise. Their fingertips were scarcely soiled.

"If you eat correctly, only your fingertips will touch the food," Mihrimah told her.

Heather blushed from the top of her head to the tips

of her toes. She reached for a slice of eggplant with her right hand.

"Eat plenty of eggplant," Safiye urged her, "and you will be fulfilled."

"What do you mean?" Heather asked.

"Eggplant is enchanted food," Safiye answered. "Your special dream will be fulfilled."

Heather looked as bewildered as she felt. "My special dream?" she echoed, reaching for another slice of eggplant.

"When a woman dreams about eggplant," Nur-U-Banu explained, "she is with child."

Heather choked on the piece of eggplant in her mouth and, as if it were hemlock, dropped the slice in her hand on the table. First abducted and then wed, Heather felt that her life was happening too quickly. Logically, her next role was motherhood. Though that thought was not displeasing to her, she wondered if she was capable of raising a child properly. Heather knew she could love her child unconditionally, but was she ready for the responsibility of nurturing a new life?

Slaves began serving them silver pitchers and basins of water for washing. They dried their hands on towels embroidered with gold.

"Mother, tell us the legend of the lacquered closet," Shasha said.

"In olden times there lived a powerful but cruel sultan," Nur-U-Banu began. "Learning that one of his favorite, most beautiful concubines had been having an affair with a handsome young man, the sultan devised a trap for the lovers. The hapless concubine and her magnificent lover, surprised in an intimate embrace, ran for their lives through the harem's maze of corridors. With his dagger drawn and ready, the sultan chased them. When the lovers reached the concubine's quarters, they hid inside a lacquered closet. The sultan threw the closet doors open, but it was empty. The lovers had disappeared.''

''Where did they go?'' Heather asked.

''The lovers stepped into eternity together,'' Nur-U-Banu replied.

''How romantic,'' Heather said with a sigh.

Shasha giggled. ''The *boza* is affecting you.''

''My favorite legend concerns the nightingale and the rose,'' Safiye said.

''Oh, yes,'' Tynna said. ''Tell Heather.''

''Once there was a nightingale who loved a perfect white rose,'' Safiye began. ''Aroused one night by the songbird's magic, the rose awoke from its slumber. Her heart fluttered when she realized he sang of her beauty. 'I love you,' whispered the nightingale. The white rose blushed, and pink roses bloomed all over the world. Closer and closer came the nightingale. When the rose opened her petals, the nightingale stole her virginity. The rose turned red with shame, and red roses bloomed all over the world. Since that long ago evening, the nightingale serenades the rose and begs for her love, but the rose keeps her petals closed.''

''How beautiful,'' Heather said, unaccountably saddened by the nightingale's love for the rose.

''I know a legend that no one has ever heard,'' Shasha said. ''In a faraway land there once lived a fierce, scarred beast who could only be controlled by his master, the sultan. Though this beast was feared and respected by all, his heart ached with loneliness because no one could love a beast. Far to the west in a mysterious island kingdom, a magical wildflower grew and blossomed. Divine *kismet* intervened in their lives. A strong wind blew, uprooted the wildflower, and carried her across the seas to the land of the sultan. As chance would have it, the wildflower dropped to the earth in front of the sultan's beast. Instead of trampling the delicate wildflower beneath his feet, the beast paused and sniffed her exotic fragrance. In the next instant, he lifted his head and in an aching voice howled his love for this wondrous blossom. Like a flower that basks in the warmth of the sun, this magical wildflower clung to the beast and basked in the warmth of his love. Since that day, the beast always appears with his wildflower by his side, and loneliness is a stranger to him.''

All the ladies clapped for Shasha. Embarrassed, Heather blushed. She never considered herself a likely candidate for the role of the heroine in a legend. Even more absurd was the notion that Khalid howled with love for her. But how else did these lovely women, these slaves of the sultan, entertain themselves?

"My favorite story is actually a riddle,'' Mihrimah said.

"Please tell us, Aunt,'' Shasha said. "I love riddles.''

Mihrimah nodded. "One day the perfect man and the perfect woman rode from Istanbul to Bursa. Along the way, their horse lost a shoe. Can you tell me which of them dismounted and fixed it?''

Shasha, Heather, and Tynna looked at each other. Turning back to Mihrimah, all three shook their heads.

"The perfect woman, of course,'' Mihrimah said. "There is no such thing as a perfect man.''

Laughter and clapping filled the harem's common room.

"Men only have two faults,'' Heather informed her mother-in-law when the laughter died down.

Mihrimah cocked a brow at her.

"Everything they say and everything they do,'' Heather told them.

Again, the listening concubines laughed and clapped.

For them, this day had become a time to cherish and remember always.

"What is happening here?" sounded a voice.

Everyone turned to see the sultan's newest *kadin* walking toward them. By her side was her arrogant eunuch Jamal, and in her arms she carried her infant son.

Of average height and voluptuously formed, Lyndar possessed sultry brown eyes and dark hair. Though harem gossip said the sultan's newest favorite already hennaed silver streaks from her hair, no one knew for certain. The truth behind that bit of gossip was a well-guarded secret. While her eunuch went to fetch her *nargileh,* her water pipe, Lyndar made herself comfortable on the divan reserved especially for her.

"Lyndar *Kadin,*" Nur-U-Banu said, forcing herself to smile at the other woman. "This is Heather, the wild-flower, Prince Khalid's bride."

"Hello," Heather said with a smile.

Lyndar deigned to nod at the newcomer.

"What a beautiful baby," Heather said, admiring the three-month-old infant.

Lyndar smiled with sincerity. "My lion is a handsome boy."

"Show her the twisted foot that prevents him from challenging Murad's right to the sultanate," Mihrimah said, making the other ladies titter behind their hands.

"*Jadis,*" Lyndar muttered.

Preventing further argument, Jamal returned with his mistress's *nargileh.* She took several puffs from the water pipe and then smiled.

"Would you care to try?" Lyndar asked Heather. Wouldn't she love to make an ally of someone close to the sultan's sister! That way, she would have a spy to keep close watch on Mihrimah.

Heather leaned close to the *nargileh* and imitated her.

She sputtered and coughed, then succumbed to the strangest feeling of sated drowsiness.

"Are you well?" Mihrimah asked, suspicious.

Heather didn't bother to reply. Instead, she stared dreamily into space.

"What are you thinking?" Shasha asked softly.

"Home . . . England."

"Tell us," Shasha urged.

"As much a paradise as the Garden of Eden, my country is a land blessed by God," Heather began. "England is wet in spring, lush in summer, vibrant in autumn, and pristine in winter. Heavy morning mists like the mythical dragon's breath shroud rolling hills and plains."

"Is your sultan as powerful and magnificent as ours?" Shasha asked.

"No sultan or king rules there," Heather answered. "Queen Elizabeth reigns in England."

The listening ladies gasped in surprise at that.

"A country ruled by a woman?" Mihrimah was definitely interested in this story.

"What about her husband?" Nur-U-Banu asked.

"Elizabeth, the virgin queen, has no husband," Heather said, enjoying their rapt attention. "Though still a young woman, I doubt she will accept any mate. My cousin would never wish to share her power with a corrupt man."

"This queen is your cousin?" Safiye echoed, impressed.

Heather nodded.

"But who will rule when this Elizabeth dies?" Lyndar asked. "Women do not live forever, and virgins cannot produce heirs."

Heather shrugged. "The queen will name someone her successor, probably another woman."

"Do the men in your land bow to this queen?" one of the ladies asked.

"As you bow to your sultan, the men of England bow to Elizabeth and leap over each other to do her bidding."

"Does she wear the veil?" Tynna asked.

Heather shook her head. "Englishwomen are free and wear no veils."

Excited chatter erupted from the sultan's women. Everyone seemed to be talking at once. Each wondered out loud how different life would be if they lived in this paradise called England.

"We English keep no slaves," Heather added for good measure. Then, embellished beyond the truth, "Englishwomen go wherever they like and do whatever they wish. Why, we can even choose our own husbands if we want."

The *agha kislar* entered as the lie slipped from her lips. His presence prevented pandemonium.

"Prince Khalid awaits his family at the carriage house," the *agha kislar* announced.

"Stay longer," Shasha begged. "Send word to Khalid that you will leave when you are ready and not one moment sooner."

The *agha kislar*'s mouth dropped open at the sultan's daughter's uncharacteristic disrespect. The chief eunuch whirled around at the sound of another's advice.

"Let him wait," Lyndar said.

"After all, Khalid is only a man," Nur-U-Banu agreed with her rival for the first and only time in her life. Like all the other ladies, the sultan's favorite had fallen under Heather's magical spell of life without a veil.

Something is wrong here, the *agha kislar* thought. Something is happening that could shatter the sultan's domestic peace.

"I will teach you English games the next time," Heather promised, rising from the cushions when her mother-in-law did.

The *agha kislar* escorted the three of them through the harem's maze of corridors. After delivering them to Khalid, he hurried back to the harem's common room. It was urgent that he discover what madness had taken control of the sultan's *kadins* and *odalisques*. His job, not to mention his life, depended on his ability to keep the harem tranquil.

When the *agha kislar* left the carriage house, Khalid arched a questioning brow at his mother. Mihrimah nodded and beamed a smile the likes of which he had never seen. Apparently, his bride had behaved in an exemplary manner.

Khalid pulled Heather close and gazed with love at her upturned face. "My heart swells with pride," he said, rewarding her good behavior with praise. "I am proud to call you my wife."

Chapter 17

His pride in his wife lasted less than two days.

On the second morning after visiting Topkapi Palace, Heather sat beside the table in her chamber and enjoyed a late breakfast that included egg yolks. Omar, recovered from his bout with the hives, busied himself with choosing his mistress's outfit for the day. Watching him, Heather was unable to understand why the little man took such pains selecting a garment that few people would ever see. After all, she went nowhere beyond the garden walls.

"You saved the egg whites for my facial mask?" Heather asked.

"Of course," Omar answered, then turned to look at her. "Again, my princess, I must tell you how proud I am of our successful visit to Topkapi."

"*Our* successful visit?"

"Without my skillful tutoring, you would have embarrassed the prince and his family," Omar replied. "To guarantee our fortunes, you need only get with the prince's—"

"*Heather!*"

From the corridor thundered the roar of an enraged beast calling her name. In the next instant, the door crashed open, and Khalid stormed into the chamber. The nervous twitch in his scarred cheek had returned.

"I am going to beat you within an inch of your life," Khalid promised, advancing on her.

Realizing this was no idle threat, Heather leaped up and ran behind the eunuch for whatever protection his stout body could offer. What had she done between last evening and this morning that had angered the prince?

"Is she with child?" Khalid asked Omar.

"No."

Khalid shoved Omar out of his way and grabbed his wife by her upper arm.

"I have done nothing wrong," Heather cried, struggling for freedom.

Cursing in his native tongue, Khalid dragged Heather across the chamber to the bed and sat down, but was unable to beat her. Instead, he gave her a rough shake.

"I did not waste Allah's bounty," Heather cried. "I am saving the whites."

That stopped him. Khalid stared down at her. "What are you talking about?" he asked.

"Eggs," Heather answered. "I am saving the whites to cure my crow's feet."

"Crow's feet?" Khalid echoed, completely bewildered.

"Egg whites discourage crow's feet around the eyes," she told him.

Khalid stared hard at her. "You do not suffer from crow's feet."

"Thanks to the egg whites," Heather said. "But you should have seen me before. Isn't that so, Omar?"

The little man nodded his head in agreement.

Frustrated beyond endurance, Khalid covered his face with his hands and muttered, "Allah, grant me patience to survive the fools who surround me."

"Fools? Are you implying—?"

"I imply nothing. You are a fool."

Heather opened her mouth to argue.

"Silence," Khalid shouted before she could utter a

word. Then, in a quiet voice, he ordered, "Tell me what you did at Topkapi."

"Topkapi?"

"We visited Topkapi Palace the day before yesterday," Khalid said. "You have no memory of that?"

"Of course I remember," Heather snapped. "I am no blinking idiot."

"That point is debatable," Khalid shot back. Heedless of her injury, he grasped her hands and yanked her against his legs. "Tell me what you did there."

"I—I played games with the women," Heather answered. "Later, we bathed and dined."

"What else did you do?" Khalid growled.

"Nothing! You are hurting me."

Khalid released her and pulled two sheets of parchment from inside his shirt. He waved the papers in front of her face, saying, "An imperial courier delivered these to me."

"What is it?"

Khalid held one of the papers up. "This, dear wife, summons you to appear before Sultan Selim and answer to the charge of treason. Punishable by death, I might add."

Heather gasped and paled. Across the chamber, Omar cried out and clutched his chest. His whole body itched at once as hives began rising on his skin. The little man could almost see his mistress—and his fortune—sinking to the bottom of the Bosporus.

"This is a mistake," Heather said. "I swear I committed no treason."

Khalid held the second parchment up, saying, "Prince Murad's personal note explains the reason for this accusation."

"What does it say?"

"Your lies about England have created a disturbance in the sultan's harem," Khalid told her. "For almost two days, my uncle's women have been in near rebellion against all male authority. As the instigator of these treasonous acts, you will be made an example."

"I never lied," Heather insisted.

"Tell me exactly what you said," Khalid ordered. "Leave nothing out."

"I—I told them how England looked," Heather began. "And I described its weather during the four seasons of the year."

Weather and scenery? No treason there.

"What else?"

"I explained that Queen Elizabeth rules in England," Heather added. "And . . ."

Here it comes, Khalid thought. Fearing what she would reveal, he steeled himself for the worst.

Heather said nothing.

"And?" Khalid prodded.

"I cannot remember."

In a flash of movement, Khalid grabbed her shoulders and gave her another rough shake. "You must remember. I cannot save your worthless life if I do not know everything."

"Englishwomen enjoy complete freedom and never wear veils to cover their faces," Mihrimah said, standing in the doorway. "Englishwomen do whatever they want and can marry whomever they choose."

Khalid groaned loudly. It was even worse than he imagined. Allah save them! Both of their lives were forfeit.

"The fault lies with Lyndar," Mihrimah said.

Khalid stared in disbelief at his mother. "You of all people defend this treason?"

"Lyndar gave her the poppy," Mihrimah said, walking into the room. "The opium spoke these lies, not your wife."

"I never lied," Heather said. "Elizabeth does rule England."

"And do Englishwomen marry whomever they choose?" Mihrimah asked.

"Well, no," Heather admitted. "I suppose I did exaggerate a bit."

"Forget everything I have ever said about lying being bad," Khalid said to her. "Now we must lie to undo the damage you have done. Our lives depend upon it. Do you understand?"

Thoroughly frightened, Heather nodded.

"When we kneel before the sultan, do whatever I say without argument," Khalid instructed her. "Raise your eyes to no one, and as you value your life, do not open your mouth. I will speak for you."

Again, Heather nodded. Lord, but she was too young to die. And so very far from home. Who would mourn her passing?

"Omar, get her dressed," Khalid ordered as he stood to leave the chamber.

"I will accompany you," Mihrimah said.

"You can only become tainted by this crime," Khalid refused.

"Nevertheless, I will accompany you."

"No, I said," Khalid snapped. "You will remain here and stay out of this."

"I am still your mother," Mihrimah reminded him in a stern voice. "You will issue no orders to me. I will go with or without your escort."

"Fools," Khalid howled, brushing past his mother. "I surround myself with fools."

Two hours later, the three of them waited outside the

Hall of the Sultans to be called into the imperial presence. Dressed completely in black, Heather stood between her husband and her mother-in-law and shook with extreme fright.

"Sultan Selim will be seated upon a throne on a dais," Khalid told her. "Standing beside him, Murad will speak for his father."

"Do not dare raise your eyes to Selim or Murad," Mihrimah said. "Do you understand?"

"Y-y-yes," Heather stammered.

"You have nothing to fear," Khalid said, warming her hands in his. "I will remain by your side, and no one will harm you."

"Liar," Mihrimah snapped. "If Selim deems her guilty of treason, she will be executed."

"If Selim does that, it will be the last order he ever issues," Khalid replied.

"What do you mean?"

"I will kill him."

"Allah protect us!" Mihrimah cried. "Her treason is infectious. What will become of us?"

"I warned you to stay home," Khalid reminded her.

With eyes large with wonder, Heather gazed at her husband. "You would avenge my death?"

"Yes, but we must try to avoid that," Khalid said. "Will you do exactly as I say?"

Surprised by his loyalty to her, Heather could only stare at him. This man who had made her his slave was willing to kill and be killed for her. If the opportunity ever presented itself, could she do less for him?

"Will you do as I say?" Khalid repeated.

"Yes."

"We will walk to the center of the chamber, face the dais, drop to our knees, and touch our foreheads to the carpet," Khalid instructed her. "Do not sit up unless commanded by Murad."

"I will walk behind you," Mihrimah said.

"You will walk nowhere," Khalid told her.

"I share my son's fate," Mihrimah insisted.

"Mother, you are an ass," Khalid said. "Stay here, or I will strangle you myself."

"Oh, very well." If the situation looked bad, she would speak in their defense, Mihrimah decided. Once she knelt in front of her brother, no one would be able to silence her.

The *agha kislar* exited the hall at that moment. The chief eunuch cast the accused a withering glance and then turned to his master's nephew.

"Follow me," the *agha kislar* said.

Khalid and Heather stepped inside the entrance to the hall. As the *agha kislar* walked toward the center of the chamber to announce their presence, Heather stole a peek at the chamber.

Long and rectangular, the Hall of the Sultans was spacious and elegantly decorated. At one end of the chamber stood a raised platform, over which hung a balcony. An embroidered carpet covered the tiled floor in front of the throne.

"The sultan uses this room to receive and entertain the entire harem," Khalid whispered.

"Am I today's entertainment?" Heather whispered back.

The *agha kislar* called them to appear before the sultan. Heather hesitated. Khalid grasped her uninjured hand and gave it an encouraging squeeze, and they started forward.

Most of the ladies of the harem were there by imperial command to watch the proceedings. Shasha, sporting a shiny black eye, stood directly opposite the entrance.

Beside her was Nur-U-Banu, her lips scabbed and swollen. Several of the other *odalisque*s also wore a variety of bruises.

Oh, what trouble had her wagging tongue wrought? Heather thought. Because of a few carelessly spoken words these women, who had so readily befriended her, had suffered. If she survived, would they ever forgive her? Guilty remorse coiled itself around her heart and made breathing painfully difficult.

Reaching the center of the chamber, Khalid and Heather turned toward the dais and dropped to their knees. In unison, they pressed their foreheads to the carpet.

"You have been summoned here to answer the charge of sowing discord and discontent in the imperial household," Prince Murad announced in a loud, clear voice.

Discord and discontent? Heather thought. A world of difference lay between treason and discord. Had Prince Murad purposefully avoided the word *treason*? Was that the signal that all would be well?

"Look up," Prince Murad commanded.

Khalid sat back on his calves. Remembering her husband's instructions, Heather kept her forehead pressed to the carpet.

"*Both* of you will look up," Murad said in a stern voice.

Heather sat back on her legs but kept her gaze fixed on the carpet.

"Sultan Selim, in his infinite wisdom, chooses to handle this troubling situation as a family problem," Murad told them. "It is for this reason you have been summoned here instead of the audience chamber."

At a gesture from the sultan, Murad leaned close and listened to his father's softly spoken words. Facing them again, the prince said, "Sultan Selim would see the infidel's face."

Without hesitation, Khalid removed the black veil that covered his wife's face. For her part, Heather concentrated on keeping her gaze glued to the carpet. There was danger in looking up at the sultan and the prince.

"Cousin, you are in no way accused of any wrongdoing," Murad said to Khalid.

"O *Padishah*, King of Kings," Khalid hailed the sultan and bowed formally. He caught his uncle's eye and said, "I share my wife's fate."

Murad's lips quirked. He had known his cousin would defend his wife to the bitter end, and the sultan was in no position to offend his most ruthless and fearless supporter. As long as the little barbarian did nothing during this audience to anger him, the sultan would assuredly forgive her.

"Why did you prevaricate to the sultan's women about this England?" Murad asked.

"My wife smoked the poppy that Lyndar offered," Khalid began. "She—"

"The sultan wants the infidel to speak for herself," the prince interrupted.

Khalid and Heather looked at each other in alarm. Their gazes locked. His eyes warned her to be cautious and prudent with her words.

"O *Padishah*, King of Kings," Heather imitated her husband. She pressed her forehead to the carpet and then sat back on her legs. Keeping her gaze fixed on the floor, she answered, "The poppy made me yearn for my native land, and the homesickness lured me to exaggerate, my lord . . . I mean, Your Highness . . . I—I mean my *padishah*, King of Kings."

"And?" Murad asked.

And what? Heather wondered, her panic rising, her tongue tasting metallic with fear. What did he expect of her?

"B-because of me, these ladies have been punished," Heather said, hoping this was the correct approach. "I regret my words, apologize to the sultan for creating this—this turmoil, and promise to smoke the poppy never again."

Sultan Selim said something to Murad. The prince turned back to Heather, saying, "The sultan wishes to hear the story of this English queen. She is truly your cousin?"

"Yes, but I have never attended her court," Heather replied. She knew she must choose her words carefully and place heavy emphasis on the importance of men. "Elizabeth is the only surviving child of the late King Henry. Her advisors are the wisest of men who guide her in all matters of state."

"So, England's queen rules through the guidance of men," Murad repeated in a voice that carried to the far corners of the enormous chamber.

"All of her ministers are men," Heather said. "They set England's policies, and the queen heeds their counsel."

"And the other women?" Murad asked.

"Other women?" Heather echoed, confused.

"Other Englishwomen," Murad said. "You, for example. Tell the sultan and these ladies about your life in England."

"I lived in my father's home and only ventured outside its walls when accompanied by an escort of armed guards," Heather admitted. Without thinking, she added, "Except for that one day . . ." She paled, and her voice trailed off as she recalled that horrifying day that was forever etched in her memory.

Khalid snapped his head around to stare at his wife. Regardless of protocol, he put his arm around her protectively and drew her close. "Outlaws attacked my unguarded wife," Khalid explained. "Though it happened many years ago, the memory of that day still disturbs her. She witnessed her father's murder."

Unexpectedly, Mihrimah marched into the hall and knelt beside Heather. She grabbed Heather's bandaged hand and yanked it high into the air for all to see.

"My *padishah,* my brother, I seek mercy for the daughter-in-law who saved my life," Mihrimah said, looking Selim straight in the eye. "Truly, Allah sent her to us. Besides, she carries my only son's child in her womb."

That simple statement got an instant reaction from everyone.

Shocked at the outrageous lie, Khalid and Heather stared at Mihrimah. The harem ladies whispered excitedly to each other. Murad leaned close to consult with his father. Finally, Sultan Selim stood without a word and left the hall.

What did that mean? Heather wondered, her heart pounding frantically. Would she be executed? Would they slaughter Khalid too?

"Sultan Selim is merciful," Murad announced. "The infidel's wife is spared on one condition." He looked at his cousin, saying, "You must punish her for this offense and control her tongue in the future."

Khalid nodded. "My wife will receive the beating she deserves."

Murad's lips quirked. "The sultan says you may postpone the punishment until the child is delivered. Next week is my mother's birthday. Return with the little barbarian then." Prince Murad left the hall, and the sultan's women followed him out.

Khalid stood and then helped Heather and Mihrimah rise. He leveled a deadly look on his mother.

"I must attend Nur-U-Banu. The poor woman appears

unwell, thanks to your wife,'' Mihrimah said. "I will stay the night and return home in the morning.''

"We are fortunate to have escaped with our lives,'' Khalid said, gazing at his wife. "We will never enjoy such luck again. Understand?''

Heather nodded. "I will become the perfect wife,'' she vowed.

And Heather was the perfect wife.

For exactly one week.

The day of Nur-U-Banu's celebration arrived. Against his better judgment, Khalid agreed to attend the small celebration at Topkapi Palace.

"Act pregnant,'' Mihrimah whispered to her daughter-in-law as they followed the *agha kislar* down the corridor toward the *bas kadin's* salon.

Act pregnant? Heather thought. How the bloody hell was she to do that? Heather closed her eyes and prayed for divine guidance. And then they arrived at Nur-U-Banu's salon.

"Hello.'' The voice belonged to Shasha.

Heather winced at the sight of the other girl's fading bruise. "I'm sorry about your injury,'' Heather apologized.

Shasha smiled to indicate her forgiveness. "A few of us are playing games in the hall. Would you care to join us?''

Heather looked at her husband for permission.

Khalid nodded, saying, "I intend to visit Murad and will send someone to fetch you later.''

As they headed toward the sultan's hall, Shasha confessed, "My bruise was worth the astonishment on Murad's face when I refused to wed Prince Mikhail next summer and demanded he find me an English nobleman.''

"Planting silly ideas in your head was wrong of me,''

Heather said. "I have learned my lesson about guarding my tongue."

"We should have realized that Istanbul is no England," Shasha replied. "Besides, the guilt lies with Lyndar. She's the one who squealed about what you told us. May Allah send her an ignominious death."

"Never wish for things you don't really want, for you may get what you wished," Heather said.

"Lyndar's death would be cause for celebration," Shasha said, then changed the subject. "How do you feel?"

"Guilty," Heather admitted. "I repaid your kindness by leading you astray."

"Not that," Shasha said. "How does it feel to carry the beast's seed inside your body?"

"As well as can be expected," Heather hedged, blushing with guilty embarrassment.

"Are you ill?

"At the moment, no."

By this time, several of the *odalisques* who'd played "Istanbul Gentlemen" with Heather had gathered around them. Some wore fading bruises, others were unmarked.

"You promised to teach us English games," one of them said.

Heather hesitated. She had no intention of kneeling in front of the sultan and begging for his mercy again. If that happened, Khalid would probably kill her himself. "I do not think—"

"Please," said another girl.

"You did promise," Shasha reminded her.

"How about 'hide and seek'?" Heather suggested, thinking there was nothing dangerous about that game.

"That sounds wild and exciting," Shasha said. All the *odalisques* nodded in agreement.

"One person is 'it,' " Heather explained. "She covers her eyes and counts to one hundred while everyone else hides. The 'it' person tries to find the others before they return and touch the goal or starting point."

"Since I am a princess by birth, I will be 'it'," Shasha said.

"Being 'it' is no honor," Heather told her.

"Nevertheless, I will be 'it'," Shasha insisted.

Heather nodded. "What shall we use as the goal?"

"My father's throne," Shasha said, her eyes sparkling with mischief. "Each girl will touch the sultan's throne."

Shasha stood in front of her father's throne and covered her eyes with her hands. Not above cheating, she kept several of her fingers parted for a better view of where each girl ran.

"Peeking is forbidden," Heather announced.

"Very well." Shasha covered her eyes completely and began to count. "*Bir, iki, uc, dort, bes, alti, yedi, sekiz, dokuz, on . . .*"

All the girls, including Heather, dashed out of the sultan's hall and scattered. Uncertain of where she was going, Heather found herself in the harem's deserted common room.

Heather raced to one of the chamber's small alcoves, piled eight enormous pillows on top of each other, dropped to the floor to hide behind them, and waited. The silence in the unfamiliar chamber became threatening. Long moments passed. She could hear a buzzing in her ears and feel her life's blood coursing with excitement through her body.

Heather had never been this alone without the sounds of another creature. As the minutes lengthened, the frightening feeling that she was alone in the world grew inside her. So powerful was that eerie feeling, Heather almost returned to the sultan's hall and let herself be caught.

Two things happened that prevented her from rising. From a distance, Heather heard faint whoops and shouts as Shasha raced for the goal before one of the other girls could reach it. The reassuring sound of humanity calmed her.

Heather wondered if she should try to reach the goal, then heard light footsteps inside the harem's common room. Was it one of the other players looking for a new hiding place or Shasha searching for her?

Heather peeked around the mountain of pillows. The footsteps belonged to Lyndar. Heather would have made her presence know, but Jamal walked into the common room to speak with his mistress.

"The little barbarian landed on her feet like a damn cat," Lyndar complained. "If it weren't for her meddling, Mihrimah would already be dead."

"Why is Mihrimah's death necessary?" Jamal argued.

"If Khalid believes Fougere killed Mihrimah, he will leave Istanbul to hunt for him," Lyndar replied, her voice filled with irritation at his stupidity. "Assassinating Murad will be easier."

"Let us assassinate Khalid first and then Murad," Jamal suggested.

"We need the Sultan's Beast to keep the empire safe for my son," Lyndar said. "When Karim reaches manhood, we will kill Selim and the beast."

Hiding in the alcove, Heather covered her mouth with both hands to keep from crying out. She had to find Khalid. *Immediately.* Should she make a run for it or wait until the conspirators left the chamber?

Peeking around the pillows, Heather saw Lyndar sit down on her divan. Jamal sat on a cushion beside her.

Apparently, the despicable conspirators were making themselves comfortable.

"Perhaps poison would be the most propitious method," Lyndar was saying. "In Nur-U-Banu's name, we would send tainted *rahat lokum* to Mihrimah and her meddling daughter-in-law."

"What if the Sultan's Beast takes a fatal taste of the delights too?" Jamal countered.

"That is a disturbing possibility," Lyndar admitted. "Do you have any suggestions?"

Treason is an evil that cannot wait, Heather decided. Lyndar and Jamal sat with their backs facing the alcove. If she could get out of the door behind them, she would somehow find her way back to the others.

Heather stood, and lifting the bottom edge of her caftan, scurried on tiptoe across the chamber toward the door. She almost made it. Glancing back at them, Heather stumbled into the side of a low table.

Lyndar whirled around and cried, "Get her."

Heather flew out the door and dashed down a long, winding corridor. Spying a mullioned-glass door that opened onto the garden, she practically crashed through it. Close on her heels were Jamal and Lyndar.

"Fire!" Heather screamed, hoping that particular alarm would draw an instant crowd.

Jamal reached out and grabbed her. His strong hands closed around her throat and squeezed. With a strength born of desperation, Heather kneed the eunuch's belly, and he doubled over.

Drawing a ragged breath, Heather turned to flee. Unfortunately, Lyndar grabbed her copper mane and yanked her to the ground.

"Drown her," Lyndar ordered.

Jamal grabbed Heather and covered her mouth with his hand. In spite of her frantic struggling, he managed to drag her to a nearby fountain. Before Jamal could push her head under the water, she bit his hand and freed her mouth for several fateful seconds.

"Khalid!" Heather shrieked, then sucked in her breath as her head plunged beneath the water's surface.

Chapter 18

"Fire!"

Standing on the terrace of his cousin's apartments, Khalid lifted his head and looked for the telltale sign of smoke. There was none. Who would falsely shout that most feared of all alarms?

"Khalid!" sounded a second, desperate wail.

Heather! Khalid leaped over the balustrade and ran in the direction of his wife's cry. Murad was one step behind him.

Crashing through a row of tall hedges, Khalid burst upon a shocking scene. Jamal was drowning Heather while Lyndar watched. Without breaking stride, Khalid reached the eunuch, yanked him away from his wife, and whirled the man around. His fist connected with the eunuch's jaw, rendering him unconscious.

"The traitor must die," Lyndar shouted.

Gasping and wheezing, Heather lay on the grass. Khalid turned her onto her stomach and rhythmically pounded on her back to empty her lungs. Heather gagged and coughed up the water she'd swallowed.

"The bitch must die," Lyndar cried, wild in her fury. She moved to attack, but Murad grabbed her arms and held her prisoner.

Khalid's heart beat frantically at the thought that he'd almost lost his wife. He held her in his arms and caressed her pale cheek. "You are safe," Khalid crooned. "No one will hurt you."

By this time a crowd had gathered and encircled them. Ready for orders, the *agha kislar* and his corps of eunuch guards stood by. Nur-U-Banu and Mihrimah, as well as Shasha and the other *odalisques,* stared in shock at Heather.

Murad gestured two of the guards to hold Lyndar's arms, then rounded on her. "You will explain why you tried to kill my cousin's wife."

"I answer only to my sultan," Lyndar replied.

"Answer me, or I will kill you here and now," Murad threatened, drawing his dagger.

"The barbarian insulted Selim," Lyndar accused, an unholy light gleaming from her dark eyes. "She must be—"

"Silence," the Sultan's Beast growled.

"Khalid," Heather whispered.

"Do not speak until your breath returns," Khalid said, stroking her cheek.

"Lyndar—wants—Murad—dead."

Khalid paled at her words. He turned to the others and ordered, "Stand back. Cousin, I need you here."

Murad knelt beside Heather. Both men leaned close.

"Lyndar plots to kill you," Heather told Murad. She looked up at her husband, adding, "And Mihrimah too."

"Say no more until you have recovered fully," Murad said. Rising, he turned to the *agha kislar.* "Guard Lyndar and Jamal until I summon them to be questioned. Afterward, I will send for my cousin's wife." Murad looked at the onlookers and announced, "The wildflower is well and wishes privacy to recover her breath. Disperse now."

"Selim will hear of this outrage," Lyndar screamed as guards dragged her away.

Nur-U-Banu stepped forward and said, "Carry your

wife to my apartments. I will send for my own physician.''

Khalid lifted Heather into his arms, then followed Nur-U-Banu and Mihrimah inside. Reaching the *bas kadin's* chamber, he set his wife on the bed and sat down beside her.

''Attend Murad,'' Mihrimah told her son as the physician rushed in. ''When your wife is recovered, the *agha kislar* will escort her there. You may question her then.''

The physician felt Heather's pulse points with his fingertips and listened to her lungs as she breathed deeply. ''The princess is well and fit,'' he said to his mistress. ''Dry her hair and keep her warm.''

After he'd gone, Mihrimah towel-dried her daughter-in-law's hair, then brushed and wove it into one thick braid. Nur-U-Banu helped her change into one of her own brocaded caftans and draped a cashmere shawl around her shoulders. A slave served them hot tea and crescent pastries.

Heather sipped her tea, relaxed against a pillow, and closed her eyes.

''Feeling better, my dear?'' Nur-U-Banu asked, sitting on the edge of the bed.

Heather opened her eyes. ''Yes, thank you.''

Mihrimah sat on the other side of the bed and patted her daughter-in-law's hand. ''Tell us what words you spoke to Murad and Khalid in the garden.''

So that was it. Heather read the expectant expressions on both of their faces. ''Perhaps you should ask Murad and Khalid,'' she said. ''I do not want my husband angry with me.''

Two pairs of eyes narrowed on her.

''Very well,'' Heather said, ''but you must promise to act surprised when they tell you.''

"We promise," the older women chorused together.

"I overheard Lyndar and Jamal plotting to murder Murad," Heather began.

"I told you so," Nur-U-Banu said to Mihrimah. "But, would anyone listen to me? No."

"What did she hope to accomplish?" Mihrimah asked. "Her son is imperfect and can never assume the sultanate."

"Lyndar thought to assassinate you and me," Heather told her mother-in-law. "She wanted to place the blame on Fougere. Khalid would leave Istanbul to search for him. Without him around, killing Murad would be easier."

"That proves it," Nur-U-Banu said. "The woman is stupid. She could have murdered Khalid first and then Murad."

"Lyndar is cunning," Heather replied. "She needed Khalid alive to keep the empire safe until her son grew to manhood. Then she planned to assassinate both Khalid and Sultan Selim."

"Treason," Nur-U-Banu cried, her hands flying to her breast.

"Come," Mihrimah said, holding her hand out to Heather. "Testify now and rest later."

The *agha kislar* arrived in a few short minutes. Mihrimah, Nur-U-banu, and the chief eunuch escorted Heather through the maze of corridors that led to the prince's apartments.

Khalid opened the door and drew his wife inside. Much to the consternation of his mother and aunt, he slammed the door in their faces.

While Murad paced back and forth across his salon, Khalid led Heather to a divan. He sat down beside her, placed an arm around her, and drew her protectively close. "Feeling better?" he asked.

Heather gazed at her husband through disarming green eyes and nodded.

Murad quit pacing and sat on the edge of a table opposite the divan. "I trust the babe you carry is well?"

Heather flicked a glance at her husband, then lowered her gaze and said in a voice no louder than a whisper, "Yes."

Murad suppressed a smile. He already knew his aunt had lied to the sultan. "Tell me everything," he said. "Leave nothing out."

"Shasha and several other ladies decided to play 'hide and seek'," Heather began.

"What is 'hide and seek'?" Murad asked.

"Does it matter?" Khalid asked. "What she overheard is important."

"I would know everything," Murad told his cousin. "Go on."

"'Hide and seek' is an English game," Heather explained. "All the players except one find a hiding place. The 'it' person searches for the others. Shasha volunteered to be the 'it' person, and everyone else, including myself, ran out of the sultan's hall. Uncertain of where I was going, I found myself in the deserted common room and hid behind a mountain of pillows. That's when Lyndar and Jamal walked in and sat down. I am no eavesdropper and would have made my presence known, but their conversation shocked me into silence."

"Of course, you would never eavesdrop," Murad said with a smile.

"What did they say?" Khalid demanded.

"Lyndar planned to kill Mihrimah and me," Heather said to her husband, "but place the blame on Fougere to get you out of Istanbul. Then Murad would be assassinated. Once her son grew to manhood, Sultan Selim and you would be eliminated."

Both men were silent. Lyndar's plan was logical and could have worked. Except for Heather and her English game of 'hide and seek.'

"That will be all," Murad said.

Khalid stood up and offered his hand to his wife. She ignored it.

"That will be all?" Heather asked.

"Careful," Khalid warned. "Your manners are slipping."

"I am nearly drowned, and you scold me for bad manners?" Heather asked, irritated.

Murad gave her a reassuring smile. "Justice will be served as soon as I consult with my father."

Khalid drew Heather to her feet and escorted her to the door. Mihrimah and Nur-U-Banu looked at him expectantly, but Khalid merely handed them Heather and shut the door again.

Murad looked at his cousin. "I believe her."

Sultan Selim, his eyes glazed with fury and wine, stepped from behind the lacquered Chinese screen. "Tell the *agha kislar* to issue death warrants for the traitors," he ordered his son. "And that crippled whelp too. Deliver the warrants to me for signing."

Selim turned on his heels and headed for the private door on the opposite side of the chamber, muttering, "Allah, I need a drink."

"You heard him," Murad said to Khalid. He opened the corridor door and ordered the chief eunuch, "Bring parchment, ink, and the sultan's seal."

Murad closed the door. Without a word to his cousin, he walked outside to the terrace. His heart felt heavy. The deaths of two traitors were of no importance, but the death of the babe was a troubling complication.

"The boy is innocent of any wrongdoing," Khalid said in a quiet voice, standing behind his cousin.

Murad whirled around. "Being a traitor's son is his crime."

"Karim is your half brother and—"

"—can be used against me by disgruntled subjects," Murad interrupted.

"But he—"

" 'Killing is better than disquiet,' " Murad quoted from the Koran.

"Falsify the death certificate and give me Karim."

"What?"

"Mihrimah told the world my wife is with child," Khalid said. "Let me take Karim home to Maiden's Castle. I will raise him as my own."

"What about Fougere?"

"Karim's life is more valuable than the weasel's death."

"Why?"

"Slaughtering innocents can make sleeping extremely difficult," Khalid told him. "I know this from experience."

"If his identity ever becomes known, the empire could erupt into civil war," Murad said.

"Eventually, you will be an aged sultan, and I will be too old to fight your battles," Khalid argued. "With my training, Karim will become the next Sultan's Beast and need never know who sired him. Trust me, Cousin."

Murad said nothing. He walked back inside and began pacing the length of his chamber. Should he kill his half brother or save him? Murad loved gold and women. He also loved the by-product of lovemaking, namely children. If he slaughtered his infant brother, would he suffer sleepless nights until the day he died?

A knock on the door interrupted his thoughts. The *agha kislar* walked into the chamber.

"Sit at the table," Murad bade him. "By Sultan Selim's order, you will write death warrants for Lyndar, Jamal, and Karim.''

The *agha kislar* nodded and began his task.

Murad flicked a glance at Khalid and then told the eunuch, ''You will drug Lyndar and drown her in the Bosporus tonight, but Jamal will be publicly executed at sunrise tomorrow.''

The *agha kislar* looked up. ''And the child?''

''How old are you?'' Murad asked abruptly. ''Thirty-five or forty?''

''Forty.''

''Young enough to be *agha kislar* when my father dies,'' Murad said. ''Would you like to remain *agha kislar* when I am sultan?''

''The honor would be mine,'' the chief eunuch replied, wondering what the prince was about.

''Your fortune is assured if you will do as I ask and remain silent about it.''

Uncertain, the *agha kislar* glanced at Khalid and then stared at Murad. Finally, he nodded.

''Give my half brother's birth certificate to Prince Khalid,'' Murad instructed. ''Send Abdul, my cousin's man, here and deliver Prince Karim to us. When you return, you will lead Abdul and Karim through the secret passageway to my barge and never repeat what transpired here tonight.''

''I have just written the boy's death warrant,'' the *agha kislar* said. ''If the sultan discovers—''

''Prince Karim will be dead to the world, drowned with his mother in the Bosporus,'' Murad told him. ''Never say otherwise to anyone.''

The chief eunuch bowed his head and said, ''I hear and obey, my prince.''

Murad smiled. ''Confine the ladies to their chambers

before you deliver Karim to us. No one must suspect my brother survived this night.''

The *agha kislar* stood and left the chamber.

Someone knocked on the door a few minutes later. Opening it, Khalid ushered Abdul inside.

''We have an important task for you,'' Khalid told him. Before he could say anything else, the *agha kislar* returned with the sleeping infant prince.

Khalid lifted him from the eunuch's arms and cuddled the baby against his chest. ''Abdul, this is my son. Guard him with your life.''

''I swear it,'' Abdul said. Nothing his master did ever surprised him.

''Take the boy and go with the agha *kislar*,'' Khalid said, handing his man the baby. ''Prince Murad's barge will stop along the way to collect Omar and your wife and then take you to Maiden's Castle. I will be home tomorrow evening.''

The *agha kislar* produced the baby's birth certificate and handed it to Khalid. Abdul, carrying the young prince, followed the chief eunuch out of the chamber.

''If I die without a male heir,'' Murad said, ''use the birth certificate to place Karim on the throne.''

''You will never regret your merciful decision,'' Khalid vowed.

Murad nodded. ''Your wildflower will attend Jamal's beheading at sunrise.''

''My wife is too sensitive to witness the execution,'' Khalid said. ''You saw her reaction today when she spoke of her father. Nightmares about his death still torment her.''

''Her testimony brought Lyndar and Jamal to this end,'' Murad replied. ''Her presence at the execution is required. She may, however, keep her eyes closed.''

"So be it," Khalid said, already dreading the dawn. Though worried about his wife's well being, Khalid knew there was nothing he could do beyond standing beside her and offering her his support.

As bright tentacles of light streaked the eastern sky, Khalid and the *agha kislar* walked down the corridor toward the *bas kadin*'s apartments. Khalid stopped in front of his aunt's door and knocked.

Nur-U-Banu stepped outside. "She refuses to accompany us," she told her nephew.

"I will speak to her," Khalid said, and walked into his aunt's salon.

With her black cloak wrapped around her, Heather sat on a pillow and stared straight ahead. Her face was deathly pale, so pale the fine freckles sprinkled across the bridge of her nose seemed darker than usual.

Beside her, an aggravated Mihrimah was saying, "By the sultan's order, you must attend."

Khalid gestured his mother out and sat down beside his wife. He held her cold hands in his. Heather gazed at him through eyes that mirrored her fright.

"When you were born, my wildflower," Khalid said in a voice as gentle as a caress, "your fate was written on your forehead. That is what we Moslems call *kismet.*"

Heather raised her chin a determined notch and insisted, "I am the mistress of my own fate."

"You testified against the traitors and are required to attend the execution," he said.

"What monstrous beasts can watch the slaughter of an innocent child?" Heather cried as tears welled up in her eyes.

So that was it, Khalid thought. His wildflower had a special fondness for children, which pleased him. Should he tell her the boy was safe? *No.* In her agitation, she would give their secret away, and then Murad and he would be executed for disobeying the sultan's order.

"Sultan Selim ordered Lyndar and her son drugged into sleep and then drowned in a sackcloth," Khalid told her. "Neither felt pain nor fear."

"That poor baby," Heather said, bowing her head. Fat teardrops fell on her hands folded in her lap.

Khalid tilted her face up and stared into the fathomless pools of sorrow that were his wife's eyes. "As soon as this is done," he promised, "we will go home to Maiden's Castle. Even now, Murad's barge awaits us."

"You let them murder that baby."

"Truly, I spoke in his defense, but my words fell on deaf ears."

Khalid stood and offered her his hand. Reluctantly, Heather placed her hand in his, and together, they walked outside where Nur-U-Banu, Mihrimah, and the *agha kislar* awaited them.

"Your attendance is required but do not watch," Khalid whispered as they walked behind the others. "At the final moment, close your eyes."

Heather glanced at him and nodded. Her hand in his shook badly, and Khalid gave it an encouraging squeeze.

Reaching the Tower of Justice, they took their places on the balcony overlooking an open courtyard. Heather stood between her husband and mother-in-law.

A corps of eunuchs already ringed the open area below. In the middle of the courtyard sat a raised slab of stone on which the hapless Jamal would bare his neck. A hooded executioner, with scimitar in hand, waited beside the forbidding death stone.

Were those bloodstains on the stone? Heather wondered, her panic rising. How many others had ended their lives here?

Sultan Selim, accompanied by Murad, walked onto

the balcony and sat upon a throne. He gestured to his son who, in turn, raised his hand for the proceedings to begin.

Flanked by two guards, Jamal was led into the open courtyard. The executioner ungently forced him to his knees and shoved his head down on the stone. He looked toward the balcony to await the sultan's signal.

Heather stared wide-eyed at the shocking scene and clutched her husband's hand. Worried, Khalid looked at her and then his uncle.

The sultan raised his hand high into the air.

"Close your eyes," Khalid whispered.

Heather, her gaze riveted on the scimitar, did not respond.

"Damn it! Close your eyes," Khalid ordered in a louder voice.

The sultan's hand came down. The scimitar followed the master's gesture and ended Jamal's life.

Heather's eyes clouded and became glazed with unspeakable pain. "Papa, blood . . . *Papa!*"

Khalid caught Heather before she hit the floor. Lifting her into his arms, he cuddled her like a baby against his chest.

"Carry her to my apartments," Nur-U-Banu said.

"No, Murad's barge is waiting to take us to Maiden's Castle."

"The weasel still lives," Mihrimah cried.

"Fougere be damned," Khalid swore. "I am taking my wife home."

"I knew she would infect you with her European ways and lure you from your chosen path," Mihrimah said, her voice filled with bitterness.

Khalid ignored her. Without a word, he turned away. Nothing was more important to him than Heather.

"Your brother and sister cry out for vengeance,"

Mihrimah shouted. ''Avenging their deaths is your responsibility.''

With contempt etched across his features, Khalid looked at his mother. ''Bitter old woman. My first responsibility lies with the living. Our revenge must wait.'' At that, he carried his unconscious wife inside.

Chapter 19

Heather opened her eyes and focused on the unfamiliar chamber. Where was she? A thick Persian carpet covered the floor, enormous cushions sat beside a marble table, and one wall of the lavishly decorated room had two portholes.

Without a doubt, Heather knew she wasn't at her mother-in-law's. As far as she knew, no chamber inside Topkapi Palace had portholes.

The shockingly gruesome scene of Jamal's execution came rushing back to her. The deadly scimitar sliced the air, and a sea of blood gushed from the eunuch's decapitated trunk.

"No," Heather groaned, struggling against the horror. That road led to certain madness.

Heather forced herself to sit up and threw her legs over the side of the bed. Hoping the sea's pungent air would revive her, she padded across the chamber to the porthole.

Staring out at the blue Bosporus was a mistake. In her mind's eye, Heather saw the bloated face of Lyndar's baby. Her stomach lurched, and she covered her mouth with her hand and gagged dryly.

The door swung open. Heather whirled around.

Carrying a tray, Khalid stood there. He cast her a measuring look, noting her stricken expression and pallor. Stepping inside, he closed the door with his booted foot and then crossed the cabin to set the tray on the table.

Khalid gave her an easy smile. "Feeling better?"

"No."

"Lie down," he suggested, starting toward her.

"I don't want to rest. Where are we?"

"Murad's barge." Khalid took her arm and guided her toward the table. "Come, refresh yourself."

"I'm not hungry."

"The tea will revive you," Khalid told her.

"Returning to England where civilized people live will revive me," Heather replied, sitting on one of the pillows.

Khalid said nothing. He sat down beside her and poured her a cup of tea. With trembling hands, Heather took the offered cup and sipped the tea.

"I warned you to close your eyes," Khalid reminded her, his voice gentle.

Heather looked up at him. Her stricken expression wrenched his heart.

"I could not," she said in a small voice. "It's my fault Jamal and Lyndar . . ."

Khalid put his arm around her shoulder and drew her close. Heather stiffened in his embrace, but he refused to let her go. Instead, Khalid stroked her shoulder in a soothing motion and said, "The traitors chose their own fates."

"And the baby?" Heather set the tea on the table and stared at her hands. How best to broach the subject of returning to England? How could she live in a land with people who slaughtered innocent babes?

"Tell me about your father," Khalid said, close to her ear.

Heather snapped her head around and stared at him, but said nothing. Their faces were merely inches apart, and his blue-eyed gaze held hers captive.

"Share the heavy burden of your nightmares," Khalid said. "The load will be lighter."

Heather shook her head.

"Fougere's fleet attacked and sank the ship transporting my sister to her new husband," Khalid said, surprising her. "I can only assume the greedy bastard seized the opportunity to pirate a lone imperial vessel. There were no survivors."

Why was he telling her this? Heather wondered. He'd never confided in her before. What was his motive?

"Swearing vengeance on him, my brother and I tracked him down," Khalid went on. "Little did we realize that finding him was part of the weasel's plan to ambush us. Aware that we sought his death, the coward was unable to rest easy until we were dead. Afterward, Karim lay dead and my cheek sliced in half. If not for Malik, I would also be dead."

"Killing Fougere is justified," Heather said. "You needn't explain yourself to me."

"That is not the point of my story," Khalid said. "I was a full grown man, trained in warfare, yet unable to save my brother's life. Feeling guilty for what happened when you were a girl is needless."

"My father died because I disobeyed his rules and rode unescorted beyond the walls," Heather insisted, her eyes clouding with pain. "Nobody said so. Their eyes told me what they were thinking. They judged me guilty."

"I find that difficult to believe."

"It's true," Heather cried, her voice rising in agitation. "Instead of freezing in fear, I should have grabbed that man's—"

"Those men murdered your father," Khalid argued.

"Stop it!" Heather covered her ears with her hands. Khalid drew her into his embrace and held her shaking body tightly. His intention had been to calm, not upset her.

"We will speak of it no more." Khalid stroked her hair and kissed the top of her head, then pulled her onto his lap and cuddled her like a baby. "I will do anything within my power to slay your demons and give you peace, even if I must travel to England to avenge your father's death."

"You would do that for me?" Heather asked, her eyes brimming with tears.

"I swear."

His gentleness and outrageous promise undid her. Heather wept against his chest. Khalid stroked her back and whispered words of comfort.

"I want to go home," Heather whispered.

"We are."

"To England, I mean."

"You are my wife," Khalid said.

"No priest married us." Heather looked up at him through tear-glazed eyes and hiccupped.

"You would be unhappy there," Khalid told her. "Returning to England would bring you no peace."

"How dare you decide what is best for me," Heather said, the fire back in her eyes.

"You suffered from nightmares in England," Khalid said. "Will you return to stand at the very spot where your father died? Besides, you would soon regret leaving me."

That unexpected statement startled Heather. "Why would I do something stupid like that?"

Khalid smiled. "Because you love me."

"Love a man who never raised a hand to save an innocent baby? Love a man who doesn't love—?"

Khalid pressed a finger across her lips. Nose to nose with her, he repeated, "You do love me."

Heather opened her mouth to deny it, but Khalid was faster. His mouth covered hers in a long, slow kiss.

Heather never had a chance. Caught in his spell, she returned his kiss in kind. They fell back on the carpet, his body covering hers.

Bang! Bang! A loud knocking sounded on the door.

Khalid lifted his head and called, "What is it?"

"Maiden's Castle in sight," a man replied.

"We will be ready."

Khalid looked down at Heather, whose eyes were glazed with passion. Unable to resist, he kissed her again and stared with love at her.

Heather's expression cleared. "I still want to go home," she said.

"You will change your mind. I have a surprise for you."

Khalid stood and helped her up. He turned away to fetch her *feridye*.

Watching him, Heather thought about his words. It was true. She had fallen in love with her captor. She'd grown so accustomed to having him near that she couldn't bear to leave him. But, more importantly, what did he feel for her? Did he return her love? Or did he consider her merely his property?

Heather was still pondering the weighty problem of her husband's feelings for her when they stepped ashore thirty minutes later. She looked up at Maiden's Castle. It appeared less forbidding than the first time she had seen it. Was that because she actually loved its lord?

Argus the saluki loped down the beach toward them. Behind the dog hurried Abdul and Omar.

Instead of greeting his master, Argus leaped on Heather who toppled backward. Khalid caught and steadied her before she fell.

Argus tried to lick her face through the *yashmak,* but Heather pushed him down. "Hiding behind this veil has merit," she said.

Khalid opened his mouth to reply, but Argus chose that moment to greet him. The dog's tongue slipped into his mouth.

"I'm certain I saw Argus washing his backside," Heather remarked, glancing sidelong at her husband.

Khalid patted the dog's head and then pushed him down. He grasped his wife's upper arm, turned her around, and lifted her veil.

"*Op beni,*" Khalid whispered, then pressed his lips to hers. Breaking the kiss, he asked, "What were you saying about Argus?"

"Never mind," Heather muttered, wiping her mouth on her sleeve.

"*Hos geldiniz,*" Omar greeted them. "Welcome, my prince and my princess."

"Escort the princess to her chamber," Khalid instructed the eunuch.

"Come, my lady," Omar said, walking down the beach with her. "You must bathe, eat, and nap."

Abdul studied his master's face for a long moment, then remarked, "You appear tired."

"The night was long and the morning even longer," Khalid told him. "The boy is well?"

Abdul nodded. "Lana has been caring for him in your absence. Does the princess know she's about to become a mother?"

"Not yet." Khalid watched Heather walking down the beach with Omar. "My wife will accept him."

"And if she refuses?"

"You need harbor no worries on that account. My wildflower has a gentle heart."

"Any news of the weasel?" Abdul asked.

"Forget about Fougere," Khalid said, starting down the beach. "If he comes looking, he will find death."

Instead of taking his mistress to her old chamber, Omar ushered Heather inside the prince's. Spacious but spartan, the chamber contained a bed, a table, and a bronze brazier for heat. A thick Persian rug covering the floor was its only luxury.

Heather rounded on the little man. "This isn't my chamber."

"Maiden's Castle is mine," Khalid said, standing in the doorway. "Every chamber belongs to me. The other one is already occupied."

Heather arched a copper brow at him. "Taken another captive, have you?"

"Unless I say otherwise, my wife will sleep beside me," Khalid said, sauntering toward her. "Very European of me, would you not agree?"

"No priest married us."

"You are my wife unless I divorce you."

"You mean, I could divorce you?" Heather asked, shocked. Except for old King Henry, she'd never known of anyone who'd been divorced.

"Women do not divorce their husbands," Khalid told her. "It is illegal."

Heather stared him straight in the eye. "Illegal, my arse."

Listening to them, Omar became dismayed. Were they still fighting? How could the princess get with child if she constantly badgered the prince?

And then it came to him, the perfect solution. As if bestowing his blessing on them, Omar grinned broadly.

"At what are you smiling?" Khalid growled at the little man. "Serve us lunch."

"I'm not hungry," Heather said.

"Hungry or not, you will eat."

"I won't."

Omar chuckled and headed out the door.

"You appear tired. Lie down until he returns."

"I'm not tired."

"Dark smudges of fatigue circle your beautiful eyes," Khalid said. "And you are as cranky as a teething baby."

"I refuse to sleep ever again," Heather announced. "Sleeping disturbs me."

Khalid laughed in her face. His wife was the most amazing woman he'd ever met. If more women like her peopled the world, men would be passing their lives behind the veil and following orders.

Khalid chucked her chin. "If anyone is capable of conquering sleep, I do believe it is you. Come, then. If we walk in my garden, the fresh air will whet your appetite and relax you."

Khalid led Heather through the doors on one side of the chamber, and they started down one of the paths. Heather had seen his garden in moonlight only. Her husband's magnificent handiwork surprised her. It was even more beautiful than the gardens of Topkapi.

White, pink, and red baby's breath were arranged with multicolored marigolds and a variety of asters, chrysanthemums, and verbena. Flowering cabbage, pansy, snapdragon, bleeding hearts, and fairy primrose bloomed, completing the autumnal display. It appeared the prince had a skilled, artist's eye for color, form, and design.

"Over there are my herbs," Khalid said, leading her down another path.

"How talented you are," Heather said, inhaling deeply of the mingling scents. "No roses?"

"The solitude of gardening brings me peace," Khalid told her. "And you should know that roses do not bloom in late autumn."

"What's that?" Heather asked, pointing at a plant with fernlike leaves.

"Yarrow, used in making a tea that helps digestion."

"What is that?" Heather asked.

"Lady's mantle," Khalid answered. "It promotes drowsiness when placed under a pillow."

Khalid reached for the velvety, fan-shaped leaves pleated into soft folds. He picked a few that glistened with dewdrops captured inside their folds.

Heather's smile enchanted him. "How can a leaf make a person sleepy?"

"I love your smile," Khalid whispered, drawing her into his embrace. "It reminds me of sunshine."

Khalid lowered his head. His warm, insistent lips captured hers in a lingering kiss.

"Are you hungry now?" he asked, breaking the kiss.

"Well, I suppose I could eat a little."

They returned to his chamber. Still wearing that stupid grin, Omar awaited them with their lunch.

Heather frowned at the platter of fried eggplant on the table. Eggplant, the enchanted food.

Heather loved her husband and wanted his children. But how could she deliver an innocent child into a culture that approved of slaughtering infants like Lyndar's son? How could she endure the constant terror that the sultan would order her own child's execution?

"Remove this at once," Heather ordered the eunuch.

Omar lost his smile. If the princess refused to eat eggplant, another way to beget a child must be found.

Puzzled, Khalid looked at the platter and then at his wife. "What is wrong with the eggplant?"

"It makes a woman pregnant," Heather informed him, "the same way a leaf makes her sleepy."

She didn't want to bear his children.

A thousand daggers pierced Khalid's heart, but he

kept his face expressionless. How could he have been so wrong about her gentle heart? She would never accept Karim. Perhaps he'd done the boy a great injustice. Khalid knew from experience how miserable a child could be with a mother unable to love him.

What was he to do now? Khalid wondered. Send the boy to Malik? Execute him? Khalid knew without a doubt that he could never order the death of another innocent.

"Remove the eggplant," Khalid said.

Omar's expression was sullen. "Shall I serve something else?"

"No," Heather said, dismissing him. The sudden hurt she saw in her husband's eyes took her appetite away. She forced a cheerfulness into her voice and asked, "Where's my surprise?"

"You must nap before the surprise."

Reluctantly, Heather lay down. Khalid placed the lady's mantle beneath her pillow and started to turn away.

Heather grabbed his hand, and when he looked down at her, said, "Please, stay a moment."

Khalid sat on the edge of the bed and gazed at her, the hurt in his eyes tugging at her heart.

Heather sat up, drew his hand to her lips, and kissed it. "I do love children, but I'm afraid."

"There is nothing to fear about giving birth," Khalid said, his relief evident in his voice. "I will send for the best midwife in Istanbul."

"I'm not afraid of that," Heather said. "At least, not overly much."

"What does frighten you?"

"Karim is dead because of his mother's actions," Heather explained. "What would happen to a child of ours if I did something wrong? There are so many unfamiliar rules . . ."

Khalid pulled her into his arms and held her close. "While I have life in my body, no man will ever harm you or our children. Did I not kneel in front of the sultan and defend you?"

Heather reached up and caressed his scarred cheek, then planted a kiss on it and murmured, "I trust you."

All would be well, Khalid decided. His wife would accept the boy with love.

"I was awake all night and need rest," Khalid said, gently forcing her back onto the pillows. He lay down beside her and gathered her into his arms.

Heather relaxed in his embrace and rested her head against his chest. The warmth of his body, and the steady rhythm of his heartbeat soon lulled her to sleep.

Khalid pressed a kiss on the top of her head and eased from the bed. After pulling the coverlet up, he paused for a long moment and studied the face he had come to love.

Khalid headed for Heather's old chamber. Inside, he found Lana feeding the boy from a flask with a make-shift nipple fashioned from lambskin.

Khalid lifted Karim into his arms, dismissed Lana, and continued feeding him. The boy's dark eyes, so much like his mother's, watched the prince with interest, but his mouth never stopped suckling on the makeshift nipple.

Marveling at how helpless and trusting children were, Khalid watched the infant prince. He set aside the flask of goat's milk and lifted the boy onto his shoulder to burp him.

With the baby cuddled against his massive chest, Khalid paced the chamber. The helpless infant and the fearless warrior made an incongruous picture.

"My son, you are a noble prince of the greatest em-pire the world has ever seen," Khalid told the baby. "As your father, I will teach you whatever you need to know. Your mother, whom you will soon meet, is a defiant angel sent by Allah to love you unconditionally. Her tender heart will temper life's harsh lessons.''

Exhausted from lack of sleep, Khalid lay on the bed with the baby snuggled against his body. Father and son dropped into a deep sleep . . .

''Wake up, my prince.'' Omar nudged him.

Opening his eyes, Khalid looked at the eunuch and then down at the baby. Karim still slept with the peacefulness of the innocent.

''The princess has eaten and bathed,'' Omar told him.

Khalid stood and lifted Karim into his arms, then turned to the little man and asked, ''What do you think of my son?''

''A fine boy,'' Omar said. ''I pray he will have many brothers to order about.''

Khalid chuckled. Awakening, Karim whimpered and fidgeted in his arms.

''The cradle?'' Omar suggested.

Khalid shook his head. ''Leave it outside my chamber.''

Omar picked the cradle up and followed the prince out of the room. Reaching his chamber, Khalid gestured him to wait there and then opened the door and stepped inside.

With her back turned toward the door, Heather gazed outside at the prince's garden where the late afternoon sun was casting long shadows. ''I thought I heard a ba—''

Heather stopped short at the unexpected sight of the prince cradling an infant in his arms.

Khalid started toward her. ''I want you to meet my son.''

''*Your son?*'' Flabbergasted, Heather stared at the squirming baby.

"You misunderstand." Khalid smiled. "I mean, our adopted son."

"*Our* adopted son?"

Khalid's smile drooped. He was bungling this badly. He crossed the chamber and sat on the edge of the bed.

"Sit here," he said.

"Not until you tell me whose baby this is."

"I said, sit." Khalid's voice rose in frustrated irritation.

Karim wailed his displeasure at the noise. Heather raced across the chamber, snatched the baby from her husband's arms, and sat down.

"Look what you've done," she scolded in a loud whisper. "You made him cry." Heather held the baby close and stroked his cheek. "Hush, you're safe now. I won't let that nasty man frighten you."

Khalid couldn't help smiling. His wife certainly acted and sounded like a mother, which was exactly what he wanted.

"Since Mihrimah told the world you were with child, Murad and I found a way to save Lyndar's son," Khalid told her. "From this moment, Karim is our son. No one, not even the boy himself, can know his true identity. Discovery means death to all involved, if not civil war."

Heather's smile told him how relieved and happy she was that he'd saved the baby.

Encouraged, Khalid asked, "Can you love the boy as if he were your own?"

So that was it, the trap to make her forget about her family and her home. Heather gazed at the baby and then her husband. "Does mothering him mean I'll never see England again?" she asked in a small voice that ached with loss.

"You would mother a son and then abandon him?" Khalid shouted.

"I could never abandon my child," Heather shouted back, startling the baby. "How dare you even suggest such a vile thing!"

Karim screeched.

"You've frightened him again," Heather said.

She cuddled and cooed to the boy, but he refused to be consoled. "He must be hungry."

"He ate," Khalid said, holding his hands out to lift the baby from her arms.

Heather clutched the baby against her breast and refused to relinquish him. "My son needs me."

Khalid smiled at that. All would indeed be well.

"For safety's sake, Karim needs a new name," Heather said, rocking the baby to quiet him. "We'll call him Walter for my father."

"Walter sounds too European," Khalid refused, offering the wailing baby his finger. "Besides, custom requires his father name him."

"Another rule?" Heather asked, arching a brow at him.

Khalid gave her a wry smile.

"Oh, he is sheer perfection," Heather exclaimed, admiring the infant.

"So be it," Khalid said. "Our son will be known as Kemal Mustafa. Kemal means 'perfection,' and Mustafa is in honor of my late uncle."

"Kemal is a fine name." Heather continued rocking the baby, who finally stopped crying. When she kissed his cheek, he gurgled and smiled toothlessly at her.

"Kemal likes me," she said.

"Gas, probably."

Heather cast her husband an unamused look and then lifted the baby against her chest. "Oh, Lord. He smells like swill."

"Custom requires the mother change the baby's napkin," Khalid told her.

''I don't know how.''

''You will learn.'' Khalid called for Omar, who rushed in. ''Bring a fresh napkin.''

Within seconds, Omar handed Heather the napkin and beamed at her. ''The Koran says, 'Paradise lies at a mother's feet.' ''

''I'm Christian, you blinking idiot,'' she shot back.

The two men watched as Heather unswaddled the baby and unfastened his soiled napkin. After wiping him clean, she placed the fresh linen beneath his buttocks.

''Look at your poor twisted foot,'' Heather cooed. She bent her head to kiss the misshapen foot but jerked back, crying, ''He squirted me.''

Khalid and Omar smiled.

After casting them a disgusted look, Heather wrapped Kemal in his swaddling and lifted him into her arms. She hummed a lullaby, and when his eyelids closed, pressed a light kiss on his forehead.

''Bring the cradle,'' Khalid whispered to Omar.

Khalid watched his wife cuddling the boy. Heather was hooked neater than any fish. His wildflower could never abandon or endanger her son; Kemal had a mother who would love him. Forever.

Chapter 20

Heather placed the sleeping Kemal in his cradle and then rounded on the prince, asking, "What's my surprise?"

Khalid stared at her blankly.

"Bring Kemal his food," Heather instructed Omar and then smiled at her husband. She thought she sounded like an experienced mother.

"The boy ate barely three hours ago," Khalid said as the little man hurried away to do his mistress's bidding.

"Apparently, you know nothing about babies."

"*I* know nothing?" Khalid countered. "What makes you an expert?"

"All women possess an inborn knowledge concerning babies," Heather informed him. "Infants have tiny stomachs and need food more often than adults. Besides that, Kemal just emptied himself on his napkin . . . Now, what's my surprise?"

"What do you mean?"

"You have a surprise for me," Heather reminded him. "One that will change my mind about wanting to go home."

What a typical woman his wife was, Khalid thought. No matter how much men gave them, they always wanted more. Adorable creatures, but mercenary.

Khalid pointed at the cradle. "Kemal is my surprise."

"Oh." Heather was disappointed.

"What other surprise would you like?" Khalid asked, correctly reading her expression. "Jewels? A letter delivered to your mother?"

"A good idea, but no."

"What the bloody hell do you want?" Khalid's voice rose in direct proportion to his irritation.

"Lower your voice, or you'll wake the baby," Heather ordered.

Khalid growled and stepped closer.

"Kemal is sleeping," Heather reminded him.

Khalid counted to twenty and then asked, "What would you like, my princess?"

"A priest."

Khalid's complexion mottled with suppressed anger, and the nervous tic in his cheek returned with a vengeance. Through clenched teeth, he told her, "For the last time, there will be no priest."

Heather reached out and touched his arm. "It's urgent. We are unmarried and cannot raise this child without benefit of marriage."

"The *imam* married us," Khalid insisted.

"I need a priest to celebrate mass," Heather pleaded, though softly for fear of waking the baby. "Dying without confession will send me directly to hell."

An amused smile softened the prince's features. His hand caressed the warm silkiness of her cheek.

"Angels like you need harbor no fear of eternal damnation," Khalid said. "Paradise awaits you." He lowered his head and brushed his lips against hers.

Frustrated, Heather drew back and glared at him. "Why must I be the one to always adjust to your wishes? Why can't you bend a little? Why are you so insufferably pigheaded?"

Khalid's scarred cheek began twitching again. "I am

your husband," he shouted. "Never speak to me in that disrespectful manner again."

In his cradle, Kemal screeched his displeasure at being so rudely awakened.

"Look what you've done," Heather accused him. She lifted the baby into her arms and stroked his back soothingly.

"There will be no priest," Khalid said with deadly finality. He stormed out of the chamber and slammed the door.

"And don't come back," Heather shouted.

Kemal wailed even louder.

"Bloody bugger," Heather muttered in English and began pacing the chamber, all the while crooning softly to the startled baby.

Marching down the corridor, Khalid came face-to-face with Omar. "Get out of my way," the prince snarled, knocking the little man over as he brushed past him.

Omar shook his head sadly and watched Khalid retreating. The prince and his princess argued too much. A strong-willed woman like the princess produced strong sons, but driving the prince to distraction discouraged lovemaking. At this rate, the princess would never get with child, and his own fortune would be lost before he ever saw it.

While Omar stood there and mulled over this sorry state of affairs, an outrageous idea popped into his mind, and a smile spread slowly across his face. The cook was skilled in the use of herbs and potions. Might her expertise extend to aphrodisiacs? The little man intended to find out.

Omar walked into Heather's chamber and handed her the flask of goat's milk. Without a word, he started to leave.

"Wait," Heather ordered.

Omar paused and looked at her.

"I need help," she said.

"Eunuchs know nothing about babies," he informed her, then hurried out.

Heather stared after him until Kemal whimpered and gained her full attention. She sat on the edge of the bed and offered him the flask. His mouth latched on to the nipple, and he quieted instantly.

Humph! Heather thought. At least, some men were easy to please . . .

His wife refused to be pleased, Khalid seethed, like every stubborn female ever born. No matter what he gave her, she wanted more. When her illogical mind fixed on an object, Heather refused to give in gracefully.

The little ingrate! Hadn't he freed her, showered her with jewels, and made her his princess? Not only had he risked his honor and his life to defend her but he'd also postponed tracking and killing Fougere.

Was the green-eyed *jadis* satisfied? No! She demanded the unreasonable. All of his efforts to please her were nothing before her desire for a priest's blessing. If he granted her that, she'd think of something else with which to badger him.

Without thinking about where he was going, Khalid burst upon the battlement high above his garden. His sudden intrusion startled the two guards who gasped and drew their daggers.

"Do cowards protect my home?" Khalid snarled at them.

"A thousand pardons," one of the warriors apologized, sheathing his dagger. "We thought you were the ghost."

"The spirit of the Christian princess," the second warrior explained.

"Flesh and blood men cannot frighten us," the first one said.

"But, how do you kill a ghost?" the other asked.

"There exists no such being as a ghost," Khalid said in a stern voice.

"If you say so," one of the warriors agreed.

"As in all things, my prince, you are correct," the other added.

"Leave me," Khalid ordered. "Wait below stairs until I come down."

The two warriors, glad to get off that battlement, hurried away and disappeared from sight.

Though the sun had set, the night had not yet vanquished the day. It was twilight, that hushed hour betwixt the two. Awash with hues of lavender, blue, and deep indigo, the sky was barren of stars and moon.

Standing near the edge of the battlement, Khalid leaned against the cold stone wall. He looked toward the bay and watched the fog, slow and silent, creeping toward the castle.

"Damn Christian *jadis,*" Khalid cursed his wife.

After luring him to love her, Heather refused to compromise for the sake of their union. She loved him, he knew, but denied him at every turn until he was half crazed with longing. Whenever he thought he was gaining ground with her, Heather called for a priest.

Khalid refused to budge in this matter. If it killed both of them, she would submit to his will. Almost as bad, the peace of his garden was denied him. He knew she would accost him there and renew her outrageous demands for a priest. Was she worth all of this turmoil and soul searching?

Yes, an inner voice replied.

Beautiful, intelligent, intrepid, and softhearted, his wild-flower was unique among all of the other women in Allah's universe . . .

Khalid blinked. Was he seeing what he thought he was seeing? In the distance, a ship sailed through the heavy mist toward the castle. Who would dare approach Maiden's Castle, the beast's lair? Certain death awaited intruders here.

And then it vanished, swallowed by the mist.

Khalid shook his head to clear it. Had he really seen a ship? Perhaps fatigue . . .

A cool breeze—no, something else—tickled the back of his neck and sent a shiver dancing down his spine. Khalid looked left and right, then relaxed.

Heavy mist swirled around him. Nothing supernatural about fog.

Khalid heard it then, the pathetic sound of a woman weeping softly. Heather, weeping for what he denied her! Khalid gazed at the garden below, but was unable to see through the dense fog.

The weeping grew louder, too loud to be drifting up from the garden. Khalid turned to the right and stared in surprise. An unveiled woman stood no more than five feet away and gazed out to sea.

"Who are you?" Khalid demanded.

Without a word, the woman turned at the sound of his voice. The hint of a welcoming smile touched her lips as she noticed him for the first time. She glided toward him.

Khalid stood motionless.

The woman reached out to touch his face. As if realizing he was a stranger, the woman lost her smile and stepped back a pace.

Khalid reached for her, but she disappeared before he could touch her.

"Where are you?" Khalid called, whirling around.

No answer. Nothing happened.

A few seconds later, the two guards rushed onto the battlement. "You called us, my prince?"

"She was here," Khalid said, feeling unaccountably saddened.

"Who?" one of the guards asked.

"The Christian princess."

Both warriors touched their *masallahs,* hidden beneath their shirts. The blue-beaded necklaces were known to ward off the evil eye.

"You are relieved of this duty," Khalid told them, gesturing them away. "No one will stand guard on this battlement."

The two guards hurried off. Lingering could change the prince's mind.

Before following them below, Khalid spared a glance at the mist-shrouded bay. Could that mysterious ship have been the princess's Moslem lover coming to rescue her . . . ?

Returning to the prince's chamber, Omar found Heather, sulking, as she sat on the edge of the bed. Kemal was asleep in his cradle.

Omar handed her the goblet of sherbet containing the aphrodisiac.

"I despise sherbet," she refused, shaking her head.

"Cook prepared this delicious lemon sherbet especially for you," he coaxed. "If you refuse it, her feelings will be hurt."

"I'd rather not."

"Is not the prince's anger enough?" Omar scolded her. "Would you have the cook angry too? While you drink, I will remove the bandage and stitches from your hand."

"Put it down. I will drink it later," Heather said. She

held her bandaged right hand out, adding, "Do your worst. The itch is driving me crazy." Then she turned her face away.

Omar unwrapped her bandage. From his pocket, he produced a pair of tiny scissors and tweezers and snipped the stitches in the palm of her hand. Omar gently pulled them out with the tweezers, then turned her hand over, and repeated the procedure on the back of her hand.

"You can look now," he said.

Heather inspected her hand. The healing wounds were pink and slightly puckered. "How lovely," she remarked dryly.

"The Moor said you would carry the faintest of scars only," Omar told her.

"If the physician says so, far be it from me to contradict him," Heather said, taking a tiny sip of sherbet and then putting it down. She had no intention of drinking it but wanted him to believe otherwise.

"The boy is sleeping so soundly," Omar said. "Perhaps removing him to another chamber before the prince returns would be wise."

"Khalid and I are his parents," Heather replied. "Kemal should stay with us."

"If the prince returns the way he departed, the baby will be awakened," Omar said.

Heather nodded. "If that happens, I will be the one pacing the floor with him."

"Remember, Princess," Omar said with a smile. " 'Paradise lies at a mother's feet.' "

Unamused, Heather curled her lip at him.

Omar chuckled and hurried across the chamber. Without disturbing Kemal, he picked the cradle up and headed for the door, whispering over his shoulder,

"Lana will care for the little prince, and I will return with your supper."

Heather stood and walked to the garden door. She opened the door and inhaled deeply of the mingling scents of the flowers, but could see nothing because of the heavy fog invading from the bay.

Where was Khalid? Heather wondered. Was he seething in anger? Why couldn't he understand that she needed a priest's blessing to feel married?

Damn the priest, Heather thought. What she needed was her husband. She needed to feel his hands caressing her flesh, feel his powerful body covering hers, feel his love.

Priest's blessing or no, Heather desired her husband. And she would have him.

Closing the garden door, Heather hurried across the chamber to her chest and dropped to her knees. She rummaged inside it and withdrew a caftan designed to seduce. Created from the sheerest ivory silk, the caftan sported three ivory satin ribbons that fastened the front.

Heather stripped down to nothing and donned the caftan. Anxious for her husband's arrival, she began pacing the chamber.

The door opened, and Heather whirled around. It was Omar returning with their supper.

Setting the plates of food and decanter of rosewater on the table, Omar saw the untouched sherbet and looked at her in surprise. Her change of attire delighted him. Apparently, his plan hadn't been needed.

Like a caged tigress, Heather paced the length of the chamber and then back. Finally, she stopped beside the table and ordered, "Fetch me the prince."

As if her words had conjured the man, the door swung

open and the prince walked in. Shaken from his encounter on the battlement, Khalid was even more startled by the sight of his seductively dressed wife. From opposite sides of the chamber, his blue-eyed gaze and her green locked on each other.

"Supper is served," Omar mumbled, and scurried out.

A soft, welcoming smile touched Heather's lips. She reached up and slowly, tantalizingly pulled each of the three ribbons, baring her nakedness to her husband's gaze. The caftan slid down the length of her body and dropped to the floor at her feet. All she wore was her glorious mane of copper hair.

Her unspoken invitation was irresistible.

Without taking his gaze from hers, Khalid crossed the chamber and stood in front of her. Heather entwined her arms around his neck and pressed her body to his. Drawing his head down, she kissed him lingeringly, thoroughly.

Breaking the kiss, Khalid stared at her upturned face. He caressed her silken cheek and lifted her hands in his, then kissed her left hand before raising her right hand to his lips.

"No, it's ugly," Heather whispered, trying to pull her hand away.

Khalid studied the puckered wound and pressed his lips to it, then repeated her own words to him, "Your beautiful scar gives you character."

Heather moaned and pressed her body to his. She rained feathery-light kisses all over his face, especially his scar, before her lips traveled down the column of his throat. Pulling his linen shirt over his head, Heather rubbed her face against the dark mat of hair covering his chest.

"My mythical beast," she murmured, seeing the glittering griffon pendant he always wore against his heart.

Licking and nipping, Heather suckled upon her husband's nipples. Khalid's breath caught raggedly in his throat.

Heather dropped to her knees and pressed her face against his groin. Desperate with wanting, she turned away and with one swipe of her hand, sent the dishes on the table crashing to the carpet.

Mesmerized by her need, Khalid sat on the edge of the table and let her have her way with him. Heather yanked his boots off, then ran her hands up his legs to unfasten and remove his pants.

And then each was naked to the other's gaze.

Heather took his manhood in her mouth and sucked until it grew too big. Licking the long length of it, she flicked her tongue this way and that. Finally, her tongue swirled around and around his ruby knob.

Unable to bear any more, Khalid drew her up. Their faces were close. He kissed her slowly, wetly, and lingeringly.

"Touch me," Heather breathed against his lips.

Khalid caressed and stroked every inch of her hot flesh, then lifted her onto his lap. He dropped his head and suckled one aroused nipple while his skillful fingers teased the sensitive jewel of her womanhood, making her moan low in her throat.

Khalid stood with her in his arms and gently laid her on the table. With his hands resting on his hips, he gazed with love at his wife.

Through eyes glazed with passion, Heather looked at him and urged, "Love me."

Khalid gave her what she craved. He mounted her there upon the table and rode her in a wild frenzy.

"Make me swell with your seed," Heather whispered.

Khalid groaned loudly and exploded with his wife, shuddering as he flooded the deepest part of her.

Their labored panting broke the silence of the chamber.

Finally, recovering himself, Khalid held Heather tightly and rolled with her in his arms onto the carpet. He pressed his lips to hers and then vowed, "I love you, my princess."

Chapter 21

"I'm dying," Heather groaned, draped across the chamber pot.

"Your illness is not fatal," Omar said, hovering over her. "If you eat this piece of flatbread, I guarantee you will feel better."

"Do not speak of food," Heather moaned. "What a nightmare I had. I was standing on the beach below the castle, and a monstrous eggplant rolled down the hill . . ."

Heather broke off. Thinking about that eggplant made her nauseous. Turning her face into the chamber pot, she gagged dryly.

Omar covered his mouth with his hand and swallowed. His mistress was making him sick.

The door swung open, and Khalid burst upon the unexpected sight of his wife gagging into the pot. He rushed across the chamber and gently held her forehead.

When her spasms ended, Heather leaned heavily against his legs. "Please, send for the priest," she begged.

Khalid arched a questioning brow at Omar, who grinned broadly and nodded. A satisfied smile spread across the prince's face.

"There will be no priest," he said. "After all these weeks of silence, why do you call for one now?"

"Would you deny me the last rites of the church?"

"You are not dying."

"I am too dying," Heather whined, irritated.

"You will live a long life," Khalid assured her, caressing the crown of her head. "Trust me."

Heather pulled herself up his legs and stared him straight in the eye. "How dare you tell me when to die."

Khalid laughed in her face.

"You dare laugh in the face of the dying?" Heather shouted with surprising strength.

"She should eat a piece of flatbread each morning before she rises," Omar told the prince. "It discourages the queasiness."

"The dead cannot eat," Heather said.

"Eat this bread," Khalid ordered, becoming exasperated, "or I will kill you myself."

Heather lost her temper. She grabbed the flatbread out of his hand and took a bite. "Are you happy tormenting the dying?" she grumbled when she'd eaten the whole piece.

Khalid pulled her into his embrace and stroked her back soothingly. After a time, he asked, "Feeling better?"

Heather paused as if thinking. Her nausea had quieted. "Why, I believe I do feel better."

"Let us walk in the garden," Khalid suggested.

"I'm too weak for that," she refused. "Later, perhaps."

"The fresh air will revive you," he told her. "Besides, I have a surprise for you."

That perked Heather up. "A surprise? What is it?"

Khalid tapped the tip of her upturned nose. "Come outside with me."

"The smell of the flowers will make me ill."

"In that event, I will hold your head."

"Very funny."

Khalid and Heather walked outside and strolled down one of the paths. When they reached the stone wall,

Khalid grabbed her hand and yanked her behind tall shrubbery, saying, ''This way, Princess.''

Hidden behind the bushes was a wooden door, and Heather found herself outside the castle's walls. Hand in hand, Khalid and Heather walked down the path toward the beach.

Argus raced up the sand to greet them. The excited dog tried to leap on Heather, but Khalid used his arm to deflect him.

''Sit,'' Khalid ordered.

Argus sat down and wagged his tail.

''Good boy,'' Khalid said, patting the dog's head. He picked a stick up and threw it. In a flash of movement, Argus dashed after it.

''Let us rest on this rock,'' Khalid said, sitting down.

Heather sat beside him, lifted her nose in the air, and sniffed. ''Low tide smells marvelous today. What's my surprise?''

Khalid smiled at her expectant expression and said, ''The arrow has left the bow.''

''The arrow . . . ?'' Heather was definitely bewildered.

''Your fate is sealed, my princess.''

''What are you talking about?'' Heather asked. ''And where's my surprise?''

''There,'' Khalid said, his gaze dropping to her belly.

Heather looked around. ''Where?''

Khalid pulled her close and gazed with love into her disarming green eyes. ''You suffer from morning sickness, Princess. You carry my child.''

''Pregnant?'' Heather cried, her hands dropping to her belly. Beneath his amused gaze, Heather stood up and stared at her belly. Was it true? she wondered, running the palm of her hand across its flatness. Heather filled with joy at the thought that she carried a new life, her husband's child, inside her.

And then a tidal wave of homesickness washed over her. With an expression of sadness on her face, Heather looked at her husband and said, "I'll never see my mother again, and she'll never know of this grandchild."

Khalid knew breeding women were highly sensitive and required gentle handling. He stood up and gazed with love at her. "I promise to take you to England for a visit. Until then, write your mother a long letter, and I will guarantee its delivery."

Touched by his offer, Heather caressed his scarred cheek and refused, "If my mother demands it, the sultan will return me to her. You said so yourself."

"Only if that is what you desire. Given a choice, you will remain here because you love me."

Khalid lowered his head, and his mouth captured hers in a persuasive kiss. "My sweet wife," he murmured before releasing her.

"Are you certain that I'm with child?" Heather asked. "How do you know?"

"Omar keeps a record of important information," Khalid said. "Knowing such things is his duty."

Heather blushed at the thought of the little man recording her menstrual cycles.

Khalid whistled for Argus, who bounded down the sand toward them. "I believe it is time for your nap."

With his arm around her shoulder, the prince and his princess retraced their steps to the garden. Khalid paused when they reached their chamber's door and ordered, "Argus, stay." The dog sat down and waited.

Once inside, Khalid escorted his wife directly to the bed and sat down on the edge.

"When I awaken," Heather called to Omar, "I want two hard-cooked eggs and a piece of flatbread."

Omar peeked at the prince. "You mean two egg yolks?" he asked his mistress.

"No, the whole egg."

"But you hate the white."

"I will force myself to eat it because it may be good for my baby," Heather said.

Rolling his eyes heavenward, Omar left them alone. If he managed to survive her pregnancy, he would consider himself lucky.

"Sleep peacefully," Khalid said, planting a kiss on her forehead. "I will be working in my garden. Call if you need me."

Heather nodded and closed her eyes. She was asleep before he left the chamber.

Heather slept for hours. By the time she had eaten her hard-cooked eggs with flatbread, bathed, and decided to catch a breath of fresh air, the late afternoon sun was casting long shadows in the garden.

Followed by Omar and Argus, Heather cuddled Kemal in her arms as she strolled leisurely down one of the garden's paths. As if the boy understood every word, she kept a steady stream of chatter up.

"God—I mean, Allah—blessed your papa with a wondrous gift for gardening," Heather told the baby, whose large dark eyes never left her face. "This is verbena, and this is—I forget. Smells pretty though, doesn't it? And over there is your papa's herb garden."

"Rest, my princess," Omar clucked, hovering around her like a mother hen. He set a stool beneath a cypress near the rear of the garden. "Tell me if you are cold, and I will fetch a shawl. Catching a chill is bad for the new baby."

Heather gave Omar a quelling look. The little man was making her nervous, but for the sake of peace, she appeased him and sat down. Argus lay beside the stool and whined.

Heather shifted the baby in her arms, giving him a

view of the dog. "This friendly fellow is Argus, who
will protect you from harm." She patted the dog's head
and said, "Won't you?"

Argus wagged his tail and barked. Startled, Kemal
began to whimper.

"Believe me, this dog's bark is worse than his bite.
It's his kisses that will kill you," Heather said, caressing
the baby's cheek. "I have a little one growing inside
me, a princess for you to protect. Your papa doesn't
know it, but I plan to fill his house with little girls."

A rumble of masculine laughter drifted through the
air.

Heather looked up and smiled at her husband, standing a few feet away. He was so damn handsome, she
thought.

Love leaped at Heather from Khalid's intense blue-
eyed gaze. Sauntering toward her, he asked, "Planning
to fill my home with dozens of demanding daughters to
pester me?"

The sounds of feminine giggles and masculine chuck-
les filled the air. At least two people were hiding behind
the hedges that bordered one side of the path.

"Who is with you?" Heather asked, trying to peek
around her husband's body.

"A pleasant surprise."

Malik and April came into view and started forward.

"Cousin!" With the baby in her arms, Heather leaped
off the stool and raced for April. One step behind her,
Khalid lifted Kemal out of harm's way.

Heather threw herself into April's arms. She buried
her face against her cousin's shoulder and wept with joy.

"I fought long and hard to get here," April teased
her. "I thought you'd be glad to see me."

"I am happy." Heather choked back a sob and wiped
the tears from her cheeks.

"Congratulations on your impending fatherhood," Malik said, slapping his friend's back in camaraderie.

"Let's refresh ourselves inside," Heather suggested, lifting the baby from her husband's arms. "This is our adopted son Kemal."

Malik cast his friend a questioning look, but Khalid's eyes warned him to silence. He would explain the situation when they were alone. After all, Malik had saved his life, and the two friends kept no secrets from each other.

Since Maiden's Castle had no salon for entertaining guests, the four of them headed for Khalid's chamber. There they made themselves comfortable on pillows set around the table.

"Lana will watch over Kemal," Omar said, lifting the baby from his mother's arms. "I will bring refreshments."

"I'm going to write a letter to my mother," Heather told her cousin. "We can send a message to yours also. My husband guaranteed its delivery."

"I'd like that." April peeked at the notorious prince, then whispered, "Are you truly well?"

"I suffer from the morning sickness," Heather said. "Guess what? Khalid is taking me to visit England. While there, he intends to avenge my father's death."

"Ten years is a long time," April remarked doubtfully. "How will he ever find those men?"

"No matter how difficult, my husband can do it." Heather smiled at Khalid. "Isn't that right?"

Before Khalid could reply, Omar returned. He served them grapes, figs, goat cheese, *boza,* and rosewater.

"My wife is the empire's newest hero," Khalid told them. "It was she who discovered the identity of the conspirators plotting Murad's death."

"Tell us this tale," Malik said.

"When my mother brought Heather and Tynna to the bazaars," Khalid began, "an assassin attacked Mihrimah, but my wife stopped the death blow with her hand."

"See," Heather said, holding her right hand out for their inspection.

"Because of her bravery, Murad invited us to Topkapi Palace," Khalid went on. "During a game of—"

" 'Hide and seek'," Heather supplied.

"A rather stupid English game," Khalid said. "From her hiding place, Heather overheard Lyndar and her eunuch plotting my cousin's death."

"I applaud your courage," Malik said to Heather, then turned to the prince. "And your search for Fougere?"

"Postponed," Khalid said, surprising his friend. "My responsibility lies with the living, not the dead."

"If you were really responsible, you'd call for a priest and marry me," Heather said, unable to resist the opening his remark gave her.

"The *imam* married us," Khalid said. "I told you a thousand times, there will be no priest."

Malik looked away. April stared at her lap. Both pretended deafness as the battle of wills began in earnest.

"Besides, I want my baby baptized," Heather added, shocking her husband.

"Her pregnancy makes her unreasonable," Khalid told their guests. He turned a dark expression on his wife and said, "No prince or princess of mine will be a damned Christian."

"I am."

"But you are married to *me*."

"We are unmarried," Heather insisted, leaping to her feet. At that, she headed for the door.

"Heather," Khalid called, leaping to his feet.

"Leave me alone!" The door slammed shut behind her.

In a blinding haze of anger, Heather stormed out of the chamber and marched down the corridor. She didn't know where she was going, only that she needed to be alone.

From the opposite end of the corridor walked Omar, carrying a tray laden with flaky pastries and Turkish coffee. "My princess?"

"Get out of my way, bloody bugger," Heather snapped, shoving the little man so hard that he and the contents of the tray fell on the floor. Realizing what she had done, Heather helped the little man up. She looked at the mess on the floor and then at him. Swallowing her tears, Heather ran down the corridor and disappeared from sight.

Heather raced up the stairs leading to the battlement that overlooked the bay and the prince's garden. Bursting upon that lonely walk, Heather breathed a sigh of relief. It was unguarded. At least, she was assured of a few moments of privacy.

Wandering to the edge of the battlement, Heather leaned against the cool stone wall and gazed at the bay in front of her. Twilight's heavy mist floated slowly but relentlessly toward the castle.

Why was Khalid unable to understand that she desperately needed a priest's blessing? Heather thought. She was carrying his child and he didn't seem to care how miserable she felt. She was a Christian, and without the priest's blessing, peace of mind would be forever denied her.

Heather rested her forehead against the wall and let out a choked sob that broke the dam of hot tears she'd been holding back. For several minutes, Heather allowed her emotions free rein. And then she realized she wasn't alone. Another's weeping mingled with hers. The tiny wisps of copper hair on the nape of her neck stood on edge, and a prickle of fear danced down her spine.

Heather glanced to the left but saw nothing. She looked to the right. The misty shape of an unveiled woman gazed at the bay and wept bitter tears.

Heather followed the woman's gaze. Was that a ship sailing toward the castle through the fog? And then it was gone, vanishing before her eyes. The mysterious woman wailed as if in agony and reached toward the bay.

Frightened, Heather made a protective sign of the cross and asked, "Are you the princess?"

Wearing a tormented expression, the woman turned to face her. Heather stepped back a pace and crossed herself again.

"Heather, where are you?" Khalid called from below stairs, drawing her attention.

Heather looked back at the princess. She had vanished.

Shocked by what she had witnessed, Heather leaned back against the wall and pressed a hand to her pounding heart. She could feel her life's blood racing wildly throughout her body. The sensation made her feel faint.

The Christian princess died pining for her Moslem lover, Heather remembered. Was there a lesson to be learned from the poor soul's misfortune? Could she live for all eternity without Khalid?

No, an inner voice told her.

Khalid was correct; she loved him. If he refused to bend, then she would.

Khalid burst upon the battlement. One look at his wife's deathly pale complexion told him she had met the princess.

"Hold me," Heather cried, throwing herself into his embrace.

"You are safe," Khalid whispered, stroking the back of her head. "Nothing can harm you when I am near."

"I love you," Heather said, her words muffled against his chest.

Khalid heard her clearly. His hand halted in midair and then continued its soothing motion. "And I love you," he vowed.

Khalid glanced at the mist-shrouded bay, closed his eyes, and sent up a silent prayer for the anonymous Christian princess who had died there.

Chapter 22

"How do you feel?" Khalid asked, looking down from where he sat astride his stallion.

Heather smiled behind her veil. "The flatbread worked."

Two hours after dawn, the sun's warming rays had chased winter's chill from the air. The morning promised a day of glorious sunshine and clear blue skies.

Khalid, Malik, and a large number of the prince's warriors were ready and anxious for a long day of hunting. Argus, catching the excitement in the courtyard, pranced around and between the horses.

"How will you entertain April today?" Khalid asked.

Heather spared a glance at her cousin.

"She insists on showing me where she saw the ghost," April told him. "I don't believe in such things, and if they exist, do not want to see them."

Khalid nodded.

"The *Saddam* should arrive later this morning," Malik interjected, looking at the prince. "Perhaps we should wait until Rashid and my men return."

Khalid turned to his wife, asking, "Would you prefer we delay our hunting until later in the day?"

Heather shook her head. "Catch me a pig," she said. "I've a mind to eat roasted pork."

Khalid gave her an exaggerated, wholly disgusted grimace.

Heather giggled.

Turning his mount, Khalid led the hunting party out of the courtyard. Though he knew no one would dare attack Maiden's Castle, his mind was uneasy, and he decided to return to his wife by early afternoon.

Two hours later, Heather led a reluctant April and a nervous Omar up the stairs to the unguarded battlement. Walking to the edge, Heather stood in the exact spot where she'd been the previous evening.

"I was standing here when I heard another woman weeping," Heather told them. "The princess stood on my right and gazed out at the bay." She turned toward the bay and exclaimed, "Bloody hell! We're being invaded!"

A large group of men approached the castle from the beach. Two men were in the lead. One was heavyset and the other lean. Both sported dark hair and mustaches. Even at this distance, Heather saw the lean man's face bore a striking resemblance to a weasel.

"Fougere!" she cried.

Grabbing her cousin's arm, Heather dragged April toward the stairs. Omar, his body a mass of rising hives, hurried after them.

Heather raced into her chamber where Lana and her sister Cyra sat with Kemal. Lifting the baby from his cradle, Heather thrust him into her cousin's arms and ordered, "Guard him with your life."

"What about you?" April asked.

"Fougere intends to kill Khalid," Heather said, already ushering the group toward the garden door. "I refuse to risk my son's life. If the weasel finds me, he won't follow you, and Kemal will be safe."

"I'm staying with you," April insisted, her voice rising with her panic.

"My son's life depends on you," Heather growled,

cuffing the side of her cousin's head. "Do as I say and be quick about it."

Heather led them outside and down one of the paths to the rear of the garden. She stepped behind the tall shrubbery that hid the secret door, then opened it.

"Omar, guard my son with your life," Heather ordered.

"I can't leave you to face those men alone," April said.

"Please, Cousin, you are wasting precious minutes." At that, Heather shoved April through the door, shut it quickly, and locked it.

Intending to confront Fougere, Heather ran back to her chamber and prepared herself for the worst. As the sounds of the embattled warriors drifted in from the corridor, she lifted the paring knife from the fruit dish on the table and hid it in her pocket.

The chamber door crashed open, and the Comte de Beaulieu swaggered in. Tall and lean, he had reddish-brown hair and a long, pointed nose that topped a thick mustache.

Heather backed up two paces before standing her ground. The comte advanced on her until he stood merely inches away.

His cold black serpentine eyes scanned the chamber. "So, this is the beast's lair?"

Heather raised her eyebrows at him. "The human weasel, I presume?"

Fougere reached out and slapped her.

Heather slapped him back and hissed, "Sniveling, servile snake."

Fougere raised his fist to strike. In a flash of movement, Heather drew her knife and pressed it against his throat.

"Have mercy," the weasel whined. "I come to rescue you."

Heather laughed without humor. Before she could reply, she felt the tip of a dagger pressed to her back and froze.

"If you please, Mademoiselle," said a deep voice. "Drop the knife."

"And if I do not please?"

"Will you force me to kill you?"

Heather dropped the paring knife and turned around slowly. The heavyset man with greasy black hair and mustache stood in front of her.

"Count Orcioni at your service, Mademoiselle," he introduced himself.

"Princess, if you please," Heather announced. "I am Prince Khalid's wife."

Fougere snorted with contempt and hurried across the chamber to the chests. He pulled a giant sackcloth from inside his doublet and started stuffing Heather's clothes into it.

"I shan't be needing a change of clothing," Heather said. "I'll be home as soon as my husband kills you."

"Silence, slut," Fougere snapped without looking up from his task. "These are not for your use."

"You prefer women's apparel to men's?" Heather asked, surprised and bewildered.

Count Orcioni chuckled at his friend's expense.

"Shut that mouth," Fougere threatened, "or I'll shut it for you."

With the sackcloth filled, Fougere grabbed her upper arm. Count Orcioni sheathed his dagger and grasped her other arm. Caught between the two of them, Heather left Maiden's Castle.

As they marched down the path to the beach, Fougere

pulled one of Heather's caftans from the sackcloth. He
tore the delicate silk into two pieces and dropped one
on the path, then left the other on the sand before climbing into the longboats awaiting them.

Heather had no idea where they were going. She did
know, however, that the Comte de Beaulieu was a
strange man who, apparently, derived pleasure from destroying women's clothing.

The comte's sailors steered the longboat along the
coastline toward an isolated cove where his ship was
anchored. Along the way, Fougere tore several articles
of clothing and dropped them out of the longboat.

"What the bloody hell do you think you're doing?"
Heather asked.

"Leaving a trail for the beast," Fougere replied.
"How can I ambush the beast if he doesn't follow me?"

Ambush? Heather's heart sank to her stomach. The
weasel had successfully ambushed her husband before.
What worked once could work again.

"Why don't you fight him like a man?" Heather
cried. "You dirty weasel!"

At that, Fougere's fist connected with her jaw and sent
her reeling. Count Orcioni caught the unconscious
Heather before she fell overboard.

"Marring her beauty is unnecessary," the count
warned. "Strike her again at your own peril."

It was late afternoon when Heather awakened. She lay
on her side near a campfire. "Where are we?" she
asked, reaching up to feel her aching jaw.

Count Orcioni smiled at her. "Near Istanbul,
Princess."

Heather caught the scent of food. Something simmered in two pots that hung over the campfire.

"Where's the weasel?" Heather asked, making the
count chuckle. "Crawled into his hole?"

Fougere walked into her line of vision, ordering, "Shut up, slut."

Heather scanned the area and wondered where the weasel's minions were hiding. Probably on guard duty, she thought, though it wouldn't do them any good. The whole lot of them were walking dead men.

She sat up and turned her attention on Fougere, fixing her startling green-eyed gaze on his. "You could have had a quick death," she told him. "For daring to strike me, you are condemned to a slow and painful death."

Fougere drew his dagger and pointed it at her. Unafraid, Heather laughed in his face.

Backing away from her, Fougere turned to Orcioni, saying, "Those green eyes mark her a witch without fear."

"Beware, little weasel," Heather said, sounding more confident that she felt. "My husband will rescue me and the babe I carry."

"Pregnant?" Fougere growled, stepping toward her.

"Remember what I said earlier," Count Orcioni warned as he stirred the contents of the pot.

Fougere stopped short and kept his distance from his captive.

"Dining before dark is uncivilized," the count complained.

"A night fire is too dangerous," Fougere whined.

Orcioni looked at him. "You did say you wanted the prince to find us. What better beacon could there be than a fire in the night?"

"I want to see him coming, you fool," Fougere snapped.

"Fool?" Count Orcioni growled low in his throat and started to rise.

"Forgive me," Fougere apologized, preventing a confrontation. "See to your boiling water."

"Sassari is the only smart one," Orcioni muttered. "He went home."

"What are you cooking?" Heather asked with a grimace. The aroma was making her nauseous.

"*Putanesca paste,*" the count answered.

"It smells like dead fish," Heather said.

"We Italians call it 'whore's sauce' because of its distinctive aroma," the count explained. "It smells like a harlot's well-used—"

Standing in front of her, Fougere laughed loudly, muffling the rest of the count's words. Regardless, Heather had the general revolting idea.

"When we finish with you, you will smell like the *putanesca,*" Fougere told her.

Heather leaped to her feet and tried to run. Fougere reached out, spun her around, and threw her to the ground. He raised his foot and aimed to kick her belly.

With a strength born of desperation, Heather grabbed his boot and halted the blow. Fougere tried to shake her away, but caught off balance, landed with a heavy thud on his backside.

"Injure my babe, and the agonies of hell will feel like paradise," Heather threatened.

"Well said, Princess," sounded a voice behind them.

Count Orcioni and Fougere leaped to their feet and whirled around. Heather smiled at the newcomer.

With scimitar in hand, the Sultan's Beast stood there.

"We are two against one," Fougere sneered. "Are you ready to die?"

"A coward and a whoremaster hardly signify against a man," Khalid said.

"Get him," Fougere ordered the count.

"You get him," Orcioni refused. "You're the one who wants him dead."

"I am waiting," Khalid said.

Fougere glanced at the count. "Together, then?"

Count Orcioni nodded and reached for his sword lying on the ground. Heather was faster. She grabbed the sword and pointed it at the count who backed away from her.

"Two against two," Heather announced. "The sides are even."

"Remain where you are, Princess," Khalid ordered. "Use the sword for self-defense only."

Fougere drew his sword and the count his dagger. Together, they advanced on the prince, and the three of them began circling one another in a macabre dance.

Orcioni hung back because of his measly dagger. He had no intention of attacking a warrior who held a scimitar in his skillful hands. Still, the odds were against the prince as long as the woman stayed out of it.

"Are you dancing or killing me?" Khalid baited them.

Unexpectedly, Fougere lunged at Khalid, who leaped back. The prince had waited a long time for this moment, and he intended to enjoy it to the fullest.

"When you're dead, Orcioni will install your beloved in his brothel," Fougere said. "Any man can use her for the right price."

Khalid refused to be baited. Killing two men required the coolest of heads.

"After I use her myself, I'll keep her naked and bound to the bed," Orcioni added. "All those men will futter your seed right out of her."

Khalid growled and glanced at the count. Lunging at the prince with his sword, Fougere jumped into the arc of his reach.

With the agility of an experienced killer, Khalid leaped back and then reversed his movement. He landed a backhanded swing with his scimitar on the count. Unprepared for the attack, Orcioni lost his head, but the scimitar flew out of the prince's hand.

"Still two against one," Fougere said, blocking the prince's path to his only weapon. "My sword and I against you." He swung wildly at the prince, who easily sidestepped to safety.

"Toss me the dagger," Khalid called to Heather.

Heather was almost beyond hearing. She stared in a horrified daze at the sea of blood gushing from the count's decapitated trunk, but saw, in her mind's eye, her own father lying there mortally wounded.

"Heather, the dagger!"

As if from a great distance, her husband's voice penetrated, calling her back to reality. Heather grabbed the hilt of the sword, leaped to her feet, and attacked. Fougere kicked her away, striking her belly dead center. Clutching her midsection, Heather went down. Terrible pains from her lower regions shot through her body.

Khalid lunged for Fougere, but the comte whirled around in time and swung. The tip of his sword grazed Khalid's chest, ripping his shirt open.

Caught off balance, Khalid fell backward, shouting, "Heather!"

"Khalid," Heather moaned, her eyes clouding as she struggled against the memory.

Ignoring the crippling pain in her belly, Heather grabbed the dagger, forced herself into a sitting position, and threw the blade at Fougere. Her aim was straight and sure. The dagger pierced the back of his neck with such force, its tip protruded out of his throat.

Khalid whacked the flat of the sword toward the right and rolled in the opposite direction. Gurgling for breath, Fougere dropped the sword, reached for his throat, and toppled over.

Khalid leaped to his feet and raced for Heather. With

her eyes closed against the pain, she lay on her side and panted for breath.

Dropping to his knees, Khalid lifted her upper body and held her close. "Awaken, Princess."

Heather opened her eyes and moaned, "I hurt."

"I will take you home," Khalid said.

"I dispatched the weasel's guards," a voice beside him said.

Khalid turned his stricken expression on Malik. "My wife has been injured."

"She is losing the baby," Malik said. "Take her to Mihrimah's. It is closer."

Khalid dropped his gaze to his wife's caftan. There was the telltale bloodstain growing larger as he stared at it.

The legendary Sultan's Beast lifted his head and howled in soul-chilling agony, lamenting his loss.

Chapter 23

Heather swam up from the dark depths of unconsciousness but was unable to break its surface. Am I dead? she wondered in the deepest recesses of her mind. Or is this a bad dream?

As if from a great distance, a murmur of hushed voices mentioned babies and bleeding. A door closed somewhere, and then all was silent.

Heather opened her eyes and focused on the chamber. Was she dreaming or dead? Moving to sit up, Heather realized she was painfully alive. Her body felt like one massive ache.

Strong hands gently pressed her back on the pillows. "Rest easy, my love."

Heather looked toward the voice. With worry etched across his face, her husband stood beside her.

Gingerly, Khalid eased himself onto the edge of the bed. He caressed her cheek, saying, "You have been injured slightly."

"I feel like the mortally wounded."

That brought the hint of a smile to his lips. "You will be climbing trees in a few days," he promised.

What injury? Heather wondered. Visions of daggers, swords, and scimitars danced across her mind's eye, but she couldn't quite recall being hurt.

"Your skill with the dagger saved my life," Khalid

said, drawing her attention. "Cutting the villain's breath off was a stroke of genius."

Heather smiled wanly. "I probably aimed for his heart."

"Allah guided your hand," Khalid said. He leaned down and picked a goblet of rosewater off the floor. "Sit up for a moment and drink this."

"I'm not thirsty," she refused.

"Do as I say."

With one hand, Khalid helped her up. Every muscle in Heather's body, especially her lower regions, protested the movement. With the pain came the awful memory of her injury.

"My baby?" she asked.

"Drink," Khalid ordered, holding the goblet to her lips.

Heather obeyed and drank every drop of the drug-laced water. When she spoke, her voice mirrored her anxiety. "My baby?"

Khalid eased toward her and gently drew her into his embrace. "The physician promised you would bear dozens of healthy children."

"This one?" she asked, her heart shining in her eyes.

"No."

Heather hid her face against his chest and wept in misery.

"You suffer for saving my life," he said. "The fault lies with me."

Holding her close, Khalid stroked her back, but Heather would not be consoled. In time, her sobbing subsided. The sleeping draft and her tears tired her until she was deadweight in his arms.

Ever so gently, Khalid pressed her back to the pillows and carefully eased off the bed. He studied her face for a long time, then leaned down and touched her lips with his own.

"Farewell, Princess," Khalid whispered. He stood up straight, wiped the moisture from his eyes, and took a deep breath.

Outside his wife's chamber, Khalid came face-to-face with his mother. "Heather is sleeping," he told her. "You may visit her in the morning."

Mihrimah nodded and started down the corridor with him. "You told her?" she asked, glancing sidelong at him.

Khalid nodded but stared straight ahead. He was controlling his own emotions with difficulty.

"How did she receive the news?"

"She wept, and then the drug put her to sleep."

Mihrimah touched his arm. Surprised by his mother's gentle gesture, Khalid halted and turned to her.

"And you?" Mihrimah asked. "How do you feel?"

"How do you think I feel?" he snapped.

"My son, I am concerned for you," she said.

"You? Concerned for me?" Khalid echoed, incredulous.

"You find that impossible to believe?" Mihrimah asked, her eyes welling up with tears. For the first time in her life, she reached up and caressed his scarred cheek. "My heart aches for your loss. You are my only living son, and I do love you."

Khalid's expression softened. "You love me?"

Mihrimah nodded. Fat teardrops rolled down her cheeks.

"Thank you for that, Mother," Khalid said. He put his arm around her shoulder and escorted her down the corridor. "Will you do something for me?"

"Anything, my son."

"Care for my wife and report on her recovery to me each night."

"Report her recovery?" Mihrimah stopped walking

and turned to him. "Do you have eyes in your head to see for yourself? Where are you going?"

"I am going nowhere." Khalid glanced down the long corridor toward his wife's chamber. "However, I will not see her again."

"You are divorcing?" Mihrimah asked, surprised.

"I am sending her home," Khalid answered.

"Your wife's home is with you."

"Her home is in England."

"But, you love her," Mihrimah said. "Do not deny what can easily be seen."

"I love my wife," Khalid admitted, "but I am sending her home. I made her my slave and forced her into a marriage she can never accept. At great risk to herself, she saved your life and mine. All she ever wanted was to return to her family in England."

"She told you that?"

"Many times," Khalid answered. "Can I now refuse her heart's desire?"

"Divorcing her requires that you tell her in the presence of witnesses," Mihrimah said.

"I will not divorce her," Khalid replied. "Heather is my wife. No other woman will enter my heart."

"Do you intend to mourn her for the remainder of your life?" Mihrimah cried.

Stunning her, Khalid leaned close and kissed both of her cheeks, then turned and walked away. Mihrimah stood there and watched her son, a lonely figure of a man, until he disappeared from sight.

If it was possible, Heather felt even worse the next morning when she awakened. Both her body and spirit were sore.

"Good morning," Mihrimah said, standing beside the bed.

Heather's gaze scanned the chamber. "My husband?"

"My son has been summoned to Topkapi Palace," Mihrimah told her, wondering why she even bothered to ask about him. "Now, how do you feel?"

"How would you feel if you'd miscarried your first child?" Heather asked.

"The physician says you will bear many children," Mihrimah said, handing her a cup of tea.

"Did he really?"

"Would I lie about such an important matter? You will rest today, but tomorrow you must get out of that bed and walk."

Heather handed her mother-in-law the empty tea cup and yawned.

"I will visit you again later," Mihrimah said, then left the chamber.

Heather tried valiantly to stay awake until Khalid returned but was unable to keep her eyes open. She slept through the day, awakening once during the night. The bed beside her was empty. Where was Khalid? Why wasn't he with her? Too groggy to ponder the matter, Heather fell back into a deep, dreamless sleep.

When Mihrimah walked into the room the next morning, Heather was sitting up with her legs thrown over the side of the bed. A warm, welcoming smile died on her lips when she saw her mother-in-law.

"Oh, it's you," Heather said, disappointed. "I thought it was my husband."

"Khalid has gone to do an errand for Sultan Selim," Mihrimah informed her.

"Did he leave last night?"

"No, why do you ask?"

"He never came to our bed."

"Perhaps he had no wish to disturb you," Mihrimah lied.

Heather stared at her. Khalid had never worried about

disturbing her before now. Something was definitely wrong. Did her husband judge her responsible for the death of their child?

"Where is Tynna?" Heather asked, forcing a light tone into her voice. "I have not seen her."

"Tynna is visiting Shasha for a few days." Mihrimah smiled. "Would you like a bath?"

"Yes, thank you." Heather forced herself to return the smile.

Later, Heather sat alone in her chamber and waited for her husband. By evening, she was more angry than hurt. At first opportunity, Heather intended to give him a large piece of her mind. How dare he treat her like this after she'd lost her baby saving his life? How did he dare profess his love and then ignore her?

Heather waited for hours.

Khalid never came.

When the door opened the next morning, Heather whirled around. "Where is he?" she growled.

"Who?" Mihrimah asked.

"My husband, you idiot!"

Pitying her, Mihrimah admitted, "Khalid refuses to see you."

Stunned, Heather sat down on the edge of the bed. She turned a heart-wrenching expression on her mother-in-law and echoed, "Refuses to see me?"

"I have good news," Mihrimah said. "Khalid has made arrangements for your return to England."

"Sending me home?"

Mihrimah smiled brightly. "In a few days, Malik will take you to Algiers. There you can board an English ship and will soon be reunited with your family."

"Get out," Heather said in a voice that ached with loss.

"What?"

"I said, get out!"

Khalid hated her because of the baby, Heather thought. How ironic that when she started loving him, he stopped loving her.

Flopping back on the bed, Heather curled up on her side and wept bitter tears.

Empty with loss, Heather passed through the next few days like a walking dead woman. Rising early each morning after a sleepless night, she bathed and ate and dressed, then waited in vain for a husband who never came. She smiled politely at Mihrimah, but initiated no conversations, nor did she reply to the other woman's remarks or questions.

On her last morning at Mihrimah's, Heather sat alone on a stone bench near the rear of the garden. She looked at the peach tree and remembered the day she climbed it. Khalid had rescued her.

Thinking of him brought tears to her eyes. Heather hid her face in her hands and gave her emotions free rein.

"Tears of joy?" Mihrimah asked, sitting down beside her.

Heather turned to the other woman. "How can you ask such a question?" Heather sobbed. "My husband hates me."

"Hates you?" Her remark surprised Mihrimah.

"Khalid cannot forgive me for miscarrying our child," Heather said, her bitterness creeping into her voice. "His hate prevents him from saying farewell."

"My son loves you," Mihrimah told her.

"Because of his undying love, he refuses to see me?" Heather countered.

"Though doing so brings him unspeakable pain, my son loves you enough to grant your wish," Mihrimah said.

"What wish?"

"Your wish to return to England."

"Are you saying this to make me feel better?" Heather asked.

"Why would I do that?" Mihrimah shot back. "I do not even like you."

Heather grinned at her.

"You smile at his pain?" Mihrimah asked.

"I would never do that," Heather replied, standing. "I love my husband."

"It is too late for a change of heart," Mihrimah said. "Khalid is on his way to Topkapi, and the litter is waiting to take you to Malik's ship."

"It is never too late for love." Heather leaned down and planted a kiss on her mother-in-law's cheek, then turned and hurried away.

Wearing a *yashmak* that left her eyes visible, Heather boarded the *Saddam* two hours later. Malik, wearing a forced smile, stepped forward to greet her.

"Welcome aboard, Mademoiselle," he said in French.

"Princess, if you please," she replied, switching to her husband's native tongue. "How long will it take to get me home?"

"A month, more or less."

Heather raised her eyebrows at him. "A month to get to Maiden's Castle?"

"You are going to England."

Heather stared at him hard. "My home is with my husband and my son, whom I love beyond words and never wish to leave."

"Very well, Princess," Malik said, his face splitting into a broad grin. "Maiden's Castle, it is . . . ."

The longboat from Prince Murad's ship glided through the water toward Maiden's Castle. Sitting in the bow, Khalid gazed through twilight's mist at his domain.

All would belong to his adopted son one day. Without Heather, there would be no more children.

And then Khalid caught sight of a hooded figure standing on the battlement that overlooked the bay. *The Christian princess!*

Leaping out of the longboat, Khalid ran up the path from the beach. Once inside, he ignored his men's greetings and dashed down the maze of corridors that led to a certain stairway.

"Wonderful news, my prince," Omar gushed, materializing from nowhere.

"Get out of my way," Khalid growled, shoving him aside.

Omar went flying. He and the tray of food in his hands landed on the floor. The little man grinned at the prince's retreating back. Life was almost normal again.

Hoping to catch a glimpse of the princess, Khalid raced up the stairs two at a time and burst upon the unguarded battlement. The apparition whirled around to confront him and lost her hood, revealing a mane of brilliant copper hair. Khalid stopped short.

Heather smiled uncertainly and took a step toward him, then lost her courage. She halted and stared at the stone floor.

"What are you doing here?" Khalid asked, advancing on her until he was merely inches away. "I sent you home."

Heather's head snapped up. She looked him straight in the eye and said, "My home is with you."

As a groan of relief escaped him, Khalid yanked her into his arms and crushed her against his body. He lowered his head, and his mouth captured hers in a demanding, earth-moving kiss.

Khalid caressed her cheek, and his smile was pure love. A figure behind her caught his eye.

"Look," he whispered.

Heather turned in the circle of his arms.

The Christian princess stood at the edge of the battlement and gazed toward the bay. Out of the swirling mist appeared her Moslem lover.

He held his hand out to her; she reached for it. Their fingers touched, and they evaporated in the mist as if they had never been there.

"He came for her," Heather whispered.

"Yes."

"Where did they go?"

"Paradise."

Khalid crushed her against his body as if he would never let go. Heather rested her cheek against the solidness of his chest, and he rested his chin on the crown of her head. They stood as one for a long, long time.

"I love you," Heather vowed, finally breaking the silence.

"And I love you," Khalid said. "Will we ever be in accord?"

"Christ only knows," Heather answered.

"You mean Allah," he corrected her.

"I mean Whomever."

Khalid smiled. "And how shall we celebrate your homecoming?"

Heather gifted him with an enchanting grin, and her eyes sparkled like emeralds. "Let's eat pork."

"Very well," Khalid agreed. "Tomorrow we will roast the biggest swine I can find."

"Tomorrow is Friday," Heather informed him. "Eating meat is forbidden."

"I know."

Heather cocked a copper brow at him, saying, "About that priest—"

"I will tell Malik to abduct the pope," Khalid offered. "We will bring him here to marry us."

Heather smiled. "A simple priest will do."

Khalid covered her mouth with his own and poured all of his love into that single stirring kiss. It melted into another. And another . . .

The Moslem prince and his Christian princess stepped into eternity together.

Let best-selling, award-winning author **Virginia Henley** capture your heart...

☐ 17161-X The Raven and the Rose $4.99

☐ 20144-6 The Hawk and the Dove $4.99

☐ 20429-1 The Falcon and the Flower $4.99

☐ 20624-3 The Dragon and the Jewel $4.99

☐ 20623-5 The Pirate and the Pagan $4.50

☐ 20625-1 Tempted $4.99

Experience the Passion and the Ecstasy

Meagan McKinney

- ☐ 16412-5 No Choice But
  Surrender $4.99

- ☐ 20301-5 My Wicked
  Enchantress $4.99

- ☐ 20521-2 When Angels Fall $4.99

- ☐ 20870-X Till Dawn Tames
  the Night $4.99

- ☐ 21230-8 Lions and Lace $4.99